THE
FIRST
48
HOURS

THE
FIRST
48
HOURS

SIMON
KERNICK

HEADLINE

First published in 2023 by
HEADLINE PUBLISHING GROUP

1

Cataloguing in Publication Data is available from the British Library

Hardback ISBN 978 1 4722 9240 7
Trade paperback ISBN 978 1 4722 9241 4

Typeset in Sabon by CC Book Production

Printed and bound in Great Britain by Clays Ltd, Elcograf S.p.A.

HEADLINE PUBLISHING GROUP
An Hachette UK Company
Carmelite House
50 Victoria Embankment
London EC4Y 0DZ

www.headline.co.uk
www.hachette.co.uk

Prologue

'If anything happens to my precious boy, I don't know what I'll do ...'

These are the words that no police officer ever wants to hear. They're delivered with such animal anguish that Cotton and I just look at each other, knowing full well we're taking a real risk here. And as the senior officer of the two of us, I'm the one whose career goes down the pan if we fail.

The woman who utters those words is forty-six-year-old Jenny Day. She's in the front passenger seat of the car fifty yards in front of ours, and she's talking to us on an open phone line. The man driving her is her husband, Nigel, and they're the parents of eighteen-year-old Henry Day, the latest victim of a team of professional kidnappers operating throughout south-east England known by both the media and the National Crime Agency's Anti Kidnap and Extortion Unit – the people who employ both Cotton and me – as the Vanishers.

These days, kidnapping's often considered something of

1

an old-fashioned crime, and one that, in the age of cameras on every street corner, has had its day. But nothing could be further from the truth. There are kidnappings and abductions happening around you all the time, whether it be drug dealers holding those who owe them money for ransom, or parents snatching kids from their partners. The difference is, they don't tend to make the headlines. For a long time, the Vanishers flew under the radar too, because they made use of the one technological development that takes out a huge amount of the risk involved in kidnapping.

Cryptocurrency.

Crypto is every criminal's friend. It may not be quite so anonymous as its proponents think it is, but it's still very hard for law enforcement to trace if you know how to move it around, and it's helped make the Vanishers' MO near-perfect.

They pick an ordinary upper-middle-class family, one that's got ready access to significant liquid savings, and then snatch the most vulnerable member. Contrary to popular belief, this isn't usually a young child. The easiest to take out are those between the ages of eighteen and twenty-three, especially if they come from a good family. They're the ones making the most of the freedom that adulthood brings them, and who are still naïve enough to trust people, as well as being generally unobservant of their surroundings. They're not going to be missed quickly, especially if they're at uni, and if the abduction's done swiftly and efficiently (potentially when they're inebriated), no one's going to notice a thing.

When the Vanishers have their victim safely stored, one of their number calls the mother (it's always the mother), using the victim's phone, and explains the situation. As long as the family cooperate and don't involve the police, then as soon as a ransom is paid into a specified crypto wallet in bitcoin (the amount varies but is usually equivalent to about half a million pounds), the son (it's been a son in every case so far) is released unharmed. However, it's made very clear that if they don't pay, or are foolish enough to involve the police, then they'll never see their child again. As an added security measure, the caller warns them that if they contact the police after the victim's release, they'll be targeted again.

It may or may not come as a surprise to find out that almost everyone cooperates and pays the ransom without involving us, and it's for that reason that we still don't know the exact number of kidnaps there've actually been. But it appears that in every instance, the Vanishers have been true to their word and have released their victim unharmed within twenty-four hours of receipt of the money. It's only afterwards that the truth has begun to seep out. When someone's been the victim of a trauma like a kidnapping, it's very hard for them to keep quiet about it to those around them, so word ends up spreading. In one case, a nineteen-year-old man who'd spent three days locked in a basement tried to commit suicide three months later, causing his family to finally report what had happened to the police, even though they were still terrified of being targeted again, and the media to pick up on the story. As a result of the press coverage, three other families came forward anonymously, which is how the NCA's Anti Kidnap team, which I head up, finally built a picture of what had been happening. The four cases we know about for sure took place over a period of just under three years, and the problem's been that the trail on all of them has long gone cold. The bitcoin ransoms have disappeared into the ether; the CCTV footage has been wiped; and there's no longer even any DNA evidence of any kind.

The Vanishers have left clues behind, of course. There was no way they could avoid that. We know for a fact that there are at least two of them: a man who liaises with the victims while they're being held (although because they're always blindfolded, there's no description of him other than that he talks in a London accent and sounds like he could be in his thirties or forties, which doesn't exactly narrow it down); and a woman aged somewhere between twenty-five and forty-five, who's taken an active part in all four abductions. They like to snatch their targets from the street at night. According to the victims, the female kidnapper approaches them pretending to be drunk or distressed, and unsteady on her feet. As they go to help her, she jabs them with a needle containing a powerful sedative, and in every case the next thing they can remember is waking up in a locked basement cell, where they're kept for the duration of their stay. During that time, they're fed and given water by the male, but they have no real communication with him. At the end of their ordeal, they're injected with a sedative again, always without warning, and the next thing they know, they're waking up in the middle of nowhere (an abandoned quarry in one case; a field in the middle of the countryside in another), often only minutes before they're discovered by their family members, who've been given the coordinates of where they are. All four known victims were released within an area of approximately fifty square miles around south-west Surrey, which suggests that the Vanishers have connections to the area and are keeping their captives somewhere in the vicinity.

But that was it. And it wasn't much to go on. The media made a big thing of the story when it first broke, but when it became clear that the Vanishers weren't going to be identified and arrested any time soon, interest faded away. Which meant we had to wait and hope and keep alive in the minds of the public the fact that there remained a dangerous kidnap gang out there somewhere, and if anyone else fell victim to them, it was imperative they contact the police straight away so they could finally be brought to justice. But our big problem is that the Vanishers are almost too reliable: every prospective victim knows that if they pay the ransom, they get their loved one back in one piece, whereas if they call the police, there's no guarantee that they'll achieve the same result.

And then three days ago, we finally got our break when we received a phone call from property developer Nigel Day to say that the Vanishers had their son, a student at Reading University, and were demanding a ransom in bitcoin just short of half a million pounds.

The first thing we did was get hold of the council camera footage for the previous twenty-four hours covering the street where Day lived. And that was when we got break number two. At 7.23 p.m. the previous night, Henry Day had walked out of his front door, turned left and gone approximately fifteen yards before a woman approached him from out of shot, appearing to ask him a question. As he paused to talk to her, she jabbed him with something. He then stumbled, and she put her arm round his shoulders and led him to where a grey Chrysler people carrier had pulled up. She slid open the rear passenger door, pushed him inside, and the car drove off.

We knew it was the Vanishers. The woman matched the basic description we'd been given of the female kidnapper, although it looked in the footage like she was wearing a long blonde wig. The driver of the Chrysler was wearing a cap, glasses and the criminal's other best friend, the face mask. As soon as we ran the car's plates through the ANPR system, we saw that they were fake. So we now had a confirmed kidnapping in progress, although the suspects had again made sure they were hard to recognise and track.

Our plan with the Days has been to keep a low profile and let them pay the ransom before simply following its trail to the kidnappers. And that's what the couple have done, paying the whole sum into a crypto wallet in the name of a non-existent individual called Arthur11138. Theoretically, any wallet can be traced back to its real owner, because every transaction is recorded on a public ledger called a blockchain. However, this process can take months, or even years, if the owner is tech-savvy enough to set up virtual barriers: fake IP addresses, logless VPNs, etc.

But that doesn't matter to us, because our plan is to wait for the Vanishers to grab the money from the wallet, at which point we'll be able to watch as they move it round the system. Because here's the thing. Eventually they'll want to turn it into hard cash – the type you can actually spend – and in order to do that, they'll need a bank, which means identifying themselves and setting up accounts. And that's when we'll pounce.

So for the last twenty-three hours, we've been waiting for Arthur11138 to take the money out of the wallet, which any self-respecting kidnapper would want to do as soon as possible so he can start the process of making it disappear.

Except it hasn't moved.

Which is something of a worry.

But then just over an hour ago, one of the kidnappers got in touch with the Days via text, using a burner phone that was then immediately switched off, acknowledging receipt of the money and telling them where they could find their son.

That's where we're heading now, to an abandoned barn two miles south of the village of Ockham, in the same general area where the other victims have been released. We haven't had time to put a surveillance team in place, nor have we told the local police what's going on, in case they inadvertently do something that tips off the kidnappers.

'Your son's going to be okay, Mrs Day,' I tell her. 'We're almost there now.'

'Then why is he not answering his phone?' she replies, an almost hysterical edge to her tone. 'The man said he would have his mobile phone with him. I've just tried to call it.'

Henry Day's mobile phone started pinging from the location we're heading to approximately five minutes after the kidnappers' call to the Days, but they were under strict instructions not to call it until 10 a.m., which was two minutes ago.

'He's almost certainly been drugged before release,' I explain, 'because that's what happened with the other victims. Which means he's probably still suffering the effects of it.'

'Will he be all right? They won't have given him an overdose, will they?'

'I very much doubt it, Mrs Day. None of the other victims suffered any tangible side effects.'

'None of the other victims' families involved the police,' she says, her voice shrill. Contacting us was her husband's idea, and Jenny Day has been something of a reluctant participant, who clearly would have kept quiet about the kidnap if she'd had her way.

'These people don't know you've involved the police,' I say, exchanging another look with Cotton. 'We've kept everything completely under wraps. Only a handful of people are aware of what's going on.'

'They could have been watching.'

'They weren't watching, Mrs Day, and even if they were, they would never have seen us together. And neither your phone nor your house was bugged, so they wouldn't have known about any phone calls either. It's going to be okay.'

'It will be,' I hear her husband telling her. 'We're nearly there.'

And we are. We have a tracker on the Days' car, and we can see on the dashboard screen that they're pulling up to a T-junction, having moved a little further ahead. Now they turn right. It's only another two hundred metres to the barn from where Henry's phone is sending its signal.

'I'm going to try him again,' says Mrs Day, and inadvertently or otherwise, she ends the call with us.

'Do you think it's a good idea to let them go first, Fish?' asks Cotton, now that we're not being overheard.

'We'll let them pull up outside. If he comes out to greet them, fine. Otherwise they wait for us to go inside.' Our plan has always been to let the Days arrive first while we stay back, just in case the kidnappers are watching the barn – although doing so would again represent the kind of needless risk that the Vanishers tend to avoid. But like all hastily made plans around kidnaps, you never know.

We're at the T-junction now, and I use the radio to tell the convoy of unmarked vehicles following us that our ETA is only one minute, and that they should keep a mile back and wait for further instructions.

Mrs Day comes on the line again, sounding worried. 'He's still not answering.'

Cotton looks at me. He mouths the words: 'I don't like this.'

I know exactly what he means. All four prior victims

we know about were drugged before release, but they'd all woken up before their families got to them. Also, none of them were in possession of their mobile phones. It's always a dangerous move for criminals to keep hold of traceable mobile phones, because even switched off, we're able to track them. And yet they've turned Henry's back on. Which is not like them.

And still the ransom money hasn't moved from the account.

The combination of all these things makes the atmosphere in the car tense. I'm ultimately responsible for this operation, and it's my head that's going to be the one rolling.

I can see from the tracker signal on my phone that the Days' car has turned onto the short track leading to the barn and is pulling up directly in front of it. I call their mobile phone, and when Mr Day answers it, putting us on speaker, I tell the two of them to stay in the car. 'Can you see any sign of Henry?' I ask.

'No, we can't,' he says. 'The place looks empty and the doors are shut.'

'I need to go in there,' says Mrs Day. 'I need to find him. It's freezing. He could die of exposure.'

I hear the passenger door opening. 'Please stay where you are, Mrs Day. I don't want either of you contaminating the scene. There may be clues we can pick up about the kidnappers.'

'I don't care,' she answers. 'I just want my boy back.'

'Please stay put,' I tell her firmly. Then, to Cotton: 'Pull in next to them.'

Cotton nods and slows down as he comes to the turning at the end of a high hedge running along the road. The barn, a large one-storey structure with a dilapidated roof, sits behind a piece of potholed waste ground. I look round as we stop next to the Days' car, and Cotton cuts the engine. The ground here is flat and open, interspersed with hedges and fences that divide the fields all around the property, and although there are a couple of outhouses and residential dwellings in the distance, there are no obvious vantage points from where we can be observed.

'The Vanishers aren't going to be watching this place,' I say, before getting out of the car and shivering against the wind. It's a dreary, cold December day, the kind that makes you wonder why you live in this country, with sleet forecast for later.

The Days are out of their car too, both looking at me. Mr Day, early fifties, dressed too young for his age, is clearly working hard to stay stoic and calm. Mrs Day, a short, intense woman brimming with nervous energy, and the look of someone who's used to being in charge, is almost bouncing up and down on her feet. 'He's going to freeze in this. Get in there if you won't let us in,' she says. 'I've called his name. There's no answer.'

'We're going in now,' I say, putting on a pair of evidence gloves and motioning for Cotton to follow me. I repeat the instruction for the Days to remain where they are. I'm feeling anxious now, although I try not to show it.

But I know Cotton can see my tension. He looks worried too. We've worked together in Kidnap for close to

11

six years and we know each other well. Every case is very different, and you can usually predict the way it's going to go. But there are alarm bells sounding all over the place with this one.

We get to the barn door. I can feel Nigel and Jenny Day's eyes boring into my back. Once again Jenny calls her son's name, her voice rising above the wind.

I knock loudly and call his name too, asking if he's in there and all right.

No answer.

There's no point hanging about. If Henry is lying in there unconscious, he will be at risk of hypothermia, so I open the door and step inside, Cotton following.

The barn is empty. Completely. Even the cobblestoned floor is comparatively clean. I look up, as if I'm going to see him there, but there's nothing but cobwebs between the beams, and a hole the size of a suitcase that looks straight out onto a relentlessly grey sky.

'The phone's got to be in here somewhere,' says Cotton, glancing at his own phone as he walks across the room. 'The signal's coming from south of the barn.'

'But where the hell's Henry?' I say, conscious of the helplessness in my voice. 'This isn't how these people operate. He should be here.' But the fact is, I'm not missing anything. He isn't here, and that's the end of it.

'Here's the phone,' says Cotton, crouching down at a spot in the corner of the building.

Then he says something that stills the room. 'There's a note with it.'

I'm at his side in two steps as he stands back up, unfolding a piece of A4 paper with gloved hands.

We both stand in silence for a moment as the bold type-written words on the page sink in.

YOU SHOULDN'T HAVE INVOLVED THE POLICE. NOW YOU'LL NEVER SEE HENRY AGAIN. CHECK THE PHOTOS SECTION. PASSCODE 999911.

It's me who picks up the phone. I do it instinctively, wanting to get this over with. Without speaking, I punch in the passcode. The home screen comes up with a photo of Henry Day looking mean and moody in a hoodie

'How could they have known, Fish?' says Cotton, in-credulous. 'We kept it tight. We kept it fucking tight.'

I don't answer. I find the photo icon, open it up, and there it is. The first picture I see. It's a close-to-full-body shot of Henry lying on a bare stone floor in the foetal position, a thick puddle of blood pooled beside him, emanating from what look like a number of stab wounds to his abdomen. His mouth is gagged, his hands tied behind his back. This photo is not faked. When you've seen as many dead bodies as I have, in twenty-one years of police work, you know what a dead person looks like. This is definitely Henry. And he is very definitely dead.

'Oh Christ,' says Cotton. 'They really did it.'

Because he knows a dead body when he sees one too.

'Have you got an evidence bag?' I say, my voice quiet, constricted. The words an effort to get out.

SIMON KERNICK

He reaches into his coat pocket and takes one out, and I hand him the phone, not wanting to look at the picture any more as the barn door opens and Jenny Day strides inside, followed closely by her husband.

'Where is he?' she demands as I turn to face her. 'Where's my son?'

But as I walk towards her, not sure how I'm going to say this, she must see the expression of defeat etched into my face, because she lets out an animal howl and comes at me. 'Where is he? What's happened to my boy?'

'We don't know yet for sure,' I say, and I could take the coward's way out and not elaborate until I've got more information, but I don't, because I owe them the truth. 'The kidnappers found out we were involved,' I continue. 'There's a possibility he may have come to harm.'

She goes for me then, and who can blame her? She slaps my face, tries to scratch me, and though I put my hands up to defend myself, such is her fury that she just keeps coming, her nails cutting my cheeks, until finally Mr Day grabs her with both arms in a bear hug and pulls her backwards, his eyes flashing a cold fury as they meet mine.

I stumble outside, just keep walking into the blessed biting cold, knowing that this whole thing is on me. That I have failed.

And I'd say that this is going to be something that haunts me for the rest of my life. But that wouldn't be true.

Because, you see, I planned the whole thing.

THREE MONTHS LATER

1

Thursday, 11.15 a.m.

Okay. So let me introduce myself. My name's Keith Fisher, but no one calls me Keith because, frankly, it's a terrible name, and I've always been known as Fish. Obviously you know by now that I'm not one of the good guys, although I suspect it was a shock to find that out.

I wouldn't say I'm evil. That would be far too simplistic. Let's just say that twenty-one years of dealing with criminals, back-stabbing bosses and an unappreciative public has left me with the opinion that if you want to get on in this world, you've got to step on a lot of toes and not worry too much about the consequences. There are plenty of arseholes out there who deserve what's coming to them.

Take the Day family, for instance. Nigel Day, the dad, is a property developer who knocks down perfectly good houses and sticks back-to-back monstrosities in their place, cutting financial corners wherever he can and basically not giving a monkey's about anyone else. He and his wife also own a portfolio of five student rental properties in various locations where they charge young people extortionate rents to live in mould-infested dumps, thereby helping them to pile up huge amounts of debt for the future. Jenny is also a Conservative local councillor, which probably helps explain why planning approval never seems to be a problem for Nigel's latest development company (he's had two others in the past, both of which went bankrupt, owing their suppliers a lot of money that none of them ever saw). He's also fucking his secretary, the dirty dog.

Both of them have behaved appallingly since the disappearance and presumed death of their son (who, incidentally, wasn't an especially nice kid either, although more on that later). They've been appearing on TV criticising the police, writing articles in newspapers about the incompetence of the Anti Kidnap unit and especially its former head (i.e., me), acting like they're the only people in the country let down by the forces of law and order. Message to the Days: you're not. Everyone gets let down by the forces of law and order these days.

So why does a man who's a bit of a villain make a career out of the police? Well, to be honest – and I feel I can be honest with you now – I wanted adventure, and power too. At first, my plan was to join the army. I'd always fancied the idea of carrying a gun and potentially firing it at people, but at that time, in the mid nineties, the only war zone the British army were involved in was Northern Ireland, where I was far more likely to get shot or blown up than have a chance to take on the bad guys face to face, and actually, when it came down to it, I really didn't want to get shot. So instead I opted for the police. And do you know what?

I've had a pretty successful career, having spent the best part of the last fifteen years as a detective (including a stint in armed surveillance), putting away some seriously bad guys in the process. Guys a lot worse than me

After the Day case and the ensuing fallout, I thought that was going to be it for me. That I'd be drummed unceremoniously out of the force, sacked with a decent pay-off and my pension intact, and that the pressure of public opprobrium would force me to leave the country and retire to a beach somewhere in southern Thailand where I could enjoy a nice relaxed life in the sunshine eating great food and drinking too many beers. Ouch!

Except it hasn't worked out like that. Right now, as you may have heard, there's a serious dearth of experience within British policing. Half of the detectives in the Met have had less than five years on the job. The people with the knowledge have been leaving in droves, and consequently, even when someone appears to have messed up like I have, the bosses can't afford to lose them, so instead of the boot, I've been demoted from the NCA equivalent of DI to DC, and Adam Cotton, the man who was my second in command, has taken over my old role, which I have to say, I'm not impressed with. Cotton's a good guy, with even longer on the job than me, but he's not leadership material, and I'd have thought the unit could have scored some serious diversity brownie points by appointing DS Riva Patel instead. She's an excellent detective and totally incorruptible, which is what you want in that kind of role.

But hey, that's not my problem. I just do my job and

attempt to line my pockets without anyone spotting it, and that's why I'm still here. I've made decent money from my side hustle helping the Vanishers avoid capture and supplying them with fruitful targets, but the problem is, it hasn't made me rich. There are too many people involved and therefore the money's spread too thinly.

But now, three months after the Henry Day debacle (which obviously didn't pay any of us anything, as it was way too dangerous to touch the money), it's time for the Vanishers to go to work again, and this time is definitely going to be the last. The payday's going to be a hell of a lot bigger too, and as the man who's set it up, I'm going to be getting a very sizeable share of it, as I both deserve and need.

And then I'm out of it. Because in truth, the whole thing's getting far too risky. Over the years I've noticed that most intelligent and resourceful criminals get caught because they don't know when to stop. The lure of easy money is simply too much. It's always just one more job, and eventually, through probability as much as decent detective work, we get them. And I tell you this. There's no way that's happening to me. I've worked too hard and planned too well to fail now.

I've got the next four days off, and I'm going to take it easy. I've just come back from a nice walk down to the river, where I sent a text from a burner phone I bought in cash to another burner phone, letting the person on the other end know that the job's on and we're ready to move. And that's pretty much the extent of my involvement. Now I sit back and let others do the work for me, and hopefully by Monday I'm going to be a wealthy man.

I'm making a coffee when my regular phone rings, and straight away I'm thinking it's probably one of the three women I'm currently talking to on Tinder, so I pick it up with a wry smile on my face, only to discover to my disappointment that it's Cotton.

This isn't good. He never calls on a day off unless it's really urgent. Of course, I'm under no obligation to take it. I've just put in seven days on call during which I worked close to eighty hours. But I also know that if it's something to do with the Vanishers case then for obvious reasons it's better I hear it now.

And that's exactly what it is. Almost as soon as I've pressed the green button, I hear Cotton's voice, sounding far too enthusiastic as he says the four words that fill me with horror.

'We've got a lead.'

2

Thursday, 11.25 a.m.

Katherine Steele-Perkins, known to her tiny circle of friends as Delvina, takes great pleasure in her corpses. She considers it a privilege to be the person tasked with preparing them for their final send-off. She is the artist who works her dark magic, breathing a freshness into their dead flesh so that they are almost brought back to life as they lie empty and cold in their open coffins while the weeping relatives file past.

Right now, she's inserting the needle that will carry the embalming fluid into the carotid artery of her latest client, Norman Whitly, a very large seventy-six-year-old Caucasian male with legs full of gout. Norman had numerous health issues over the years, according to his relatives, but what finally got him was a blood clot to the brain that had somehow evaded the blood thinners and every other drug he'd been existing on. It's a foolish thing, thinks Delvina, keeping the old and infirm just alive enough so that they crumble and fall apart slowly. But then the road to hell has always been paved with the best of intentions.

'Look at you,' she whispers, running a nail lightly across

his face. 'Fat, helpless and ugly. And today I'm going to make you look far better than you ever did in your miserable little life.'

There's a knock on the embalming room door, followed by a pause. Her husband and submissive knows better than to come in before Delvina gives him permission.

'Enter,' she calls sharply, and Vincent Steele-Perkins steps inside, shutting the door behind him.

He's a short, hard-looking man of thirty-eight, which makes him close to a decade Delvina's junior, and a former amateur lightweight boxer. When she met him five years ago, he was something of a rough diamond, to say the least, an ex-con known as Vinnie Slice by his friends because he once slashed a man's face from ear to ear with a Stanley knife in an argument over something so petty that he can't even remember what it was. But somehow Delvina (who's good at such things) saw potential there, and in the intervening years she's moulded him into exactly the kind of man she likes: obedient, industrious, well mannered and utterly expendable. Now he's her co-director of the Travellers Rest Funeral Home and the one who tends to act front of house, which just shows how well she's trained him, and makes her very proud.

He gives her a little bow, part of their ritual when they're alone, and Delvina steps in front of Norman Whitly's bloated corpse so that her husband doesn't have to see the embalming fluid being pumped into the neck. She knows he gets creeped out by this part of her work, which is strange considering he's a naturally violent man.

23

'What can I do for you, Goddess?' he asks. His accent is still rough around the edges, as befits his upbringing, but the effort he puts into improving it pleases her immensely.

'I've heard from McBride,' she tells him. 'He's given us the go-ahead. He wants the snatch done tonight. Are we ready?'

He nods, his demeanour less subservient now they're talking business. 'We're ready. Has he paid us the first chunk yet?'

Delvina frowns a little. 'It's a tranche, pet. Not a chunk.' This first tranche is 7.7 bitcoin, which at the previous night's exchange rate is approximately £150,000, although the way the bitcoin price swings, it's almost certainly different now. This represents one third of the agreed price for the job they are about to do. The other two thirds will become payable as soon as their victim is safely stowed.

Now, this isn't the way Vincent and Delvina usually work. As professional kidnappers, they've always used a tried-and-tested technique of abducting individuals for a set ransom, paid by the victim's family. The names and details of the victims are supplied by Delvina's contact, Keith Fisher, who insists that she call him by the codename McBride in front of Vincent because he doesn't want Vincent to know his real identity. Fisher is a man you wouldn't trust a millimetre, but she has no choice but to work with him. He knows things about her that can never be made public, which is the main reason he always gets to take a decent cut of the proceeds. But the job he's getting them to do this time is different. There's no ransom involved. Fisher has provided the details of the victim, and he's the one who's paying them a third upfront, which means he's almost certainly working on behalf of someone else, and Delvina knows that her husband has doubts about this.

'Are you sure you want to go ahead with this, Goddess? I don't like it that McBride's working for people we don't know.'

'McBride has always been reliable and we need to trust that he knows what he's doing this time, pet. We're making the equivalent of four hundred and fifty thousand pounds for this.' She smiles at him. 'Then we retire from the game.'

'Just one last job, eh?' he says, with a hint of doubt.

'Yes. Just one last job.' And in truth, she knows that this will indeed be his last job, and possibly hers too, but only possibly. Because, you see, Delvina enjoys the power she wields too much not to take big risks like this. She's a natural hunter, and although she feels the same twinge of fear she always feels before a job, she also experiences a warm glow of pleasure.

Because tonight she's hunting again.

3

Thursday, 11.30 a.m.

The thing you notice about prison is the number of doors you have to go through to get to your destination, all of which have to be unlocked then locked behind you as you go further and further inside. And when you're visiting an inmate in Belmarsh, the UK's most secure penal establishment, which even has its very own prison within a prison, that's a lot of doors; Becca Barraclough counts fourteen before she finally enters the High Security Unit.

Becca is the kind of barrister any defendant wants on their side. And that's because she's a winner. In her seventy-seven criminal defence cases since coming to the Bar almost two decades ago now, she's won sixty-six. She's quick and ruthless, but also comes across as empathetic, even kind.

Becca knows that some people absolutely despise her, particularly so after the now infamous Tamzan case four years ago, when she secured an acquittal for her client, a failed asylum seeker, on a double murder charge. The victims – Oliver Tamzan's girlfriend and her thirteen-year-old daughter – were bludgeoned to death in the girlfriend's flat in an especially brutal crime. Becca was convinced Tamzan was innocent, even though he didn't have an alibi and had been at the flat earlier that evening. He wasn't a violent man, and he had no motive, but far more importantly than that, the prosecution offered no forensic evidence testifying to his guilt. Their case was weak. All Becca had done was exploit that to create a perfectly reasonable doubt in the jury's mind.

In fact she was convinced of Tamzan's innocence right up until eighteen months ago, when he was charged with the attempted murder of a businesswoman who'd taken pity on him and allowed him to stay in a flat she owned. The woman had visited him there one evening and had ended up with injuries that included a broken jaw, a broken wrist, six broken ribs and a detached retina, as well as marks on her neck where she'd been strangled unconscious. Tamzan had fled the scene when a neighbour, hearing the commotion, had knocked on the door and threatened to call the police, and he'd been arrested four days later.

Once again Becca had defended him in court, but this time the jury weren't swayed by her argument that he was suffering from PTSD and therefore had diminished responsibility when he carried out the assault. He was found guilty and sentenced to eighteen years. What Becca hadn't been prepared for was the media storm that followed. She was named and vilified in the press as the lawyer who'd got a murderer off the hook and then tried to help him evade justice a second time, leaving behind a victim with life-changing injuries, something that was made even more heinous by the fact that Becca was herself a single mother of a daughter.

The result of all this was a slew of anonymous death threats for months afterwards, and even the offer of police protection, which she'd turned down.

Because Becca knows you can't let things get to you. She does her job even if sometimes that makes her unpopular, and she's going to continue to do it until she – and no one else – decides it's time to do something else. There's no shortage of work either. Her reputation has spread far and wide in legal circles, and so there are plenty of clients vying for her services, the latest of whom is the enigmatic and undeniably handsome Logan Quinn.

Quinn is being held in Belmarsh's maximum-security wing on remand while awaiting trial for murder. And it's one of the strangest cases Becca's ever come across in her time in the legal profession. What happened, at least according to Quinn, was this: he was driving on an isolated Essex road through woodland on an unseasonably warm November night four months ago when he went to overtake the car in front of him. As he pulled out, the driver of the car in front, thirty-one-year-old Jess O'Sullivan, inexplicably did the same. The two cars collided, and Jess's Renault Clio left the road, went down a steep bank and travelled a further twenty yards before hitting a tree head-on.

Quinn immediately stopped his own car, climbed down the bank and went to check if Ms O'Sullivan was all right. However, as soon as he got to her, he could see that she was badly hurt. Her head was resting against the wheel and she was bleeding badly from a head injury. He reached inside her open window and felt for a pulse, first on her neck, then on her wrist, but could find nothing. Realising that he could get into serious trouble for what had just happened, he ran back to his car and drove away without reporting it to the police.

And there it might have ended, with Ms O'Sullivan's death being treated as a tragic accident and Logan Quinn off the hook. But unfortunately for Quinn, a young couple were wild camping on the edge of a river only fifty metres from the spot where Ms O'Sullivan's Clio left the road. They were both asleep at the time (it was 12.50 a.m.), but alerted by the commotion, the male half of the couple, Josh Harvey, climbed out of the tent and went to investigate what had happened.

The Clio still had its headlights on, and as he approached it through the trees, still unsure what was going on, he saw a man heading towards the vehicle from the road at what he described as a run. The man reached through the open window, looking like he was feeling for the driver's pulse, although it was hard to tell for sure from where Harvey was watching. But he was definitely sure of what he witnessed next, which was the man opening the door, grabbing Ms O'Sullivan by the hair and smashing her forehead repeatedly and violently into the dashboard for a period lasting as long as thirty seconds. He then closed the door and reached beneath the Clio's rear driver's-side wheel to retrieve something, which he placed in his jacket pocket before running back up to the road.

Harvey followed at a safe distance and saw the man get into a car, which he described as a dark-coloured saloon with the letters NB on the number plate, and drive away at speed. He then returned to the Clio and felt for Ms O'Sullivan's pulse himself. She was apparently still breathing at this point, but it was some minutes before he was able to call the emergency services for help, because the signal in the area was poor, and by the time she reached hospital, she was already dead.

As a result of Josh Harvey's testimony, Essex Police launched a murder investigation, and were quickly able to identify the suspect's car using footage from a CCTV camera at a junction three miles from the scene of the crash. Its registered owner was Logan Quinn, who, when arrested, gave the account he still stands by: that he panicked and fled the scene without reporting it but did nothing to harm Ms O'Sullivan, who was, according to him, already dead when he reached her car immediately after the crash.

Even so, he was still charged with murder and remanded in Belmarsh to await trial, which was when he made contact with Becca through his solicitor.

The case intrigues her. Logan Quinn is a self-styled property developer who lives in Buckinghamshire and had no prior contact with the victim, nor any obvious motive for killing her. The police and the Crown Prosecution Service hold a different view, however, as became clear when Becca met up with her CPS counterparts to discuss the evidence against her client. Forty-two-year-old Quinn might be a property developer but he's also a former commando with over ten years' military service, including two tours in Afghanistan, where he saw action and won several medals. And according to the police, he's a contract killer who murdered Jess O'Sullivan for money, although the evidence that Becca's seen so far to back up this claim (and as Quinn's defence barrister she's entitled to see everything the CPS have) is scant to say the least.

There's no mention of who hired him to kill Ms O'Sullivan, or why. According to the CPS, friends of the victim said that she'd been acting strangely recently and had appeared worried about something. She'd also contacted a national newspaper, telling the reporter who answered that she had a potentially very big story about her employer, a large multinational mining company for whom she worked as a marketing manager, but refused to go into further details over the phone. She'd wanted to meet, but the reporter had been reluctant to without some idea of what the story was actually about. Ms O'Sullivan had given no further details and had promised to come back to him. But she never did, and nine days later she was dead.

And that's it. The sum total of the case against Logan Quinn. In Becca's opinion, as it stands, even with a very average defence barrister representing him (and she's a hell of a lot better than average), there's no more than a twenty per cent chance of a conviction. In reality, all the CPS have is one witness who, by his own admission, had just woken up and could easily have mistaken what he thought he'd seen in the darkness. And yet they're still going ahead with the trial, which is set to begin in two months' time. It isn't unheard of for the CPS to try cases with only a slim chance of conviction (and which almost always end in acquittal), but they do try to avoid it, so Becca is certain that the police are holding him on this charge while they try to find evidence against him for other murders.

Does she believe Logan Quinn is innocent of Jess O'Sullivan's murder? The truth is, she's not sure, but then that's the case with plenty of the suspects she's defended, including Oliver Tamzan. Where the client has declared his or her innocence, and where the evidence isn't so overwhelming that it's wasting everyone's time, then Becca will always do her utmost to secure an acquittal, because that's her job.

Logan Quinn is a good-looking guy with plenty of charm and a winning smile. He doesn't look like an archetypal killer, and yet he's seen action in Afghanistan and almost certainly killed enemy fighters there. And his background is sketchy. Though he claims to be a property developer, apart from flipping three houses over a period of nine years, there's no obvious evidence that he's done any actual developing. Since leaving the army in 2009, he's worked in a variety of security jobs for blue-chip companies and private clients, but always in a freelance capacity, and in the last four years, his official earnings total less than £40,000 annually, yet he owns two properties with a total value in excess of a million pounds, as well as two cars, and has investments in his name worth another hundred thousand. So he's getting the money from somewhere. More damningly, he had no good reason for being in the vicinity of the accident, a distance of sixty-seven miles from his home. His claim that he'd been driving round looking at possible houses to buy doesn't sound plausible at all.

But again, none of this is evidence. And right now, Becca's main aim is to get Quinn out of the zoo that is Belmarsh and into a less brutal and dangerous Category B or, ideally, C prison to await trial. At least then she won't have to come to this place, which always fills her with a deep sense of unease.

It's Quinn who's called her in today. He said it was urgent that they talk face to face but didn't tell her why on the phone, although as soon as she entered the prison, Belmarsh's health-and-safety manager took her aside to explain that the previous day Quinn had been attacked on the wing during recreation by a prisoner armed with a sharpened spoon.

'He's all right, though,' insisted the manager, who clearly had one eye on a potential lawsuit for negligence. 'And we've moved him off the block and into a segregation unit in maximum security, away from the other prisoners. He'll be safe there.'

'He'd better be,' Becca told him sharply. 'You owe him a duty of care.'

From her brief discussion with the manager, it appears that the attack on Quinn was sudden and apparently unprovoked, but he managed to fight off his attacker, sustaining a minor injury on his forearm in the altercation, before prison staff intervened. He was checked over and patched up before being given a clean bill of health, none of which he mentioned in his phone call to Becca the previous evening.

A meeting room has been set aside for them in the middle of the maximum-security block next to the small indoor garden with its large skylights, where the inmates are encouraged to tend the plants and grow vegetables. Becca thanks the guard as he unlocks the door and lets her inside.

Logan Quinn's already there, sitting on the other side of a large wooden table. Because he's on remand and hasn't yet been convicted of any crime, he's wearing civilian clothes: a neatly pressed checked shirt with the sleeves rolled up and a white T-shirt beneath, and jeans. Only the bandage covering part of his exposed left forearm looks out of place.

He stands up and smiles at her, his blue eyes twinkling. Quinn knows he's good-looking and charming and he plays to those two strengths, something Becca doesn't much like, although she knows a jury will. It's like he's constantly trying to convince her he's a nice guy, but he's working too hard at it, which tells her he's probably not.

'Good to see you, Becca,' he says, his voice deep and resonant, the handshake firm. 'Thanks for coming in at such short notice. I hope it wasn't too much trouble.'

'I heard about what happened to you in here,' she says, motioning towards the bandage as they sit down opposite each other. 'What was that all about?'

'It's one of the things I wanted to talk to you about,' he says, leaning forward with his elbows on the table. 'I was deliberately targeted. That prisoner came straight at me from out of an open cell door. It was an ambush. He had a home-made knife and was trying to stab me in the neck. In other words, he wanted to kill me.' He speaks slowly, carefully, emphasising the importance of his words.

'Why would he do that?'

'I've never even seen him before, and from what I can gather, he's not talking to the authorities. But I'm certain I know the reason behind it.'

'Go on.'

Quinn looks thoughtful. 'You said that at your last meeting with the CPS you were told the police think I'm responsible for another two murders?'

'That's their theory. They named two men. Avtar Singh and Victor Otogo. Killed two years apart. The first in Glasgow. Found drowned in his bath. The second in London. Shot dead outside his home. And as I recall, you told me you didn't know either of them, or anything about their deaths.'

'Have the police got any evidence at all to back up their claims?'

Becca's instincts tell her that Quinn might well be about to come up with some revelations. When defending a client against a charge, she always asks them whether they're guilty or innocent. Not one has ever told her they were guilty. In some cases she didn't believe their denials, but that was irrelevant.

'They haven't given me any details yet,' she tells him, 'which I take to mean they don't have much. But I expect they'll want to question you about the murders at some point in the near future.'

Quinn nods, taking this in.

'Have you got something you want to tell me, Logan?' Becca's tone is firm.

He sits up in his seat, his back ramrod straight, looking right into her eyes, which is a habit of his. He's the very opposite of evasive. 'I've got a lot of information that would be very, very useful to the CPS and the police,' he says carefully. 'That's why there was an attempt on my life.'

'I'm your lawyer. You can tell me what that information is in confidence.'

Quinn hesitates, and Becca can see he's not entirely convinced. Finally he speaks. 'I can help them solve a number of murders and bring to justice the people who ordered those murders.'

'So I take it from that that you are who the police say you are. A contract killer.'

Again he hesitates. And this time he looks away.

'Did you murder Jessica O'Sullivan?'

He sighs, runs a hand through his thick black hair. 'My actions resulted in her death, yes.'

'Was it deliberate?'

'That depends on who I'm talking to.'

Becca's getting tired of this. 'You're talking to me, and I need to know the answer in order to build a successful defence. When we first met, and in all our subsequent conversations, you stated that Ms O'Sullivan's death was, in your words, an accident. If you want me to defend you in court, you have to tell me the whole truth. No evasions.'

This time Quinn doesn't pause. 'Yes,' he says. 'I killed

her deliberately. And yes, I suppose I am what the police would call a contract killer. But that's not my whole story. You have to believe that.'

Becca isn't sure what to believe. She wasn't expecting Quinn's admission and it makes her evaluate him very differently. She's no longer sure she wants to represent him.

'I'm not an evil man, Becca,' he continues. 'I'm a deeply troubled one, I'll admit that, but—'

'How many?'

'How many what?'

'How many victims?'

'This goes no further, right?'

'I told you it won't.'

He takes a deep breath, looks her straight in the eye. 'Twenty-three.'

4

Thursday, 12.10 p.m.

So here I am in the Kidnap Unit's offices, located in a quiet corner of the NCA HQ in Waterloo, and the place is empty apart from Cotton, who's taken up residence in my old office without the slightest concern for my feelings. Cheeky bastard.

It's not unusual for the offices to be quiet. As the NCA website will tell you, the Kidnap Unit's remit is wide. We're not just involved in leading criminal kidnap cases. We also deal with blackmail and extortion (and there's plenty of that going round) and product contamination. We give support and tactical advice to local police forces, the Foreign Office, Interpol and, believe it or not, even the United Nations. And on top of that, we deliver anti-kidnap training to foreign governments and private companies. All with a very limited number of officers and an even more limited budget.

'You all on your lonesome, Cott?' I say with fake jauntiness as I give a cursory knock on the open door before taking a seat opposite my new boss. I don't call him 'sir'. We go way too far back for that, and after we swapped places in the pecking order, he took me aside to tell me that on a personal level he didn't agree with my demotion, and that he'd lobbied hard for me to stay on the team, which is something of a blessing in reverse. 'As far as I'm concerned, we're still equals,' he said. Which is bullshit – I'm a far better detective than him – but of course I never let on. I just smiled, thanked him for his support and carried on with the job.

'You know what it's like, Fish,' he says. 'No shortage of cases to look at, and everyone wants to work from home. It's never busy in here any more, is it? Not like it used to be.'

Cotton is three years older than me, at forty-eight, which these days isn't actually that old, but he still talks like Ol' Man River banging on about the good old days.

'Very true,' I say, vaguely. I need to know what he's got, because this could make things very complicated, so I ask him what the lead is.

Cotton's a big lad, and he leans his head forward so his double chin's almost resting on his chest, his lip jutting out at the same time, the kind of sad face a clown pulls. To people who don't know him, it can look slightly disconcerting, but I know it's the expression he wears when he's got something important to say, and it just looks more exaggerated these days because he's put on a good few stone, a decent portion of which is sitting on his face.

'About an hour ago, I got a call from Major Incident Command,' he says, and straight away I'm nervous. 'They've got an ongoing undercover operation to infiltrate a small but nasty organised crime gang led by an individual called

39

Blake Burns. Apparently Burns's crew have a little sideline going that involves them kidnapping big-time drug dealers and holding them until their wives or girlfriends pay a ransom. They've done it three times so far, without any of the crimes ever being reported, and they're just about to do another one.'

'I thought it was a lead on the Vanishers case,' I say, looking and sounding disappointed, but secretly pleased.

'It is,' says Cotton, with a small smile that's almost lost in his face. The fucker really needs to lose some weight. 'At least indirectly. The gang are short on manpower, so they're using an associate of Burns's called Marv to help with the kidnap. The undercover operative was with Burns when he made a call to Marv earlier this morning, and he managed to eavesdrop on some of the conversation. From what we can gather, Marv said that if Burns wanted to use him, he'd have to hurry up, the reason being that he was on standby for another job – apparently one that's very well paid and just involves, quote, "some babysitting".'

'And that's it? What makes you think this guy's got anything to do with the Vanishers?'

Cotton sighs and leans back in my old swivel chair, which bangs against the wall behind him. 'I don't know if he does or not, but it was the undercover oppo who picked up on it. He couldn't hear Marv talking because Burns had the phone to his ear, but it seemed to him that the job that Marv was on standby for was a kidnap, and because it was well paid and kidnap's not that common a crime, he thought he'd bring it to our attention. It might be nothing, but it's worth looking into. I mean, it's not like we've got any other leads on the Vanishers case.'

Which is true. And I don't think this isn't going to be one either. I happen to know that the Vanishers are a husband-and-wife team: the scary Delvina and her partner, Vincent Steele-Perkins, aka Vinnie 'Slice' Cunningham, a short-arsed thug with a penchant for GBH who now masquerades as a funeral director. Even so, I don't like the timing of this particular lead (it's worryingly coincidental given that there's going to be another snatch tonight), so I ask if we've got an ID for this mysterious Marv.

Cotton shakes his head. 'No. The difficulty is the undercover oppo's new to the gang, so he can't ask too many questions. All he knows is that Marv is some scumbag who's used as muscle.'

'Which doesn't really narrow it down round this neck of the woods,' I say, thinking about the numerous scumbags I've had to deal with over the years. They're always the ones who breed more too, giving me very little hope for the future of the human race. 'And what do we know about Burns, the man who's hiring him?'

'I looked him up on the system. Thirty-four years old, long record for violence. He served four years for GBH; three for intent to supply class A; six months as a kid for possession of a knife. Plenty of other minor stuff. He runs the dealing on the Hillview estate in Harlesden, supposedly with an iron fist.'

'But he still sounds pretty low-level,' I say, concluding that it probably is just coincidental and I've been dragged in here under false pretences. Wanting to discredit this lead as soon as possible, I add: 'We know the Vanishers are a sophisticated team. They don't use muscle in their abductions. With Henry Day, they used a woman who appeared to drug him with something, then they had him in the back of a car before he even knew what was happening. It was smooth. It was professional. It wasn't done by a thug for hire.'

Cotton shrugs. 'It might be nothing, but apparently the undercover oppo wants to meet this afternoon, so he might have some more information that we don't know about yet. I want to solve the Vanishers case just as much as you do, Fish. It's personal to both of us. And to the team, because our reputation's taken a big hit after what happened to the Day boy. It made us look incompetent. And we're not.'

'I know we're not,' I say, 'and I still don't understand how those bastards got on to us.' I even consider mentioning a suspicion I have that there's someone on the inside, but that would be too cocky.

'We just have to be even more careful next time. We'll get them, Fish. We've always got the bad guys in the past. And you know the drill. These people always make a mistake in the end.' He smiles again, a twinkle in his eye. 'Who knows? You might even get your old job and this office back.'

I allow myself a light chuckle. 'Imagine that. You and me running the show together.'

'Two old white men with one foot in retirement? I doubt that.'

I'm slightly peeved at being called an old white man, if I'm honest with you. I'm white, but I'm only forty-five, and

I look good on it. 'We're not old, Cott. We're men about town. And didn't you say you've got another date with that woman you've been seeing, tomorrow night?'

'Yeah, it's going pretty well too,' he says with real pride in his voice.

'I'm glad for you,' I tell him. 'You've got to enjoy life.'

He smiles, and we fall silent for a moment. I know old Cott feels there's a shared bond between us, and that we're great friends. I also know he's embarrassed that he's now the equivalent to a DI while I'm suddenly a DC, and well he should be, since the new positions don't reflect our relative talents. But the truth is, I do like him. Though if and when the time comes to throw him to the wolves to save myself, I won't hesitate. Because in the end, you've always got to look after number one.

'So what's the plan then?' I ask, going back to the subject at hand.

'Well, the Blake Burns case is a potential kidnapping, so it falls within our remit anyway. And apparently it's going down tonight. I'm going to ride along, and hopefully get a chance to talk to this Marv, or maybe one of the others arrested along with him. Because as you know, Fish, there's a fifty-grand reward for helping put the Vanishers behind bars, and that might get people's tongues wagging. But it's your day off, so if you don't fancy it . . .'

'Of course I fancy it,' I tell him, thinking that I can't imagine anything worse on my day off, but I also know that I need to keep control of the situation, and that means making sure that this lead is a non-starter.

The problem is, I'm already getting just a little twinge of nerves. It's the timing. As a copper of many years' standing, I don't believe in coincidences.

Which means I'm going to have to do something I hate doing. And that's meet with Delvina.

5

Thursday, 12.15 p.m.

'It's not how you think it is,' says Logan Quinn with a long, melodramatic sigh as he runs a hand through his hair. 'I'm not some kind of monster.'

Becca, still shocked, says: 'You've just told me you've killed twenty-three people. How *should* I think of it?'

'Think of me as a fallen hero.'

'A fallen hero?' She looks at him aghast. 'There's nothing heroic about what you've done.'

'I know. But it's not the whole story, Becca. I didn't start out like this. In the army, I was a hero. I won two medals. I was mentioned in dispatches. But it wasn't enough to help me when the MoD investigators came sniffing around.'

'You were accused of torturing a prisoner.'

'A violent Taliban thug who we knew had been planting the IEDs that had killed two members of our unit. And we didn't torture him. We questioned him robustly to find out where he'd hidden some others.'

'I think it might possibly be the same thing,' says Becca.

'It's easy for civilians, for people like yourself, for the

MoD investigators, all of you, to cast judgement on us, but we were out there fighting a bad war against people who didn't play by any of the rules, and which none of us actually wanted to be involved in. We may have over-stepped the mark, but I didn't deserve to be thrown out and threatened with prosecution, not after more than ten years of good service.'

Having examined the details of the case, Becca isn't sure she agrees with Quinn's version of events. At the time, he was a lieutenant in the Royal Irish Rangers, and he and three of his subordinates tied and hooded their prisoner, Tawab Khan, and repeatedly dunked his head in a cattle trough to simulate drowning until they got the answers they were looking for. Quinn was the one doing the dunking, and another member of the unit filmed what was happening and afterwards released the footage to the UK media.

Some say that the end justified the means, since the pris-oner told them the location of three other IEDs, which were subsequently made safe, potentially saving the lives of soldiers and civilians alike. But on a personal level, Becca doesn't subscribe to that point of view. The law's the law, and if enough people choose to bypass it, however justified they feel, anarchy prevails. Yes, as a defence lawyer she tries to make the law work best for her and her clients, but she would never countenance doing anything illegal to win a case, whatever her detractors might think.

'Anyway,' Quinn continues, calmer now, 'when I left, I was on the scrapheap. No one wanted to employ me. I was having constant nightmares. Remember, I saw men I cared about – men I was personally responsible for as their commanding officer – die horribly. I saw others lose limbs, or have their faces ripped apart by shrapnel. And in one case, both. I was diagnosed with PTSD; my mother died around the same time. My life was falling apart. I didn't know what to do.' He pauses. Takes a deep breath.

Becca can see the pain in his eyes. Whether it's real or not is another matter.

'One day, about ten years ago, when I was on my uppers, I got a call from an ex-serviceman called Sean Callahan, who ran a consultancy offering security services to blue-chip clients. He wanted me to come and work with him on a freelance basis. His main client was a big mining company with operations in Africa and South America. The money was good. Very good. But I was told that sometimes I might have to cut corners, break rules to earn it.' He sighed. 'I was an angry man back then. I felt I'd been let down by my country, a public that really didn't understand or care how bad things were, and most of all the army, which I'd always thought of as my family. So I said: "Fine. I'll do what it takes."' He pauses. 'Well, it turned out that what it took was a lot more than I'd been expecting. This mining company were involved in some very controversial pro-jects, digging up virgin rainforest, building mines in national parks and bribing local governments. There was a potential whistleblower in their Nairobi office, a manager who was threatening to lift the lid on one of the projects. So Callahan and I were given the job of neutralising the problem.' He paused. 'I promise you, Becca, I never knew until the last second what the actual plan was. I thought we were there purely to abduct him from his quarters and rough him up a little. Scare him into keeping his mouth shut.'

'But you killed him?'

'Callahan did. We took him to this stretch of waste ground just outside the city. He was handcuffed, gagged and blindfolded. We walked him over to an isolated spot. I punched him in the back. Then the side of the head. Told him that if he opened his mouth about the company, we'd get to him wherever he was. I didn't like doing it. It felt like bullying, but I figured he'd get over it. Then Callahan just walked up and put a bullet in the back of his head.' Quinn sits back in his seat, staring up at the ceiling. 'And that's when I started my new career.'

'You could have walked away,' says Becca, surprised at her own lack of surprise on hearing Quinn's revelations for the first time. 'You weren't the one who killed him.'

He shakes his head. 'It doesn't work like that, sadly. I was intimately involved in the abduction. Plus, Callahan secretly filmed me punching the victim while he was bound and blindfolded, and told me in no uncertain terms that if I said anything to anyone, that footage would come out. And I believed him.' He shrugs. 'After that, it got easier. We didn't just work for the mining company. We were employed by other people, including representatives of foreign governments.'

'Killing people?'

'Sometimes.'

'Where's Callahan now?'

'He died three years ago.'

'Did you kill him?'

'Officially it was an accident.' He sits back, rolls his shoulders and fixes her with his stare, his eyes almost glistening in the dull light of the prison meeting room. 'But yes, I killed him. I wanted to be free of his blackmail. It seemed like the only way.'

Becca exhales audibly. 'I'll be honest, I don't think any of this is going to help your case.'

Quinn sighs. 'Look, the police have a good idea who I am. They're digging for evidence all over the place. They'll find it eventually. They may even have found it already. I'll be straight with you. I killed Avtar Singh and Victor Otogo, so I run the risk of being charged with their murders as well. That's why I want to cooperate. I can name names. The people who hired me and who hired Callahan. I have evidence as well, backing up my claims. Evidence that's well hidden. And these are senior figures. Members of the establishment. High-ranking diplomats representing hostile states. I can help bring them to justice.'

'What are you looking for in return?'

'I want a deal.'

'What kind of deal?'

'I know I won't get immunity.'

'No, you definitely won't get that.'

'First and foremost, I want protection. I'm not safe here. The people who've used my services want me dead, precisely because my testimony can put them away. They'll do whatever it takes to get to me. That's why I was attacked

49

yesterday. It failed, but they'll try again. So I want to be put in a safe house.'

'Belmarsh has a contingency unit where you can be completely isolated from other prisoners.'

Quinn shakes his head. 'No way. Other prisoners still prepare my food. The guards can be bribed. I need to be in a safe house. That's non-negotiable. I'm prepared to serve time for what I've done, but no more than five years, and I want that time served in a very secure setting where I'm not going to be got at. After that, I want a completely new identity.'

Becca raises her eyebrows, something she's always managed to do to very good effect. 'I think you have to realise, Logan, that you're not in a position to make those kinds of demands. Judges decide sentences, not police officers or the CPS. And no one will entertain the idea of giving a five-year sentence to a mass killer.'

'They will if the public are fed the right narrative. So far I'm only charged with one murder. There'll be no need to charge me with any others. Almost all my evidence against the people who hired me is digital, but there's plenty of it. Taped admissions, secret filming, transparent money trails that lead straight back to them. These people can be prosecuted without it ever being public knowledge that the information came from me. And the CPS can easily change my charge on the O'Sullivan case to manslaughter.'

'I really don't think it's as easy as that.'

'If the will is there, it is. And I'm prepared to give the CPS a taster of what I've got.'

In spite of herself, Becca is curious. 'What kind of taster?'

'I've done some work on a freelance basis as well. I advertised myself discreetly on the dark web and was approached by several people wanting me to kill individuals on their behalf. One of them was the owner of a private company with a turnover in excess of fifty million pounds a year. He wanted to avoid a costly divorce from his wife, and the best way to manage that was if she died in an accident, so he paid me one hundred and fifty thousand pounds in bitcoin to make sure it happened.'

Becca's heard plenty of bad things about her clients in her time, occasionally even from their own mouths. But the matter-of-fact way Quinn describes the act of murder is probably the most shocking of all.

He clearly sees her reaction, because his expression morphs into one of regret. 'I'm not proud of what I've done, Becca. I know it looks awful, but I think that over the years I've just become inured to it.'

'What evidence have you got against the husband?' she asks, ignoring his justifications.

'Firstly, the payment came from a public wallet directly linked to him. Secondly, we talked online and I used some fairly basic software to trace the URL of the laptop he was talking to me from. I can prove that it was his. And finally, most damning of all, I have him on film discovering his wife's body in the bath of the hotel room they were staying in, and you can quite clearly see his rather pleased reaction. He's actually grinning from ear to ear in the moments before he calls reception to report her death, and it's also blindingly obvious that finding her was no surprise to him.'

'You put a hidden camera in the room?'

Quinn nods. 'That's right. A very small one. I retrieved it a couple of weeks later with no one any the wiser.'

'You really planned this out, didn't you?'

'It was insurance. I always wondered if this day would come.'

'It never occurred to you to just stop killing people for money?'

He places his hands together in a prayer-like posture that looks deliberate. 'I've been trying to withdraw from the business for a long time,' he says, 'but certain figures don't want me to do so. I've been too useful to them. And now that I'm here, I'm dangerous to them, which is why I've got to do something now. The evidence against the man I've just told you about is on a memory stick. It's also hidden securely online. I can point you in its direction easily enough.'

They both sit there in silence for several seconds.

Quinn breaks it. 'Will you help me? I need you for this.'

People often describe lawyers as devoid of conscience. Some have called Becca a lot worse, especially after the Oliver Tamzan incident, but she's always felt that, on the contrary, she has a very strong moral compass. She believes in giving a voice to the weak, to helping those who are downtrodden by an uncaring society and who otherwise might be the victims of a miscarriage of justice. She isn't naïve enough to think that all the clients she's defended are pleasant people – some of them really weren't – but she's always been able to justify that on the basis that they were entitled to a fair hearing, and this is something she can give them.

But in the last half an hour, Logan Quinn has gone from being an enigmatic character with questions to answer about the death of a young woman to a committed and largely unrepentant mass murderer. It's a transformation she's never seen before.

'I'll do what I can,' she says at last, keeping the uncertainty out of her voice, 'but you'll still need more than this to get the CPS to take you seriously.'

Quinn nods slowly. He doesn't appear concerned. 'Okay,' he says. 'I'm going to give you the name of someone the security services have been after for years. You tell them that name, and say that I can give them that man. Then they'll want to talk. I guarantee it.'

6

Thursday, 2.10 p.m.

I first met Delvina Steele-Perkins when she was still just plain Delvina Perkins and I was investigating the mysterious death of her first husband, Philip. That was eight years ago now, while I was still a DI in one of the Met's Murder Investigation Teams.

Delvina and Philip had been holidaying on Italy's picturesque Amalfi Coast when Philip had fallen more than a hundred feet to his death while hiking alone along the Path of the Gods, a well-used trail linking the famous coastal resort of Positano with the clifftop town of Bomerano.

Straight away, things didn't look quite right. The weather conditions on the day had been very good and the path was dry without any loose rocks. Although the point on the path from where he'd fallen was narrow and didn't have any safety railings, it wasn't considered dangerous, and no one had ever fallen from there before. A post-mortem carried out by the Italian coroner had also shown no obvious health issues that might have caused him to fall. He had, it seemed, been a perfectly fit fifty-five-year-old man with a strong heart. The local police made a plea for witnesses, but although there were walkers on the path at the same time, no one saw anything, and his body was not discovered until early the next morning, some hours after Delvina had reported him missing.

Delvina was his second wife, and there was a sixteen-year age gap between them. She'd joined his undertaking business as an embalmer, of all things. His first wife had died of cancer eighteen months before that, and within a year, he and Delvina were engaged. They'd been married for five years at the time of his death, and he'd changed his will so that his business, the Travellers Rest Funeral Home, including the freehold of the building, was left entirely to her. This represented around seventy per cent of the value of his estate, with the other thirty per cent being shared between his three children.

Needless to say, it was his kids who'd kicked up a fuss about the death being suspicious, muttering darkly about Delvina being behind it. Of course, they had no evidence whatsoever to back up their accusations. She hadn't even been with him at the time. She didn't share her old man's passion for walking, something she'd freely admitted, and preferred to stay behind at the hotel, where she was seen by at least a dozen witnesses by the pool. The local cops weren't interested in it being anything more than an accident, and to be honest, the Met weren't either – we have plenty of our own killings of one form or another without bothering with anyone else's. But the kids weren't taking it lying down, and one of them contacted his local MP, who finally got my Murder Investigation Team to take a look, just to see that everything was above board.

That meant me visiting Delvina at her home in the flat above the Travellers Rest offices, along with one of my DCs, just to go over her version of events.

It was three weeks after her husband's death, and she was dressed conservatively in a black blouse and black jeans, devoid of make-up. Even so, as we sat in her sumptuously decorated lounge and she explained in a soft, quiet voice what had happened, she oozed sexuality. She's a tall, slender woman with fine angular features and long dark hair that curls down below her shoulders, but it's the eyes that get you. They sparkle with all kinds of promises, and when she first fixed me with them, I remember going hard beneath my trousers. And given that her husband, whose photos were lined up across the mantelpiece, was, to put it bluntly, no looker, I guessed immediately that she was involved. It was as if I could smell the badness on her, and the way she met my gaze left me in no doubt that she could smell it on me too.

But her answers made sense, she didn't contradict herself, and it was clear that she hadn't physically pushed her husband to his death, so what were we going to do? Luckily, in one of those rare strokes of good fortune, I was able to travel with one of my colleagues to the Amalfi Coast to liaise with the local force and see for myself the spot where the late Mr Perkins had met his end. We were there three days, staying in Bomerano, during which time I hiked the whole trail myself, as well as the path over the other side down to Amalfi town, and I have to tell you, it is indeed picturesque.

56

Anyway, there was still no proof that Mr Perkins' demise was anything other than an accident, and so the case was officially closed, with the UK coroner recording a verdict of accidental death. Of course, I didn't have to visit Delvina again to give her the good news – I could have just done it over the phone – but something told me that seeing her again would be profitable.

When I turned up alone on her doorstep, having called ahead, she was no longer dressed conservatively. Instead, she was wearing a black satin corset with leather trousers, her pale feet bare, the toenails painted black.

I looked at her and I don't think we even spoke. We simply fell on each other. It was some of the best sex I've ever had, and when we finally came up for air on the king-size bed that up until two months earlier she'd shared with her husband, she looked at me and purred: 'You and me, we're kindred spirits.'

And we are, that's the thing. But I'm also no fool, and although we became lovers, I knew full well that she was using me as a potentially useful contact, so I refused to let myself fall for her. And Delvina doesn't like it if men don't fall for her, or bend to her will, so it didn't take long for our affair to end.

But that didn't matter, because as kindred spirits, our business relationship had just begun. And it's led all the way through the years to here: a park in south-west London, roughly equidistant between my flat and the Travellers Rest, where hopefully no one will recognise either of us.

I've arrived five minutes early for our meeting. There's

no sign of Delvina, so I stroll the length of the park, subtly checking out the few other people around. It's a sunny March day, but there's still a chill in the air, and the place is quiet, with most of the activity set around the kids' play park at one end.

When I turn round and start back the other way, I see her coming towards me. She's wearing a long black coat, jeans and white trainers, and her hair's hidden under a beanie cap. She still looks damn good, though, and thankfully a lot different than the street-camera footage we've got of her from the Henry Day abduction. When we made that shot public after the whole op went tits-up, we got a slow stream of callers phoning in to name who they thought it was, and of course none of them mentioned Delvina, who was always heavily disguised.

I don't see her much at all these days, but I still get a twinge deep in my groin whenever I do, something that annoys me, because it shows that despite my best efforts, she still retains some power over me.

'Mr McBride,' she says, using my codename as we hug like two old friends meeting up after a long time apart, although in truth we don't actually give a shit about each other. But her words when she speaks are cold and businesslike. 'This is a surprise, and I haven't got a lot of time to spare. What do you want?'

We break free of each other and walk side by side, staying close.

I don't beat about the bush. 'Do you by any chance work with someone called Marv?'

She looks at me and frowns. 'Why?'

I'd been hoping that she would answer a resounding no and that Cotton's lead was just a false alarm, but I can tell by her expression that it isn't. This is really bad news. 'Because his name came up as a possible member of the Vanishers,' I say quietly, stealing a quick look back over my shoulder just to check there's no one nearby.

'How did it come up?'

'Just answer the question. Do you work with him or not?'

Her frown deepens. 'Yes.'

'Shit. That's all we need. I thought it was just you and your old man involved. What part does Marv play? And who the hell is he?'

'He's my husband's cousin, and we use him to look after the guests.'

I'm aghast. 'Christ. Can't you two manage it?'

Her eyes flare angrily like this is somehow my fault. 'It's important we put a buffer between us and them. Just like you like to put buffers between yourself and us. He's the only person the guests have any contact with after the snatch is made. It makes good security sense.'

'Well, it might if he wasn't shooting his mouth off.' I tell her what Cotton told me. 'We haven't got an ID on him yet, but that's only a matter of time.'

'That arsehole,' she hisses under her breath. 'I always knew he'd fuck it up.'

I feel like asking her what the hell she was using him for then, but don't. There's no point getting into an argument about it. Right now, we need to focus on fixing the problem before it gets out of hand. 'Where is he now?'

'I don't know. Probably at home. He knows the snatch is going down tonight.'

'Get him out of home as soon as possible and to the place where he'll be looking after your guest. Make sure he leaves his phone behind.'

She nods. 'We always make him do that anyway. Then what?'

I take another glance over my shoulder. 'Then you'll need to get rid of him. Permanently.'

'Shit,' she says. 'He's family.'

'You've got no choice,' I tell her, and she hasn't. 'If they catch him and he talks, he'll lead them to you straight away.'

'He won't talk.'

'Don't bet on it. If he's looking at life in prison for murder and kidnap, he'll spill his guts. And even if he doesn't, they'll still be able to follow a trail to you and your old man. But if he's out of the picture, they've got nothing.'

'Will you do it?' she purrs, moving in close to me. She usually smells divine, but today her smell is neutral, which I know is deliberate. When she's making a snatch, she doesn't wear perfume, to minimise anything that the victim might remember about her. She's very professional like that, which is why I'm amazed she's made the mistake of bringing someone unreliable into her tight-knit team.

'No way,' I say, impervious to her charm when it's being used against me like this. 'That's not my remit. But I know you can manage it.'

'It's as much in your interests as ours to have him out of the way,' she says, her expression hardening.

Mine hardens as well. 'It's a problem of your making, Miss D. You sort it. But first things first, get him away from home. I'll do my best to make sure we don't actually get an ID for him. But cousin or not, he's a loose end, and he's got to go.'

She nods. 'Leave it with me. By the way, my husband's asking a lot of questions about this particular operation. He doesn't like the fact that it's not a standard ransom job. And neither do I. What you want us to do is guaranteed to create major publicity, and we've always tried to avoid that.'

'We've already had this conversation,' I say. 'You're being paid four hundred and fifty grand to cover the risk, though there isn't going to be any real risk to you as long as you get rid of Marv. You snatch the target, follow the instructions, and then release her unharmed as soon as you get the go-ahead. There'll be publicity, but it'll be no worse than Henry Day, and it'll blow over again. After this, as agreed, we all take a nice long break.'

Delvina stops walking and takes a seat on an empty bench, before eyeing me in a way I don't like. 'I won't ask who you're working for this time, Mr McBride, because I know you won't tell me. But I know you're being paid a lot more than four hundred and fifty, so if you want us to do this, we need half a mil. And that's non-negotiable.'

I can't believe I'm being strong-armed. The bitch. 'I'm not doing this in the middle of a park,' I say, faking a smile for appearances' sake as I lean in close to her. 'I called this meeting because of a problem you've caused. Not so you could blackmail me for more cash.'

But it's not working. Her eyes are flint. 'We do the hard work. Half a million.'

I'm being paid six fifty, which still leaves me with a tidy profit, and one that I can potentially play with, but it's the principle that irks me. We made an agreement and now she's not sticking to it. But I'm also a pragmatist. 'Half a million. That's it.'

'Shake on it?' she says, with a vague smirk she can't quite hide. That's the thing with Delvina. It's all power play. It wouldn't surprise me if she'd just decided to try it on on the spot.

'No thanks,' I say, getting to my feet and wondering what I can do to get that fifty grand back somehow.

Because mark my words, no one puts one over on me for long.

7

Thursday, 2.25 p.m.

Delvina watches him go and thinks what a snake he is, and how dangerous to her. She only became his lover all those years ago so that she'd have a heads-up if ever Philip's case was reopened. But she has to admit, he's been a useful business associate, even if he's always done very well out of the relationship without having to do any of the heavy lifting.

Still, he's proving his worth now with that tip-off about Marv. She's always thought her husband's cousin was a weak link in the chain. Marv is an uncouth thug who consumes too much drink and drugs to be truly reliable. As she explained to Fisher, he's fulfilled a role for them as the main liaison with their kidnap victims, and it was him they used to dispatch Henry Day. But now he has to go, and her husband's not going to like it. He and Marv are close. Delvina knows she'll have to play this very carefully, because she needs to keep her husband on side, at least for the time being. Eventually she plans to get rid of him, like she did Philip, but that'll only be once they've moved abroad to somewhere the police don't know her history.

Then she can finally be free. And with the business sold and the proceeds from the kidnappings, she'll be a wealthy woman who won't have to worry about money for a long, long time.

It's a far cry from her upbringing on a rough council estate in Dagenham. The daughter of a feckless mother and a father who, when she was three, left home one day to go to the pub and never came back, leaving Delvina with a permanent fear of abandonment. God, she had it hard as a kid and she hates to think of her childhood now, except to remind herself how far she's come, and always under her own steam. She's never had any real help from anyone, with the possible exception of her first husband, Philip, who did genuinely love her and who taught her so much about the business, making the transition to owning it a far easier one for her. She will always be grateful to him for that, and she feels she paid him back by giving him a life of sexual excitement. He found being a submissive hugely satisfying, and he served her faithfully, doing her every bidding without any fuss, for the whole of the six years they were together. Until he finally outlived his usefulness.

And now husband number two will soon have outlived his. No matter. All she has to do is survive this weekend and a golden future beckons. But first she has to deal with the Marv problem. She ponders the best move for a few minutes, and during that time, she comes up with a plan of action that pleases her with its ingenuity.

So much so that she's smiling to herself as she exits the park.

8

Thursday, 3.00 p.m.

Vincent Steele-Perkins doesn't enjoy being called Vincent Steele-Perkins. But Delvina told him that he needed an unthreatening name, and when he married her, she made him lose the Vinnie and change his last name by deed poll.

He's used to doing what Delvina tells him. It's just the way it is with her. She brings out a side of him that he's never known before. A need to serve, and to take orders. If any of his old mates (mates he's now largely lost touch with) knew that he's completely in thrall to his wife, calls her Goddess and obeys her every command, whatever it is, they'd be aghast, because they'd never guess that he was that sort of bloke. But if the truth be known, he's happy with his position as the submissive in their relationship. He adores Delvina and would do anything for her.

Even so, right now he's worried. The kidnapping gig has always worked well for them. It's big money, and although there are significant risks involved, it's also exciting. Because Delvina is such a planner, who thinks of everything, they've minimised those risks and always got away with it. In all they've carried out six kidnappings over a period of five years, starting only a few months after they first met. Delvina has always been the driving force. She got the idea from a previous relationship she'd had with a corrupt detective called McBride, who had some experience of investigating kidnaps and who'd given her all the information she needed about how to avoid getting caught.

Vinnie has never met McBride. Delvina has always told him that the less he knows about the other man, the better, and Vinnie has been prepared to accept that. She's still in touch with him, but insists that the relationship is now purely business, and indeed, over the years McBride has given them valuable information and tip-offs, including the fact that the police were involved in the Henry Day case, allowing them to take radical measures. For this service, he takes a big cut of their ransom payments, which pisses Vinnie off (he's always had a healthy hatred of the police), but even he has to admit that McBride has proved himself valuable and trustworthy, and that without him, they'd probably have been caught by now.

The problem for Vinnie is that suddenly the goalposts have moved. Now it seems he and Delvina are working directly for McBride, who's the one picking the target and paying them to do the job. The money's the same as they'd get normally, but Vinnie still doesn't like it, because the way he sees it, a crooked cop like McBride has to be working for someone else. There's no way he has that kind of money, which just adds another layer of unknown people into the mix, people who will almost certainly have no problem betraying them.

But in the end, none of Vinnie's doubts matter. He's said his piece and Delvina has still decided to go ahead, so he knows he simply has to live with it. She makes the rules.

And now she's told him to pick up Marv straight away and drive him to the place they refer to as 'the hotel', where they keep their victims while they wait for the ransom to be paid. Vinnie asked her what the urgency was, but all Delvina would say was that she didn't trust Marv to get there by himself, even though he's always managed before. Vinnie has an uneasy feeling in his gut that she's hiding something from him, but he's not sure what.

Marv is Vinnie's cousin, and someone he's hung out with since they were tiny kids, and he still lives in Vinnie's old stomping ground in Harlesden, way across town from Sutton, where he lives now.

Vinnie always has a wave of nostalgia when he comes home, and it's because he rarely makes the journey these days. Delvina discourages him from going back. She says that part of his life is behind him so why revisit a past that involved limited prospects, long stretches of unemployment, and prison? She also thinks he should avoid spending too much time with Marv now that they're working together professionally. And the truth is, Vinnie understands where she's coming from. But still . . .

Marv has a ground-floor flat in a run-down block thrown up at some point in the 1970s, when cheap and ugly were the main building criteria, and it's barely a mile down the road from the estate where the two of them grew up. Vinnie parks round the corner, several hundred metres away.

Delvina has always told him how important it is not to be seen publicly with Marv any more because of security concerns, so as he exits the car, he pulls a baseball cap low over his face, and keeps his head down as he walks to his cousin's front door and rings the bell.

Marv must have been waiting right behind it, because he yanks the door open so quickly that Vinnie takes an involuntary step backwards.

To be fair, most people would take an involuntary step backwards if they ran into Marv. He's a big, lumbering hulk of a man with a face like a gargoyle and an outlandishly large chin that tends to jut out like a weapon whenever he looks angry, which is most of the time. Marv is not a nice man. He's a violent outsider who people want to give a wide berth to. Even so, Vinnie has always been protective of him. After all, he's family. But the reason he and Delvina work him with isn't through any sense of family loyalty. It's because they both know he's ruthless enough to do whatever nasty job needs to be done.

'Blimey, you're in a hurry,' says Vinnie, recovering himself and stepping inside quickly, keen not to linger on Marv's doorstep. If his cousin is ever fingered for any of the kidnaps, Vinnie knows he'll never talk, but Delvina has taught him how easy it is for the police to identify associates of criminals and come after them.

'You said there's a job on,' says Marv, moving out the way so Vinnie can come through. 'I was just getting ready.'

'You don't look very ready,' Vinnie replies, taking a seat at the two-man table that sits between the kitchenette and the sofa in Marv's cramped, messy living area.

Marv's wearing jeans, a wife-beater vest that's seen better days, and not much else. His feet are bare, the toenails like yellow claws. He is, thinks Vinnie, his own worst enemy. No wonder he can never get a woman.

'How long's this one going to take?' asks Marv, leaning against the wall and fishing out a pack of cigarettes.

Vinnie doesn't actually know but figures it won't be that long. He shrugs. 'Three, maybe four days. It's just the usual. Keep her fed, quiet and definitely unharmed.'

'I ain't going to kill a woman,' Marv says. 'Even if it goes tits-up. No way. I'm not an animal.'

Vinnie knows that for all his violence, Marv has an almost old-fashioned criminal moral code, and he respects that. He's got one too. 'Don't worry, you won't have to,' he says.

Marv lights his cigarette, takes a loud drag. 'What's the pay?'

'The usual. Ten grand. Cash or bitcoin. Your choice. Payable at the end.'

'I'll take cash. I don't fucking understand bitcoin.'

'Just be careful how you spend it, Marv. You don't want to draw attention to yourself.'

Marv's eyes narrow. 'You don't have to talk to me like I'm a kid. I know how to keep shtum. I've been doing this a while, remember?'

'I'm not talking to you like you're a kid. I just know we can all get a bit slack sometimes. It's important to keep everything tight.'

'Well, I don't get slack. I'm careful.'

'I'm glad to hear it.' Marv has never done anything foolish before, but he has a gambling habit, and drinks far too much, so Vinnie knows he has to keep an eye on him. If he's honest with himself, another reason they use Marv is because he's the only person the victims will remember afterwards. In other words, he's their fall guy. Which makes Vinnie feel guilty sometimes. 'We need to get up to the hotel straight away,' he says. 'I'll drive you.'

'I'll drive myself. I like my fucking car with me.'

'Why? You can't leave her on her own.'

'I just want my car, all right. It's never been a problem before.' Marv glares at him, his chin jutting out. It doesn't take much to get him going. 'So why the change now?'

The reason for the change, as always, is Delvina. She's told Vinnie that he has to drive Marv to the safe house, because that way he won't be tempted to disappear off somewhere while on babysitting duties – not that he's ever done that before. But there's no way Vinnie is going to tell him that. 'No reason,' he says. 'But I'm here now and I thought it would be easier.'

'I'll drive,' says Marv, and Vinnie knows that this is the end of the conversation.

'I need your phone, though,' says Vinnie. 'And that's non-negotiable. I don't want you using it while you're at the safe house. We don't use ours there because the law can trace the signal.' He pulls another of their pay-as-you-go burner phones out of his jacket pocket and slides it along the table in Marv's direction. 'This is for you, just for the next few days. Our new numbers are on it.'

Marv looks peeved. 'Come on, Vinnie, help me out here. I'm seeing someone. I need to stay in touch with her.'

'Blimey, this is news. Who's that, then?' Someone who definitely isn't fussy, thinks Vinnie.

Marv looks uncharacteristically shy. 'Just some woman I met online. Been going on for a few weeks now.'

Vinnie grins, genuinely happy that his cousin has miraculously found someone. 'I'm pleased for you, bro. You got any photos of her?'

'A couple,' Marv says. 'I'll show you them another time.'

'Well, all you have to do is put her number into the burner phone and tell her you've lost your real phone, then when the job's over, you say you've found it. Simples.'

'I'd better get it back,' says Marv, pulling out his iPhone and giving it a quick look before sliding it across to Vinnie.

'You will. The minute we're done.' Vinnie powers off Marv's phone and places it in a Faraday bag so it stops sending any kind of signal.

Marv picks up the other phone. 'This one isn't even a smartphone. I can't send pictures.'

'Your girl will just have to wait a few days. Buy her some flowers with your earnings.'

'Is this you deciding about the phone and car and all that shit, Vinnie, or is it her?' Marv sneers the 'her'.

Vinnie gets to his feet, keen now to get out of here, because he knows what's coming. '"Her" is my wife, Marv. Delvina.'

'She orders you around. Makes you her bitch. You're better than that, Vinnie.'

'Easy, Marv. I don't like disrespect. I'm helping you out here. *We're* helping you out. Don't forget that.' Vinnie's angry now and Marv's blocking his way. The problem is he doesn't think he could take him out even if he wanted to. The bastard's like the Incredible Hulk.

And it seems his cousin's got more to say. 'How much are you two getting for this job? 'Cos I read somewhere that the ransoms being paid are in the hundreds of thousands. That's one fuck of a lot more than I'm getting.'

Vinnie faces him down, even though he's almost eight inches shorter than his cousin, who seemed to have got all the height genes in the family. 'We take the risks. We identify the target. We do the snatch. The handover. The lot. That's more than ninety per cent of the work.'

'I fucking killed that kid for you, Vinnie,' says Marv quietly, his words hanging in the room's stale air.

'And you were paid extra for that. Another ten grand. Plus it was us who got rid of the body. It was just a couple of minutes' work for you.'

'It was murder. And I did it because you didn't have the balls to.'

Which Vinnie has to admit is true. He *doesn't* have the balls for murder. Never had. Whereas Marv didn't have a single qualm about stabbing that boy to death. He did it with a casual shrug. Vinnie saw the body afterwards and it made him feel sick. It still does.

'Do you want this job or not, Marv?' he says. 'If not, we'll get someone else.'

'I'm not doing a girl.'

'You won't have to. This time it's going to run a lot smoother. Just babysitting, and keeping her alive and healthy.'

'I can do that.'

'Good. We make the snatch tonight. Get yourself up to the hotel asap.' Having taken back control of the situation, Vinnie moves past Marv, who finally gets out of the way.

But as he reaches the front door, Marv calls out from behind him: 'I don't know why you hang round with that bitch. You used to be a good bloke, Vinnie. Now no one ever sees you any more, and you treat me – your own family – like I'm your fucking employee.'

Vinnie turns round, sees the almost hurt expression on his cousin's face and tries to ignore it. This is business, and he has to show he's a businessman. 'I'm using you for this *because* you're family and I trust you. But don't push it. Or next time we won't, and you'll be saying goodbye to easy money. Understood?'

Marv grunts something, which Vinnie knows is the best he's going to get. And then he's out of there and heading up the street with Marv's phone, which he'll hide in woods a few miles from the safe house so there's no way on God's earth its signal can be picked up.

But he's worried, because Delvina has already told him that when this job's finished they're not letting the girl go. The instructions are that she has to die, and if Marv won't kill her, Vinnie knows it's going to have to be him.

9

Thursday, 3.30 p.m.

Becca Barraclough's not the kind of woman who gets riven by indecision. She's always been focused on the task in hand, and once she decides something, she sticks to it. But the conversation with Logan Quinn has hit her hard. He may have tried to justify what he's done, but the fact remains he's a mass murderer and she's loath to help him. It's possible for her as a lawyer to release him as a client because he hasn't been entirely truthful with her, but it won't be that easy. In truth, Becca remains intrigued by this case and the information that Logan Quinn allegedly possesses, which could potentially convict some very high-powered individuals. In other words, she could do some good from this.

And that's why she's now sitting in her office at the Herman Bell Chambers in Gray's Inn, her laptop open in front of her, looking up information on Mr Graham Wallace, the founder and chief executive of a successful Manchester-based engineering company who lost his wife in June 2019. According to the limited, mainly local news stories on Mrs Wallace's death, she drowned in a bath in a hotel room during a visit to London with her husband. He was out at the time at a business dinner, which Mrs Wallace hadn't attended because she was allegedly feeling unwell, and when he returned at just after midnight, she was dead. A coroner's report stated that she'd had a blood-alcohol level of close to 200 mg, more than two and a half times the drink-drive limit, as well as Valium in her system. Mr Wallace testified that his wife was a heavy drinker who'd also suffered from depression, and the coroner's verdict was that her death was a result of misadventure (in other words, an accident).

Having digested this information and made some brief notes, Becca now logs onto a data storage site that offers high levels of security for its users, using login details supplied to her by Quinn. A prompt asks her a security question: *What is your favourite colour?* She types in the answer Quinn gave her. *Black.* Which seems apt somehow. She's then told that a six-digit authorisation code has been sent to the user's email address, so she logs into the email account Quinn supplied her with (all of this off the top of his head). There's only one new email in it. In fact there's only one email full stop. The one just sent from the data storage site.

And this is what unnerves her about Quinn. It's the fact that he's been preparing for this day for a long time. He knows how to clear up everything behind him so that she (or anyone else) can only access what he wants them to access. Apparently the search of his home was the same.

The police found nothing that linked him to any crime at all. His personal desktop computer, laptop and phone were all wiped clean of information, and repeated attempts by police technicians to retrieve it have failed.

Becca types in the six-digit security code, and now she's allowed into the site. Five files appear on the screen, numbered 1 to 5. She's been directed to number 1, and when she clicks on it, there's another password prompt. Checking the notes that she took from her meeting with Quinn, she enters the password, and she's finally in.

She spends the next half an hour perusing the information the file contains. First there's the email correspondence between Quinn and the man who's hiring him to murder his wife. The man, who calls himself John, sends an introductory email from a Hotmail address, asking about Quinn's services. Quinn sends a message back suggesting that they liaise in the drafts section of a new email address (he provides the details) so that everything they write to each other can be deleted without any of it being sent electronically. John, clearly pleased that Quinn is so security-conscious, is far more expansive in the messages that follow, all of which have been photographed by Quinn. In them, he gives details of his wife's drink problem and her prescription Valium, and provides a full rundown of where they're going to be in the coming weeks as the two men try to find a suitable venue for the job. It won't take much, Becca realises, to tie these messages to Graham Wallace, especially as the URL of where he logged into the account from is shown quite clearly.

And then there are the details of Wallace's bitcoin payment to Quinn, which did indeed come from a public wallet in his name.

But of course, the *coup de grâce* is the four-and-a-half-minute video clip, taken using not one camera but two, showing Wallace returning to the hotel room and discovering his wife's body. The quality of the footage, and the audio, is extremely high, and it's obvious that Quinn was filming the scene in real time remotely, allowing him to switch between the cameras for maximum effect. It's a really professional video, and the smile on Wallace's face as he turns away from his wife's corpse is both obvious and chilling, making Becca think how she'd love to bring down a bastard like that who thought he'd got away with his crime.

Whether any of it is admissible in court, however, is another matter. The video has been taken illegally. It also doesn't actually show Wallace killing his wife, because of course he didn't. Yes, it shows him grinning, but that's not evidence of guilt, and the emails and the bitcoin payment, though damning, are also deniable. If she herself was defending him, she's confident she'd be able to get him off. And any half-decent lawyer would advise him not to co-operate with the police and to take a 'no comment' defence under questioning.

So it's not necessarily enough on its own to whet the CPS's interest.

The only other thing Quinn has given her is a name. 'You tell them that name. Then they'll want to talk,' he said.

She decides to find out if that's the case.

Her main contact in the CPS is Clyde Faulkner, one of its most senior lawyers and the man in charge of prosecuting Logan Quinn for the Jess O'Sullivan murder. He's also, ironically enough, Becca's former partner. They were together eight years, and cohabiting for two of those, and it's still the longest relationship she's ever had. The most important, too. Clyde acted as stepfather to Becca's daughter, Elle, during her all-important teenage years. They might have broken up five years ago now, but Becca and Clyde (Bonnie and Clyde, people called them) are still good friends, and it feels weird being on the opposite side of the fence to him. They've always managed to keep their professional lives separate, but in the end, with him in the CPS and her as a defence lawyer, this day was always going to come.

Before she calls Clyde, she gets an Americano from the machine outside in the corridor and puts in a call to Elle.

Her daughter is twenty-one, and very different to her mother. Rather than taking a degree in law as Becca, by her own admission, had pushed her hard to do, she's gone into nursing. 'I've got no interest in the law,' she said. 'I want to help people.'

'I help people,' Becca said with some indignation.

'You defend criminals,' Elle responded, with a withering tone to her voice. But that's the thing with youth – everything's so black and white to them.

They fell out about it for a while, but Becca is no pushy tiger mother, nor is she completely stubborn, and eventually she got used to the idea of Elle being a nurse and doing something she was passionate about.

Once she accepted Elle's decision, they got on pretty well for a while, and Elle was actually very supportive when Becca secured an acquittal for Oliver Tamzan and was vilified in the press. But then when he was found guilty of the second crime, her view changed entirely. Like most of the rest of the public, she suddenly regarded her mum as someone who'd got a killer off from his rightful sentence and therefore was at least partly responsible for the subsequent attack he'd committed. Becca tried to explain that she'd defended him in good faith and had done her job by questioning the evidence against him and finding it wanting. But Elle was dismissive. She still is, not realising that the Tamzan acquittal has weighed on Becca's conscience too.

The two of them haven't talked much recently, and haven't seen each other in four months. Becca misses her. Elle is her only child, born when Becca herself was only twenty-five and still doing her legal training, the product of a short but passionate relationship with an Australian bar manager called Brad that ended pretty much the moment she announced she was pregnant. She thought long and hard about termination. It would have made her life a great deal easier, but by the time she realised she was pregnant, she was already more than three months along, and in the end, she simply couldn't bring herself to do it.

Bringing Elle up as a single parent was hard, especially as Becca had to work long hours as a trainee lawyer, but with the help of her parents and some fantastic nannies, she managed it. And sometimes she resents the fact that this is the thanks she gets. A daughter who judges her and doesn't, it seems, want much to do with her.

But she's determined to persevere. She's never been the sort to give up easily. Elle hasn't returned her last message, left three days ago, and it seems she's not answering this time either. After about ten rings, the voicemail clicks in.

'Hey, honey,' Becca says brightly into the phone, 'it's only Mum. Try and give me a call, please. I'm tired of relying on Facebook and Instagram for my updates. Miss you.'

She can't think of anything else to say, so she ends the call, wondering how her daughter would react if she knew Becca was defending a man accused of murdering a woman not much older than Elle herself. A man who has just admitted to numerous other killings. Not well, she thinks. Not well at all.

Even so, it doesn't stop her calling Clyde Faulkner before she's even put the phone down. Strike while the iron's hot, she tells herself, not wanting to give herself any time to have doubts about what she's doing.

Unlike Elle, Clyde answers. Almost on the first ring.

'Ms Barraclough, how are you?' he says, his voice a deep, confident baritone. One that's made for a courtroom. 'Ringing with a guilty plea for Logan Quinn?'

He's being playful and she can imagine the smile on his face. 'I'm good, thank you, Mr Faulkner. And what I'm ringing about, aside from to hear your lovely voice, is to offer you a deal.'

'What kind of deal?' he asks cautiously.

Becca gives him the details of what she wants.

'Are you serious?' is his response.

'Absolutely. My client has very valuable information on a lot of people. He's already shown me evidence of a murder that was recorded as a death by misadventure.'

'A murder that he committed?'

'My client's not admitting to anything until he's been moved into a safe house and has a deal approved, a deal whereby he only serves a maximum of five years.'

'I'll be frank, Becca,' says Clyde, 'because I know you appreciate frankness. I think your client's deluded if he believes he can ever secure a deal like that. And I'm surprised you're encouraging him in those thoughts.'

Becca's been expecting this reaction. She plays what Quinn has told her is his trump card. 'He tells me that he can give you evidence that indicts an individual called Kalian Roman.'

Clyde doesn't say anything for a moment. It's clear the name means something to him. 'What evidence does your client have against Kalian Roman, and for what crimes?'

'Strictly off the record . . .'

'Of course.'

'He claims Kalian Roman hired him, via an intermediary, to commit murder. Apparently the intermediary reports directly to Roman.'

'I need to see the evidence that your client has.'

'He won't give you that until he's in a safe house. His life's in danger in Belmarsh. As I'm sure you're aware, he was violently assaulted by another prisoner yesterday, and could have been killed.'

'I heard about it. I also heard that he's been moved to a segregation unit within the prison.'

'He still believes his life is in danger. So do I.'

'I can't get him into a safe house, Becca. It's unrealistic. He's been charged with murder.'

But Becca detects something in Clyde's voice that suggests he's more open to negotiation than he's letting on. 'You can. And if you do, you'll get a string of convictions to your name. And that can't do you any harm in your bid.'

'What bid?'

'You know you're aiming for Director of Public Prosecutions. And you deserve it too. This could really help.'

'You know, you're better than cheap flattery, Becca.'

Which is true, but she also knows it's working. 'Look, Clyde,' she says with a sigh, 'I've given you the option to do a very good deal, but it's not going to happen unless my client's in a safe house. End of story.'

She's bluffing. In the end, she may well have to persuade Quinn to do a deal while remaining in Belmarsh. But right now, there's no point showing flexibility.

'Okay,' he says, after a pause. 'I need to talk to some people. I'll come back to you shortly.'

With that, he ends the call, and Becca smiles.

He's bitten.

10

Thursday, 4.25 p.m.

The place where we're meeting the undercover operative is the KFC in Shepherd's Bush, a most insalubrious-looking establishment on a litter-strewn section of the Uxbridge Road. He only wants to talk to one of us, and everything's got to be very subtle in case he's being followed. Ordinarily, as the senior officer, Cotton would be the one to go in, but as we pull up, he gets a call from our boss at the NCA about an upcoming trial resulting from one of our other cases, and as he flicks on the hazards, he motions for me to go in instead of him.

Which is a nice stroke of luck really. It's far easier if I speak to the undercover and work out how far he's got in ID'ing Marv. Then hopefully I can chuck a spanner in the works.

I get out of the car before Cotton can change his mind, leaving the keys in the ignition, while he shuffles over into the driving seat.

It's 4.30 and the KFC's still got remnants of the after-school crowd, so the downstairs tables are filled with rowdy kids throwing things at each other while the few ordinary people in the place pretend it's not happening. A couple of the kids push past me with their orders as I approach the counter, as if I'm utterly insignificant to them, and it makes me think that if they represent this country's future, then we really are truly fucked. Although luckily for me, I won't be around to see it. The youth are much more respectful in Thailand.

This place might be a dump of the highest order, but the smell of frying food is already getting my mouth watering, and I order three pieces of chicken and a large fries, along with a bottle of water for the sake of my arteries, then make my way upstairs, which is thankfully a lot quieter, with just a handful of people scattered about the place.

The man I'm looking for – well built, with a shaved head and a beard, and wearing an Adidas hoodie – turns my way briefly as I enter but gives no sign of recognition. He's sitting at a long counter on the back wall, and I wander over and take a seat next to him, pulling out one of my chicken pieces and giving it a blow before taking a tentative bite. A mirror runs the length of the table at head height, so we can see what's going on behind us, which right now is basically nothing except people eating.

'I'm Fish from the NCA,' I say, giving him a sideways look. There's background music playing over the speakers and no one's near enough to hear my words.

'I don't know if Marv's your man or not,' says the op, continuing to eat as he talks. 'But he's pulled out of the job we're doing tonight.'

84

'That's a pity,' I say, not meaning it. 'What makes you think he might be the man we're after?'

The op glances at me for the first time. He's early thirties, hard-looking, the kind who wouldn't take any shit from the kids downstairs and who they'd give a wide berth to. 'You know about my role, don't you?'

I nod. 'Yeah, I do.' And I'm impressed, too. Doing the job he does requires balls of steel. I've been in frightening positions before, particularly during my time in armed surveillance, but I was always part of a team with plenty of backup, knowing that the chances of me ever being put in a situation where I had to shoot or be shot were minuscule. This guy's walking into danger completely alone, knowing his cover could be blown at any time.

The op goes back to his chicken. 'The way I work, I can't afford to ask too many questions. I'm new to this outfit, and they're still suspicious of me. But I pick things up. This morning we had a meeting round the flat of the guy who runs the show, Blake. There were four of us there discussing the job tonight. That's when Blake decides we need a fifth man, so he calls this associate of theirs, Marv.'

'I heard. He's got some other job. That's why he's not going to help.'

'That's right. Anyway, afterwards I was talking to one of the other boys, Leon Dennay, just shooting the breeze, being subtle, because you've got to be subtle with these people. One wrong move and suddenly everyone's suspicious of you, and then it's all over. And these boys are violent . . . very, very violent.'

He swallows his chicken, smacks his lips with satisfaction.

'Anyway,' he continues, 'Dennay makes a comment that immediately gets alarm bells going. He says he reckons Marv's got something to do with the Vanishers. I ask him why and he says it's because he always has money. And not just a little bit. Wads of the stuff.'

'It's still not much, though, is it?'

'That's what I said to Dennay. But he said there's other reasons too. Except he wouldn't tell me what they were. And then he shut up about it. I think he thought I might go to the cops and claim the reward if he told me any more. But I get the feeling he knows Marv quite well, and that he'll talk if you get to him.'

'Okay. Thanks for that. It's useful.'

'You're riding along tonight, right? Because that's when we're going to take the gang down.'

'Definitely,' I say, cogs whirring as I try to work out how to scupper this operation. 'You think Dennay will cooperate?'

The op appears to ponder this a moment as he takes another bite of his chicken. 'He's the weakest of the group. If anyone's going to blab to save their skin, it'll be him.' He looks at me properly for the first time. His gaze is cool and confident. 'I heard about all the shit you got after the Vanishers killed that kid they kidnapped. It seemed like they were blaming you personally for it.'

I exhale loudly. 'That's what it felt like.'

'I feel for you, buddy. I know you were doing your best.

But the problem is, these days we're everyone's whipping boys, aren't we? They expect us to keep them safe, but any of us put even a toe out of place, and we're hung out to dry.'

'Too right,' I say, because I can hardly disagree. The life of a copper in the Met these days is hard, thankless and lonely. 'I'm just hoping that this leads to something and takes some of the pressure off.'

'You still short on leads?'

'Totally bereft is a better description. Those bastards are slippery as hell. They don't make mistakes.'

The op finishes his chicken and meticulously cleans his mouth and fingers using the wet wipe. 'Everyone makes mistakes, buddy. You know that.' He gets to his feet, leaves the empties on the table. 'I've got to go. People to meet. See you later.'

I give him a good-luck nod and turn back to the mirror on the wall just to make sure that no one's taken any interest in the fact that we've been sitting together talking. As I demolish my cardboard box full of greasy goodness, I try to figure out a way to scupper the operation tonight.

The problem is, there's no way I can do it without exposing myself. If I call Blake Burns, the target, even anonymously and from a burner phone, and let him know that he's got an undercover police officer on his team, it'll cause a real shit show. The undercover might well end up dead or seriously injured and there won't be a stone left unturned trying to catch the person who betrayed him. With virtually no one in the know about the operation, it won't take them long to get to me.

Whichever way I look at it, I've got no choice but to let everything go ahead and do what I can to minimise the chance of it leading anywhere. If Delvina's already got Marv over to their safe house, even if he is ID'd we're not going to be able to arrest him. The important thing is to make sure he never makes it out, and then I need to work out how to get Delvina and her husband out of the picture.

I can't help feeling in my gut, though, that events are beginning to move out of my control, which is something I'm neither used to nor comfortable with. I don't know if it's the nerves or the chicken, but I'm feeling vaguely nauseous as I head out the front door, dodging kids and flying French fries.

'What about the lead? Find out anything new?' asks Cotton when I'm back in the car and we pull away from the kerb.

I shake my head wearily. 'To be honest, Cott, I don't think it's a goer.'

11

Thursday, 10.05 p.m.

Delvina knows that the key to success in the kidnapping business is research. You need to know your target. Habits, relationships, movements. All of it.

She and her husband have had ten days to scope out their latest one, twenty-one-year-old Elle Barraclough, and they've used the time wisely. Elle is a prolific poster on Instagram and even Facebook, which the young tend to shun these days, as well as a sometime user of Twitter. Her profiles are all public too, thus allowing Delvina to get a very good insight into how she spends her time. She lives in Brighton, which is where she went to uni. It seems she works hard, gets on well with her colleagues at the hospital where she's been a nurse for the past nine months, since graduating, but also enjoys nights out in Brighton and can sometimes drink far too much, as is often the way with young women of that age. On her Facebook profile, she's listed as single, which is also good to know, because it's unlikely anyone will get hugely suspicious for a few days if she disappears.

Best of all, from Delvina's point of view, is the fact that Elle is a driver who uses her car regularly. Vincent planted a tracking device (one of six he'd bought for cash from a Halfords in Croydon the previous May) in the wheel arch of her Mini Coupé (a birthday gift from her mother) right back on day one, and so they've also been able to watch where she goes in real time without her being any the wiser, and, more importantly, without them having to get too close to her and risk getting spotted themselves.

The tracker tells them that Elle works long hours at the hospital and that she had three days off earlier in the week before starting work again two days ago, doing the midday-to-10 p.m. shift, coming straight home both nights.

And today, if all goes to plan, she'll come straight home again. If she doesn't, they'll just have to wait. It's all well and good Fisher wanting the snatch made tonight, but Delvina knows there's no point in rushing things. The reason they've been successful for so long is because they're methodical. If push comes to shove, Vincent can break into Elle's flat. He possesses excellent lock-picking skills picked up from his stints in prison, but she'd rather avoid that. It would mean drugging Elle inside the flat then transporting her through the terraced house in which it's situated and out onto the street, which is far too risky. It might also mean leaving behind physical evidence, and while Delvina's DNA might not be on file, Vincent's certainly is.

She's not nervous, though, because she's certain it'll go to plan, just like it has all the other times before. Delvina's a professional hunter. It's something she takes pleasure in and it'll be something she misses.

She and Vincent have been in Brighton for the past two hours. They brought sandwiches with them, not wanting to risk eating out and getting caught on camera, and now they're parked in Vincent's Chrysler people carrier on Freeland Avenue, a long residential road of terraced houses about a mile north of the city centre, waiting for their target to return home. It's the same vehicle they used in the Henry Day snatch, and on the way down here from their home in Sutton, they pulled into a wooded lay-by on a back road off the A23, where Vincent swapped the real number plates for a fake set cloned from an identical Chrysler registered to a forty-two-year-old woman in St Albans (you can, Delvina knows, never be too careful).

At the same time, the two of them disguised their appearance. Delvina put on wide black-rimmed glasses and a good-quality wig of curly auburn hair that she's had for years and used on several of the early snatches, and filled her cheeks with cotton wool to fatten out her narrow, sculpted face. She added a stab-proof vest beneath her sweater and jacket to add more bulk to her body too, and now she looks very different. The disguise won't pass muster if someone is standing right next to her, but no CCTV cameras are going to be able to ID her, especially with the hat she'll be wearing, and that's the most important thing. Vincent meanwhile chose a baseball cap, tortoiseshell glasses and, of course, his trusty surgical face mask.

It's dark and Freeland Avenue is quiet, with only the

occasional pedestrian and a car every minute or so. They're parked approximately fifty yards from Elle Barraclough's flat, on the other side of the road, the closest they could get. This place has a largely transient student population, so even though they've been sitting in the same spot for twenty minutes now, they don't particularly look out of place, and no one who passes pays them any heed. The only problem is, being March, it's quite cold, and they can't afford to draw attention to themselves by leaving the engine on.

Delvina notices that her husband seems subdued tonight as he checks the tracker app to make sure that Elle's car is still at the hospital. She's very in tune with his moods and it's unusual for him to be like this when they're on a job.

She asks him what's wrong.

He looks at her, and there's sadness in those sharp, flinty eyes of his. 'Why do we have to kill the girl, Goddess?' he asks. 'I don't understand.'

'I don't know,' she answers, which is a lie. She knows exactly why the girl has to die. 'But that's what McBride wants and he's paying us the money. And that's why we're using your cousin. He can do the unpleasant part, like he did last time, so we don't have to. It's just business, pet.'

Vincent shakes his head. 'Marv ain't going to do it,' he says quietly. 'He won't kill a girl.'

'*Isn't* going to do it,' she corrects him. 'And what do you mean, he won't kill a girl?'

'He doesn't like hurting women and kids.'

Delvina unleashes a deep sigh of displeasure. It fills the

car and causes her husband to cringe slightly, which pleases her. 'Then tell me. What the fuck are we using him for?'

'He's always done a good job,' he answers, not meeting her eye. Delvina knows this is definitely not true. 'And I don't see a reason for killing the girl either. It doesn't fit in with anything. And she's young, you know. Just seems harsh.'

'The world is harsh, pet. We just have to deal with it. Anyway, you weren't concerned about Henry Day dying, so why the worry now?'

'He was a man. That's different.'

'He was a teenager.'

Vincent shrugs. 'He was old enough. And it's just that this one, she's a nurse and all that. A good person. I don't mind snatching her and holding her prisoner, but killing her?'

Delvina gives him one of her sterner looks. 'You're not going soft on me, are you, pet? We do this and we can retire from the game. That's got to be worth it, right?'

Vincent pauses, looks away.

Delvina doesn't like this. It's not in her plan for her husband to suddenly get an attack of conscience. After all, he sliced half a man's face off without a moment's contrition. She keeps looking at him. 'Right?'

He takes a breath, nods. 'Right.'

'Right what?'

He gives a small bow. 'Right, Goddess.'

'And don't forget that I *am* your Goddess,' she tells him. 'What I say goes. And what I'm saying now is we need to be strong, do what McBride is paying us a lot of money to do and not keep asking pointless questions.'

'I'm sorry, Goddess,' he says, sounding suitably mollified.

Delvina looks down, sees that he's getting hard beneath his jeans, already forgetting about his moral scruples as he slips back into his role as her subservient.

She smiles, touches a rouge fingernail to his lips and watches him quiver. 'You're mine,' she whispers. 'You know that, don't you?'

'I'm yours, Goddess,' he answers, joyful surrender in his eyes.

Delvina sits back in her seat, looks out of the window into the darkness, pleased that she's got him back on side. Vincent, she thinks, is like a puppy. Always doting, but sometimes in need of a harsh word. And the truth is, for a while now she's been bored of him. Intellectually he's not stimulating enough, and although he's a good, solid sub, an excellent lover and a useful business partner, he's always been a stepping stone, someone for her to use and then discard when his usefulness ends. Delvina knows that soon it's going to be time for her to move on. The thought of new adventures in a new setting excites her, and she allows herself a small, knowing smile as she thinks about her potential new life, until Vincent interrupts her reverie.

'The target's on the move,' he says, staring at his phone. 'And she's coming this way.'

12

Thursday, 10.20 p.m.

Elle Barraclough is already exhausted and it's only three days into her six-day work block. Halfway, and yet she feels like she could sleep for a week. She's currently looking after eight patients on the vascular ward, four of whom have just had legs removed thanks to complications resulting from diabetes, and of the others, two more look like they might be losing a limb imminently. All of them require regular checks, medicine and dressing changes, as well as ongoing emotional support. And there are other patients desperately in need of help coming in all the time, meaning they never have a spare bed, or even a spare moment.

Elle is a caring woman and that's what keeps her going. She knows she's doing good. Sometimes she feels she's making up for the fact that her mum is doing a lot less good. Elle loves her mum, and admires the fact that she did the best she could bringing her up, working long hours and making sacrifices so that they had a roof over their heads and food on the table. But sometimes Elle wishes that she'd actually spent more time at home, so that they could have spent quality time together instead of her mother defending people who, in at least one famous case, shouldn't have been defended. The really sad thing is that Elle can hardly remember anything she and her mum did together before the age of ten, but she remembers the three different nannies she had really, really well, and frankly that can't be right.

So yes, Elle loves her mother. But she's not at all sure she likes her, and as she parks her Mini Coupé (which yes, was a present from her mum and something she really does appreciate) just up the road from her flat, she sees she's got another message from her.

She sighs, knowing that she has to return the call. It's late, but if she doesn't do it now, Mum'll probably get worried, and she doesn't want that. She thinks about texting instead, but then decides to bite the bullet and makes the call as she climbs out of the car.

'Hey, honey,' says her mum. 'Where have you been?'

'Working, Mother,' Elle answers, already impatient. 'I've also got a job that involves long hours. It may not pay as well as yours—'

'I know, I know. I didn't mean it like that,' says Mum, injecting a playful tone into her voice. 'I just haven't heard from you in a while, and I wondered if you're busy Sunday. I thought I might pay a visit to the coast.'

In truth, Elle would actually like to see her mum. It's been ages. And she knows she'll buy her dinner somewhere nice, and who's going to turn that down? 'I'm working Sunday. It's my last day. I could do Monday, though.'

As she speaks, Elle is walking along the pavement towards

the flat. She sees a hippyish-looking woman in a big floppy hat and long suede coat staggering towards her. The woman looks drunk, and as Elle watches, she stumbles and goes down on one knee, putting a hand out against a parked car to steady herself.

Elle immediately feels the need to help. 'Listen, Mum,' she says, cutting her mother off mid flow as she talks about coming down Monday, 'I'll have to call you back. I think someone might be in trouble.'

'What are you talking about, Elle?' says Mum, sounding worried. 'Where are you?'

'I'll call you back in five, okay,' answers Elle, and ends the call.

She goes over to the woman, who's trying to get to her feet. 'Are you all right?' she asks. 'I'm a nurse. I might be able to help.' Putting her phone in her pocket, she takes one of the woman's arms to help her up.

Which is when she notices that her long red hair is a wig.

And then they're face to face and something dark flashes in the woman's eyes, and Elle immediately senses danger. But, as she lets go of the woman's arm and tries to turn away, she suddenly feels a sharp pinprick in her upper thigh.

Looking down, she can see she's been stabbed with a syringe, and almost immediately, she feels light-headed. At the same time, the woman drops the syringe into her handbag and stands up quickly, linking arms with Elle, her grip strong as she pulls her between two parked cars and out into the road.

Elle can feel herself weakening, but the shock of the

assault has released enough adrenaline to temporarily overcome whatever drug she's been injected with, and she struggles hard, trying to break free, looking round desperately for anyone who might be witnessing what's going on. She starts to scream, the noise rising in her throat, but nothing's really coming out, and then the woman is facing her again, her features full of fury as she hisses: 'Shut your fucking mouth, bitch.'

As Elle continues to struggle, the woman elbows her hard in the face from close range. There's no pain, just shock, and she starts to fall, but the woman's holding her up, and then a car's pulling up beside them and the woman's sliding open the back door and pushing Elle inside. Elle puts out a hand to grab the door frame because she knows it's the only thing that's going to help, but she hasn't got the strength, and she stumbles forward across the back seats while the woman jumps in behind her, slamming the door shut as the car pulls away.

And amidst the fog that's shrouding her brain, Elle still has the wherewithal to know that she's in real danger, and that she has to get out.

13

Thursday, 10.25 p.m.

Delvina curses as she grabs Elle Barraclough's legs and shoves them into the gap between the front and back seats so she can sit down. Elle is still struggling, her head hanging slightly off the seat, so Delvina leans over so she's right above her, then punches her hard in the face, three times in rapid succession, and that finally seems to shut her up.

'Christ, what's happening back there?' asks Vincent worriedly as he takes a right at the end of the road.

'I don't think I gave her a big enough dose,' answers Delvina, sitting back up but keeping her head down to avoid any street cameras as she rearranges her wig, which has become somewhat askew in the struggle. 'She put up a bit of resistance.'

'No one saw, did they?'

'Of course they didn't,' Delvina snaps, annoyed at his tone. But she's not a hundred per cent sure of this. There were lights on in plenty of windows, and she thinks she might have seen someone looking out of one, but it could be that she imagined it. Still, it's left her flustered and she knows it's important they put as much distance between them and the crime scene as possible. 'Just keep driving, okay. Let's get the fuck out of here.'

Vincent nods but keeps his speed steady and only just over the 30 mph limit. Right now, with an unconscious and clearly injured woman in the back of the car, they don't want to draw any unwanted attention to themselves. Delvina takes a couple of deep breaths, forces herself to relax. They've done it, and in a couple of hours they'll be tucked up at home in bed.

'I saw she was on the phone just before you got to her,' says Vincent without turning round. He's got his head down too.

'I know,' says Delvina. 'But she'd already ended the call. I heard her say something about calling whoever it was back.' She reaches down into the front pocket of Elle Barraclough's scrubs and quickly locates her phone, which she takes out. Elle doesn't stir. She's out for the count, bleeding from the nose and with her left cheek already beginning to swell.

The phone is a newish-model iPhone, which asks for a passcode or face ID, so Delvina leans across and lifts her up by her hair, putting the phone in front of her face. Elle's injuries don't bother Delvina, at least not on a moral level. She's going to die anyway, so it doesn't really matter, and if her mum sees a video of her with a few bruises, it'll make her keener to cooperate.

At first the face ID doesn't work, so Delvina changes the angle, and bang, there it is. Open. She drops Elle's head back so that it's propped in the gap between the two seats and examines the recent calls. 'She was talking to her mum,' she says.

'Shall we make the call now?' asks Vincent. 'She might start getting worried.'

'No. Too early. Let her stew for a bit.' Delvina sends a quick text to the mother, ostensibly from Elle, saying she's exhausted and will call her back first thing in the morning before she starts her next shift. She sees that Elle usually ends her messages to her mother with three kisses, so she adds them and then switches off the phone and places it in a Faraday bag she's brought with her, before settling back in her seat and looking down at their latest victim.

She's a pretty young thing. Sweet-looking. Even in the horrible staid set of overalls they make nurses wear these days. Usually Delvina doesn't interfere with the hostages, because it just complicates things, although she's always fantasised about it. But since this is their last job and there's no obvious benefit in releasing Elle unharmed (and no financial cost to not releasing her), Delvina has decided that she's going to die. She's always enjoyed the idea of inflicting pain during sex, which is why for a number of years she was a professional dominatrix. There's no shortage of men who enjoy being beaten, slapped, kicked and generally humiliated. And Delvina has always been more than happy to indulge them, especially when they pay good money for it, or do exactly what they're told, like her husband. But to her mind, there's always been something magnificently exciting about dominating an innocent young woman who has no choice in the matter, taking her hard and fast and then . . .

101

And that's where her fantasy is really off the scale, because she can't get the idea out of her mind of strangling that innocent young woman with her bare hands just as she's coming herself. There's something so sweetly personal about it.

14

Thursday, 10.25 p.m.

Becca looks at the text from her daughter and wonders what she's done wrong. She finally talks to Elle after weeks and almost immediately gets cut off. And now apparently, five minutes later, she's suddenly too tired to talk to her.

The text reads: *Hi Mum. Very tired. Call you tomorrow before next shift. Xxx*

At least she got the full quota of kisses.

Becca sighs and pours herself a glass of wine. She's back home now and tired. It's been a long, stressful day, the kind that makes her wish she did a simpler, more relaxing job. She thinks about calling Elle back anyway but knows it'll be a waste of time. If her daughter doesn't want to talk, she won't answer. But it does sadden her. She's always tried to be a good mother and she hopes that Elle understands how much she truly loves her, because she knows that sometimes she hasn't been good enough at showing it.

She texts back: *Okay honey. I love you. Let's speak tomorrow. Monday sounds great. Looking forward to it a lot. Sleep well. Mama xxx*

Becca has to be in court on Wednesday in a high-profile corporate manslaughter case that requires several days of further detailed preparation, but she's just going to have to fit it all in at the weekend and on Tuesday, because there's no way she's missing out on the all-too-rare opportunity of spending time with Elle. She starts planning in her head what they're going to do: a walk down to the seafront, some shopping in the Lanes, dinner at a nice restaurant. They'll have Thai, because it's always been Elle's favourite. When she was younger, in the days before she was out with friends at weekends, the two of them would religiously have a Thai takeaway every Saturday night from the restaurant down the road in Crouch End, and eat it in front of the TV, watching whatever crap happened to be on.

Good times, thinks Becca. The days when Elle still looked up to her and didn't answer back. Long gone now. But she's determined to reinvigorate their relationship, get their closeness back, because when Elle was young, they really were close. It's a thought she's determined not to let go of, even though sometimes a nagging voice in her head tells her that actually she's deluding herself, and that she was never around when her daughter most needed her, which is why they're so distant now.

Her thoughts are interrupted by the sound of her mobile ringing.

It's Clyde, and she picks up immediately.

'You said your client can deliver us Kalian Roman?' he says without preamble.

'That's right,' says Becca, ignoring the fact that what

Quinn actually said was that he could give the CPS information on Roman, and in legal circles that's a very different thing.

'Can you get to my office at nine a.m. tomorrow?' There's impatience in his voice. And something else too. Excitement?

'Let me check my diary,' she answers, putting the phone on her lap and taking a long sip of the wine before coming back on the line. 'Yes, I can do that.'

'I'm not promising anything. I still think your client's demands are ridiculous.'

'I'll be there, Clyde,' she says, too tired to get into a verbal tug of war with him. She'd had enough of that when they were together.

'Can I just offer you a piece of advice, Becca?'

'I'm sure you're going to anyway, so fire away.'

'Be careful of Logan Quinn. He's a dangerous man.'

'Allegedly, Clyde. And thank you for the advice. I'll see you tomorrow.'

She ends the call and sits back on the sofa with a big sigh, thinking that Clyde hasn't told her anything she doesn't already know.

15

Thursday, 11.35 p.m.

There are numerous places I'd rather be than some gloomy street in south Kilburn on a cold March night chasing scumbags I don't even want to catch. I torment myself with thoughts of sitting at a beach bar in Phuket watching the sun set over the Andaman Sea and sipping a cold Singha, with a woman on each arm. Instead, I'm in the back of an unmarked Land Rover sitting next to Cotton, while in the front, next to the driver, is a female DI from Serious Crime Command called Fiona Lindsay, who's been designated Silver Commander, meaning she's the lead officer on the ground in the operation to arrest Blake Burns and his gang before they carry out their planned kidnap.

We're parked round the corner from Blake's flat, well out of sight, one of a total of seven unmarked vehicles involved tonight. The undercover I met earlier is wearing a hidden mic, and the conversation he and the other three members of the gang are having is clearly audible in the car. Marv, the man we're ostensibly interested in, isn't there, of course, and his absence is noted angrily by Blake, who describes him as unreliable before moving on to discussing the gang's target, a wholesale coke and meth dealer, now identified as Kayden Hoffer, who lives with his girlfriend and young son a few miles away in Wood Green.

The gang's expletive- and slang-filled conversation, complete with loud banging drill music in the background, centres round how much ransom they can charge for Hoffer's safe return (they settle on thirty grand after a bit of to-and-froing); whether he'll have drugs on the premises they can steal as well; whether he has access to firearms (they conclude he doesn't); and even whether it's worth abducting his son instead and doubling the ransom. One of them uses the Vanishers as an example of how to successfully kidnap kids (which ought to impress me but coming from these idiots doesn't). In the end, though, they decide that it's easier to stick to basics and just snatch Hoffer.

Unfortunately for them, there's not going to be any snatch. Blake has already said over the mic that en route to Hoffer's place they're stopping to pick up a gun from a man he identifies only as Chalkman. Once the gun is in Blake's car, they'll all be arrested and charged with possession of the firearm under the law of joint enterprise, as well as conspiracy to kidnap. Chalkman can be ID'd and picked up later, as doubtless his DNA and fingerprints will be all over the gun.

The thing I've got to hope for is that they all clam up and refuse to cooperate, which of course is most career criminals' immediate instinct – and let's be honest, from a crim's point of view it's by far the best thing to do in most circumstances. There's never anything to be gained by shooting your mouth off when you're arrested. It's always better to take a wait-and-see approach and let the lawyers prepare a decent defence (or a guilty plea) further down the line.

So I should be sitting pretty.

Except I'm not. And that's because there's a fifty-grand reward on offer, half of it put up by the Met, the other half by the Day family, to anyone whose information leads to the conviction of the Vanishers gang, and that's a problem, because fifty grand is a lot of money, even in these inflationary times, and it may well loosen tongues.

Luckily, I'm not a worrier, and with Marv out of the picture for the moment, I've got time to come up with a plan.

'Silver to all units, be prepared. It looks like they're on the move,' says DI Lindsay over the radio as Blake loudly announces that it's time to go and make some serious money.

'What if Hoffer's missus doesn't pay up?' the undercover asks.

'Then we'll send her his fucking ear and tell her the kid's next,' Blake guffaws, blissfully unaware of how much he's incriminating himself. I might be a bit of a villain, but that doesn't mean I identify with scumbags like Blake Burns, and I sincerely hope the arrest team give him a bit of a kicking before he's taken into custody.

A tablet-sized video screen has been set up on the Land Rover's dashboard showing a live camera shot of the front of Blake's ground-floor flat. Apparently the flat next door to his is empty, its occupants having been driven out by the gang, and is now used as their makeshift prison/torture chamber. The last man they abducted was held for eighteen hours, during which time he was burnt with a steam iron, slashed on the buttocks with a knife, and had bleach sprayed in one eye, leaving him with partial sight loss.

These are the kind of people we have to deal with, and I'm looking forward to leaving them all behind.

On the screen, we watch as the door to the flat opens and Blake leads his gang out with a deliberate swagger. Immediately behind him is a big bodybuilder type, with muscles almost popping out of his tracksuit top, carrying a holdall.

DI Lindsay turns round slightly in her seat. 'That's your man, Leon Dennay.'

Cotton says: 'I'm glad I'm not the one who's got to take him down.'

I don't say anything. I'm too busy watching Dennay on the screen, wondering if he's the type who'll talk. He's doing all the big macho posing, but that doesn't mean anything. The ones who look the toughest often aren't.

Behind Dennay comes a much smaller guy with a naturally fierce expression who looks straight out of 'violent thug' casting, and bringing up the rear is our undercover man, his expression almost nonchalant as he closes the door behind him. I have to hand it to him, the guy's ice cool.

The four of them get into Blake's car, the kind of gleamingly clean black BMW 5 Series so beloved of drug dealers everywhere, and which acts like a beacon demanding attention. The undercover's wearing a microscopic tracking device sewn into the material of his jeans, so there's no need for the arrest team to follow the BMW too closely until they're ready to make the strike.

I relax a little and sit back in my seat as the camera feed on the tablet screen changes to a GPS map of the surrounding area and the Land Rover pulls away from the kerb, the driver taking us through the night streets of Harlesden, which are still busy enough at this time of night that we don't stand out too much. There's a steady chatter over the radio between the vehicles involved, and the tone is tense. This is an armed op. Things can easily go wrong, and I'm pleased that we're just along for the ride and not actually taking part in any of the tough stuff. I know Cotton feels the same.

Not much happens for the first fifteen minutes of our slow-motion pursuit, but then things move up a gear as the BMW turns into a quiet residential road running parallel to a railway line. It's clear from the map that this road doesn't lead anywhere in particular, which means that the man with the gun, Chalkman, lives down there somewhere.

'Beta to Silver,' comes a voice from the lead car over the radio. 'How close do you want us to follow?'

'Give them one minute, Beta,' says DI Lindsay, 'then go down there slowly and check it out. All other cars hold back on All Saints Avenue.'

On the screen, the BMW stops about two hundred metres down the residential road. The undercover's mic's still on, and we can clearly hear Blake say that he'll be back in a minute before exiting the car.

Our Land Rover pulls up at the kerb on the main road, some three hundred metres away from where the BMW's just stopped. DI Lindsay leans over and expands the tablet screen as far as it will go. 'It looks like they're parked outside a church,' she says, switching the screen to Street View. A photo taken in daylight shows an end-of-terrace house with a single-storey extension. The words *God Will Deliver. Seventh Day Adventist Church of St Luke* have been painted in bold black letters on the side wall.

'It's a good cover for a gun dealer,' I say, impressed in spite of myself. That's the thing about criminals. Some are clever and entrepreneurial and are wasting their talents in the short-term world of crime.

DI Lindsay asks Gold Commander, who's running the whole show back at the control centre at Paddington Green nick, to check who owns the building, then tells Alpha and Gamma cars, which are both armed-response vehicles, to take up position at the other end of the residential street so that they're in front of the target. 'Remember,' she continues into the radio, 'as soon as our man gives the signal that they're in possession of the gun, with the words "That's some piece", we move to amber and prepare to go in with the hard stop.'

While she's talking, I'm looking at the tablet screen. It strikes me that the street the gang are stopped on is particularly narrow, and in the Street View photo there are cars lining both sides. No one else seems to have noticed this, so when DI Lindsay has finished speaking into the mic, I say: 'It may not be such a good idea sending Beta down there. He might get stuck behind the target car.'

She flashes me the kind of look that says, 'Mind what you're saying, you're just a guest here', but then she glances back at the screen and tells Beta to disregard her last instruction and remain on the main road.

'Beta to Silver. We're already proceeding down there,' comes the reply.

'Is it possible to turn round?' she asks.

'Target car's forty metres ahead, blocking the road, it's possible to turn round, but it's a squeeze and it might draw attention to us.'

Straight off I can see that DI Lindsay knows she's made a mistake, but that's the problem with high-end police pursuits using multiple vehicles. The person in charge on the ground has to make a lot of decisions in quick succession.

As she presses a couple of buttons on the screen and the feed changes to the dashboard camera in Beta's car, we can now all see the BMW in the middle of the road with its driver's door wide open and blocking the street, which is the typical cockiness you get from these kinds of thugs and just makes me dislike them even more.

As we watch, Blake emerges from the house and walks round the back of the car, carrying a plastic bag. He stops and looks towards Beta's car, which is slowing down. Even from a distance and on the tablet screen, I can see from the expression on his face that he's clocked them as cops. It's just sheer bad luck. However well planned an op is, you still need an element of luck, and tonight it looks like no one's got any except me, because Blake doesn't hang around. He immediately drops the bag and takes off on foot round the side of the house, disappearing from view. At the same time, the BMW doors fly open and the other three leap out. Dennay, the big muscle man who supposedly knows Marv, heads in the same direction, as does the undercover, while the fourth member of the gang runs up the road in the opposite direction to the Beta car.

'Suspects are heading for the railway track,' hisses the undercover over the mic, while Beta disgorges its officers, who take off after suspect number four, guns drawn.

DI Lindsay is barking orders while fiddling with the screen so that it's showing the map again. 'Turn the car round,' she snaps at the driver. 'We need to cut them off on the other side of the tracks.'

The driver does as he's told and starts heading back the way we came. He slows as we come to a bridge over the railway, and I can just make out two shadowy figures scrambling down the embankment, followed a short distance behind by the undercover.

The car accelerates again before taking a right on the other side of the tracks, which is when I realise, somewhat belatedly, that we're now the lead car in the pursuit. This wouldn't be quite so bad if we were armed (or if I actually wanted to catch these idiots), but we're not.

Two unmarked ARVs with flashing lights appear behind us and that reassures me that we're not completely on our own, because let's be fair, the occupants of the car I'm in are not exactly Delta Force. DI Lindsay looks like she could handle herself, true, but the driver resembles an underfed trainee accountant, and Cotton might have the bulk, but with a top speed of 'amble', he won't be much help.

'Blake and Dennay are splitting up,' pants the undercover over the mic. 'I'm sticking with Blake. Dennay's coming your way and he's coming fast. I think he's going to climb the signal box a hundred metres north of the bridge. It's his only way over.'

Sure enough, twenty seconds later, as we drive steadily down the street with the ARVs following, a silhouetted figure appears on top of the signal box on the other side of the fence no more than ten metres in front of us, and jumps over it onto the pavement.

'Go! Go! Go!' shouts Lindsay as our car screeches to a halt, almost knocking Dennay over as he races across the road with an impressive turn of speed for a guy who's already covered a couple of hundred metres at what must have been a fair old sprint.

Usually in this kind of situation I'd hang back just long enough for a couple of the others to get ahead of me, so that if things turn nasty during the arrest, they get the brunt of it. Unfortunately, I'm in that bizarre position where I need the bad guy to get away, and the best way for that to happen is if I'm the lead pursuer. So, wondering how the hell I got myself in this situation when I could have been lounging at home on the first evening of a long weekend, I'm out of the car like a ball from a malfunctioning cannon, half tripping over myself but somehow suddenly in the lead, with no one between me and Dennay.

I can't quite believe this is happening. It's been the best

part of five years since I've been involved in a foot chase, and the suspect that time was five foot six and scraggy and there were two cops in front of me. Now it feels like I'm on my own, and what's more, I'm actually gaining on the bastard, probably because Dennay's got to be knackered.

He's about ten metres ahead of me when he makes a sharp left turn down an alleyway that cuts through the row of houses. I take a quick look over my shoulder and I'm shocked to see Cotton only a few metres behind me, already puffing and panting but showing no sign of slowing up. He did mention something about joining the gym, but I didn't think he'd actually turned up there. He's followed closely by Silver and our driver, and then just behind them, several armed uniforms who've decamped from one of the cars.

Up ahead, I can see a wooden fence a good three metres high blocking access to the backs of the houses. But that's not stopping Dennay, who takes a running jump and grabs the top of it with both hands before hauling himself up.

I slow up a little, hoping to give him just enough time to get over it, but he's not moving fast enough, and as he throws one leg over, I can hear Cotton at my shoulder.

'Get him, Fish!' he gasps, starting to come alongside me.

And that's it. I've got no choice now but to act the hero, otherwise I'm going to look a right idiot (if not a little suspicious, too).

Dennay's other leg is still dangling, and although he's lifting it fast as we approach, I jump up and manage to get hold of the ankle, giving it a hard yank. He tries to kick me away, but Cotton's getting in on things now, and he wraps both arms round the leg just above the knee and pulls.

With our combined weight acting as a drag on him, even a guy of Dennay's size has no chance, and eventually gravity wins out and he comes crashing down, all twenty-odd stone of him. We end up in a tangled heap in the dirt, with me, winded, at the bottom and Dennay and Cotton wrestling on top of me.

Which is when Cotton says something I'm really not expecting. 'We only want to talk about Marv,' he hisses in Dennay's ear. 'There's a fifty-grand reward.'

Dennay pauses for a second, and straight off I can tell he's intrigued, but then he gives Cotton a hard shove and scrambles to his feet, still wearing a puzzled expression, as if he's trying to work out if it's a trick or not.

But this time he doesn't get far. As I roll over onto my side, DI Lindsay appears above me, jumping over my prone form and sidestepping Cotton before firing a dose of pepper spray into Dennay's face. Even now, Dennay has the where-withal to lash out at her, catching her with a roundhouse punch that sends her backwards and into the driver, before kicking his leg free from Cotton's grip and stumbling blindly back towards the fence. The guy's got determination, you have to give him that, and it gives me hope that someone this hell-bent on escaping justice won't want to cooperate with the forces of law and order.

But determined or not, it's the end of the line for Dennay. As I crawl out of the way, feeling like I've been crushed by a dumper truck, the armed uniforms appear. One of them yells, 'Taser! Taser! Taser!' and our fugitive goes down in a crackle of electricity, luckily managing to avoid me this time and landing on Cotton, who actually squeals.

Even so, I feel like I've somehow snatched defeat from the jaws of victory.

16

Friday, 12.12 a.m.

Delvina owns a small detached house just south of Cobham in Surrey, set back down a private drive with fields on either side. It was a wreck when she bought it six years ago, after the death of her first husband. Since then, she's worked hard to do it up, with Vincent helping her after they got together, and now it represents a very tidy income stream through Airbnb rentals. It's situated in a lovely part of the world, only an hour's drive from central London yet a million miles from the madding crowds, and is very popular with walkers. She's even given it a new, suitably twee name to attract the punters: Acorn Cottage.

Which is ironic really, because it's also where they keep their kidnap victims – the place they refer to as 'the hotel'. She and Vincent have built a makeshift soundproofed dungeon in the cottage's basement, accessible only via a secret locked trapdoor in the middle of the living room, hidden under a thick rug.

And it's here that they've brought their latest abductee. The journey has taken them an hour and fifty minutes and they stopped twice. Once at the same lay-by as their journey down, where they switched the fake plates back to the real ones, just to make it even harder for the police's ANPR cameras to track them. And the second time at a small stretch of woodland five miles from the hotel, where Delvina hid Elle's phone in bushes a few yards from the road. She knows you have to be ultra-careful these days if you want to avoid the attention of law enforcement, so she leaves absolutely nothing to chance, which is what angers her so much about that idiot Marv shooting his mouth off. She hopes Fisher's sorting that end of things but doesn't hold her breath. In the end, she knows that the only person you can truly rely on in this world is yourself.

Right now, as they turn into the cottage's driveway, Elle is still flat out, and Delvina calculates they've got roughly another half-hour before the effects of the ketamine she injected into her wear off. This will be the last dose she administers for a while. She likes to keep her victims nice and docile, but she doesn't want to give them an actual overdose, at least not while she still needs the parents to be cooperative.

The lights are on inside, which means Marv is here, as he's meant to be, but as Vincent pulls up and stops, Delvina's face darkens when she sees that so is Marv's silver Ford Mondeo. 'What's his car doing here?' she demands, leaning forward between the seats. 'I told you to drive him here.'

Vincent turns round, and she's surprised to see that he looks annoyed with her. 'I tried, but he wanted to bring his own car, and I can't force him.'

119

Delvina knows when to pick her battles. She can see Vincent is stressed, as he has been all evening. She toys with the idea of telling him about the police's interest in Marv, but decides that now's not the time. 'Okay,' she says with a sigh.

She gets out of the car and stretches, relishing the fresh country air. She's stiff from sitting down all night, and makes a note to call her chiropractor tomorrow and see if he can fit her in for a session at some point. 'I'll leave it to you two to get her down to the cellar,' she tells Vincent as the outside light comes on and the looming silhouetted figure of Marv opens the front door, looking like some demented horror-film butler.

It's no secret that he and Delvina don't get on. She's never liked him. He's a petty thug with ideas above his station, and definitely their weak link. Her husband she can manipulate, and he has no secrets from her. But Marv is very much his own man, and now his big mouth has proved to be a real issue. She doesn't think he'd give them up if he was caught. He's old school like that, and he has huge loyalty to Vincent, but even so, it's far too dangerous to keep him alive. Unfortunately, Vincent has huge loyalty to Marv as well, and that's likely to be a problem.

'Hey, bro,' says Vincent, looking genuinely pleased to see his cousin.

Marv looks pleased to see him too, and they do some complicated handshake. He ignores Delvina.

'You'd better get her inside,' says Delvina, hurrying them along. 'I don't want her waking up.'

Marv gives her a contemptuous look but follows Vincent back to the car. Delvina goes into the cottage, noticing the half-eaten takeaway pizza still in its box on the kitchen top, as well as two empty Coke cans and an empty 500 ml bottle of Peroni. Slovenly bastard, she thinks, walking into the neatly decorated living room, where *Love Island* is playing on the TV. There's another empty Peroni bottle on the coffee table, without a coaster, too. She's tempted to tear a strip off Marv but decides against it. He's belligerent enough as it is. There's no point riling him further. She comforts herself with the knowledge that after this weekend, she'll never see him again.

The hotel is more than two hundred years old and has bare stone floors. Marv hasn't bothered getting anything ready, so Delvina moves the coffee table and the sofa a couple of feet to one side and pulls up the rug, revealing the trapdoor beneath. It's double-locked, just in case some inquisitive Airbnb guest ever discovers it, and once Delvina has unlocked and opened it, she leans inside and switches the light on.

The basement's a grim place, with a flight of uneven stone steps leading down into the gloom, and it always sends a little shudder up her spine. She's claustrophobic, and the thought of being trapped down there terrifies her. Not that it will ever happen. Vincent always has her back.

The other two come into the room, propping Elle up between them. She looks so vulnerable and helpless with her head lolling to one side and her feet dragging. Delvina tries not to let the lust show on her face as she moves out of the way to let them manhandle the young woman over to the trapdoor. Vincent goes backwards down the steps taking Elle's legs, with Marv following holding her shoulders. The trapdoor isn't a particularly big opening, and Marv has to slide down on his behind, although Delvina notes with interest that both he and Vincent are very careful with Elle, as if they're transporting something incredibly fragile and valuable, and she remembers what her husband said earlier about not wanting to kill her because she's a young, female nurse.

She gives them a few seconds, then follows them down the steps, through a heavy iron door and into the fully soundproofed cell, which is lit by a single naked bulb. The room measures a reasonably spacious four by three metres, and is just over two metres high, meaning Marv comes close to brushing the padded ceiling with his head. There's a sink and toilet at the far end, so although it's pretty basic, it could be a lot worse. It was Delvina who insisted on the toilet, even though Vincent had to plumb it in himself, because she's a stickler for hygiene and doesn't want to have to clean up anyone's bodily waste or deal with a fetid stench.

Vincent and Marv place Elle down on the bed with her head on the pillow, like she's Sleeping Beauty, then they both stare down at her for a moment in silence.

'She's a looker,' says Marv, and Delvina sees the glint in his eye. The dirty bastard. He's never interfered with any of their victims before, but that's because they've all been men.

'No one's allowed to touch her,' she says sharply. 'You've

just got to keep her fed and watered. Nothing else. And make sure she gives you her phone passcode.'

He glares at her. 'All right. I know.'

'We can trust Marv,' says Vincent, ever the peacemaker. 'He's always reliable.'

Marv nods. 'Exactly. I'm a pro. I know what I'm doing.'

Delvina gives him a withering look, but doesn't state the obvious. 'Good. Because there's a lot of money riding on this.'

'How much?' he demands, his tone disrespectful.

'None of your business. You're getting paid extremely well for a straightforward job. Leave it at that.'

'Come on, mate,' says Vincent, patting his cousin on the back. 'Let's grab a beer upstairs.'

Marv grunts something and follows him back up the steps. Delvina remains where she is. 'Leave the hatch open,' she calls after them, suppressing a brief shudder at the thought of Marv locking her in here and never letting her out.

The cell door is open, so she can hear their voices disappearing into the kitchen. When they're finally out of earshot, she gets to work, taking off Elle's shoes and socks before locking a chain round her right ankle and another round her right wrist. The ends of the chains are attached to secure plates in the bare wall, so there's no way she can break free, but there's enough slack in them that she can move round the room and use the toilet and sink.

When she's finished with the chains, she leans over and releases Elle's hair from its severe ponytail, rearranging it

SIMON KERNICK

so that it flows out across the pillow. She's a very pretty girl, even if her face is a little bruised from earlier. In a way, the bruising adds something to her character. Delvina takes a bottle of mineral water from her bag and places it on the floor next to the bed, and then stands staring at her victim in silence, feeling the excitement build. She thinks about stripping her, but then sees Elle's eyelids flickering and knows it's time to go.

Whipping out one of her burner phones, she takes a couple of photos of her prone on the bed, making sure to get the chains in, then turns away.

But she'll be back. She's going to take her time with this one, and eat her right up.

17

Friday, 12.24 a.m.

Elle comes round slowly, her head thick, vision foggy. She senses movement somewhere in her peripheral vision and then the muffled sound of footsteps disappearing. She's in a dark room with a single light burning. There's more light coming from a doorway to her left, but then that suddenly disappears, and everything is silent.

She tries to sit up, but the effort's too much for her. Her mouth is bone dry and she just has time to realise she's feeling extremely nauseous before she retches. She rolls over on her side and dry-heaves so hard it feels like her ribs are going to break. But nothing comes out and her mouth feels even drier. She vaguely registers a sink and toilet in the corner of the room before seeing the bottle of mineral water on the bare stone floor, and that's what immediately grabs her attention. Instinctively she reaches out and grabs it, pulling open the cap and putting the bottle to her lips. She drinks half of it down, rests for a few moments as her mind begins to clear, then takes another big gulp and puts the bottle back on the floor.

She's been kidnapped. She knows that. Someone snatched her on the street. The memory's vague, but as she lies back on the bed looking up at the ceiling, it begins to return. Getting out of her car after another long shift at the hospital and talking to her mum on the phone. Seeing the drunk woman in front of her, and the way she stumbled. Stopping to help, then . . . nothing.

She vaguely remembers lying down in the back of a car, and someone hitting her in the face – the blows a real shock. As that particular memory resurfaces, her face suddenly starts to hurt, and she touches it. The skin feels tender. That's when she realises that there's some kind of iron cuff on her wrist attached to a chain. She pulls the chain and it rattles. Her phone and wallet were in her bag, but as she looks round, she sees there's no sign of it, or them. She feels in her scrubs, hoping that by some chance she'd put her phone in there, but the pockets are empty. Her watch is missing too.

A tiny part of her was hoping this was some kind of horrible vivid dream, or maybe a really nasty practical joke played by one of her friends, but of course it isn't. It was a deliberate abduction, and now she's chained to a bed in a dungeon-like room with what look like foam tiles covering the walls and ceiling to soundproof it from any noise she might make.

But why? What possible reason could there be to abduct her? Her first terrified thought is that the motive is sexual. That she's going to be kept here for days, weeks, months on end, tortured and assaulted, then murdered and buried in a shallow grave somewhere. And yet she's still wearing her shift scrubs. Only her feet are bare, and a cuff has been placed round her right ankle, but otherwise she's intact. No one's assaulted her. At least not yet. And it occurs to her that whoever has taken her has gone to a hell of a lot of trouble, probably too much for it to be just a simple sexual motive.

This leads on to her second thought. That it's something to do with her mother. It's no secret that her mum has made enemies over the years through her work as a lawyer. She's successfully sued corporations, the government, Unionist politicians in Northern Ireland . . . the type of people who might seek revenge on her. She also got herself a public profile – and a very negative one at that – after her successful defence of Oliver Tamzan. She even had her photo published in the *Daily Mail* alongside an unpleasant caption along the lines of 'How does she sleep at night?' Elle knew her mum had received a slew of death threats after that and was even offered police protection, which (typical Mum) she turned down. Maybe someone has finally decided to get back at her using Elle. It isn't such an outlandish prospect. But it's definitely a scary one, because it means that whoever is holding her is probably not planning on letting her go.

So the third possibility, that this is the work of the Vanishers, is actually quite a welcome one, because it means that this is a simple kidnap for ransom, and if her mum pays up, she'll be freed. Elle read about the Vanishers when the media story about them broke following the death of one of their hostages a few months earlier. Her mum even warned her to be careful when approached by strangers on the street and to keep her wits about her, which she always has (until tonight anyway). Elle knows that however big the ransom for her release, her mum will get hold of the money somehow. She has no idea how much Mum is worth – she's never been interested in finding out – but it doesn't matter. Whatever else anyone says about her, she has the kind of steely determination that's put her right at the top of her profession, and Elle's proud of her for that. As well as thankful.

She focuses on her breathing as she's been taught in her regular yoga class, and feels herself calming down. She's always been a level-headed person, not given to panic. You have to be if you're a nurse working on a busy vascular ward where clinical emergencies are happening all the time, and where the worst-case scenario is always death. So lying here now, she takes solace in the fact that she's still alive, and that so far no one has threatened or tried to hurt her. She needs to stay strong, develop some kind of relationship with her captors, and most of all, look for potential ways to escape.

'You'll get through this, Elle,' she says aloud, her voice croaking, but even as she speaks the words into the gloom, a part of her is already fearful that it isn't true.

And that she'll die here, helpless and alone.

18

Friday, 2.15 a.m.

It's late and way past my bedtime when me and Cotton are finally allowed to see Leon Dennay, who, along with his two fellow gang members, is being held at Paddington Green station for questioning. All three have lawyered up, and Dennay's already had two hours with the officers from Serious Crime, during which time he's answered every question put to him with the classic 'no comment'. So far, so typical.

However, we still have our secret weapon, the reward money, and as soon as we walk into the room, Dennay's eyes light up.

Christ, he's a big unit sitting there behind the pockmarked desk. It looks like he could break out of here single-handed, and I'm amazed that he didn't cause more damage when he fell on me earlier.

His lawyer, meanwhile, is a miserable-looking bald guy with a long head and thick-rimmed black glasses who has an iPad in front of him on which he's currently making notes. He looks up with little obvious interest as we sit down and introduce ourselves for the benefit of the tape.

'Are you here about the cash?' says Dennay before his lawyer can open his mouth.

'That's right,' says Cotton, who as the new boss takes the lead (an injustice I still can't get used to, although I'm impressed how he mentioned the reward to Dennay mid fight). 'I understand you've got information that may help us with the Vanishers case.'

'I want immunity,' says Dennay, somewhat optimistically.

'We can't help with that,' Cotton explains. 'It's a separate matter.'

Dennay shrugs his massive shoulders. 'Then I've got nothing to say.'

'You can still claim the reward even without immunity for any other charges you might face,' I tell him, 'because those crimes have got nothing to do with what we're investigating.'

'Is that true?' Dennay asks the lawyer.

'I'd have to check the details,' he answers, 'but I can't see why you'd be denied reward money if your information leads to the apprehension of criminals for a separate crime, as long as you didn't have anything to do with that crime.'

'I didn't,' says Dennay.

'So you can tell us,' says Cotton.

'I need it in writing first.'

'We haven't got time for that,' I tell him. I really don't want to sit here any longer than I have to. 'If you've got information, give it to us. And like your lawyer says, if it leads to a conviction, you'll get the reward money. '

'How do I know you won't renege on it?' demands Dennay.

'Because we're on fucking camera,' I say, exasperated, pointing up at the ceiling. 'We can hardly go back on it.'

Dennay sits and considers this for a moment. Then he says: 'I'm not a snitch.'

Neither of us bothers responding to that. We just sit there waiting. I'm hoping he'll stay shtum at least for a few days, because I have a plan that will effectively put a huge and impenetrable buffer between me and the Vanishers. But I need time.

Unfortunately, Dennay's not going to give me it.

'Marvin Cunningham,' he says. 'I reckon he's one of the Vanishers. And if he is, I get fifty grand, right? Whatever happens?' He looks at his lawyer for support.

The lawyer nods, but not quite with a hundred per cent conviction. 'It's on camera,' he says.

'If your information leads directly to Cunningham's conviction for the Vanishers kidnappings, you will get at least a portion of that fifty-thousand-pound reward, and the whole lot if the entire gang are convicted because of you,' says Cotton.

'I'd better fucking do,' says Dennay darkly, glaring at both of us in turn.

What he doesn't realise, though, is that by giving us Cunningham's name, he's effectively lost all his bargaining power.

'Why do you think he's one of the Vanishers?' I ask, keen to find out exactly how much he knows.

'He told me.'

This makes both of us sit up. It's the way he says it. Without hesitation.

'What did he say exactly?' asks Cotton, getting in there first.

'We were in the pub one time a few months back, and I asked him how come he'd always got money, because, you know, he always has. Normally he doesn't tell you too much about his business. He's not a big talker, but he'd had a few drinks and he told me he'd kidnapped a couple of students and held them for ransom. Made some big money off of it as well. Said you had to know what you were doing. I thought he was joking at first. You know, he's not the brightest of sparks. But when I asked him more about it, he clammed up. Wouldn't say any more.'

Dennay pauses to stretch in his seat, rolling his shoulders back and forward and cricking his neck before continuing. 'This was before that stuff about the Vanishers was all over the news, you know. Then, when the story broke and they killed that student, Marv called and told me never to mention a word about him doing those kidnaps. Said it was all bullshit. Except, you know, when he said it like that, it made me think he was definitely involved.'

So there you have it. Marv really did shoot his mouth off.

I exchange looks with Cotton and look suitably excited by this new development. It's not solid evidence, but it's more than either of us was expecting.

'Apparently he wasn't available tonight for your job, was he?' says Cotton.

'No. Bit of good luck on his part, wasn't it?'

'Did he say why?'

'Blake said he had a job for good money doing some babysitting. That's what made me think it might be another one of those kidnaps.'

'He wouldn't be doing it on his own, though, would he?' I say, because someone's going to ask these questions and it might as well be me. 'Did he ever mention any associates? Or is there someone else you can think of who might be involved with him?'

'I've told you what I know,' he replies, and although we continue to question him for a further ten minutes, it's clear he hasn't got any more useful information.

It might be late, but as soon as we're out of the interview room, we find a spare computer terminal in the CID offices and look up Marvin Cunningham on the PND. The image of a grim-faced unshaven guy with broad shoulders, big bug eyes and a chin that juts at a weird angle like it might be dislocated appears on the screen.

'Blimey, he's an ugly bastard,' says Cotton, and there's no way I can argue with that.

Cunningham is thirty-eight years old, with a long criminal history. Aside from the usual theft and drug dealing, it includes four counts of assault on a police officer, three of assault causing ABH, and a further two of assault causing GBH. The GBH convictions both led to prison sentences, of two and six years respectively, with the latter one involving him putting a man in a week-long coma and causing brain damage. It pisses me off that he served less than four years of his sentence for inflicting that kind of injury. It's no wonder that these people remain professional criminals when the punishments they receive are so soft. You might think that's a bit hypocritical of me, but as I've said already, just because I commit some crimes myself doesn't mean I root for the bad guys. I don't. Like everyone else, I want to see justice prevail. Except, obviously, when it affects me.

'And a real charmer as well,' I say, staring at the screen. 'With a record like that, he's definitely capable of committing kidnap and murder, but I can't see him being the mastermind. The guy looks small-time.' This, of course, is me being disingenuous. I can't be seen to be anything other than relentless in my pursuit of the Vanishers, the people who ruined my public reputation.

'Well, we know there's a woman involved,' says Cotton. 'Check any known associates.'

I scroll down the screen and am relieved to see that the column containing known associates is empty. Cunningham really is small-time. He's been out of nick four years and hasn't been in any trouble since. There are no active investigations into him, and it seems he hasn't been on anyone else's radar either.

I sigh, feigning frustration. 'There's not a lot, is there? And the kidnaps started while he was still behind bars.' Which they did. From memory, it seems that Marv missed the first one. I guess they recruited him because they were struggling to do everything with just two of them, but I don't see why. The hard part's the snatch. Everything else is just babysitting.

'They could have recruited him afterwards,' says Cotton, whose detecting skills seem to be improving.

'That's true,' I say. 'Look, I've still got the footage from the Day abduction on here.' I pull out my phone. 'Let's have a look if it's Cunningham driving.'

It only takes me a few seconds to find it, because it's kept in the Favourites section of my photos to show the world how obsessed I am with solving the case. While Cotton looks over my shoulder, I scroll through the grainy footage of Day walking along the pavement in the direction of his girlfriend's house. I feel a twinge of something – I think it might be guilt – at seeing him on the screen alive and well and knowing that he's now dead, but I push the feeling aside. I can't be getting emotional about anything right now.

Focus, Fish. Focus.

On the screen, Day sees Delvina come into shot in front of him. She's pretending to stagger, and as he moves to one side to pass her (he's definitely no Good Samaritan), she deliberately bumps into him before appearing to jab a needle into his arm. Now it's Day's turn to stumble, and as he does, Delvina puts an arm round him and guides him across the road as the Chrysler people carrier being driven by her co-conspirator pulls up. She manhandles him into the back before jumping in herself. I have to admit, it's a very slick operation, and one that requires some serious cojones, given that it was done at 7.30 at night. But then that's Delvina for you. She's a high-risk kind of woman.

I stop the video as the car moves towards the camera, focusing in on the driver, who wears a plain black baseball cap, glasses and a surgical mask and who I know for a fact is her husband, Vincent. We've had the footage enhanced using the best available software, but even so, it's still not great quality, which is another of those things that always amazes me. We've got telescopes that can see stars literally trillions and trillions of miles away absolutely perfectly, and yet you try to get some decent camera footage of someone a few metres past the end of the lens here on planet Earth, and all you manage is a blurry face. Anyway, on our enhanced footage, you can see that the driver's white, medium build and height, dark-haired, and that he's most likely in his thirties or forties.

Which narrows it down to about two million people.

'That's definitely not Cunningham,' says Cotton, stating the obvious. 'It says on his file that he's six feet three, and he definitely doesn't look like the one on here.' He points at the screen. 'This guy's a lot smaller. Look how far down he is in the seat. He's no more than five nine tops.'

'It's possible there's more than two of them in the gang, though, Cott. At the very least we need to get Cunningham put under surveillance, after what Dennay told us,' I say, knowing full well that Marv is already in the wind.

Cotton shakes his head. 'Come on, Fish. You know there's no way I can get it approved with what we've got.'

Of course I know that. But I've got to act the part. 'So where do we go with it?' I ask him, sounding exasperated. 'It's not like we've got any other leads, and we're under constant pressure to solve this. I believe what Dennay says, and if Cunningham's been kidnapping students, it'll be as part of the Vanishers. If it was something separate, we'd know about it.'

Cotton sighs. 'Look, I'll take it upstairs, see if we can start an investigation into him, check his bank accounts and his credit card history. But that's about the best we're going to get on the evidence we're holding. And you know how much it costs and how much hassle it is to get twenty-four-hour surveillance authorised.' He shrugs wearily. 'We're just not going to get it.'

I know exactly where he's coming from. Resources are scarce and getting constantly scarcer. Which suits me fine.

We sit there in silence for a moment. 'So tonight was a complete waste of time, then?' I say. 'I get crushed by a twenty-stone lowlife and all for nothing.'

'Course it wasn't a waste of time,' says Cotton, giving my shoulder an affectionate squeeze. 'You know how it works, Fish. It takes time to build a case. We've got Cunningham on our radar now. If he's involved, we'll get him. Listen,' he adds, seeing that I'm still looking mildly despondent, 'a couple of the victims spoke to one of the male kidnappers while they were being held. Let's play them a recording of Cunningham's voice. We can get one easily enough from old interview tapes. See if they recognise it as his.'

It's a good idea and I tell him so. 'I don't mind going to see them,' I continue, wanting to remain right at the forefront of any developments and knowing I can muddy the waters better if I'm the only one involved. 'I'll start with Jonathan Syed. He was the most recent victim before Day. I seem to recall he mentioned talking to one of the kidnappers.'

'You don't have to do it, Fish. Tomorrow's your day off. I can send someone else.'

I appreciate Cotton's kindness. He's one of the good guys. My only criticism is that he's probably a bit too soft for the role he's in. You need some steel to lead a unit like ours. 'I'd rather go myself, to be honest, Cott,' I tell him. 'It's my reputation on the line.'

'It's not just yours, Fish. It's all of ours. We bear collective responsibility for what went wrong. I've told you before, you shouldn't torture yourself.'

But I bravely insist, and fifteen minutes later I'm back in my car heading home, with an audio recording of Marv Cunningham's dulcet tones on my phone and a vague feeling that I should be feeling a bit guilty about what I'm doing but unable to quite manage it.

To me, it's just a business, and let's be frank: I've always been a little crooked in my dealings, at least since I first went plain clothes the best part of twenty years ago. That's meant me taking money from the wrong kinds of people for services that I was able to render by virtue of my position as a detective. Even so, I didn't join the Anti Kidnap unit in order to organise kidnaps; it was just something I fell into when I saw a gap in the market, so to speak. Cryptocurrencies might not be as anonymous as some criminals think, but they take away a huge amount of the risk because there's no need for any contact between the kidnappers and those paying the ransom. That's what gave me the idea to get involved, and I had the perfect amoral and clever accomplice in Delvina.

I've never wanted anyone to die, of course. I'm not an animal. I just want everything done smoothly, with the minimum of pain and fuss and the victim delivered back suffering from as little trauma as possible. I've always been the one to pick the victims, spending an extensive amount of time looking for the right ones. Obviously they've got to have a decent amount of money and be in a position where they can be snatched easily without unduly alarming anyone close to them. But I also tend to go for families I consider to be deserving of this kind of upheaval. One of the earliest victims was the student son of a high-ranking executive in a well-known payday loan company. You know, one of those outfits that pick on the very poor and sting them for everything they haven't got, while making heaps of money in the process.

Look, I'm not pretending I'm doing this for any kind of noble reason (I'm not), but I'd still rather avoid going for the really nice ones. Take Henry Day, for example. Now, the reason I picked him wasn't just because of his obnoxious parents, although they're bad enough. It was because of something he'd done aged sixteen that I initially read about in the papers. He and three friends, drunk on cheap booze and whatever else, had broken into a village hall a few miles from the Day family home one night. Apparently the hall was playing host to a meeting of model-railway enthusiasts that weekend and they'd spent literally days setting up a huge tabletop model so they could do whatever it is they do with their model trains. Day and his mates had smashed the whole thing to pieces, and then, as if this wasn't bad enough, had then broken all the windows and let off the fire extinguisher, causing thousands of pounds of damage and wrecking the plans of a whole lot of people. They'd been arrested after their faces were caught on CCTV, but probably because they were middle class and from well-off families, they'd been let off with police cautions and a poxy letter of apology each to the model-train people.

Now, you can say it was just teenage high jinks that got out of hand, and that plenty of kids make mistakes like that and go on to be decent citizens, but I'm not so sure. They were old enough to know what they were doing and arrogant and selfish enough to derive real pleasure from other people's misery. In my mind, they deserved serious punishment, which was what I'd planned for Henry Day. I hadn't wanted him to die, though, and I still feel bad about it, even though the kid was clearly something of an arsehole. But we'd been put in a position whereby letting him go would mean the Vanishers wouldn't be taken seriously, and we couldn't have that either. Like I say, it was business, pure and simple, and sometimes you've just got to be ruthless.

The important thing now is to navigate through the next few days, collect the remainder of my money and extricate myself from the Vanishers without drawing any suspicion on myself.

When I've put some distance between me and Paddington Green station, I pull over on a quiet residential road in Brentford, still a couple of miles from home, and remove the burner phone I'm currently using to liaise with Delvina from the glove compartment. Switching it on, I immediately see a message from her delivered at just after midnight. It's short and not very sweet: *We have the target safe and sound. Marv here without his phone. Send balance as agreed.*

She's not getting it yet. I need access to my laptop, and anyway it's now gone four and I need to sleep. I'll sort it out in the morning. I'm pleased at least that Cunningham is away from his home and at the hotel where Delvina and her little crew keep their victims. I decide to give her a hundred and fifty grand tomorrow, as we agreed last week, and then the balance, including that fifty grand she strong-armed out of me, when Becca Barraclough has carried out her end of the bargain, and when I've got confirmation they've got rid of Marv.

The big problem I have is that once it becomes public knowledge that there's been another Vanishers kidnap, with all the ensuing publicity (and this one's going to have a hell of a lot of publicity), Cotton and the rest of us are going to have no choice but to look a lot closer at Cunningham, which means unearthing his contacts while probably increasing the reward money at the same time. In other words, it's only a matter of time before Vinnie and Delvina's names come up. I've got a plan in motion to make sure they don't get to me even if Delvina opens her mouth (and I have no doubt the bitch will if she gets half a chance), but it means I have to be very careful in every aspect of my dealings with her so that there's no trail that my colleagues can follow from her to me.

Obviously, as I told you right at the beginning, cryptos

aren't as anonymous as most people think they are, which means that if the police get into Delvina's bitcoin wallet, they'll be looking at big transactions going into it and trying to find out where they came from. Now, on this particular kidnap you've probably already guessed that I'm working for someone else. That individual has already paid me in bitcoin and I've spent the last three days moving the money round the cryptoverse using something called a cryptocurrency tumbler, which mixes up the bitcoin in my name with that of multiple other users before returning it to me, successfully laundered, and from where I can then send it to anonymous private wallets that I've set up using the Tor browser. It's time-consuming work, and it's not foolproof, but it does make it extremely hard to identify me as the man who paid Delvina.

They could still ID me of course, if they're prepared to look long and hard enough. The key therefore is to give them someone else so that they don't feel the need to, and that's exactly what I'm going to do. It's treachery of the highest order, but needs must when the devil calls.

And unfortunately for my new boss, Cotton, he's the potential fall guy.

19

Friday, 8.50 a.m.

The venue for the meeting with Clyde is the CPS's head office in Petty France, right in the heart of the West End. It's a bland, monolithic building, doubtless designed to look brutalist and suitably imposing, built sometime in the 1960s or 70s, when architectural merit was way down the agenda, and it reminds Becca of a multistorey car park with windows.

As she signs in at the front desk, she checks her phone once again. Still no word from Elle. It irritates her that her daughter is being so evasive. All she wants is a five-minute chat. She sends a quick text, careful not to display her frustration: *Hey honey. Give me a call this morning. Am in meeting for next hour then free. We need to arrange Monday. M xxx*

She puts her phone away and sits down to wait. Before she left home this morning, Becca had a prearranged phone call with Logan Quinn in which she got him to supply some more details with which to tempt the CPS. He was polite, profuse in his thanks for all Becca was doing for him and, as always, came across like a friendly, good-mannered guy who was just trying to sort out a minor misunderstanding rather than avoid multiple murder charges. Becca could imagine him in his cell: tall, dark and handsome with a big smile on his face as he chatted to her. The kind of man you'd want your daughter to bring home. At least until you got to know him.

She doesn't ask herself whether Quinn is a good man turned bad by the terrible things he saw and took part in during his tours in Afghanistan, or whether he's simply a sociopath, so devoid of a moral compass that he's able to kill for money. She doesn't ask herself this because ultimately it's not her business. He's her client, and that's the end of it.

'Becca, how are you?'

It's Clyde. Talk about tall, dark and handsome. Dressed immaculately as always in a beautifully tailored midnight-blue suit and handmade tan brogues, he approaches her with a big smile, looking like he's really missed her.

She still misses him. That's the truth. It's why she's never fully moved on, even after all this time.

'Hey, Clyde, good to see you,' she says, standing up.

Usually they'd greet each other with a peck on both cheeks, but this is a formal occasion, so they shake hands. 'How are you doing?' he asks, leading her towards the lifts. 'It feels like a long time since we've seen each other.'

'It has been,' she says. 'It was at that gala dinner at the Park Lane Hilton.'

'My God. That must have been a year ago.'

'Two, I think.'

Clyde greets a couple of young women walking past who both look at him with barely concealed interest, and Becca actually feels a pang of jealousy. He's always been a charmer.

'Is it really?' he says, moving aside to allow her into the lift first. 'I know I sound like my mother now, but time really flies.'

They make more small talk as they head up to an office on the fourth floor. Clyde asks her about Elle, who he was always very fond of, even though as far as Becca knows they haven't spoken to each other in a long time. He also asks if she's still getting flak from the Oliver Tamzan case, and she tells him that no, she isn't any more, and they leave it at that. To be fair, he did call her while it was all going on to offer moral support, but he hasn't exactly been beating a path to her door these past years, and she knows that this is because he moved on from their relationship a lot faster than she did. It was his decision to break up, not hers. He said she was just too wrapped up in her work to make time for anyone else. At the time, she thought that was a bit rich coming from a man like him, who regularly used to put in twelve-hour days, but now she can see he had a point. Clyde might have worked hard, but she's always been obsessed with getting to the top of her profession, showing the world that she can be a success, and in the end, although she's loath to admit it, it's been to the detriment of everything else.

'This is a colleague of mine, Jeff Taylor,' he says as he

145

leads her into a spacious office where a nondescript middle-aged man in a suit sits behind a large desk. 'He's going to be joining us for the meeting.'

Becca and Taylor shake hands, and Clyde takes a seat next to him and across the desk from her. He offers her coffee from a thermal jug, and she accepts gratefully. She may already have had two cups this morning, but she can always fit another one in.

'You said your client, Mr Quinn, can give us Kalian Roman,' says Clyde, getting straight down to business. 'Do you know who Mr Roman is?'

'I only know what my client has told me,' says Becca, taking a sip of the coffee. 'That he's an individual who sponsors terrorist attacks and other acts of espionage within the UK, aimed at destabilising the country, and that the security services have been after him for more than twenty years.'

'And how does your client know him?' asks Taylor.

'He's carried out work for him.'

'What kind of work?'

'I'm not prepared to go into details at this juncture.'

'This meeting's off the record, Becca,' says Clyde. 'Whatever you tell us here can't be used as evidence against your client. You can speak freely.'

'He's carried out three assassinations on behalf of Kalian Roman,' she answers, reiterating what Quinn told her on the phone this morning.

Clyde leans forward over the desk. 'Does he know Roman's real identity?'

'Yes.'

'Has he met him?'

'No, he hasn't. He dealt through an intermediary.'

'So what evidence has he got against Roman himself?' asks Taylor. There's scepticism in his tone.

'My client has strong evidence against the intermediary, who works directly for Mr Roman. If you lean on the intermediary, he'll testify against Roman. My client's certain of that.'

The two CPS lawyers look at each other, then back at her, trying to keep poker faces but not really managing it. It's clear she's piqued their curiosity, even though she has no real idea who this Kalian Roman character they're both so interested in is.

'It's not just Roman my client can give you,' she continues. 'He also claims to have operated as a freelance assassin on the dark web, and says he has evidence to implicate no fewer than eight other individuals for murder, in particular the CEO of a large public company for whom he's worked freelance for a number of years, work that involved committing two murders that were made to look like accidents.'

'He sounds like a fantasist,' says Taylor.

Becca gives him a look. 'He's no fantasist. He's already provided me with evidence of one murder.'

'What kind of evidence?' asks Clyde.

She tells them what's on the memory stick she retrieved the previous day.

'The video won't be any use in a court of law if it's been illegally made and not independently verified,' says Taylor.

'The paper trail leading to Quinn's client is direct and

obvious and there's more than enough evidence on there to secure a murder conviction. And I can provide you with it right now.'

'Okay,' says Clyde. 'Let's see it.'

She hands him a memory stick with a copy of all the evidence and he plugs it into Taylor's laptop.

Becca waits while they view the contents, watching their expressions. Both men make a very obvious attempt to hide their interest, but they're not entirely successful. She can see they're surprised by the quality of what they're seeing.

'Where did you get this?' Clyde asks her.

'Quinn provided me with the location.'

'Which means he definitely planned for this kind of eventuality. And that's precisely why we shouldn't be doing a deal with him. By his own admission, he's a ruthless serial murderer. And you want to get him off.' Clyde makes the distaste obvious in his expression, but Becca's used to getting this kind of reaction from prosecution lawyers. It's all part of the game.

'He has information that can put a lot of people away for a long time, people who would otherwise avoid justice.'

'People you'll probably be defending in a few months,' says Taylor.

She ignores the jibe and addresses Clyde. 'Your job is to prosecute wrongdoers and provide the jury with enough evidence for a guilty verdict. Logan Quinn can give you that evidence. All he requests is that you get him to a safe house where his life's not in danger and where he can stay until he's testified against the people he's worked for and they've been put behind bars. Then he's prepared to serve a sentence for his crimes, but no more than five years. After that he wants to be released with a new identity.'

'Our understanding is that Quinn's now been moved to the contingency unit at Belmarsh, where he's the only inmate,' says Taylor. 'He's perfectly safe there.'

Becca shakes her head. 'No, he's not. The people he's worked for, including Kalian Roman, want him dead, and they've got the resources to do it. They've already tried once, and of course they can get to him in the contingency unit. Prisoners prepare his food; guards can be bribed. And if that happens, and he dies, all his secrets die with him.' Her expression lets them both know that she's not going to back down.

Clyde leans forward, putting his elbows on the table and returning her gaze. It's a look she's seen him use more than once in court. He's a big man, and even when he's totally calm, as he is now, he can be intimidating. 'Any decision on how much time Logan Quinn serves will be a political one. He's too high-profile for it to be otherwise. And no one is going to agree to a five-year sentence for someone who by his own admission is a mass murderer.'

Becca's been expecting this, and she knows it's something she has to be prepared to negotiate on. 'What sentence would you consider?'

'It all depends on what evidence he has.'

'Get him to a safe house and we can discuss it.'

'It doesn't work like that,' says Taylor.

Becca doesn't even look at him. 'It does this time.'

149

'Give us something else on Kalian Roman,' says Clyde, 'so we know that Quinn hasn't just heard the name somewhere and is trying it on.'

'You're being very cynical, Clyde.'

'Well?'

She repeats what Quinn told her earlier. 'Roman is attached to the foreign embassy of a potentially hostile nation.'

'We need more than that,' says Taylor.

'That's all you're getting for now. Get my client to a safe house and there'll be more.' She knows she's gone as far with these two as she can for now. It's time to leave the ball in their court. She can see Clyde's interested. He's an ambitious man. He wants to be attorney general, and Logan Quinn's testimony could help get him there.

'I want a list of all the individuals your client claims to have evidence against, and the murders they're supposedly responsible for,' he says, 'and that's non-negotiable. If what he provides is of sufficient interest, we can talk again.' With that, he gets to his feet, signalling that the meeting is over and giving her an almost pitying look. 'I'm surprised you're getting involved with another lowlife, Becca, after what happened with Tamzan.'

The words sting her coming from him, and in front of his colleague too, but she doesn't show it. Instead she stands and says: 'He's my client, and like everyone else, he's entitled to the best defence available.'

'It's not defence, though, is it? He's already as good as admitted his guilt.'

'He's still my client.'

Taylor hasn't even bothered standing up, and he gives her a contemptuous look. 'I don't know how you sleep at night.'

'My conscience is clear,' she answers, and without shaking hands with either of them, she turns on her heel and walks out.

But Clyde's words nag her, and as Becca travels back down in the lift, standing alone and ignoring her reflection in the mirror, she wonders for the first time in a long time whether her conscience really is that clear.

20

Friday, 9.30 a.m.

Elle Barraclough lies in her prison cell, staring up at the ceiling. It was a grim night's sleep. She drifted in and out of consciousness for a while, then woke up very cold, and only dropped off again what felt like hours later, although it's hard to tell because there's no natural light in this room.

They've taken her watch so she has no idea what time it is, which she assumes is so they can keep her disorientated, but it feels like it's probably sometime in the morning. She's finished the bottle of water by the side of the bed, and she's thirsty and hungry. She also needs the loo.

Slowly, stiffly, she gets up from the bed and walks over to the toilet, the chain rattling on the padded floor beneath her feet. There's just enough slack for her to reach the bowl, and she sits down and goes quickly, thankful that paper's been provided. It gives her a scrap of hope that her kidnappers are providing the bare essentials. If this was some kind of revenge thing against her mum, she doesn't think they would have bothered.

As she washes her hands and dries them on a hand towel

that actually smells quite clean, she replays the events of the previous night. It's actually coming back to her now. Finishing the shift, having a quick chat with Chantel and Ahmed as they left the building together, then the uneventful drive home. Talking to her mum as she got out of the car. The next bit's still vague, but as she stands at the sink and concentrates, she remembers their conversation being interrupted when she saw a woman staggering up the street, clearly needing help.

It was this woman who drugged her, she's sure of that. She remembers reading a newspaper article about the kidnapping of that boy who was killed, Henry Day. Apparently he'd been accosted on the street by a woman who appeared drunk, in much the same way Elle was. This again gives her some room for optimism. Henry Day was definitely kidnapped by the gang the media nicknamed the Vanishers, and it's too much of a coincidence that she was abducted in the same manner.

Which means that as long as her mum cooperates with them (and Elle is certain she will, because she doesn't trust the police at the best of times), the likelihood is she'll go free, and hopefully quickly.

She goes back to the bed and sits down, wondering when they're going to give her some food, and it's then that with impeccable timing she hears the sound of locks being turned in the door.

Instinctively she retreats on the bed until her back is against the cast-iron headboard. She's both scared and curious.

153

The door opens a few inches.

'Are you on the bed?' says a voice. Male, harsh, a London accent.

'Yes,' she says.

'There's a blindfold by your bed. Put it on, and don't try to look over it or there'll be real trouble.'

She tells him she won't. Elle's sensible enough not to do anything to antagonise her captors, and to appear compliant so they won't see her as a threat.

With her eyes shut behind the blindfold and hugging her knees to her chest, she waits as he enters the room, closing the door behind him, his steps quiet on the padded floor as he approaches the bed.

'I've got food and water,' he says, putting down what sounds like a tray.

'Thank you.'

She can sense that he's standing there watching her. 'Are you all right?' he asks, his voice softening.

'I'm okay, but I'm scared,' she tells him, knowing how important it is that she gets at least one of her abductors on side.

'You don't need to be. As long as your family do what they're told, you'll be free soon.'

'Do you have any idea how long?'

'Shouldn't be more than a few days at most.'

'Will you be the one looking after me here?'

'Yeah,' he says, something close to pride in his voice. 'And I'll make sure you're okay.'

She thanks him again. 'Do you think I'll be able to speak to my mum? She'll be really worried. I'm all she's got.'

'I'll see what I can do,' he says. Then: 'We need to contact your work. Let them know you're not going to be in for a few days.'

'The hospital? How are you planning on doing that?'

'We just need the code for your phone and the person you contact if you're off sick. We'll send them a text.'

Elle tries to think of a way she can somehow get a message out that she's being held against her will, but her head's still fuzzy from the drugs and the lack of decent sleep, and she knows it's not worth the risk. She gives him the passcode and the name of her supervisor, and she can hear him writing it down. 'If you just text her, she'll sort it out. I do need to get back to work soon, though. I'm a nurse. I'm needed there.' She hopes the fact that she's a nurse will gain her some extra sympathy. Most people like nurses, in her experience.

'Where do you work?' he asks.

'The General, in Brighton. In the vascular ward. We help people with blood clots and diabetes.'

'Do you enjoy it?'

'Yes,' she says without hesitation. 'I do. Making people better is the most rewarding work I can imagine.'

'Yeah,' he says, and she thinks she catches a hint of regret in his voice. 'I bet it is. Look, I'll see what I can do about talking to your mum, okay?'

'That's very kind of you.'

155

He doesn't reply, and she hears him leaving the room and locking the door behind him. Then silence again.

She pulls off the blindfold and looks down at the contents of the tray. What appears to be a ham sandwich in white bread, a fruit cereal bar, and another half-litre bottle of water. It's not exactly appetising, especially considering Elle's been a vegetarian for the past three years, but right now she's not fussy. The most important thing is the water. She checks that the seal on the cap is in place, then drinks down half of it in one go. Next goes the cereal bar, and finally she's left with the sandwich. She wonders if it's been laced with drugs. Clearly these people have access to powerful sedatives, and they might think it best to keep her out of it for the duration of her stay here. She doesn't want that. She knows her chances of escape are limited, but she still has to keep her wits about her just in case.

In the end, though, hunger trumps everything and she eats the sandwich, ham and all.

Five minutes later, she's flat out asleep, and she doesn't stir as Delvina enters the room and touches a perfectly varnished nail to her forehead. She doesn't hear Delvina's heavy breathing either, or feel her nails digging into the flesh of her cheeks as she runs them down her face and onto her neck, before stopping at her collarbone.

She doesn't hear Delvina's whispered words either, because if she had, they'd have terrified her.

21

Friday, 9.55 a.m.

Because the meeting finished early, Becca takes the opportunity to walk the two miles back to her chambers and get some fresh air. She's crossing St James's Park when her phone rings. As she retrieves it from her bag, she sees it's Elle, and she smiles, because it means her daughter's making the effort.

'Better late than never, I suppose,' she answers playfully. 'How are you, honey?'

'I'm well,' says a distorted, robotic-sounding voice at the other end, and Becca almost jumps back in shock.

She feels a rush of fear. No one but Elle has ever answered this phone, and she's certain her daughter doesn't have a boyfriend. And definitely not one who talks like this. 'Who's this?' she demands. 'And what are you doing on my daughter's phone?'

'She's staying with us for a while,' says the voice, 'and if you do what you're told, she'll come back to you.'

'What do you mean, she's staying with you?' says Becca, trying hard to keep her voice down so she's not overheard by passers-by. The shock she's experiencing makes it hard for her to make sense of what's happening, but it's dawning on her fast that this is not good. Not good at all.

'I think you know what I mean.' The voice – and right now she can't tell if it's a man or a woman – is calm, but there's something mean and mocking in the tone.

'What have you done with her?' hisses Becca into the phone. 'She'd better be all right.'

'She's fine right now, and if you do what you're told, she'll be released unharmed like all the others whose parents didn't go to the police. Or you can get them involved and she'll end up like Henry Day. Never seen again.'

'I want to speak to her.' Becca knows she can't show weakness. She has to be strong, even though the fear's washing over her in intense waves so powerful it's hard to stay upright.

'That's not possible, I'm afraid.'

Becca steps off the path and walks under a tree, leaning against the trunk and taking a deep breath to calm herself. 'You're not getting anything until I speak to my daughter. Period. How do I know you've even got her?'

'I'm just texting you a couple of photos, so you can see for yourself.'

Becca removes the phone from her ear as it bleeps twice to signal incoming texts. Feeling a sense of dread, she opens the first one and gasps audibly.

There, chained to a single cast-iron bed in a dimly lit room, lies her daughter. She's blindfolded and wearing her blue nurse's scrubs, her head to one side as if she's asleep.

Becca zooms in on the picture. It becomes more blurred, but even so, there's an obvious red mark on Elle's face, as if she's been hit with something. She zooms back out, checks the other photo. It's taken from slightly further away, and she can see Elle's feet in it. They're bare, and there's a chain attached to her ankle by some kind of metal cuff.

She knows the technology's out there to fake photos, but she also knows that there's no way these ones are fake. They're too realistic for that. Trying hard not to panic, but conscious of her shaking hands, she puts the phone back to her ear.

'Did you see them?' asks the voice in the same mocking tone.

'Don't hurt her, whatever you do,' she says quietly.

'We won't if you do what you're told.'

'How much do you want?'

'There's no need to talk money yet, darling. I want you to continue with your day, and don't worry. Your daughter's safe. You'll be hearing from me later but on a different phone. Make sure you answer first time.'

Before Becca can say anything else, the connection's cut. She starts to call back – there are still a lot of questions she needs to ask – but then stops herself. There's no point. Right now, the caller's told her everything they want her to know. This is their way of keeping her on edge. The most important thing is for her to stay calm. Panicking won't help. She tells herself that these people are rational. If they'd wanted to kill Elle, they would have done. If it's the Vanishers, they'll be after money, which means they can be reasoned with, and that Elle will indeed be returned to her.

It's hard to believe that the Vanishers would target her, though. What are the odds of that? There must be tens of thousands of people in their target wealth bracket in the south-east of England, maybe even more than that, but they've gone after her. Yes, she's got money, but in the main it's tied up in her house and pension. And yet something in the way the caller said 'darling' makes her think it was a woman, and she remembers from the media story that it was a woman who abducted Henry Day from the street.

She starts doing rapid calculations in her head, working out how much she can raise in the next forty-eight hours. It's the weekend tomorrow, so it's not good timing, but she thinks she could probably get two hundred grand by Monday if she cashes in her ISA. Maybe another thirty grand through her various savings and current accounts. If they want any more, it's going to take more time, and she doesn't want to leave Elle with these people any longer than she has to.

'Christ, why me?' she says audibly through gritted teeth.

And that's when a horrible thought strikes her. What if this isn't the Vanishers? What if she's been targeted by someone else? Someone who heard about her defence of Oliver Tamzan and decided to get revenge. This isn't as strange a theory as it might first appear. Becca had more than a thousand death threats, delivered variously via social media, her office email and even the post. People claiming they were going to burn her alive, rape then crucify her, and of course the one where an anonymous letter writer said he was going to make her watch while he violated then skinned her daughter.

Jesus Christ. What if it's him, or one of the other psychos? Would they really have gone this far? A former client of hers, who was allegedly a very high-ranking organised-crime figure, once told her that people who threatened you indirectly were never going to do you any harm. They were just keyboard warriors. Which would have made her feel better except for the fact that he then added that it was the ones who didn't threaten you that you had to watch out for, as if that was even possible.

Becca didn't take the police protection that was offered to her at the time, preferring to brazen things out. She tried to get protection for Elle, but Elle refused it too. In hindsight, that was a mistake.

Because if this is someone with a personal grudge against Becca, then it isn't about money at all. It's about revenge. About getting to her.

And by far the most effective way to do that is to kill Elle.

22

Friday, 10.55 a.m.

I'm parked in a quiet road of grand three-storey town-houses in what's known colloquially as Dulwich Village, an affluent, relatively green area of south London. It's the home of the Syed family, whose son, twenty-year-old Jonathan, or Jonny as he prefers to be called, was abducted by the Vanishers in May last year, barely a hundred metres from where I'm standing now.

The Syeds, who were the last people to be targeted before the Days, were sensible enough to follow Delvina's instructions and pay the approximately £490,000 ransom without involving the police, and consequently young Jonny was delivered back to them physically unharmed three days later. It was only after the Henry Day case that they finally came forward, by which time any security camera footage from the street had been wiped clean, leaving us with no clues. You can hardly blame them. Like most people these days, they've lost faith in the police, and having been threatened by the kidnappers with being targeted again, they opted to stay silent and deal with the situation in their own way.

I stifle a yawn. I didn't get to sleep until gone 4.30 and was awake three and a half hours later, so I feel like dogshit as I stare down at the five-word message in block capitals I've just received from Delvina on my burner phone: *WHERE'S THE OTHER TWO HUNDRED??*

I paid a hundred and fifty grand in crypto into Delvina's wallet, as per the original contract, an hour ago, but I'm still holding back on the money she strong-armed out of me yesterday, as well as the last hundred and fifty. I text back: *M has been identified. You need to act fast. Rest of money comes at end. As agreed!*

I know she won't like it, but I'm not prepared to negotiate with her. If you agree a fixed price with someone, you don't pay them the final instalment until they've done the job. She and Vinnie have to coax Becca Barraclough to do something that will destroy her career, and only if they succeed will the rest of the money be theirs.

Having sent the text, I exit the car and walk past all these million-pound-plus houses filled with wealthy people who don't appreciate what they've got, until I reach the Syeds' place. I've called ahead to let them know I'm coming, and sure enough, the door is answered almost immediately by Larry Syed, a short, bald sales director with big glasses and what I can only assume is a naturally angry face. He's dressed casually in an unpleasant lime-green polo shirt tucked into beige chinos, along with tasselled loafers in an alarming chestnut hue and, of course, no socks, giving him the sartorial look of a low-level Mafia lounge lizard at a golf-club do.

163

'Agent Fisher, NCA,' I say by way of introduction, putting out a hand. We didn't meet last December when the Syeds first came forward, because it was just after Henry Day and I was in the process of being demoted.

Syed nods curtly, eyeing me with disdain from behind the big glasses. He just about manages to shake my hand before making a vague motion for me to come inside. 'So, you finally have a lead,' he says, leading me through the hallway towards the back of the house, which is a lot more spacious inside than it looks from the outside. On the way, we pass the kitchen where Syed's wife, Breona, is sitting at the table staring at her phone screen. She doesn't bother looking up.

'That's right, we have a possible suspect,' I say to his back, thinking that these people are remarkably rude given that they got their son back in one piece. At least the Days had a decent excuse for treating me like shit.

Syed stops outside a door under the stairs and turns to me. 'I've got to say, it's about time. It's been three months since that poor boy was murdered and almost a year since they took Jonny.'

'Sometimes these things take time,' I tell him, trying to stay patient. 'Especially when the public aren't especially cooperative.'

'I hope you're not alluding to us,' he says. 'I'm glad we didn't go to the police, given what happened when the Days did. So, who's this suspect?'

'I can't give you any further details at the moment. But I think your son might be able to help us.'

'Go easy on him,' he demands. 'He's been through hell these past months. He can't work. He hardly goes out. What those bastards did to him has wrecked his mental health.'

'I'm very sorry to hear that,' I say, with probably not quite enough sincerity.

We stare at each other for a moment, and I realise he's trying some sort of power play, like he's dealing with one of his underlings at the IT company where he works. It makes me think that this is another of the problems about being a copper these days. No one respects you. You're everyone's whipping boy. The middle classes demand that you keep them safe, but as soon as a cop even looks like he or she might have put a foot wrong, they demand their head, and usually get it too. And in some ways the parents are worse than the kids.

I picked the Syeds as targets for two reasons, and one was that I read that Larry, the man who's trying to intimidate me now, even though he's having to look up at me to do it, had been accused of bullying several of his team members, and had actually been named in two wrongful-dismissal lawsuits, both of which the plaintiffs won. He still kept his job, though, with little more than a slap on the wrist and a promise to go on an anger management course, which clearly didn't work.

I meet his stare with one of my own, and he's the first to look away.

'I'll come down with you,' he says, knocking on the door then opening it.

We descend some stairs into a large, cluttered basement

room, which looks like it belongs to a sixteen- rather than twenty-two-year-old. There are dirty clothes all over the floor, several overflowing ashtrays, and a general fetid stink of young, unwashed man.

The young, unwashed man in question, Jonny Syed, is sitting on the edge of his unmade double bed playing a video game on a huge TV on the opposite wall. He briefly looks my way but keeps playing, his fingers bouncing across the console.

'This is Agent Fisher from the NCA,' says Syed senior, sitting in the room's only chair while I remain standing, doubtless another fucking power play.

I give the kid what's meant to look like a reassuring smile. 'How are you, Jonny?'

To be fair, he doesn't look great. He's wearing dirty sweatpants and a black hoodie, which is pulled up over his head. His feet are bare, the nails dirty and gnarly, and his eyes are big and bug-like, like he's on something.

'Look, I told my dad I don't want to talk,' he says without looking at me, the rude little bastard. I feel like clouting him, but unfortunately we're not allowed to do that.

'I just need you to listen to something for one minute,' I tell him.

'I just want to forget about it all,' he answers, staring at the TV screen, where it appears he's some kind of soldier shooting the shit out of various enemy operatives, who all die with lots of blood.

'You don't want someone else to go through what you had to, do you?'

'It's not my problem.'

'You don't even want to get back at the people who did this and make them pay?' I persist like this because it's far less suspicious that way. And also because I genuinely don't understand why he wouldn't want to get them back if he could, especially when it requires only minimal effort from him.

This time he does look my way, pausing the game and putting down the console, and I can see I've piqued something in him. Maybe it's pride.

'Look, Jonny,' I continue, 'we have a potential suspect, and I have a recording of his voice here. I want you to see if you recognise it as one of the people who kidnapped you. That's it.'

'It won't mean I have to testify in court, will it?' he asks. 'There's no way I'm doing that.'

'Course you won't,' says his dad. 'You don't have to do anything you don't want to do.'

'This is just to help work out whether we have the right suspect,' I tell him soothingly. In truth, I feel sorry for the kid. The experience has obviously damaged him, and I know that that's my fault, because I picked the family. But before you feel too much sympathy for young Jonny, remember there were two reasons I chose these people. Five years ago, when Jonny was seventeen, he was done for driving while impaired, having crashed his car at 65 mph in a 30 zone, hitting a number of parked cars and narrowly missing a couple walking their dog. He was found to be twice the drink-drive limit, as well as having traces of cannabis and cocaine in his system, and ended up with a fine and community service. That didn't seem much like a punishment to me, and I thought that suffering a bit might do him good.

I can see now, though, that it really hasn't.

I've got two snippets of Cunningham's voice from his last police interview, the only things he says that aren't 'No comment.' One is: 'This is all bullshit. I need a piss.' The other is: 'I can't believe you lot are always trying to fucking fit me up like this.' In other words, the usual hackneyed criminal bravado.

Anyway, I've downloaded them to my phone, and I crouch down in front of Jonny now and ask him if he's ready.

The kid nods, but he suddenly looks nervous, his own bravado having receded rapidly. I know he's desperate not to get involved, which suits me fine. The fewer clues leading back to Cunningham the better.

I press play, and Cunningham's growling, cocky voice comes out of the speaker.

Jonny visibly cringes, his whole body instinctively leaning away from the phone, and I know exactly what's coming.

'That's him,' he says quickly. 'Definitely.'

'Are you absolutely sure, Jonny? It's been ten months,' I say, taken aback by his decisiveness. This kid doesn't look like he's decisive about anything.

He nods. 'I'll never forget that voice.'

'Have you arrested this man yet?' demands Syed senior from the chair.

'Not yet,' I say, hoping that Marv's dead by now, 'but

we're keeping him under surveillance and he has no idea we're on to him.' I turn back to Jonny, wanting to find out what else he knows. 'Was he the only person you had contact with when you were being held in the basement?'

'How do you know Jonny was being held in a basement?' says Syed senior.

'I don't know if I was in a basement or not,' adds Jonny unhelpfully. 'It was just a room.'

Straight away, I realise my mistake. *I* know that the victims have always been kept in a soundproofed basement, of course, because Delvina told me about it, but none of the released victims would know that, given that they were drugged when they went in and drugged before they came out.

Luckily for me, I'm a fast thinker with a half-decent poker face. 'One of the other victims mentioned it was a basement,' I say to Syed senior. 'We assume that everyone was kept in the same soundproofed cell. Now,' I continue, turning back to Jonny before I get any more awkward questions from Dad, 'as I was saying, was the man on the recording the only person you had contact with when you were being held?'

He nods. 'Yeah, he was the only one. He used to bring me food and water. I tried to talk to him once because I heard that you're meant to try and be friendly with your kidnappers, but he told me to keep my mouth shut and said if I didn't he'd break my jaw. He was a bastard.'

'Thank you, Jonny,' I say, keen to get out of here before I put my foot in it any further. 'You've been a real help.'

'Have you caught the woman yet? The one who abducted me from the street?' he asks as I get to my feet, putting my phone away.

'Not yet, but once we ID one, we usually get the others.'

'I remember *her* voice,' he says.

I stop, frowning. 'Really?'

'Yeah, it was when they first shoved me in the car. She'd jabbed me with a needle so I was drugged up and only half-conscious, but I can remember her talking to the driver as we pulled away.'

'What did she say?'

He shakes his head. 'I don't know. But her voice, it was very distinctive.'

'In what way?'

He steals a glance at his dad before answering. 'It was a hot voice. She, er, just sounded hot. If I ever heard it again, I'd remember.'

This I wasn't expecting. And it's not good either. Admittedly, it's not exactly a detailed description, but the point is, the kid's right. Delvina does have a hot voice. Soft, sultry, laden with the promise of excitement. It's not evidence, of course, and it would be laughed out of court, but it's another piece of the puzzle, and it won't help Delvina. Or me.

I thank Jonny once again and tell them both that I'll keep them posted about any developments.

Syed senior sees me to the front door. 'Do you know something?' he says, his hand on the door handle. 'You didn't write anything down in there.' He gives me an accusing look.

I can feel my anger mounting. I'm a patient man (you have to be in this job), but this guy is really yanking my chain. 'I didn't have to,' I tell him. 'I remember what he told me. It wasn't that long or that complicated.'

'I hope you people are putting some proper effort into finding these individuals now, because it's an embarrassment how long it's taken.'

I know there's no point getting involved in an argument, but I can't seem to stop myself. 'It wasn't helped by people like you who didn't bother coming forward. And it's easy to be an armchair detective.'

'Hold on, I hope you're not fucking blaming me for your incompetence!' he snaps, leaning forward so he's right in my personal space.

'Get out of my fucking face,' I hiss, grabbing him by the collar and lifting him onto his tiptoes before giving him a hard shove back against the wall. 'And watch what you're saying.'

He looks utterly shocked, but that's bullies for you. They don't like the tables being turned.

'I'll have your job for this,' he says, retreating down the hallway out of range as I open the front door.

'Go fuck yourself,' I tell him, and walk out of there.

I can't help feeling a certain satisfaction about what I've just done, even though I know it'll cause me plenty of grief. Syed's the kind of guy who'll make good on his threats and be bleating to the bosses about police brutality by the time I'm back at the car. Not only that, but the fact that his son recognised Cunningham's voice, as well as his description of Delvina's, further complicates things, and I'm just thinking that it can't get much worse for me today when my phone rings.

I can see it's Cotton and I pick up my pace. He can't have spoken to Syed already, so it must be about something else.

And it is. 'We've got another potential lead, Fish,' he says, and he sounds a little too excited for my liking. 'Sussex CID have just been on the phone about a potential abduction in Brighton.'

Since the Vanishers made the news in December with Henry Day's murder, every potential abduction in England and Wales where the circumstances behind it aren't immediately clear have to be reported to us. There've been several dozen during that time, but all the previous ones have been discounted as being the work of the Vanishers.

'Tell me more,' I say, my heart sinking.

'According to the DC who called, a witness saw a woman being manhandled into a dark people carrier by another woman. This was last night at approximately ten thirty, and the witness was looking out of her window. It all happened very fast and she didn't see a lot, but it looked strange so she reported it online on 111. Which obviously delayed it.'

When you report a crime on 111, it often gets lost in what passes for the system, and it's sometimes days before you got a response, meaning it's both useless and counterproductive, like a lot of the police cost-cutting measures that are supposed to increase efficiency and don't.

'No one saw the report until about an hour ago,' continues Cotton, 'then it was shown to someone in CID and they got in touch with us. The only description of the woman is that she had long hair and glasses and was wearing a wide-brimmed hat.'

It seems that Delvina hasn't done much to vary her disguise, making me think she's getting sloppy, which often happens when you've got away with something for too long. 'It could be the Vanishers, then,' I say. 'It's a similar description to the Day abductor.'

'And the timing, Fish. It's no coincidence, is it? Cunningham suddenly going off the radar? How did it go with Jonathan Syed, by the way? Have you spoken to him yet?'

Cotton's not usually this excitable, but it's clear he's got the bit between his teeth and it's not hard to work out why. If we solve the Vanishers case under his leadership – and for him, it must look like the cards are falling into place – he gets all the credit for it, which means the possibility of an even bigger promotion. And he's definitely ambitious.

'Yeah, I was about to call you,' I say. 'Some more good news. He says it's definitely Cunningham's voice on the recording.' I don't add anything about him describing Delvina's voice.

'Perfect. That's exactly what I want to hear,' he says. 'I've got a meeting with the DG at two o'clock. With all this evidence mounting up, we should be able to get access to Cunningham's bank and phone records.'

'We need to move fast if they've already kidnapped someone,' I say, once again showing that I'm right at the forefront of trying to crack the case. 'Let me go down to

Brighton and speak to the local CID and the witness, see what I can find out.'

'It's your day off, Fish, the second in a row you've worked, and I can't pay you overtime, mate. We haven't got the budget. I'll send one of the others down.'

'No, let me go. I want to be part of solving this and I've got the experience to dig out leads.'

Cotton doesn't need any more persuading. He knows that I'm the best person for the job. 'Thanks, Fish. I appreciate that. You're one of the good ones.'

Which is nice to hear, even though it's not the truth. 'I'll keep you posted about anything I find out. Not that I want to disturb your date,' I add with a chuckle, knowing that he's been seeing a woman for a while now and they're meant to be meeting tonight.

'To be honest, I think I'm going to have to cancel with all this going on.'

'No way, you don't need to do that. If I hear anything useful at all, I'll be straight in touch, but don't put this girl off. She sounds like a keeper.'

He sighs at the other end of the phone. 'You don't think it'll look bad me seeing her, Fish?'

'Course not. You can't work 24/7, and we've already put a hell of a lot of hours in since yesterday morning.'

'Yeah, you're right,' he says.

Which is exactly what I want to hear. Because it's essential he keeps that date, otherwise my plans are going to be ruined.

23

Friday, 12.05 p.m.

'Why do we have to kill him?' asks Vincent when Delvina breaks the news to him about Marv.

They're sitting in the living room of their apartment above the funeral home, and it's clear that her husband is having difficulty processing this information. His face is almost comically anguished, and Delvina thinks that – God forbid – he might actually cry.

'You know why we have to do it, pet,' she says quietly, her arm round his shoulders, holding him to her, recognising that right now he needs her love and support if he's to get through this. She can't have him giving up now. 'The police have ID'd him.'

'How do we know that?' he demands, sitting up suddenly. 'McBride might be lying.'

Jesus. There are actually tears in his eyes. She's only ever seen him like this twice before, both times when she broke off their relationship. Otherwise he's always kept his emotions in check.

'McBride has no motivation to lie about this,' she tells

him. 'He didn't even know Marv existed until he heard about him through the Vanishers case.'

'So is McBride working on the case? I need to know.'

Delvina gives him a hard look, but she can see that it doesn't seem to penetrate in the way it usually does. Her husband still looks angry and upset. 'You need to trust me,' she says firmly. 'McBride's information is good. He says that someone informed on Marv for the reward money after he was arrested for something else.'

'Who's the informant?' His voice is sharp.

'I don't know,' she says, because she doesn't. 'But I can find out easily enough.'

He sighs and looks away. 'This is my flesh and blood we're talking about,' he says, quieter now. 'I grew up with him. We've always had each other's backs. He'd do anything for me, and I'd do anything for him.' He turns back. 'That's the kind of bond we've got, babe.'

Ordinarily Delvina would have physically chastised him for calling her 'babe', but at the moment, the whole fantasy dynamic of their relationship has evaporated in the face of this new development, so she holds back. It concerns her, though. If she loses her power over Vincent, he'll be far harder to manipulate.

She leans over and pulls him close, stroking his head. His whole body is tense but he doesn't try to move. 'I know, pet. But we've got to face the facts. The police know who he is and they suspect he's involved. They'll be looking for evidence, and if they look too closely, they'll find us. And we can't have that. We've got a future together, a whole life.'

'I want to pull out of this, do something different. You know, move to Spain or something. Open a bar.'

'I agree,' she says, although she can't think of anything worse. He'll want to go somewhere shitty as well, like Torremolinos or Benidorm. Luckily, however, it'll never happen. She's got plans for Vincent and they don't involve living in some Spanish shithole full of ignorant expats. 'We can definitely do something like that,' she continues, 'and never come back. It'll be beautiful. A new life in the sun.'

He moves away from her embrace, although she can see he's calmer now.

'Is there no way we can smuggle him out of the country, Goddess?' he asks.

She shakes her head. 'No. They'll find him. Look how he stands out. He's got to go, pet. I'm sorry.'

'This fucking McBride,' he says darkly. 'I don't like the way he controls everything. Telling us to get rid of Marv. Making us kill the girl. It's like he's this fucking lord of life and death.'

Delvina can see he's getting angry again and she hardens her tone, knowing she's got to keep him in line.

'He's a professional, and he's always been reliable. We do this, it protects us. Then we can call it a day. But we have to do it, pet. There's no choice.'

Her husband gets up, paces the room. 'I can't do it, babe. I can't kill my own flesh and blood.'

Delvina gets to her feet as well. 'You don't have to. I will.'

'How? No offence, but he could break you in half. And he hates you. You'll never get close enough.'

God, how little imagination he has. How has she ever managed to tolerate him all these years? 'Don't worry about that,' she says, a confidence in her voice that tells him she's not going to fail.

He nods slowly, seeming to accept the inevitable. 'When are you going to do it?'

'When the time is right,' she says, taking him by the hand. 'When the time is right.'

24

Friday, 1.10 p.m.

Becca is working flat out to keep things together. She can't believe this is happening to her. She's used to taking hard knocks. Her profession puts her in the firing line, as the controversy and the death threats that resulted from the Tamzan case have shown. But thanks to her training and experience, she's always felt prepared for anything being thrown at her.

This is completely different. No one in a civilised society expects to have their loved one abducted and held prisoner. It's the suddenness of it all. It makes the shock so intense it feels almost surreal. And the shock is followed by a deep and terrible sense of impotence. There is nothing she can do of her own volition to bring Elle back to her. Matters are entirely out of her control, and for a strong, independent woman like Becca, who's used to fighting alone, that's hard.

And what she can't understand is why, if this is the work of the Vanishers, they haven't asked her for money yet. According to all the media reports, they're a professional kidnap gang. They would know that Becca, like most other people, doesn't have immediate access to hundreds of thousands in ready cash. It'll take her time to dispose of her assets and raise the ransom, so why didn't they get her doing that straight away?

All morning she's thought about getting the police involved. Because if this isn't the Vanishers – if it's someone targeting her for the legal work she's done – then Becca's not going to get Elle back by cooperating. It'll be a race against time to find her before something bad happens, and the police at least have the resources to be able to do that.

Two things have stopped her. First, the obvious one. The police failed last time, when they were trying to track down Henry Day, and that was the National Crime Agency's specialist kidnap unit no less. Becca's had enough dealings with the police over the years to know that their ranks aren't full of top-drawer detectives. Many of them are inexperienced and incompetent, and whoever the people are who've abducted Elle, they're definitely neither of those things.

Second, and more important, the motive might not be revenge. Because if it is revenge, why hasn't the caller already started tormenting her? Surely if you've poured all those resources into abducting a young woman from the street (and Becca has worked in the justice system long enough to know that kidnapping is a very hard crime to pull off) just so you can get back at her mother, you'd want to make the mother suffer immediately. There'd be all kinds of threats. Grimmer pictures of Elle. Yet there's been none of that. Becca has just been told to go about her business and await another call.

And that's what makes her think, finally, that this might have something to do with Logan Quinn, the man who's already admitted to her that he's a target for various powerful individuals.

Becca's frustration mounts as she's led through Belmarsh prison to the contingency unit, a detached building in the shadow of one of the wings. She knows she needs to calm down and cut out all the white noise – the constant gut-wrenching fear she's experiencing – and look for ways to turn the tables, because however clever these people are, they will have weaknesses. She just has to locate them.

The contingency unit is a lot smaller than the maximum-security wing and Logan Quinn is the only inmate. He's waiting for her in his cell when she arrives. It has a single bed and a small desk and chair next to a surprisingly large barred window with a view out onto the prison yard. He's sitting on the bed and gets up as she comes in.

'That was quick,' he says, shaking her hand and motioning for her to sit at the desk. 'Do you have any news?'

Becca waits until the guard has shut the door and left before she answers. 'I need some more information from you.'

He glances at the door, then leans forward, his voice quiet. 'I don't trust anyone in here, Becca. Especially the guards. We need to keep our voices down, if you don't mind.' Quinn looks genuinely worried, his features set in a deep frown.

'I understand,' she says, conscious that she can hear her heart beating in her chest. A part of her wants to confide in him. To tell him what's happened to Elle and to ask his advice. After all, this man is a former soldier, a trained and ruthless killer and possibly someone with good criminal contacts. He might know exactly who's behind the kidnap and be able to help.

But she resists the urge. Right now, her best bet is to keep her own counsel and wait for the kidnappers to call back, however frustrating it is.

'You need to give the CPS a list of every individual you have evidence against,' she tells him in a whisper, 'and a list of all the killings you've committed on their behalf before they'll consider putting you in a safe house.'

He shakes his head. 'No way. Once they have that, I lose at least half my leverage. What's wrong with what I've already given them?'

'It's not enough. Not to move you out of Belmarsh.'

'I gave them a man who murdered his wife,' he hisses.

Becca doesn't bother mentioning that it was Quinn himself who murdered the man's wife. 'You gave them an illegally made video that may not be admissible in a court of law, and the man you're offering up isn't high-profile enough to sway anyone. If you want them to move you, you need to give them what they ask for.' She wonders now if this list of victims and perpetrators will be useful to the kidnappers, and considers how she might use it.

'I don't want to give them everything, Becca.'

'It's just a list. You can still hold back all the evidence you've got against the people involved until we've signed a deal with the CPS. One that limits their charges against you and gets you a reduced sentence.'

'How about I give them another two names? Maybe some evidence too to whet their appetites?'

But Becca's had enough of this horse trading. She's got far bigger fish to fry. 'They're not going to back down. Give them what they ask for and then we'll clam up until they move you.'

Quinn furrows his brow as he thinks about this. It looks like he's lost a couple of pounds just in the last twenty-four hours, and for some reason, the observation makes Becca think of Elle chained to a cast-iron bed in a darkened room, completely at the mercy of people who may have killed before. She swallows, forcing the thought to one side.

'Are you all right?' Quinn's looking at her with concern in his eyes.

Again she considers unburdening herself. There's something about him that feels trustworthy, which she knows sounds ridiculous given who he is and what he's admitted to doing, but there it is. 'Yes, I'm fine. Just tired. I have a lot on.'

'I appreciate what you're doing for me, Becca. I really do.'

Logan Quinn might look and sound a like a nice guy, but Becca's met enough sociopaths to know they're good at hiding their true nature. She reminds herself that Ted Bundy also looked and sounded like a nice guy.

'It's my job, Mr Quinn.'

'And you do it well.'

'How do you live with yourself? You know, killing so many innocent people?'

He bows his head and sighs, then sits back up again, running his fingers through his thick dark hair. 'With a lot more difficulty than you think. I try to tell myself that I'm doing a job, and that if I didn't do it, someone else would.'

'Why not just let that someone else do it and keep a clear conscience?'

'In hindsight, I wish I had. But I was an angry man after I came out of the army. I was diagnosed with PTSD and it had a huge effect on my moods. My whole state of mind. And once you've killed once, it's easier to do it a second time, and it's also easier to justify it to yourself if you feel you've been betrayed by your government and the public who elect them.' He pauses, steeples his fingers. 'I know that doesn't sound like much of a justification, and that's probably why I find it hard to live with myself.'

His expression seems to be asking her to believe him, and she wants to. But she's still not sure.

They're both silent for a few moments. It's Becca who breaks it. 'I need that list.'

'You're sure there's no other way?'

She nods. 'I'm sure.'

'Okay,' he says with another sigh, looking surprisingly vulnerable. 'I trust you.'

'I'm giving your case my all, Logan,' she says, passing him a pen and an A4 notebook from the desk.

Quinn takes close to five minutes to write everything down, pausing every so often to ponder something. Finally he rips the page from the notebook and hands it to her. 'The names in the left-hand column are the clients. The ones in the right-hand column are the victims.'

Becca inspects the list. There are twelve names in the left-hand column. At the top is Kalian Roman. Number six is a name that's also vaguely familiar to her, but she can't immediately place where from. The others she doesn't recognise.

'Who among these twelve people do you think is responsible for the attack on you in here?' she asks, wondering if one of them has something to do with Elle's abduction.

'I can't say for certain,' he answers carefully, 'but there are two who definitely have the resources necessary to carry out multiple attempts on my life. Kalian Roman and Jeff Barris.'

The latter name is the one that's vaguely familiar to her, and she's trying hard to remember why. 'Tell me about Roman. You said earlier he's tied to a foreign embassy. Which one?'

'I can't tell you that, Becca. Not yet anyway. I can't risk your legal colleagues in the CPS finding out before I've signed my deal. But what I can tell you is that he has the full resources of a major and largely hostile foreign power behind him. And he and they are totally ruthless. They've killed a number of times inside the UK.'

Becca swallows. Quinn's words make her feel sick. If she's up against a foreign power, what chance does she have? 'And Jeff Barris? What can you tell me about him?'

'He's the chief executive of the mining company I worked

for in a freelance capacity through my old army colleague, remember?'

She nods. 'I remember. You really think he'd do this?'

'I have evidence that directly implicates him. The kind that's irrefutable and will put him away for the rest of his life. He'll do everything he can to avoid that. He's a very rich man and he has people who'll help him. That's why I need to get out of here fast. Whoever's behind this will try again very soon.'

Becca had hoped this information might help her, but even with these names, there's nothing she can do. It's not like any of them are going to admit it, and even asking the question might get Elle killed.

She takes another deep breath and looks at the twenty-three names in the right-hand column, tallying with the number Quinn quoted to her yesterday. They include not only the woman whose murder he's charged with, thirty-one-year-old Jess O'Sullivan, but five others whose names she recognises from media coverage over the past few years. It makes grim reading. Twenty-three people whose lives were snuffed out by the man sitting opposite her, the man for whom she's trying to secure a reduced sentence that will potentially represent less than three months for each victim.

The thought makes her feel ill.

But nothing like as ill as the thought that Logan Quinn's fate might somehow be tied in with the fate of her only child.

25

Friday, 1.55 p.m.

The first lesson in being a successful criminal is not leaving behind any clues at the scene of the crime, and the only effective way to achieve that is not to be there in the first place, which as you know is what I've done, preferring to take a supervisory role instead. However, it's still essential to learn the second lesson as well, which is how to successfully deflect blame elsewhere should suspicion somehow fall on you.

Now the way I've always seen it is that, if caught and looking at a long sentence, Delvina will cooperate with the authorities and make her own attempt to deflect blame. I have no doubt she'll accuse her husband of being the dominant partner, and because of his criminal background, she'll almost certainly be believed. After all, it's a plausible narrative, and she's a good actress. I also know that if push comes to shove and she thinks it'll help her case, Delvina will give me up. She might not have concrete proof of my involvement (I doubt she would have recorded any of our conversations because they'd implicate her too), but she could easily say that her husband and I were in contact, and that the two of us were the main players, with me providing all the inside information, including the particularly damning fact that the Day family had gone to the police. Again, it's a plausible narrative, and that's what my colleagues and juries are interested in.

So the second lesson is all about forming a plausible alternative narrative, one that puts the blame for all that inside knowledge the Vanishers have been getting on someone else. And that someone else, unfortunately for him, is my old buddy Cotton. Now, Cotton got divorced from his wife five years back. From what I can gather, it had been a pretty loveless marriage, particularly in its last years, and old Cott has always been very keen to meet someone else and live happily ever after. Unfortunately, he's never been successful with women. He's awkward, hardly a barrel of laughs (his twin conversation subjects are police work and carp fishing), and not exactly a picture to look at either. Consequently, things were barren on the female front for a long time, and he was often moaning to me about it, which eventually gave me an idea. The thing is, Cotton's a blabbermouth. He can't keep a secret, especially if pushed.

So six months ago, I did a little matchmaking. Janice Boothby (aka Misty) is what these days is termed a mature escort. She's forty-two years old and I've known her for close to fifteen years, ever since I arrested her for fraud after she was caught using several of her punters' credit cards for illegal purchases. I've got to be honest, I liked her. She was fun, attractive, and took being caught with a rare good grace. Somehow we stayed in contact. I never paid for her services, I can promise you that, because I'm not that kind of guy, but we did have occasional trysts, and I bought her dinner a couple of times. Anyway, Misty (a far better name than Janice) is still involved in the sale of sex for money, and because we have a history, I was able to get her (for payment, of course) to make contact with Cotton on Tinder, which I knew from looking over his shoulder was his dating site of choice, and set up a date. Not surprisingly, he fell for her, and the rest is history. She only sees him about once a month (I can't afford to pay her for more than that), but when they do meet, she often gets him to talk about the Vanishers case and helpfully records the conversations for me.

Look, I know what you think. That it's a real betrayal and I'm an utter bastard for doing it. You may be right, but it's only a fallback option. I've always hoped I wouldn't have to use the recordings, and I still might not have to, but it's essential I have them in reserve, because if I can frame Cotton as the insider leak, no one's going to believe it if Delvina then tries to blame me. I'll just say that it's some kind of demented act of revenge on her part because she propositioned me when I was investigating her first husband's death and I turned her down.

Not foolproof, but certainly good enough.

However, there are elements of the plan that still need sorting. And that's why I'm on the phone to Misty now, stuck in traffic somewhere in Croydon.

'He says he's had to cancel tonight,' she says. Cotton, it

189

seems, has suddenly got the bit between his teeth in a way he's never managed before.

'He can't cancel,' I tell her. 'It messes up everything. And it means I can't pay you that thousand pounds you've got coming.'

'Well, what am I meant to do about it? I can't make him come.'

'Of course you can,' I say, disappointed but not surprised by her lack of imagination. 'Tell him if he can't make tonight you can't see him for a couple of weeks. Say you've got to go away, see your mum up north, anything. Tell him how disappointed you'll be. And you will be disappointed, because you won't be getting that grand.' The thousand pounds is effectively her final payment, including a fat bonus, because I won't need her any more after this.

'Can't we just put it off until tomorrow or Sunday?'

'No,' I say firmly. 'It's got to be tonight.' And the reason for that is because with all the developments on the case, I'm planning to call Cott when he's with Misty to discuss it. Even if she leaves the room, the device will still record him chatting away to me.

'What's so important?' she says suspiciously. 'I don't understand what it is you're trying to do to him.'

'And you don't need to understand, Misty. I'm just paying you to do a service, and you've been doing it very well so far,' I add, hoping flattery will soothe her angst.

It doesn't.

'I actually like him, Fish,' she says firmly. 'You know, properly like him. He's a gentleman, and you don't get many of them these days. I don't want to see him hurt. He's a nice guy. And do you know what? He always talks highly of you, although I don't know why given what you're doing to him.'

'I like him too,' I say, rolling my eyes, 'and nothing will happen to him because of these recordings.'

'Why do you need them then?' she demands.

'It's insurance. But they'll never see the light of day.'

'Do you promise?'

And that's it. Misty's given herself a let-off. If I promise not to use the recordings to harm Cott, that'll take away the guilt she's feeling.

So obviously that's what I do. 'I promise. Just get him to see you tonight, then my involvement's over and you can both live happily ever after.'

'I'll see what I can do, Fish.'

'Make it happen, Misty,' I say. 'Please. And keep me posted.'

I could have resorted to threats and told her that I'd tell Cotton what she's been up to, but I'm not a cheap blackmailer, and I have faith in the power of financial incentives.

Talking of cheap blackmailers, I've had another text from Delvina trying to get the remainder of her money and saying we need to talk urgently.

Knowing there's no point putting off the inevitable, and knowing too that I still have to keep her on side, I call her on the current burner phone we're using.

She takes her time answering, and when she does, her voice is a hoarse whisper. 'I need a gun.'

Christ, this is all I need. 'Who do you think I am?' I demand. 'Al Capone?'

'I know you can get one at short notice and I need it to deal with Marv.'

She's right, I can. I have a very good contact, but the last thing I need is Delvina running round with a gun, because I have no doubt she wouldn't hesitate to use it on me. 'I can't do that. I can probably get you some poison. That'll be a lot easier and far less messy.'

'Poisoning's too risky. I can't get close enough to him, and if he saw me putting it in his food, he'd kill me. And Vincent won't do it. He's too squeamish. I need something that evens the odds.'

'If you don't know how to use a gun properly, it's even more dangerous. He could take it off you, and then that really fucks things up.'

'I know how to use a gun,' she says coldly. 'I've fired one plenty of times. Get me one and he's dead.'

I'm just about to say no when it occurs to me that giving her a gun might not be such a bad idea after all. Because if Delvina's armed, should the police investigation into the Vanishers lead to her, she might actually try to shoot it out with them rather than be taken alive, and since she's the only person who can finger me, her death would be seriously convenient.

It also gives me an excuse to meet her again so I can plant the drive with the Cotton recordings somewhere close to her, thereby killing two birds with the same stone.

'I'll see what I can do,' I tell her. 'Have you told Barraclough what she has to do yet?'

'Not yet. I'm softening her up. We need time for it to sink in that her daughter's life is in danger.'

'Look, forget the psychology stuff,' I say, beginning to lose patience (which I rarely do). 'Just give her the instructions and get things moving. We haven't got much time. You're not getting the balance of the money until the job's done and Marv's dead. The sooner that happens, the sooner we can all go our separate ways.'

'You get me the gun, make sure it works and is reliable, and I'll wait for the last part of the money.'

'Done,' I say, as the Croydon traffic finally begins to move. 'I'll be in touch later.'

26

Friday, 2.15 p.m.

During the hour she's been in Belmarsh, Becca hasn't had a phone signal. The authorities do whatever they can to blunt mobile reception within the prison for obvious security reasons, and any official calls made by the prisoners are on monitored landlines, so it's not until she gets out to the car park that her phone kicks back into life.

Becca's missed three calls. One from her friend Tamara, who she's meant to be meeting for dinner sometime next week; one from Nisha, her legal assistant; and the last from an unknown number, barely ten minutes ago. There's only one voicemail and that's from Nisha. Becca ignores it and gets back into the car, worried that the unknown call is from the kidnappers and she's missed them. They gave her strict instructions to pick up immediately, and she hasn't kept to them.

She calls the number back now and an automated message tells her the phone is either switched off or out of service. She curses. She can't even leave a message apologising and asking them to call her. Once again, she's just got to wait.

Thankfully, the wait's not long. She's barely out on the main road when the phone rings again, but this time it's a different unknown number, which tells her how careful these people are.

'Why didn't you answer earlier?' demands the same disguised voice that first called her.

'I was inside Belmarsh prison with a client. You told me to go about my day as normal, and that's what I'm doing. There's no signal in there.'

'There's no need to get annoyed with me, darling,' says the voice playfully.

'I'm not,' says Becca. 'I'm just very stressed, as you can imagine. Are you a father?'

There's hesitation at the other end, which once again makes her think she's talking to a woman. Then: 'Yes.'

'Then you must know how I feel.'

'I do. But this is business. Now, let me guess. The client you've just been seeing was Logan Quinn.'

So there it is. Becca's suspicions were right. This is about Quinn. 'Yes,' she answers, knowing there's no point lying.

'And what's he been saying?'

'About what?' she asks carefully.

'You know exactly what about. Is he planning on doing a deal with the authorities?'

Becca hesitates. It's a long-standing lawyer habit to think about what you say before you say it.

But it's not going to work here. 'Don't even think about lying to me,' hisses the voice threateningly. 'Because it'll be Elle who suffers if you do.'

'Yes, he is.'

'Do you know the names of the people he's intending to testify against?'

This time Becca doesn't hesitate. It's not worth the risk to Elle. 'Yes. He's given me a list.' She wonders if she's now going to find out who's behind the kidnap.

'Have you given it to the authorities?'

'Not yet. But they're expecting it imminently.'

'Give it to them. It's important you act normally. But stall Quinn. Do not let him say anything to them until you've received further instructions from us.'

Becca's confused. 'I don't understand.'

'You don't need to understand. Just do as you're told.'

'I have money. I can raise three hundred thousand by tomorrow. I can pay it to you personally, in any format you want, and wherever in the world. If you just let Elle go, I won't involve the police, I promise.' She knows they won't go for it, and even if they did, there's no way she'd be able to raise that amount of money that fast, but when you're desperate, anything's worth trying.

'I'm not interested,' says the voice. 'Just do as you're told if you ever want to see her again.'

'I need to speak to her. I have to know she's all right.'

'I'm afraid that's not possible.'

'Please. Have some pity.'

'No.' There's a firmness in the voice that brooks no dissent.

But even in her flustered state, Becca's aware that the kidnappers need her to cooperate, so she has at least some bargaining power, and it's time to use it. 'If you want me to help you, I have to know that Elle's alive.'

'You don't get to make demands, Becca. But I'll be charitable here. Ask me a question that only Elle knows the answer to.'

Becca tries to think, which is hard when you're suddenly put on the spot like this. Then she remembers. 'What's her all-time favourite takeaway restaurant? And what dish does she always go for?'

'I'll ask and get back to you with an answer,' says the voice. 'In the meantime, make sure Quinn doesn't talk. The minute he does, Elle dies. And look on the bright side. At least you get to keep your money.'

The connection's severed before Becca has a chance to respond. It seems these people are not in the business of negotiating. But that's not surprising. They hold the trump card. Elle is everything to Becca. Without her, life isn't worth living. It's that simple. Some people carry on after the death of a child, even though in most cases they're never the same again. But Becca couldn't. It's not just that Elle's an only child. It's that she's the one constant good thing in a life that in truth hasn't been easy, and although they haven't seen each other anything like as much as they should have done since Elle moved to Brighton, it hasn't dimmed Becca's burning, unstoppable love for her. The hole she'd leave behind is just too great to contemplate.

And yet right now, she has to contemplate it, because she's not dealing with a kidnap for ransom. She's being blackmailed into doing something, and the worst thing is she doesn't even know what that something is. Because none of this makes sense. If they don't want Quinn to talk, why didn't they just tell her that when they first made contact? And why allow her to hand over the list of names?

She sits there in the car, breathing deeply and trying to think, but it's impossible to second-guess the kidnappers or their motives, especially given her current state of mind. But at least she can be confident that Elle's still alive.

And with that, there's hope.

27

Friday, 2.20 p.m.

Running an undertaker's is hard, hard work. No two funerals are the same. Sometimes it involves not just arranging the transportation and storage of the body but organising the cars to the service; the flowers; the order of service; the embalming, of course (Delvina's speciality); and any unusual requests from the deceased's family, of which there are far too many. If someone dies at home at three in the morning, the family expect their local funeral directors to turn up pretty much immediately and take the body away.

Delvina has been involved in the running of the Travellers Rest Funeral Home for almost ten years now, having been promoted by her late husband, Philip, to be his assistant manager. Aside from her and Vincent, there are six employees at the company. There were fourteen, but she's been winding down operations for some months now. In truth, she could shut down the business easily, but it serves a purpose. People don't suspect legitimate business owners of being criminals, and it's a useful conduit for laundering some of their illegal proceeds too.

Also, the funeral they have this afternoon will help keep Vincent occupied at this time of crisis for him. It's no surprise to Delvina how upset he is at the prospect of them having to kill Marv, even though the idiot effectively dug his own grave by shooting his mouth off to the wrong people. But she's certain she can get him to go along with it, as long as she keeps the two men apart until after she's taken out Marv. She doesn't want Vincent seeing him and then saying something in a moment of weakness, giving Marv the opportunity to disappear somewhere into the ether, where he'll remain an ongoing threat.

Delvina's feeling the strain of trying to keep the strands of her plan together, but she prides herself on nerves of steel, and knows she can get through this. The gun will be a real help if Fisher can come through with it (which she's certain the corrupt bastard can, given the extensive illicit contacts he's built up over the years). Not only to kill Marv but also to deal with any other problems that might arise. She smiles, remembering Fisher's patronising comments about her not being able to use a gun. The naïve fool. Delvina has taken no fewer than three firearms courses in Prague and Budapest, where she was taught to shoot anything from a .357 Magnum revolver to an AK-47. One instructor described her as a crack shot, and she once got five out of ten rounds, fired in quick succession from a SIG Sauer pistol, within the bullseye section of the target. Taking out a lumbering oaf like Marv will be easy. And it'll also be a pleasure.

And of course, no one knows Delvina's biggest secret. That she's killed before, and at close quarters.

It happened when she was thirteen. Two years earlier, her mother had met a man called Terry. Delvina's father had left when she was two, moving back home to Scotland and starting a second family, effectively cutting his daughter off. Her mother had also taken it very hard and had blamed Delvina for his leaving. Consequently, she'd shown her daughter very little love, even though as a young girl, Delvina had craved it. Her mother had had a number of boyfriends, none of whom stayed long, and again Delvina always felt that she was being held responsible for their departure.

But then along came Terry, and suddenly her mother seemed happy. She even treated Delvina better. Terry moved in and all seemed like happy families, even though he could treat her mother roughly sometimes, and occasionally he showed Delvina a bit too much attention. Then, just before her thirteenth birthday, he sexually assaulted her. She didn't fight back, not quite sure what to do. After that, she avoided him when she could, but in a small flat, it was impossible, and a few weeks later, he did it again. This time he was rougher. Once again, she didn't fight back, and afterwards he even apologised. But Delvina was worldly-wise enough to know that he wouldn't stop, and that her mother wouldn't do anything about it either.

She was right. He did do it again, two weeks later. And then again two weeks after that.

Which was when she decided to do something about it once and for all.

It was another three months and quite a few more assaults

before Delvina finally put the plan she'd been carefully working on into action. Her mother and Terry liked to drink a lot, usually at home while watching the TV, and Saturday nights tended to be their biggest night for the booze. When they were drinking like that, Delvina usually stayed hidden in her room, where she had a small portable TV that had been a present from her grandma. That was the thing in those days: Delvina didn't really have any proper friends she could confide in or whose houses she could escape to. She'd always been a loner. It kept her safe, but it also meant that when the time came to make a big decision and follow it through, she was entirely on her own.

That night, she lay in bed and waited until she could hear Terry and her mother's snoring from across the hallway. Then she got to her feet, removed her nightdress so she was completely naked (she'd read that the police looked for bloodstains on clothes, so if she wasn't wearing any, she'd be safe) and tiptoed into the kitchen, which was still a mess from the evening's cooking. Terry had made home-made pizzas, which was the only thing she'd ever seen him cook, but which he was inordinately proud of and liked to do at least once a week.

Heading to the sink, she put on her mother's kitchen gloves, then picked up the chopping knife, which was still speckled with bits of veg and meat. It was no ordinary knife but one of those ultra-sharp Japanese ones, which Terry had apparently bought on a whim before he met her mother, and was the size of a small carving knife. Holding it in her hand, feeling its weight, was the moment it all felt very real.

Delvina remembers that she had absolutely no doubt about what she had to do. She didn't even hesitate, but crept slowly back down the hall, gently opening the door to be greeted by Terry's loud, pig-like snoring. Ignoring the smell of stale alcohol and body odour, she stepped inside, leaving the door open a crack so she could see what she was doing, and moved slowly towards the bed, a delicious excitement building in her as she gripped the knife tightly in her gloved right hand.

Oh, the power she felt in those moments. For the first time in her entire life.

Terry was sleeping closest to the door because he usually had to get up in the night to go to the toilet (he'd assaulted her twice en route back from it before, but that was never going to happen again). He was lying on his back, mouth open, with one bare leg hanging out of the bed.

She stopped above him, looking down, revelling in his helplessness. One thrust was all it would take and he'd be gone.

But Delvina had different plans for Terry.

Slowly she crept round the bed until she was standing above her mother, who was lying on her side in the foetal position, wrapped up in the duvet with only her head above it. Her snores were more gentle than Terry's, but she was just as comatose.

Delvina pulled back the duvet and pushed her mother ever so gently onto her back so that her breasts were exposed. Her mother began to stir, eyes flickering, and that was when Delvina raised the knife high above her head, feeling the

203

excitement build to new levels but knowing too that she had to move fast and decisively.

As her mother's hand lazily grabbed at the duvet, her eyes still closed, Delvina leant over and carefully positioned herself, then shoved a hand over her mother's mouth before bringing the knife down with all the power she had and driving it into the spot where she'd read the heart was situated.

Her mother stiffened and gasped, her eyes widening, but Delvina kept the hand over her mouth and pushed the knife in as far as it would go, putting all her strength into it.

Her mother kicked out. Beside her, Terry stirred, his snoring suddenly silenced. Delvina started to panic. Why wouldn't she die? She kicked out again, her eyes trying to focus on Delvina – was that shock in them? – and lifted an arm towards her.

And then, just like that, her eyes closed, the arm dropped, and she finally stopped breathing, the knife with Terry's fingerprints all over it sticking out of her chest. Delvina still remembers how little blood there was. It was, in effect, a perfect knife-thrust delivered to exactly the right spot, something she's always been proud of.

The whole thing almost ended in disaster, though, because Terry turned onto his side towards her mother, and placed one of his hands on her shoulder, grunting something. Delvina was convinced he was going to wake up and catch her there, but then his snoring began again in earnest, and she knew she was safe.

Leaving the room and shutting the door behind her, she

returned to the kitchen and removed the gloves, putting them back where she'd found them, then quickly washed herself in the bathroom before returning to bed, feeling strangely deflated.

But the feeling didn't last long, and she was soon fast asleep, only to be woken hours later by Terry's hysterical screaming. Throwing on some clothes, she'd run into her mother's room, ostensibly to see what the fuss was about, and saw her mother lying there while Terry stood above her, stark naked, his face white with shock, saying 'I don't know what happened, I don't know what happened' over and over again.

Again the whole thing went to plan. Delvina screamed too, then ran round to the neighbours, breathlessly telling them that Terry had murdered her mum. He was arrested and, despite his protestations of innocence, found guilty of murder, while Delvina herself was sent first to live with her father (which didn't last long), and then her grandmother, which wasn't a lot of fun but was better than being with her mother and Terry.

No one ever suspected Delvina of any involvement, and she played the part of the innocent victim caught up in a brutal domestic tragedy perfectly. While Terry went off to begin a life sentence (he died of cancer in prison eleven years later, still protesting his innocence), she blossomed into a clever, cunning young woman who wasn't about to let anyone get the better of her.

To this day, no one ever has, and she plans to keep it that way.

After coming off the phone to Becca Barraclough, having made the latest call to her from the relatively wide-open spaces of Richmond Park, she changes phones and immediately calls Marv.

He takes a long time to answer, which is typical of him. He's probably asleep, the lazy bastard.

'Yeah?'

She considers berating him for his belligerent tone, but knows it's not worth the effort. 'Did you drug the girl's food this morning?' she demands. She likes to keep the victims drugged for much of their time in the basement so they remain pliable and can't remember any little details of their captivity.

Marv grunts something that sounds like a yes.

'Go down there and see if she's awake. If she is, find out what her favourite takeaway restaurant is, and what the favourite meal she has from there. I need to tell her mother. I'll stay on the line.'

Marv grunts something else and Delvina can hear him as he lifts the trapdoor and starts down the steps. She imagines his expression when she points the gun at his head. The fear he'll experience as he sees the smile on her face. Just before she pulls the trigger. She hears him unlocking the door and telling the girl to put her blindfold on. His tone is gentle and she doesn't like that. Nor does she understand it. Marv is, and has always been, a brutal thug who thought nothing of killing Henry Day.

But now suddenly he's Mr Nice Guy.

The girl asks him if she can have some water, and perhaps

some fruit, her tone submissive, the voice deliberately soft. Manipulative little bitch, thinks Delvina. And wide awake too. She'll have to get Marv to increase the dose of ketamine.

He says he'll get her water and try to find fruit, and it's clear the lumbering oaf is already putty in her hands. Finally he asks the question about the takeaway and the favourite meal.

The girl tells him both without hesitation. Delvina doesn't need to write any of it down. She's got a good memory. She considers berating Marv for getting too close to the girl, but decides against it. It'll just anger him, and it won't make any difference either. She's learnt over the years to control her own temper and to stay calm even when people infuriate her. Because, as she knows, you can always get even at a later date. And she's going to be getting even with Marv very, very soon.

She's not going to call Becca back with the answer to her question yet. Let her stew for a while. It's always part of their MO to keep the payer, as she likes to refer to the victim's parents, off balance, and not give them an opportunity to think straight. Keep them panicking, that's her motto. Plus she doesn't like the way Fisher ordered her to get on with it. Fuck him. He doesn't appreciate the psychology involved here.

Because there's a bigger reason for Delvina's delay this time. When she finally calls Becca back, she'll tell her what she has to do to secure her daughter's release.

And committing murder is something only a parent desperate to save their child's life would contemplate.

28

Friday, 2.35 p.m.

Elle knows that they drugged her again with the food. Whatever they used was tasteless and odourless, but also very effective, so she suspects it was something like ketamine. She guesses she slept for several hours, and she's been awake now, albeit groggy, for a while. Ketamine in continuous doses is very bad for you, as well as rendering you completely ineffective, and she needs to keep her wits about her. Elle senses that the man who's keeping her here can be reasoned with. She's tried being nice to him and it seems to work. He's not rough or unpleasant with her, like the woman who abducted her from the street outside her home and punched her in the face. She was hard and ruthless. The man doesn't sound like that, and he seemed interested earlier in the fact that she was a nurse, and almost respectful.

The cell door opens a crack and he calls out, telling her to put her blindfold on. He was only down here a short while ago, asking her what her favourite takeaway restaurant and dish was, which confused her at the time but which she now realises must be some kind of proof-of-life questions that her mum demanded the answer to. That's typical of Mum. Even in an emergency like this one, she's still level-headed and tough enough not to be cowed into submission.

Elle slips on the blindfold and sits up in the bed.

'I found a tin of fruit cocktail,' he says, 'so I've got you that and another bottle of water.'

'Thank you,' she says, with a grateful smile. 'I really appreciate that.'

He puts the bottle of water down on the bed so it's resting against her leg, and guides her hand to the tin of fruit, which is lidless and has a spoon sticking out of it. Up close, she can smell him, a mix of cheap, pungent deodorant and just a faint odour of sweat. It doesn't bother her. She's used to bad smells working on a hospital ward where so many of the patients are bedridden.

'Can I ask you a question?' she says.

'It depends what it is.' His tone is suspicious.

She doesn't want to annoy him so tries to word it carefully, sounding as vulnerable and unthreatening as possible. 'Is this food drugged? It's just, I think the last meal was, and it's been making me feel really sick. You don't need to drug me. I promise I'll behave and do what I'm told.'

'It's not drugged,' he replies.

Elle has no choice but to believe him. She's hungry and desperately thirsty. If he's lying, she'll just have to rethink the situation next time.

'Thank you,' she says, and eats the fruit rapidly, before slurping down all the juice.

'You enjoyed that, eh?' he says.

'Yeah, I really needed it. I still feel a bit sick from the drugs, though.'

'I won't put drugs in again,' he says firmly. 'I'm meant to, so if anyone else comes down here apart from me, you've got to pretend to be asleep, all right?'

'I will,' she says, thanking him again. She unscrews the cap on the water bottle, relieved to hear the click of the seal breaking, and takes several huge gulps, before turning in her captor's direction. 'I guess it wasn't possible to speak to my mum, then?'

'Nah, it's a bit hard at the moment. But don't worry. You'll be seeing her again soon, as long as she does what she's told.'

'She'll do whatever she has to do.'

'What about your dad? Is he around?'

Elle shakes her head. 'My mum had me when she was young. My dad was never there. I don't even know who he is.' It's never bothered her either. What you've never experienced, you don't miss. And for those more difficult years when she needed a father, she had her mum's partner, Clyde, who was always a support. 'How about you?' she asks, knowing how important it is to bond with this man. 'Have you got both parents?'

'Yeah,' he says, not elaborating.

'And kids?'

'Look, I'm not here to answer your questions,' he says, his tone changing.

She bows her head. 'I'm sorry, I didn't mean to pry. It's

none of my business. I'm just always interested in people, you know. It goes with the territory when you're a nurse.'

'Is your mum rich?' he asks.

'I don't think so,' she answers. 'She works hard at what she does, and she's been successful, I suppose. But not rich. She's a defence lawyer.' Elle adds this thinking that, as she's dealing with a criminal, it might make him more sympathetic towards her.

'Oh yeah?' he says, sounding interested now. He sits on the edge of the bed and she can feel from the weight of his landing that he's a big guy. 'Has she ever defended anyone famous?'

'She defended a man once called Colin Blisterfield.'

Elle senses his whole body stiffening. He knows exactly who she's referring to.

'*The* Colin Blisterfield?' he asks. 'The gangster?'

She knows that if it was her mum answering the question, she'd reply, 'The *alleged* gangster.' But Elle's not her mum. 'Yes, him.'

'Jesus,' he says, and she wonders if she's gone too far by mentioning this man's name. 'I didn't know that.'

'My mum wanted me to be a lawyer,' she says, changing the subject. 'I think me becoming a nurse was my act of rebellion. I'm glad I did.'

Her captor grunts something, but it's clear he's lost interest in the conversation. He gets to his feet and says that he'll come down later to check on her, then she hears him locking the door and the world is silence once again.

Elle's worried now. Mentioning Colin Blisterfield, a

211

well-known organised-crime figure her mum secured an acquittal for a few years ago, seemed like a good idea at the time, but in hindsight, it might make her captor, and the woman he works with, even less likely to release her for fear she might remember details that a vengeful Blisterfield could use to find them.

Other people might curse themselves for making a mistake like this, but Elle's not that kind of person. Even so, she knows she has to be on her guard now and look for any opportunity to escape.

29

Friday, 2.45 p.m.

Becca sits in the car waiting for the kidnapper to ring back with the answer to her security questions, but the call doesn't come. This is when she makes the decision not to do anything they ask of her until she's got proof that Elle is alive and well. She needs some kind of plan to ensure Elle's release, given that once she's done what they tell her, the kidnappers' incentive to let her daughter go will diminish rapidly, but until she knows what it is they want, it's difficult to come up with anything.

After ten minutes of just sitting there staring at her phone, she finally kicks herself into life and calls Clyde. 'I've got the names you asked for,' she tells him. 'His clients and their victims.'

'How many are there?' he asks.

She tells him the numbers and he whistles through his teeth.

'He's been a busy boy. Twenty-three murders. You're not going to win any new friends by defending him, Becca.'

'You've told me that already, Clyde.'

'I worry about you, you know.'

She didn't know, but she's glad to hear it. She's missed his strong presence, his calmness under pressure. And she has a sudden, almost unstoppable urge to confide in him now. Clyde might be able to help her. He has the resources behind him, and he'd be careful enough not to alert the kidnappers to what's happening. He also has skin in the game. He and Elle always got on well. He'd want to help find her.

But what happens if he *can't* find her? That's the thing that stops Becca in her tracks. Because if what the kidnappers want her to do is illegal or dangerous, Clyde (or his bosses) might stop it happening, which means that Elle will be killed anyway, and Becca can't risk that.

'You don't need to worry about me,' she tells him. 'I know what I'm doing.'

'Do you? You became a hate figure after Oliver Tamzan. You'll draw even more attention to yourself with this. And you don't need it. There's plenty of other work out there.'

'What do you care anyway, Clyde? We haven't been together for over five years and we hardly ever talk, so it's not like you're a good friend.' The words come flying out, angrier than she was expecting, but that's because right now her whole life is on a knife edge.

He takes a deep breath. 'I still care.'

His words pause her anger and she's about to apologise, but he's already back to business, a reminder that she's totally on her own here. 'Send over the list straight away. We'll study it then get back to you.'

THE FIRST 48 HOURS

'Do that. And please be quick. Because my client's in danger at the moment.'

'I'll be as quick as I can, Becca, but as I'm sure you can appreciate, the safety of a man who's committed twenty-three murders is not our top priority.'

'He hasn't admitted to anything yet, Clyde. And I'm only going to send this list as it is: just two columns of names. You're not getting anything else until my client's in a safe house and we've signed a contract that protects his rights.'

'I know all that. Email it to me now and I'll be back in contact when I can.'

Becca ends the call with a hurried goodbye, and screenshots the crumpled piece of A4 paper before sending it to Clyde's official email address in a ZIP file. Then she sits and looks again at the list of people Logan Quinn has worked for. They are all men. This doesn't surprise her. Women often got a bad rep as vindictive and manipulative, and phrases like 'hell hath no fury like a woman scorned' still do the rounds regularly, but in her experience, men are by far the more dangerous sex, and more likely to resort to violence to solve a problem, as they have done here.

She decides to google the names on the list to see what she can find out about them. The first is the infamous Kalian Roman, the man both Clyde and the CPS seem most interested in. Except there's nothing on him at all. Not a single mention. This doesn't surprise her. If he's some shadowy character linked to a hostile foreign power, he's not going to be public news.

The next on the list is Jeff Barris, the CEO and founder

of the mining company. A burly, balding man of fifty-eight, with the same hard expression in every photo even when he's smiling, he has his own Wikipedia page detailing a long and illustrious business career. Apparently he has a net worth of £150 million, the bulk of which is tied up in shares in his company, so he's got plenty of reasons to resort to underhand means to keep it profitable.

She looks back through the companies he's worked for, and that's when she sees it. Tollwick Finance.

As a young lawyer, close to twenty years ago now, her chambers took out a class action against Tollwick, a company that specialised in equity release loans, whereby borrowers signed over equity in their homes in return for cash. Tollwick's management were the worst kind of shysters. They used hard-sell techniques on prospective clients, who were often elderly and typically financially naïve, signing them up to appalling deals, the details of which often only came to light after the client was dead. Becca was one of the lawyers in charge of the action, her first big case, and they secured compensation of more than £35 million for the six hundred victims they were representing, putting Tollwick out of business.

Barris had been Tollwick's CFO but had left four years before the class action and wasn't mentioned by name in it, which was why she hadn't remembered him. On a whim, she googles the words *Barris*, *Tollwick* and *shareholder* together, and a number of matches show up, one in particular catching her eye. It's an article (and not an especially flattering one) in the *Guardian* from 2011, and it mentions that as a significant shareholder in 'disgraced firm' Tollwick, Barris had lost an estimated two million pounds when it went bust.

Two million pounds. It might well have been a lot of money for him back then, but was it enough to want revenge on Becca?

The phone rings, interrupting her thoughts. It's the kidnappers' number.

'Well?' says Becca, trying to put some confidence into her tone.

'Elle's favourite takeaway is from the Thai Orchid,' says the disguised voice. 'And her dish of choice is the seafood pad cha with steamed rice and vegetables in oyster sauce on the side.'

Becca sighs audibly. She's alive.

'I take it that's the answer you were looking for,' says the kidnapper, and once again Becca gets the feeling that she's enjoying this.

'It is, thank you.'

'So now you know your daughter's alive and well, and she'll stay that way as long as you don't do anything foolish.'

'I've told you I won't. I just want her back.'

'I know. And the good news is that if you do as we say, we'll release her unharmed. But I also have some bad news for you.'

Becca stiffens. 'What bad news?'

'When you get home, keep walking down the street until you get to number 38. They currently have a black bin just inside their front gate. Tucked behind the top bin bag is an envelope. Retrieve it and take it home with you. Don't try to find out who delivered it. If you start snooping, Elle will suffer. And it won't help you locate her. Only open the envelope when you're back inside your house. Inside will be a set of instructions.'

'What kind of instructions?'

'The type that tell you how you're going to kill Logan Quinn.'

30

Friday, 4.00 p.m.

Obviously, it being a Friday afternoon, and with the sun shining on an unseasonably mild March day, the traffic on the M23 down to Brighton is grim, and the journey takes me the best part of two and a half hours.

One piece of good news I get en route is from Misty telling me that she's persuaded Cotton to keep the date. I was always confident the dirty old sod wouldn't be able to say no, and it's nice to have my judgement confirmed.

'Where are you going to be? His place or yours?'

'I don't know. He's taking me out to dinner somewhere. I think the table's booked for eight.'

Christ, he didn't hang about. 'Sorry, that's no good for me. I'm calling him tonight at about eight thirty, and you need to be in a position to record the conversation. Tell him you don't want to go out, that you'd prefer just to relax with a takeaway and a bottle of wine. Then get him into bed fast so he's there when I call.'

'I can't just do that. He might not want to. He likes taking me out.'

'Of course you can do it. You're an attractive woman offering him sex. He's a man who's never had enough of it. I promise you he won't argue. And I need that call recorded. It's urgent.'

'I don't like this. I really don't.'

'You've said that already,' I say, playing hardball now. 'But it's the last time. And I'll need the recording by ten thirty tonight at the absolute latest. You can either download it and send it across to the usual email, or you can cut the date short and meet me in person. But I need it by then, otherwise there's no bonus.'

'You're going to bring the money you owe me if we meet, right?' she asks, greed clearly winning the day.

'Absolutely,' I say, annoyed that this is another piece of my increasingly meagre profit from the Logan Quinn job that I'm giving away but knowing too that there's no alternative.

With that part of the plan sorted, I'm able to think about the next move, which is planting the recording device in Delvina's vicinity, somewhere she won't find it. That way it'll look like she was somehow using Cotton to get her inside knowledge of the police investigation into the Vanishers, however much she might deny it. I've already put in a call to a contact to see if he can get me a gun, and if he can (and I suspect he will), that means everything will be in place.

Now that I'm in Brighton, I quickly find the street where yesterday's abduction happened. Freeland Avenue is a straight road about half a mile long that runs downhill then back up again and sits between two main junctions, one of which leads straight to London. It's mainly two-storey terraced housing and, like a lot of Brighton, which is a very compact town, the parking is terrible. Two marked squad cars are pulled up at the side of the road about two thirds of the way along, and I can see two uniformed officers, a man and a woman, talking to a woman in jeans and a shirt, wearing a lanyard, who I'm guessing is DC Elaine McMahon, my contact here.

I finally find a parking spot further up the road and walk back down to where they're standing. I like Brighton. It's got a cool vibe, and hearing the sound of gulls overhead and knowing that I'm less than a mile from the sea always puts me in a good mood. On a day like today, I need that.

The woman wearing the lanyard, who's in her early to mid thirties, with a short bob and one of those faces you automatically trust, peels away from the two uniforms, giving them some instructions, then turns my way with a smile, clearly guessing who I am. 'Agent Fisher? Is that what they call NCA officers these days, agents?' She smiles, showing big white teeth. Maybe too big.

'I honestly don't know, but everyone calls me Fish,' I say as we shake hands. 'Except the bad guys.'

'And I'm DC Elaine McMahon, but you look like a good guy so you can call me Elaine. Thanks for coming down.'

Well, at least she's not a good judge of character. 'Thanks for reporting this,' I say. 'It could be very important.' I look around with a suitably concerned expression at the fact that, including Elaine, there are only four cops here, hardly enough for a vigorous door-to-door inquiry. 'What have we got so far?'

'I've requested footage from the council cameras at both junctions. I've put a priority on it, but everything seems to be taking ages at the moment. We've canvassed the street, but so far no one else saw anything, and we haven't been able to locate any private camera footage as yet. The problem is, most of these houses are student rentals, so it's a pretty transient population and people tend to keep themselves to themselves.'

I nod sagely. 'Do we have an exact time when the abduction occurred?'

'The witness says it was about ten twenty-five. She checked her phone straight away. Before she dialled 111.'

'I understand she didn't get the make of the car, or the reg?'

Elaine shakes her head. 'A dark people carrier is all she's said.'

'Can I speak to her?'

'Sure. She lives at number 97, just across the road there. I'll come with you.'

Today for me is all about damage limitation, the most important part of which is finding out exactly who compromised Delvina and her old man. As we cross the road together, Elaine gives me some background on the witness. 'Her name's Jody Hallam. She's a young mother, thirty-two. Lives with her partner and two-year-old son. She seems reliable. This is the only time she's called the police in her whole life, apparently.'

She knocks on the door, which is answered a few seconds later by a harassed-looking woman in a T-shirt and track pants. She doesn't look pleased to see us, but Elaine doesn't seem deterred, giving her a big smile. 'Sorry to bother you again, Jody. This is Agent Fisher from the National Crime Agency. He'd like a word.'

'I've told you everything already,' Jody says, making no move to let us in. A kid's shouting from somewhere further inside. She turns round and yells, 'Ethan, quiet!' so loudly that it hurts my ears.

'I've come down from London, Ms Hallam,' I say, making myself sound important. 'We think this may have something to do with the Vanishers case. You may have heard about it. A group who've kidnapped several young people and murdered one of them.'

'Yeah, I've read about it,' she says, and now suddenly there's a glint in her eye. 'There's a reward for information, isn't there?'

Christ, whatever happened to community spirit. 'There is,' I tell her. 'Up to fifty thousand pounds for information leading to the gang's conviction.'

'Will I be able to get some of it?' she asks. The kid's still shrieking – it sounds like he's trying to win a competition for loudest tantrum – but she's ignoring him now.

'Absolutely,' I say, 'if we get somewhere with this lead.'

Now she lets us in, and after settling the kid down in front of *Peppa Pig* with a big, chewy bar of something very sugary, she leads us up to the main bedroom, where she was standing when she witnessed the abduction.

223

I walk round the bed and look out of the window. It's got a good, clear view of the street outside in both directions.

'I was just pulling the curtains,' says Jody, stopping beside me, while Elaine stands further back by the door, 'when I saw this red-haired woman in a hat walking out into the road with her arm round this other woman, who looked well out of it. I thought at first they were friends. But then the other woman starts to struggle, and the redhead hits her, and before I could really get a grip on what was going on, a car pulls up in the middle of the road right next to them, and the redhead opens the back door and shoves the other girl in and gets in the back with her. Then the car drives off that way.' She points up the hill.

I turn to her. 'Did it look to you like the other woman was being taken against her will?'

'She didn't seem too happy about it. But I didn't think it was a kidnapping. Not at first. I thought it might be an argument between two drunks. We get a lot of them round here.'

'What made you change your mind?'

Jody's face furrows in concentration. 'I think it was the fact that the car just pulled up then pulled away again really quickly. Because it wasn't a taxi. Or it didn't have a taxi sign on the roof anyway. Something just seemed off, you know.'

I ask her to describe the female kidnapper, and she gives a suitably basic description – mid height; long hair that could be a wig; in her thirties (Delvina would like that part); floppy hat and a suede coat with tassels. I've got no choice but to show her the security camera close-up I've got of Delvina on my phone, and I ask her if she thinks it might be the same person.

She looks at the screen closely for a long time. 'It's a different hat, and the hair's different, but that might be a wig too. But yeah . . . she looks similar.'

'But you couldn't say for sure?'

She shakes her head. 'Not for sure. It was all very quick.'

'And the vehicle?' I show her the picture of the Chrysler from the Day abduction with a masked Vincent driving, and once again she says similar.

I'm happy enough with this. The key right now is to slow everything down so that this part of the investigation doesn't move forward enough to identify our victim, at least not until after her mother has killed Logan Quinn. I ask Jody if she recognised the woman being pushed into the car.

'I don't know her, but she looked familiar. I think I've seen her around.'

This is slightly worrying, and I have no choice but to ask the next question. 'Can you describe her?'

'She was shorter, about five four, younger too, maybe early twenties, with dark hair, tied back, and wearing dark clothes – almost like nurse's scrubs – and bright white trainers.'

Oh shit. This isn't good.

'You didn't mention nurse's scrubs before, Jody,' says Elaine, sounding interested.

'Well, they might not have been, but thinking about it now, I might have seen her in scrubs before. The thing is,

225

she looked drunk last night, swaying about and unsteady on her feet, so it never occurred to me that she was like a doctor or nurse.'

'It's possible she could have been drugged,' says Elaine.

Jody shrugs. 'That would explain it.'

And there we have it. A giant step forward in identifying our victim. And there's nothing I can do about it. I ask a few more cursory questions (which direction were the two women coming from, etc.), and make detailed notes in my notepad, and then, having thanked Jody for her time and promised to put in a good word regarding the possibility of reward money, Elaine and I are back out on the street.

'You've obviously got a talent for getting information out of witnesses,' she says. 'That's the first time she's mentioned anything about nursing scrubs.'

I sigh and give her a boyish smile, trying to digest these new developments but, as always, showing nothing of my fear. 'Just dumb luck,' I say.

31

Friday, 4.35 p.m.

The envelope is in Becca's hands. There's no address or name or stamp or anything on it. It's white and plain, the size and feel of a greetings card.

There was no way she could go back to her offices today, so she phoned her assistant, Nisha, to say she'd be working remotely and came straight home, then followed the kidnapper's instructions and fished out the envelope from its hiding place in the black wheelie bin at number 38, hoping that no one saw her.

And now she's standing in her kitchen, with its view over the garden, a deep silence bathing the house, and she doesn't want to open it because she knows it represents the next stage of the nightmare and she doesn't know how much more of this she can handle. Becca has always believed herself to be a strong character, and yet she knows that right now she's only just keeping things together, that at any moment the walls that she's built up over the years to protect herself from the outside world might come crashing down.

But she also knows that there's no point in delaying the inevitable, and with a deep breath, she rips open the envelope.

The card inside has a picture of a Labrador sitting in a garden on the front, but no writing. She opens it up and a folded sheet of paper falls out, along with a small clear tube of white powder the size of a pen cartridge. She unfolds the paper and reads the typewritten contents.

ENCLOSED IS ONE GRAM OF POTASSIUM CYANIDE. YOU WILL SMUGGLE IT TUCKED INSIDE YOUR CHEEK WHEN YOU GO TO SEE LOGAN QUINN. YOU WILL PLACE IT IN HIS DRINK WHEN HE IS DISTRACTED AND WAIT WHILE HE CONSUMES IT, KEEPING HIM TALKING. THE EFFECTS WILL BE FAST. WHEN HE BEGINS TO SHOW SYMPTOMS, YOU MAY ALERT THE GUARDS. WHEN HIS DEATH HAS BEEN INDEPENDENTLY CONFIRMED, YOU WILL HAVE FULFILLED YOUR TASK AND YOUR DAUGHTER WILL BE RETURNED. DESTROY THIS NOTE NOW.

Becca reads through the note three times, then places it on the worktop next to the tube of poison. In a way, she knew this was coming. That the only reason to target her is because she's one of the few people who can get close enough to kill Quinn. And kill him she definitely would with a dose that size. One of her former colleagues was once asked to defend a man accused of killing his wife with cyanide. Apparently he had claimed that he was just trying to make her ill by giving her only a tiny amount (less than an eighth of a teaspoonful, in his words), but she'd died in minutes.

Becca is in possession of at least ten times that amount. If she's successful in getting it into Quinn's drink, she too will be found guilty of murder. There might be extenuating circumstances if Elle's kidnap and the fact that she's being blackmailed came to light, but it won't be enough to save her career, and it will almost certainly mean significant prison time.

Effectively, then, her life will be ruined.

She knows she can tolerate this if it means Elle is released unharmed. The problem is, there's no hard-and-fast guarantee that this will happen even if Becca carries out her side of the bargain. Yes, apparently they've released victims before after a ransom was paid, but they've also shown themselves ruthless enough to murder Henry Day when his parents cooperated with the police. And this kidnap is different. It's not for ransom. There's no guarantee it's even the Vanishers. And surely it would be easier and safer amidst all the chaos and recriminations that the murder of Logan Quinn would bring just to get rid of Elle and make her body disappear, like they did with Henry Day.

And that's something that Becca can't countenance. She has to get her daughter back. There has to be a way.

There's always a solution. A way to win, however good the opposition is. Because even the people at the top of their game have their weak spots. You just have to find them.

And there's no question, they've already made one

229

mistake. Someone placed that envelope in the bin, and given its highly sensitive contents, it has to be one of the Vanishers. The letter says they'll find out if Becca starts trying to find out who left it there, but how will they find out? They're not going to be sitting there watching the street. That would be far too dangerous.

Becca has an idea. Leaving the envelope on the kitchen top, she heads out the front door and walks back up to number 38. She might have lived on this street for almost fifteen years, but she has no idea who is at that address. But that's London for you. It's rare to know anyone other than your immediate neighbours, and often you don't even know them.

She can't see any suspicious-looking people in cars, so without hesitating, she turns in through number 38's front gate. As she approaches the door, she sees that the bell is one of the new smart ones, like her own, with a camera inside. She rings it, then waits, getting her story straight in her head and trying to look as confident as possible.

She sees a figure approaching behind the frosted glass and deliberately smiles at the camera. Becca's dressed smartly in a long jacket over a navy-blue trouser suit and hopes she looks as unthreatening as possible.

A second later, the door's opened by a cheerful-looking woman in her early seventies. The woman smiles uncertainly, glancing briefly over Becca's shoulder in case there's someone else lurking there, because that's another thing about London. People don't usually ring your doorbell unless they're trying to sell you something, or worse.

'Good afternoon, sorry to bother you, I'm your neighbour from number 21,' says Becca, beginning her briefly prepared spiel.

'I thought I recognised you,' says the woman with a smile, and Becca relaxes a little. 'What can I do for you?'

'Well, sadly I was assaulted this afternoon.'

'Oh dear, what happened?'

'I saw a man and a woman trying car doors up and down the street. They looked suspicious, and when I challenged them, the man hit me.'

The woman frowns, concerned. 'Are you all right?'

Becca nods. 'Yes, I'm fine. It was a bit traumatic, though. The reason I'm here is that I also saw them rummaging in your bin, and I wondered if you've got a security camera here that might have recorded them.'

'I don't, I'm afraid. I've got a camera on my doorbell, but it only starts recording if someone approaches the front door, and then it alerts me on my phone. The only alert I've had today is just now, when you rang.'

Shit, thinks Becca. 'Do you know if any of your neighbours have cameras?' She's fairly certain she knows the answer to this one, having checked the outside of the houses on the way up here.

'I don't think so, but I do know that the man at number 34 works from home most of the time and his office is in the front room.' She leans forward, her voice dropping to a whisper. 'He's a writer. A bit of a strange one. But he might have seen something. He's often there. I'm surprised you haven't seen him.'

Becca vaguely remembers a man sitting in the front window, but he's never been on her radar, so that's about all she can remember about him. That he's a man.

'Okay, I'll ask him,' she says.

'I know him slightly, I'll come with you. Let me get my coat. My name's Ann, by the way.'

'I'm Becca,' she says, shaking hands, touched by the other woman's kindness. She knows that if someone knocked on her door with a story like the one she's just told, she'd be helpful but brusque, because in the end, she's never had much time for people she doesn't know. And that now seems shallow and wrong. She tells herself that if she ever gets through this, she's going to change. Be more thoughtful and community-minded.

Ann and Becca go to number 34's front door together. Again Becca scans the street, hoping she's not making a mistake by trying to hunt down leads when she's been ordered by the kidnappers not to, but it's too late now.

They ring the bell (another camera one), and a few moments later the door's opened by a very large man with a thick grey beard, dressed in a tatty leisure suit. He eyes the two of them suspiciously.

'Hello, Tom,' says Ann. 'This is Becca from number 21. She was assaulted out here this afternoon. Did you see anything?'

'What time?' he demands, inspecting Becca as if he doesn't believe a word of it.

And this, of course, is the problem. Becca has no idea what time that envelope was delivered. For all she knows, it could have been days ago. 'I honestly can't remember,' she says. 'It was such a shock to be hit by someone. It was sort of mid afternoon. I saw this couple trying car doors then rummaging in Ann's bin, and that's when I approached them. I asked them what they were doing, and the man told me to mind my own business, then punched me. Then they ran off.' She tries to make herself look suitably distraught, but Tom's sympathy seems to be lacking.

He shakes his head. 'I didn't see anything like that,' he says, then looks at Ann. 'I saw a woman put something in your bin, but I just thought it might be some rubbish.'

'That might have been her,' says Becca quickly. 'Can you describe her?'

Again he eyes her suspiciously, and she wonders what she's done to make him dislike her this much barely thirty seconds after they've met. Maybe he recognises her photo from the papers. 'What did the woman you saw look like?' he says.

Becca guesses that whoever left the envelope has to be one of the Vanishers, and she remembers the camera still of the female suspect who abducted Henry Day. 'She was white, around forty or so, wearing a hat.'

'That could have been her – she was definitely wearing a hat – but I didn't see a man with her or anything like that. She just kept walking and I didn't see her again.'

But that's fine. Becca has what she needs. She knows who she's dealing with now and she thanks them both for their help. 'I'll call the police again and try to get them to come out,' she says wearily. 'They're taking their time about it.'

'They're never around when you need them,' says Ann, but Becca's no longer listening. Because she's had another idea. One that's risky and very, very dangerous but that right now may well be her best bet.

So, as soon as she's back home, she pulls out her phone and punches in a number she hasn't called in close to five years and hoped she'd never have to call again, and when he answers, she says just five words.

'I need your help now.'

32

Friday, 5.10 p.m.

There's an inevitability about the way the pieces begin falling into place now that I've managed, completely by accident, to unearth the information that our potential kidnap victim was probably wearing nurse's scrubs when she was taken, and it doesn't take long for us to find out that a nurse called Elle lives alone in the top-floor flat of number 128. There's no one answering there, or in the ground-floor flat either, but by now it doesn't matter. The residents of Freeland Avenue, many of them returning from work or college, are getting interested in the activity on their street and coming forward to help. Several are checking the footage on their home security cameras, and as I'm talking to an old lady – one of those who loves to ramble on while at the same time imparting no information of any use whatsoever – a scraggy student type who looks like he's only just risen from the grave sidles up and interrupts the conversation without a by-your-leave.

'The nurse you're looking for drives a white Mini,' he says. 'It's parked up there.' He points up the hill.

The old lady looks put out and does a bit of tut-tutting at the youth's impudence, but at least it gives me an opportunity to end the conversation with her.

'Show me,' I tell him, and we walk up the street together. There, sure enough, is the white Mini. I thank him, and from there it only takes a quick check of the PND, our police database, which I have access to on my phone, to confirm Elle Barraclough as the registered owner.

Now, I've already mentioned the importance of the second lesson of being a successful criminal, which is deflecting blame. But the fact is, the blame doesn't always have to be sent on to someone else. You just have to make it completely illogical to suspect *you*, and the way to do that, in my current situation, is to act like I'm desperate to solve the case, because now that we're getting somewhere, it needs to be me who's seen to be at the forefront of developments.

So now that I officially have the name of our potential kidnap victim, I hurry back down the street to Elaine, who's standing by one of the patrol cars talking on the phone.

She ends her call as I approach, and I tell her the good news.

She smiles. 'Even better, because the council camera footage has just come through.'

We retire to her car, where she pulls out a laptop from under the driver's seat and logs in. I can tell she's excited to potentially be part of something big. Most policework is mundane and pretty depressing, if I'm honest, and Elaine looks old enough to have lost that shine of idealism that so many new recruits to the police have before the penny drops and they realise they're fighting a constantly losing battle. But she's still got a sense of optimism, I can see that, and it almost makes me jealous. Sometimes I think I'd love to be like that – you know, see the good in people, wake up each morning with a smile on my face, count my blessings, etc., etc. – but I can't quite manage it.

I feel like asking her what keeps her smiling, but instead I decide on a whim to test the water with her. 'If this turns out to be the Vanishers, I'll buy you a drink,' I say. I'm smiling to demonstrate that I'm joking, but of course I'm not. She's not wearing a wedding ring and I have this instinctive feeling she's single.

'I'll settle for a good word with my DI,' she says with a smile of her own before pressing a few buttons and bringing up footage showing one of the junctions at the end of Freeland Avenue. She runs it forward until the digital clock in the bottom left corner says 22:15, then begins to slow it down. 'If she's driving from the main hospital, she'll have come this way,' she adds, staring at the screen.

I lean in so I can watch as well, conscious of Elaine's clean-smelling, vaguely flowery scent, which for some reason makes me yearn for female company.

Of course, it doesn't take long to spot the white Mini Coupé arriving into shot at 22:20. 'That's the car,' I say, as Elaine pauses the footage and zooms in on the driver. The quality's not good, but we can both see it's a young woman at the wheel. 'And that's our victim.'

'The kidnappers' vehicle should appear in a few minutes coming the other way,' she says, speeding up the film again

237

until at 22:28, it does indeed come into view, stopping at the junction.

Elaine pauses the recording again, and I take down the registration number.

'I think we're getting somewhere, Fish,' she says, moving the footage frame by frame now until we've got the male driver in view, before zooming in on him. Again, thankfully, the film is not top quality, although I know our technical team will be able to enhance it. It doesn't matter, though. Vincent's wearing a cap, tinted glasses and a surgical mask, making an ID impossible. I fish out my phone and find the close-up we've got of him from the Day abduction, then place it against the one on the screen.

'What do you think?' I ask Elaine.

'I think it's the same guy,' she says, no doubt in her voice.

'It's the same car too, with different plates. They were fake last time, and I'm sure they will be this time too. This is looking like the Vanishers.'

Elaine zooms in further. 'Look,' she says. 'You can just make out a figure in the back.'

I lean further forward and can just make out the silhouette of a figure in the back seat, head bowed as if she knows the camera's there, which I'm sure she did. Again, there's no way of ID'ing her as Delvina, but in the end, it doesn't matter. The damage has been done and the net is closing in on these two, and by extension, me.

I continue deflecting. 'That'll be our female suspect. The two of them must have been sitting there on the street waiting for our victim to come home. Now, either they've been watching her for weeks or, far more likely, they planted a tracker on her car so they could follow her movements that way. And unless they came back last night or sometime today to collect it, it'll still be on the car.'

'Let's go and take a look,' she says, real excitement in her voice.

I have to admit it makes me smile inside to know that Elaine is blissfully ignorant of the fact that she's talking to the man who organised this whole thing. What she'll remember is a friendly, helpful (and hopefully good-looking) guy who was trying his best to crack the case and whose idea it was to check Elle Barraclough's car for a tracking device.

It doesn't take long to find it, either. It's stuck to the inside of the wheel arch on the rear passenger side, a typical spot, and it's me who locates it, even though I didn't know where they'd planted it, or indeed whether they'd removed it afterwards. It doesn't matter either way. I know for a fact that Vinnie bought all the tracking devices they use over the counter and in cash, some months back, so there'll be no record of the purchase anywhere now, making it worse than useless as a lead.

Which is the real reason I've got a smile on my face as I emerge from behind the Mini with the tracker in my hand.

'Bingo,' I say. 'Now we definitely have our victim.'

33

Friday, 5.35 p.m.

Vinnie still can't believe that Marv's got to die. The two of them are like brothers. Same age, same upbringing, they've been together right from the beginning. Sure, they might have drifted apart these last few years, although that was more Delvina's doing than his, but Vinnie's always been proud about the fact that he's helped his cousin financially by bringing him on board with the abductions, even against his wife's better judgement. Delvina didn't want Marv involved, and usually Vinnie would have gone with what she said, but on that occasion he insisted, and now look where it's got him.

He always told Marv to keep his mouth firmly closed about the work they were doing, but it doesn't entirely shock him that he hasn't. Marv's never been a blabbermouth, but he likes his booze and coke, and it only takes one moment of stupidity and then someone else knows their secret.

And now he has to go to protect Vinnie and Delvina. Vinnie recognises that and he's accepted it, but he can't resist coming here to the hotel to say goodbye. Even so, he's nervous and jumpy as he unlocks the front door and calls out to announce his arrival.

Marv calls back from the direction of the lounge. 'I'm in here.'

Vinnie walks through, knowing that soon he'll never hear his cousin's voice again. It'll be part of the past, a memory that fades, like that of his mum. He tries to think about the bar in Spain he'll be running soon. The endless days of blue sky and sunshine; the banter with the regulars; Sky Sports on all day on the big screen; decent lager on tap; Delvina in a black swimsuit showing off those long legs of hers . . . But today, none of those thoughts stick. Because he can't get what has to happen out of his head.

'Hello, mate, are you all right?' he says, walking into the room, surprised at how calm he sounds. Like he hasn't got a care in the world. But inside he's retching.

Marv's sitting on the sofa nursing a can of Stella. There's an empty one on the table beside him but he looks sober enough. 'I've been better,' he says.

Vinnie sits down on the chair opposite, wondering if somehow Marv knows he's messed up. 'What's wrong?'

'You do know who the girl downstairs is, don't you?'

Vinnie frowns. 'What do you mean?'

'Her mum was the defence lawyer for Colin Blisterfield.'

'I didn't know that,' says Vinnie, because he didn't. And he's not happy to find it out either. 'How do you know?'

'She told me.'

'You've been talking to her?'

'Course I've been talking to her. I'm the one babysitting her, aren't I? And I googled her name on your iPad and the mum definitely was his lawyer. There are photos of them leaving court together.'

Vinnie knows this is even more reason to cut their ties with Marv. If someone like Blisterfield finds out they're involved, they'll be dead rather than in jail.

'What are we going to do about it?' asks Marv, looking at his cousin expectantly.

'We're not going to do anything,' says Vinnie. 'We're just going to keep quiet, and when this is over, we let the girl go. And that's it.'

Marv nods, but he looks troubled, which isn't like him. He's usually a calm, if belligerent, presence.

'You haven't told anybody about what we're doing here, have you, Marv?' Vinnie asks, leaning forward in his seat.

'No, course not,' Marv replies defensively, but straight away Vinnie can tell he's lying. It's the way he tries to make eye contact but can't quite manage it. The problem is, Vinnie knows Marv too well, and this just confirms that his cousin, his great mate, has been shooting his mouth off, and by doing so put them all in danger.

'Good, because we've got to keep absolutely shtum on this,' says Vinnie. 'That's the way we get through it all with no problems.' But he also knows that there are bigger problems ahead, like Delvina's insistence that the girl has to die, because with Colin Blisterfield's involvement, that now seems like a distinctly dodgy plan.

'So what brings you here now?' asks Marv.

'I've got a big box of gym weights I'm selling on eBay. They're in the shed and I need a hand getting them out to the car.'

'What are you selling stuff on eBay for? You don't need the money.'

'I always need the money.' Vinnie gets to his feet. 'Come on. I'll buy you a drink if you help me, and it'll only take five minutes.' He claps his cousin on the shoulder and heads through the kitchen to the back door, with Marv reluctantly following. 'Have you spoken to that girlfriend of yours yet?' he says over his shoulder.

'Nah, I just sent her a text on the burner, said I'd lost my phone and I was waiting for a replacement, and that I had to go away for a couple of days. When do you reckon this job'll be over?'

Vinnie unlocks the back door and steps out into the garden, a small, sheltered space with a patio and lawn, and a shed that Vinnie himself constructed down in the far corner. 'I'm hoping tomorrow,' he says. 'Sunday at the latest. But don't make any plans before Monday. Just in case.'

'Don't fuck this up, Vinnie,' says Marv, before lowering his voice. 'I don't want someone like Blisterfield after me.'

It's funny seeing Marv scared, thinks Vinnie. He's always seemed pretty fearless, and for good reason given the size of him. 'Don't worry, it'll all run fine, I promise. It always does.' As he says this, he goes through the keys on his key ring, looking for the one that fits the padlock on the shed door, but none of them do. 'Have you got a key, Marv?'

Marv shakes his head.

'I'll have to grab the spare. Wait here.' Vinnie starts back to the house but only goes about five yards before he leans down and picks up the loaded crossbow from where he secreted it under a bush a few minutes earlier. Marv's currently got his back to him as he leans over to light a cigarette, sheltering the flame from the breeze, and because of that Vinnie doesn't hesitate. He lifts the bow to his shoulder, aims down the sights, and as Marv turns back, blissfully unaware, he fires.

Vinnie's a good shot. He's had the crossbow for years, more for security than anything else, but he's used it for target practice plenty of times. The heavy-duty aluminium bolt strikes Marv full in the chest, sending him stumbling. It's got a razor-sharp blade designed for maximum penetration, so it's very likely fatal even if doesn't hit him in the heart, and Vinnie's pretty certain he's got him there.

But Marv's a big man and he doesn't go straight down. Instead, he wobbles on his feet for a couple of long seconds, dropping his cigarette on the grass and putting a hand against the shed door in a vain effort to keep himself upright.

It's the expression on his face that gets Vinnie. There's obvious shock, but it's more than that. Vinnie can see the hurt there, the knowledge that he's been betrayed by the man he cares about most in the world. Vinnie feels his eyes sting with tears as the guilt rushes over him in a hot, shaming flush, and he suddenly wishes that, standing there staring at Marv, he could turn back time to one minute ago, because it feels so fucking wrong.

Marv falls back against the shed door, then slides down it until he's sat on his behind, his arms by his sides, still staring at Vinnie with his eyes wide open, his mouth opening and closing as a thin rivulet of blood runs out of one corner.

Vinnie looks down, unable to watch his cousin die like this. He was hoping that he'd only need one bolt for the job, but now he realises he'll have to use a second. There's a built-in quiver under the crossbow's barrel, and he removes a new bolt, going through the laborious task of reloading, and trying not to think about what he's doing.

Marv makes a noise. It's almost like a wail. No one will hear him. The garden's sheltered and not overlooked from the road, and their nearest neighbour is more than two hundred yards away. But that's not the point. He's dying in pain, and in those last seconds he's got, he knows it's Vinnie who's betrayed him, and that hurts the most. Vinnie planned to catch him off guard so that he'd never actually know what had happened, but of course it hasn't worked out like that. Nothing in Vinnie's life ever really runs smoothly.

With the crossbow cocked and ready, he strides over to where Marv is sitting, keeping his head down so that he doesn't have to see the consequences of his actions until he's standing right over him.

Marv makes a grunting noise and tries to look up, but he hasn't got the strength. He manages to raise an arm, though, and shakily reaches out towards Vinnie's leg. Once again, Vinnie doesn't hesitate, firing the bolt into the top of his cousin's head at point-blank range. This time the effect is instantaneous. The arm drops, the head tilts to one side, and Vinnie immediately turns away and walks rapidly back to the house, leaving Marv where he's fallen.

It's over.

34

Friday, 5.50 p.m.

It's hard to imagine what it's like to be locked in a sound-proofed room with no natural light until you've actually experienced it. You'd think it might get easier with time, as you got used to the situation, but Elle is actually finding it progressively harder. It's not just the fear of what's going to happen to her. She's less worried about that now that she's beginning to develop the beginnings of a rapport with the man looking after her. It's the frustration of being caged that is getting to her this afternoon. She feels permanently nauseous and hungry, which isn't helping either, and although she knows she's got to conserve her strength, she finds herself constantly pacing the room as far as the chain round her ankle will allow, and sometimes stopping to pull on it in a vain attempt to get it to loosen.

Finally Elle sits back on the bed and tries to take her mind off her current predicament by thinking about some of her patients. There are people among them who are truly inspiring, like Graham, the seventy-five-year-old who's just lost both his legs below the knees thanks to diabetes, and yet who never ceases to smile and chat, demonstrating an optimism that Elle is certain she would never be able to manage. She tries to imagine how Graham would react if he was in this situation, and she tells herself he'd be stoical. That he wouldn't let it get to him. That he'd use his time to look on the bright side. The bright side for Elle is that she's probably going to be released at some point in the next couple of days, with a terrifying and yet remarkable story to tell, and that'll be the end of it. As long as she just holds out and is patient.

She hears the door unlocking and it opens a crack.

'Put your blindfold on,' says a male voice. But it's a different one, and there's something angry about it.

'I'm just doing it,' she says submissively, pulling it over her eyes and leaning back against the pillow. 'Okay.'

She hears him come in and she sits still, staring straight ahead.

'I've brought you some supplies,' he says, making a cursory attempt to disguise his voice, which doesn't really work. Elle notices he has a similar London accent to the other man.

'Thank you. Where's your friend? He was nice to me.'

'He's a good bloke,' says the man, and his voice cracks with emotion.

Elle can sense something's wrong, but she's not sure what. She waits while he puts the supplies on the bedside table. 'Is there any news about when I can go home?'

'Soon.'

'Is it possible to give me some idea?'

'Just shut the fuck up, all right?' he snaps. 'I'm not interested. I've got my own shit to sort out.'

'I'm sorry,' she says meekly. His anger makes her feel like crying, and she allows herself to, hoping it might make him feel some pity for her.

It seems to work. 'Look, it's going to be fine, okay?' he says, not bothering to disguise his voice any more. 'I'll try and get back later, but if I can't, I'll be here tomorrow. I've left you enough stuff. Hopefully I'll have some good news then.'

'Thank you,' she says, bowing her head.

He doesn't say anything else, and a few seconds later she hears the door closing.

Elle immediately pulls off her blindfold and looks at the supplies he's left for her. There's a bag containing four or five slices of white bread, a six-pack of salt and vinegar crisps, and three half-litre bottles of water. It's not a lot, but at least it'll keep her going.

Once again, she feels like crying. It's the injustice of it all. Elle's always tried to do the right thing. She considers herself a kind, caring person. It's one of the reasons she became a nurse. And yet she's been treated like an animal by these people just so they can make some money from her misery and her mum's fear.

But this time she doesn't allow herself the luxury of tears. There are two ways you can go, she tells herself. You can give in to your fears and allow yourself to become a helpless victim, or you can stay strong and positive, like Graham, and make yourself ready for whatever comes your way.

Elle knows more than ever that she has to take the latter option.

35

Friday, 7.00 p.m.

Delvina's in the kitchen, preparing the ingredients for stir-fried curried seafood, one of her signature recipes, while listening to the soothing sounds of Miles Davis's classic jazz album *Kind of Blue* when Vincent enters.

Straight away, she can see that there's something wrong. The pain is etched all over his face and it even looks as if he might have been crying, which is almost unheard of for Vincent. He's not that kind of man.

'What is it?' she asks, putting down the chopping knife.

'It's Marv,' he says, leaning against the counter like he needs the support. 'He's gone.'

Delvina frowns. 'What do you mean, gone?'

'He's not going to be a problem no more. He's dead.'

This is an unexpected piece of good news, she thinks. And one she wants to hear more about. 'Go and sit down in the lounge,' she tells him as she removes the rubber gloves she always wears when she's chopping fresh chilli and garlic. 'I'll get you a drink.'

He dutifully obeys, sloping out of the room with his

shoulders hunched and head down like a beaten dog, while she pours him a large whisky and pops an ice cube into it. Then, knowing that any confession she can get on tape might prove to be useful later if she wants to paint him as the driving force behind the Vanishers, she presses the record app on her phone, before slipping it into the back pocket of her jeans, and taking the drink through.

She joins him on the sofa, sitting deliberately close, letting him know that she's there for him.

He takes the proffered drink and downs it in one go, ice cube and all. She asks him what happened, putting a slightly nervous tone in her voice for the benefit of the recording.

He sighs and stares into space as he answers. 'I went up to the house after the funeral and told him I needed some help getting stuff out of the shed. When his back was turned, I shot him with my crossbow.'

Delvina's impressed. She didn't think Vincent had it in him to kill. Especially his own flesh and blood. And at least now he won't go soft on her. She puts an arm round his shoulders, drawing him to her, and whispers in his ear quietly enough that it won't be picked up: 'It was the only way, pet. I'm so sorry.'

'I feel like shit,' he says, moving away. 'I didn't want to have to do that.'

She doesn't say anything. Instead she gives him a sympathetic smile, then picks up his empty glass and goes back to the kitchen, turning off the app now that she's got his confession on tape. She doesn't want him drinking too much

251

(he can get both maudlin and aggressive when he's had too many), but decides that one more won't hurt him.

'Who's going to look after the girl?' she asks, sitting back down and handing him the second drink. 'Have you fed her?'

He nods. 'I gave her enough to keep her going until tomorrow. She's staying calm.'

'We'll still have to drug her again to keep her that way. I don't want her getting any ideas. And we need to bring Marv back here.'

'He's still out by the shed. Where he fell.'

'Well, we don't want him staying there.' Delvina resists asking whether Marv is definitely dead. She knows Vincent will have been thorough. 'We'll go back later and pick him up.'

'What are we going to do with him?'

She looks at him gravely. 'You know what we have to do, pet. What we did last time.' What they did last time, to the corpse of the unfortunate Henry Day, was to cut him into pieces, which were then frozen, before being defrosted one by one and packed into separate coffins alongside dead clients and cremated at their respective funerals. It took four altogether to dispose of him, and Delvina had done the dismembering.

'Jesus, babe. We can't do that,' says Vincent, with a real look of anguish on his face. 'He's family. He needs a proper burial. I owe him that.'

'We can't, pet,' she says firmly. 'It's too risky. He has to disappear.' She puts a hand on his shoulder. 'I'm sorry, my love. It's the only way.'

'My mum would never forgive me,' he says, shaking his head.

Thankfully, Vincent's mother is long dead. 'But you don't have to worry about her, any more,' Delvina says soothingly. 'I'm here for you now.' Once again she places an arm round his shoulders, drawing him towards her so that his head is buried in her breasts.

He doesn't try to move, just stays there silently while she strokes his neck and head, knowing exactly where his erogenous zones are as she gently but firmly stimulates him.

Within moments, she can feel him getting hard against her leg, and she rises slowly to her feet and leads her little puppy by the hand into the bedroom, knowing that he's already forgetting the fact that he's just murdered his own cousin.

Men. They're so fucking predictable.

36

Friday, 7.25 p.m.

Another of Becca Barraclough's controversial past clients was Colin Blisterfield.

If you were to talk to Blisterfield himself, he'd tell you that he's a wealthy businessman who's made his money in property development and in buying failing businesses, particularly bars and restaurants, and making them viable again. If you talk to the Metropolitan Police, however, they will give you a different story. To them, he's a ruthless east London gangster who's made huge amounts of money illegally (mainly through drugs, fraud and prostitution) and then laundered it through his legitimate businesses.

When Blisterfield was charged five years ago with a number of offences, including the importation of several million pounds' worth of heroin and cocaine, and the murder of two business rivals, it was Becca who defended him and ultimately gained his acquittal. Virtually all the evidence implicating him in the crimes came from a former police officer who already had convictions for corruption, and so it wasn't hard for her to discredit it. She tore him apart in the witness box, where it became clear that his testimony was unreliable, and since nothing linked Blisterfield forensically to either the drugs or the murders, he was found not guilty at the end of a four-week trial.

Afterwards, friends asked Becca if she felt guilty herself for securing an acquittal verdict for a known gangster, but her answer was the same as it was when she won the same verdict for Oliver Tamzan. Everyone is entitled to a defence; it's one of the keystones of English law and it's something to be proud of. The state didn't prove its case, and Becca offered her own evidence, with the jury reaching their verdict based on that.

Colin Blisterfield had been very, very grateful to her. He'd been looking at a life sentence, and at the age of fifty-one, it might very well have been the rest of his life too, so he'd invited her to join him for a celebration dinner with friends and family. She hadn't wanted to go – she never mixed business with pleasure – but he'd been insistent. The lavish affair at a high-end Mayfair restaurant had been hard work. Blisterfield was a frightening individual who clearly intimidated all those around him even when he was trying to be charming, and so the other guests spent their whole time competing with each other to be the most obsequious towards him. Becca couldn't wait to get out of there, and she hoped that would be the end of their relationship.

It wasn't. Three days later, she received a delivery of a diamond-encrusted necklace that she later found out was worth more than £30,000. A simple gesture of appreciation for a job well done, Blisterfield called it, but she sent it back, saying that she didn't accept gifts, and that her payment and satisfaction at gaining him an acquittal were enough.

To be fair, Blisterfield took her refusal to accept the necklace (and his subsequent attempt to buy her a Tesla convertible) without rancour, but he made a point of telling her that if she ever needed him for anything – anything at all – she should contact him immediately. The following year, when it seemed the whole world was against her after the Tamzan acquittal and she'd been receiving death threats, he'd offered her round-the-clock protection of his own. She'd rejected his offer as she'd rejected the police's, but for different reasons. Blisterfield was not someone you'd ever want to be in debt to. There might not have been the evidence to convict him when he was her client, but she's never been naïve enough to think he wasn't – and isn't – a very dangerous man. In the five years since she defended him, he's increased his wealth and business interests, and there are still persistent rumours that he's heavily involved in underworld activities, but no new charges have been brought against him. It seems he's more careful these days.

And Becca now realises that he may well be her only hope of getting Elle back. Which is why she's here now, standing in the lobby of the Crafty Fox, a small members-only club situated on a quiet square in Belgravia made up of grand townhouses, most of which have been converted into offices. The Crafty Fox belongs to Colin Blisterfield and it's where he's told Becca to come for their meeting.

The smartly dressed woman at the reception desk smiles

when Becca gives her name. 'Mr Blisterfield's expecting you, Ms Barraclough. He's in his office on the second floor. He said you'd know where to go.'

Becca's been here several times before, albeit not for a long time. She remembers it as Blisterfield's home from home, the place where he comes to relax and spend time with his close friends and business associates. The main bar and sitting area is on the first floor, but when he wants privacy, he retires to his suite of offices on the floor above.

She doesn't want anyone to see her here, for obvious reasons, so instead of taking the staircase, with its trad-itional paintings of hunting scenes and depictions of rural life lining the walls, she takes the private elevator, typing in the code that Blisterfield gave her as the doors close. A camera in the ceiling watches her as the elevator moves slowly up between the floors, making a slightly alarming cranking sound. Colin Blisterfield is notoriously paranoid, which is why, Becca thinks, he's still at liberty, and she's glad that he's paranoid, because there's no way she wants the conversation she's about to have with him to get out.

The doors open, and as she steps out of the elevator into a wide, thickly carpeted corridor, a well-built man in a suit that's too tight for him appears at her side. He doesn't bother with an introduction, just runs a plastic wand similar to the kind they have in airport security up and down her, checking for anything that might be a threat to his boss. He also asks for her mobile phone, and when she's given it to him, he points her to a door at the end of the corridor. 'Mr Blisterfield's waiting for you.'

257

Becca takes a deep breath. There's no going back from this, but she has no choice. Elle's life might depend on it.

There's a camera right outside the door, and as she stops in front of it, lifting her hand to knock, the door opens and she's looking straight at the man she's here to see.

Colin Blisterfield is short, with a shiny bald head and a goatee beard, and unfeasibly large, gnarly hands for someone of his size. He's quite good-looking, but his eyes are narrow and furious, as if constantly responding to an invisible threat, and when he smiles, as he does now, it doesn't reach anywhere near those eyes.

'Becca Barraclough, as I live and breathe. It's good to see you, darling.' His accent is old-school east London, as are his manners. He leans forward and kisses her on both cheeks, and she smells expensive cologne. Most of the times she's seen him he's been in a suit, but today he's wearing a neatly ironed polo shirt revealing hairy tattooed arms, and dark jeans.

'And you, Colin. You look well.' Although she's not sure he does. His face has got thinner and more hollowed out, making his malevolent little eyes even more sunken, and there's a rash that might be eczema in one corner of his mouth, only partly covered by the beard.

'Come inside,' he says, moving out of the way so she can enter his expansive office with its immense desk taking up half the room and its view over the square, which right now is beautifully lit up. 'Can I offer you a drink?'

She sees that he's got a large brandy sitting on his desk, and although she knows she's got to keep her wits about her, the lure of a drink, just to ease the pressure a little, is too much. 'I'll have one of those, please, with ice,' she says, pointing at his tumbler.

'I don't remember you being a brandy kind of girl,' he growls with a raised eyebrow. 'It must be serious.'

She sighs. 'It is.'

He prepares her drink at a bar that takes up one wall of the room (the other holds a huge mirror, which she's heard he likes to use as a prop when he's in here with one of his many lovers), and hands it to her before taking a seat opposite with his back to the window, watching her carefully. 'Tell me,' he demands.

There's a confidence in his voice, like there's nothing that fazes him, and that makes Becca feel at ease for the first time since she was contacted by the kidnappers and her life was turned upside down.

She takes a decent-sized sip of the brandy and tells him. About the call this morning. The fact that they definitely have Elle. And what it is they want her to do in order to secure her release.

'So,' he says when she's finished, 'your client is a grass who's going to put a lot of people away. Why don't you just drop him?'

'I wish I had,' she says. 'It's too late now. They have my daughter. My only child. Please, Colin. I know Quinn might not be your cup of tea, and I'm happy to tell him not to talk to the authorities, or to drop him altogether, but only after I've got Elle back.'

'All right, all right, I understand,' he says, leaning forward and patting her hand with his huge paw, keeping it there just a little too long. 'I've heard about these people, the Vanishers. But only what I've seen on the news. I don't hear anything else on the jungle drums. They obviously keep themselves very much to themselves. I can put feelers out. I know a lot of people, but it's going to take time.'

'I haven't got time, Colin. They want me to kill Logan Quinn as soon as possible. They've already supplied me with the poison. It could even be tomorrow.'

'See, this is what I don't understand,' says Blisterfield. 'I thought they did kidnaps for ransom. You pay them, you get your kid back.'

'I don't understand it either. But the woman I'm talking to basically admitted that they're part of the Vanishers.'

'A woman?'

'It's definitely a female I'm dealing with.' She tells him about the woman who delivered the envelope.

Blisterfield sips his brandy, thinks for a minute. 'It still doesn't mean it's definitely them,' he says.

'How many teams of professional kidnappers like that are there out there?'

He shrugs. 'Not many. It's not really the kind of crime that most people do. Way too risky, and with big sentences attached. So yeah, I suppose it could be them. Listen, I can get my people asking questions, I can put up a reward for information. But I'll be straight with you. I don't see what else I can do.'

'There is something,' says Becca, and she knows that

what she says now could alter her life for ever. 'I think I might know who's behind it.'

'Go on.'

'A long time ago, I led a class action that cost a man called Jeff Barris a huge amount of money. He's now the CEO and part owner of a mining company. He's also on the list of people that Logan Quinn worked for. If he is involved, I need to know.'

'He's not likely to tell you, is he?'

'No,' she says, leaning forward. 'But he'll tell you.'

Blisterfield sits back, folds his arms and stares at her, a small smile playing round his bloodless lips. 'You want me to get the information out of him, do you?'

Becca closes her eyes, takes a deep breath. Knows exactly what she's asking, and how unethical, not to mention dangerous, this is. 'Yes.'

'You want me to torture him? Get the information out of him that way? Is that what you want? Torture?'

She knows he's toying with her, demonstrating his power. But knows too that she's got no choice. 'Whatever it takes,' she says.

Blisterfield nods slowly, as if this is the answer he wanted to hear. 'I'll see what I can do. You know, after this is over, we should go out sometime. Grab a drink, dinner. Just you and me. How does that sound?'

Becca feels her skin crawl. When she defended him, he was always respectful with her, but now that she needs him and the boot is on the other foot, she's seeing his true colours. 'That sounds good, Colin. I'd like that.'

'You'd like that?' He's giving her his full burning gaze now, as if daring her to change her mind.

'Yes,' she says, nodding. 'I would.'

'Good girl.' His half-smile turns into an arrogant smirk. 'That's what I like to hear. I'll get us a nice hotel room afterwards.'

'That'll be lovely.' She forces a smile, telling herself that she's got no other choice but to go this route, and that any sacrifice is worth it if it gets her daughter back.

'Then it's settled.' He reaches over, strokes the back of her hand with his forefinger, looking right into her eyes. 'Leave it with me, babe. If the cunt knows anything, I'll get it out of him.'

37

Friday, 7.50 p.m.

Afterwards, when she and Vincent are lying in bed, with Vincent looking very sated, one of Delvina's burner phones rings. From the tone – a loud alarm bell – she knows it's the one she uses for conversations with Fisher. She's been keeping it in the back pocket of her jeans, which are now lying on the bedroom floor, and she climbs out of bed and grabs it.

'Why don't you leave it, Goddess?' says Vincent. 'I'd love to stay in bed with you all night.'

'It's McBride,' she says, wondering what he wants. 'I have to take it.'

She walks naked out of the room, putting the phone to her ear. 'What is it?' she says quietly.

'Two things,' says Fisher. 'One, I have the thing you requested. Two – and this is very urgent – you need to call our mutual friend, tell her the authorities know about her daughter, and make sure she doesn't say anything to them.'

Delvina stops dead, a pit of fear in her stomach. 'How do they know about her?'

'Someone witnessed last night. No one got a good look. Meet me at eleven tonight. Location B. I'll fill you in then.'

'Do we need to worry?'

'Not yet,' he says. 'See you at eleven.'

He ends the call, and Delvina takes a deep breath and leans back against the wall. Things are getting complicated. She'd had an idea last night that they'd been spotted, but had hoped she was wrong. It means she needs to put all her plans into action much faster than she was intending. Fisher told her there was no need to worry just yet, and he's got her the gun. That means she still has time to turn things in her favour.

'What did he want?' asks Vincent, who's now sitting up in bed trying to look angry.

'I need to meet him tonight.'

He looks suspicious. 'Why?'

'Don't take that tone with me,' she snaps, knowing she needs to get him back under control.

They stare at each other for a couple of seconds, and then Vincent lowers his gaze. 'I'm sorry, Goddess.'

'Good. I know it's been a difficult day, but you need to remember your place.'

He nods, gaze still averted. 'I understand, Goddess.'

That's better, Delvina thinks. 'McBride's got information he doesn't want to tell me over the phone. That's why I need to meet him.'

'Can I ask what kind of information?'

'I don't know yet, pet,' she says, trying to mask her exasperation as she pulls on her underwear, 'because he hasn't told me. That's why I'm meeting him.'

'That bastard,' he hisses, real venom in his voice. 'Probably planning some other kid's murder and letting us do all the hard work.'

'Don't worry. After tonight, we'll never see him again.'

'I don't trust him,' he says. 'May I come with you, Goddess?'

'I'll be fine. He probably wants to brief me on where the police are with their investigation.' Delvina decides against telling him about the potential witness to last night's abduction. Not until she's found out more.

'Yeah, but he might also be planning to double-cross us.'

This thought has already occurred to her, but she dismisses it. 'I've got too much on him. He wouldn't dare. But thank you for offering.' She walks to the bed and leans over, kissing him full on the lips. She lets him draw her into an embrace and their kiss becomes more passionate. Delvina gives it a full minute before she pulls away. 'We'll have time for pleasure later. We've got other things to do first.'

Vincent looks up at her with sad, puppy-like eyes. 'I don't want to lose you,' he says.

She smiles down at him. 'You won't, darling.' But of course he never really had her in the first place.

'And I'm still worried about this job, you know.'

'McBride's never let us down. And he's paying us over the odds. That should be enough. This is the last job, remember? Then we can sell the business and move to Spain, and we'll be free.'

He nods slowly, like he wants to believe her but isn't sure that he can. He's a simple soul, she thinks, but in many ways

265

that actually makes him more dangerous. She knows better than to underestimate his capacity for violence, especially after what he did to Marv earlier.

'In forty-eight hours we'll have the rest of our money. Barraclough will have the poison by now. She'll want her daughter back, so she'll set up a meeting, kill her client, and then it's all over.'

'Okay,' he says, with a small, boyish smile. 'I do fancy that bar in Spain. I want to call it the London Legend.'

God, Delvina doesn't know why she bothers sometimes. All that training – five years' worth – and her husband is still an ignorant peasant at heart. The London Legend. She wouldn't be seen dead in an establishment with a name like that.

'You call it whatever you want, darling,' she says, with a lot more enthusiasm than she feels.

38

Friday, 8.00 p.m.

I'm still in Brighton, on the street where Elle Barraclough was abducted, when I come off the phone to Delvina. I had no choice but to tell her to let Becca know that she'll be contacted by the police and to make sure she doesn't cooperate.

The problem is, the leads are piling up fast. Earlier, I went with DC Elaine McMahon to Brighton General Hospital to talk to Elle's colleagues in the vascular ward (which is a truly grim place, I can tell you). Not only did they confirm that Elle had texted in sick and hadn't been seen since the previous evening, but one of them also had her on her Live 360 app. This meant she could tell us that Elle's phone had been turned off near her home at 10.30 last night and hadn't been switched on again until 9.47 this morning, where it showed that she was more than fifty miles away, in Surrey. Twenty minutes later, it had been switched off again and had not been turned on since. At this point, it was blindingly obvious that Elle was a victim of the Vanishers, and as we left the hospital, Elaine turned

267

to me and said with her trademark big smile: 'It looks like your luck's changing, Fish.'

That's for fucking sure.

Anyway, I've delayed calling Cotton for as long as possible, giving him time to get to Misty's so she can record him, but if I delay any longer, it'll start to look suspicious.

It takes him a good eight rings to answer, and when he does, he sounds flustered. I can tell that Misty's already dragged him off to the bedroom, doubtless keen to earn that bonus.

'Sorry to bother you, Cott, but I've got an update. Are you free to talk?'

'Yeah, yeah,' he says. 'Fire away.'

'It definitely looks like the Vanishers,' I tell him, giving him a rundown of everything we've got. 'But,' I add, sounding a deliberate note of caution, because I don't want Becca Barraclough interfered with before she's done her job, 'the witness couldn't say for sure that it was the same woman as in the Henry Day abduction, and also we haven't heard anything from a member of the public to say that their daughter's been kidnapped, so I'm not sure what we can do right now. We've still got no hard evidence that a crime's taken place, and if the girl suddenly turns up, we'll look very stupid, and no one wants that.' I know Cotton doesn't, anyway. He's one of those guys who doesn't want to do anything to unsteady the ship.

'But we'll look worse if it is the Vanishers and we haven't done anything. And it sounds like them, Fish. That tracker on the car, the fact that the girl's phone was turned on in

Surrey. How far away was the phone from where we discovered Henry Day's?'

'Less than ten miles.'

'Exactly. It's them, Fish. It's too much of a coincidence
otherwise.'

Which is a fair point. 'We need to find out who the
parents are,' I tell him. 'We can approach them subtly, tell
them we know what's going on. But even doing that risks
scaring them off, especially after what happened with the
Days. I know it sounds counter-productive, but it might be
best to wait and keep pushing for leads down here, then
as soon as the girl's released, we can zero in on the family
and chase the money trail, which'll be a hell of a lot fresher
and might actually lead to something.'

'Jesus. But that basically means sitting on it and doing
nothing while a girl is potentially locked in a basement
somewhere. How's that going to look?'

Bad, I suspect. Although at least not on me this time.
'Yeah, but we took charge last time and it fucked up. The
kidnappers knew we were on to them. God knows how, but
they did. How about Cunningham? Have we got anywhere
with him?' I ask, knowing they won't have done.

'Nothing yet,' he says. 'I can't even get a warrant for his
phone records yet. According to the DG, we're still short
on hard evidence.'

Ah, the huge limitations of the British justice system,
finally working in my favour after all these years. 'Jesus,' I
say. 'Whose side are the bosses meant to be on?'

Cotton makes a loud tutting sound. Then takes the classic

line-manager stance and makes it someone else's problem. 'I think this needs to go upstairs,' he says. 'Let them make a decision. Shit, that's my date out the window.'

'Are you with her now?'

'Yeah,' he says quietly. 'We're just getting ready to go out.'

'I'm sorry, Cott,' I lie. 'I didn't want to mess things up for you, but I knew you'd prefer to know.'

'It's fine, Fish. I'm glad you've told me. And thanks for all your hard work.' He sighs. 'I ought to be down there with you.'

And we all know why you're not, Fatty.

'Don't worry about that now. I'll stay here a while longer. We're still doing house-to-house. I'll keep you posted if we get anything else.'

'Thanks, Fish. That sounds like a good plan.'

I end the call and start walking back towards where Elaine and four officers are clustered, talking. She's managed to get some extra resources from her boss in CID, which, given that it's Friday night, is no mean achievement, and she's determined to continue with the door-to-door inquiries even though she should have clocked off three hours ago and the night's beginning to get cold. It's a devotion to duty I'm impressed by.

I'm halfway there when my phone rings. I pull it back out of my pocket and check the screen.

A photo of a snarling T-rex appears alongside two words in block capitals to identify the caller: *SLAPHEAD WANKER.*

It's the man I'm working for. Who I've worked for on and

THE FIRST 48 HOURS

off for far too long. I wonder if it's about the gun I asked him to supply, but I know that's unlikely. I'd be getting a call from one of his minions if it was about that.

I groan inwardly, make a quick about-turn so I'm well out of earshot, hoping like hell it isn't more bad news.

'Yeah,' I say, shivering against the cold. Or maybe because I'm nervous.

'Is that how you greet me these days?' growls the voice on the other end.

'Sorry, Colin. I'm under a bit of pressure at the moment.'

'Ooh, poor you. That's a fucking shame, it really is. Problem is, I ain't got time for your little fucking dramas. We need an urgent meet. You and me. Usual place. One hour.'

'That's not going to be easy. I'm in Brighton at the moment.'

'Having a much-needed night off, are you? Enjoying the sights? Walking down the Golden Mile or whatever it's fucking called? I don't give a fuck. Get back here.'

'Have you got the, er, thing I requested?'

'The gun? Yeah, I got it.'

Which could, of course, mean anything.

'Because I'm nice, Fisher, I'm giving you until nine thirty to get that bony arse of yours here. See you then. And don't be late.'

And with that, he ends the call, making me wonder why on earth I ever chose to do business with a deranged psychopath like Colin Blisterfield.

39

Friday, 9.15 p.m.

Becca has set wheels in motion that now can't be stopped. By the end of the weekend, she'll either be reunited with her daughter or Elle will be dead, and perhaps Becca herself will be in prison if she goes through with what the kidnappers are demanding of her.

She prays Colin Blisterfield can supply her with a lead. That he might somehow be able to ID the kidnappers and free Elle. It's a long shot. And that's the big problem. Everything's a long shot.

She's back at home now, pacing the living room in darkness, her phone in her hand, waiting for news of any kind. She has a desperate need for a cigarette. She quit smoking fifteen years ago, having had a ten-a-day habit before then, and she hasn't had one since, but in a small act of rebellion, she bought a pack of twenty Marlboro Lights and a disposable lighter from a newsagent's on the way home, and she's contemplating lighting one. It might be a personal defeat, but right now she hasn't got much to lose. The chances of her coming out of the next couple of days intact are low, to say the least, and somehow she knows that smoking will alleviate the heart-thumping stress, if only just a little.

Her phone rings and she checks the screen. She was hoping it would be Blisterfield but realises it's probably too soon. And it's not him. It's a number she doesn't recognise, and she knows what that means.

As soon as she takes the call, the disguised voice kicks in. 'The police know that Elle's been abducted.'

Becca's heart does a lurching somersault. 'How? I haven't said anything, I swear it.'

'I know you haven't,' says the voice. 'But our information's good. We have people on the inside.'

It terrifies Becca that the people she's up against have these kinds of resources. 'What do you want me to do?' she asks, wondering if she's talking to the woman in the hat.

'If you receive a call from the police, don't make the mistake Henry Day's parents made. You tell them that Elle's fine and get them off the phone straight away.'

'Won't they follow me, or put me under surveillance?'

'If they do, you need to lose them. Elle's life depends on it.' A pause. 'Did you pick up the package we sent?'

Becca takes a deep breath. 'Yes, I did, but I can't do it. I can't kill someone.'

'Of course you can if it'll save your daughter. And it will.'

'If I kill Logan Quinn' – and just saying the words sounds odd to her ears – 'what guarantee do I have that you'll release Elle unharmed?'

'Because we always keep our word. We've let plenty of people go. The only one you ever hear about is Henry

273

Day. And that's because his parents were foolish enough to believe the police could help them. They couldn't. And they can't help you now.'

The voice is confident. Cold. In control. Not that of someone who's ever going to show compassion. But Elle has to believe that they're going to keep their word.

'Killing him will destroy me. I'll go to prison. Surely there must be some other way.'

'There'll be extenuating circumstances. Your daughter will be released and she'll be able to back up your story that you did it under duress. You have no choice, Becca. And think of the person you're getting rid of. A brutal mass murderer. You'll be doing the world a favour, instead of your usual trick of getting them off.'

Becca ignores the jibe, realising how much she hates this person. This woman. Because she knows it's a woman. Just like she knew Elle was a girl when she was in her belly. It's a gut instinct. But she also knows she's cornered, so she has to appear to cooperate.

'Look, I don't see how I'm going to be able to do it,' she says. 'I can't just slip it in his drink. He'll see me.'

'You have to be subtle. I don't know how you're going to do it, frankly. But do it you will. And as soon as we have independently verified confirmation that Quinn is dead, Elle will be released.'

'By which time I'll be behind bars without any leverage.'

'Unfortunately, Becca, that's the way the cookie crumbles.'

The cruel power in the voice makes Becca want to scream. She's desperate to tell this person that she knows who she is, but something stops her. If she is indeed one of the Vanishers, there's a good chance she'll keep her word and release Elle, and that's got to be worth everything else. She takes a deep breath. 'How am I meant to get the poison into the prison?'

'It's very simple, darling. In your mouth, like you were told in the note. They won't search there. Then distract him, put it in his drink and you're all done.'

In more ways than one, thinks Becca. Can she really do this? Murder a man in cold blood? The problem is, she doesn't know the answer. It's one thing thinking you'll do whatever it takes to protect your daughter, but to actually kill someone when they're sitting right in front of you requires a ruthlessness she's not entirely sure she can find.

'When are you seeing him next?' asks the voice, interrupting her thoughts.

'We're waiting to find out if they're going to put him in a safe house after what happened to him in prison. He's refusing to talk until they do. I wasn't planning on meeting him until after the decision's been made.'

'And when will that be?'

'I honestly don't know. It needs to be authorised at a very high level. I'm hoping soon. Within the next day or two. He definitely won't talk to anyone without going through me first, I promise you that.'

'Put pressure on your old boyfriend at the CPS to get things moving. That way, you get Elle back faster.'

Christ, Becca thinks. These people know everything.

'I'll be back in touch for an update.'

'I'm not doing anything until I've spoken to Elle.'

'We've had this conversation. You know that's not possible.'

'You're asking me to kill someone. Make it possible.' Becca knows she can't be a pushover. She has to at least keep some power. They need her. But once she's taken down Quinn, they won't.

'Becca, Becca,' chides the voice. 'You're not in a position to make demands. Don't you understand that? We have the most precious thing in your life in our possession, and any time we want to, we can destroy it.'

'Then my client talks. And you lose.'

There's a click and the call ends, and Becca stands there with the phone in her hand, knowing they have her over a barrel.

But they're in trouble too. The police know they've got Elle and it's possible they could already have clues to her whereabouts. She could try to delay things. And yet every minute that Elle is with them increases the danger she's in.

Becca's mind's a maelstrom of conflicting decisions, and she finally relents and lights a cigarette, puffing on it rapidly as she continues to pace the room, feeling utterly impotent, knowing there's nothing more she can do except talk to the police. And even that's out for now. The Vanishers have an inside contact. The moment Becca opens her mouth, they'll know.

She's trapped. Delaying the killing of Quinn is her only option.

And then suddenly it isn't, because as she's stubbing out

the cigarette in a saucer, her phone starts ringing again, and this time she recognises the number immediately. Even before Clyde starts speaking, she knows what he's going to say.

'Good news, Becca. Your client's out of Belmarsh and on his way to a safe house.'

He keeps talking, telling her the information they're going to need from Quinn, when they're going to need it, the contracts that will have to be signed, but Becca is only half listening, because she knows now that there can be no delay.

The next time she sees Logan Quinn, she will have to commit murder.

40

Friday, 9.31 p.m.

To describe Colin Blisterfield as a cunt would be an insult to cunts everywhere.

He's worse than that, and unfortunately I'm sitting across a desk from him in his oversized office on what should have been my Friday night off. I've been here close to a minute now while he stares at me with those beady little eyes of his in dead silence. It's a move that's designed to intimidate, and it works. I also know better than to break the silence. With Blisterfield, sometimes known in gangland circles (I think with some irony) as the Voice of Reason, or simply the Voice, you have to wait until he's ready.

'You didn't tell me she was my defence lawyer,' he barks, slamming his hand on the desk, causing me to flinch involuntarily.

'Who, Colin?'

'The woman whose daughter you took. Who do you fucking think? Mother Teresa?'

'That's because I didn't know,' I say calmly. With Colin Blisterfield, you have to always stay calm. Raise your voice to him, express exasperation, anything like that, and he turns his full poison on you. 'You wanted her client, Mr Quinn, dead. And it's the only way we can get to him.'

'I owe that woman a lot. She came to see me today. Very, very distressed. As you'd expect with her daughter in that situation. She wants me to find the perpetrators. Bring them to justice. I'm keen to help. Course I am. I'm not an animal.'

'If she does what she's told, she gets her kid back and all will be well. But it sounds like she's not doing what she's told.'

'It's a problem,' says Blisterfield, 'because the man she thinks is behind the kidnapping is the one who hired me to make the problem go away.'

This surprises me. 'So Logan Quinn doesn't have anything on you?'

'Not a fucking jot. As far as I know, he doesn't even know who I am. And that's why I've done so well, Fisher.' He wags a finger at me. 'Because I fly under the radar. I keep it on the down-low. You get me?'

'I get you,' I say, keeping my tone neutral and thinking that this whole job with Logan Quinn is extremely convoluted. Someone who wants to get Quinn hires Blisterfield to do the work, who then subcontracts it to me before I in turn subcontract it to Delvina and her old man. It's capitalism at its finest, although in the end I'm not making enough out of it, especially now that Delvina's trying to sting me for an extra fifty grand. I wonder how much Blisterfield's getting and guess that it's the lion's share. And he doesn't have to do a thing.

'I'm doing this job as a favour to this bloke, because he's a friend of mine,' he says, as if reading my mind.

'Well, I've paid my people the bulk of the money now, so there's no going back. Ms Barraclough's had the delivery of the poison and I expect she'll be doing the deed within the next day or two. By the way, I read somewhere that there was an attempt on Quinn's life in Belmarsh yesterday. Was that you?'

Now Blisterfield looks surprised. 'Nothing to do with me.' He shrugs. 'Maybe he's just made himself unpopular in there. It's a dog-eat-dog world in Belmarsh. I was there myself for a couple of weeks.'

This is interesting, because I genuinely thought yesterday was Blisterfield's doing when I saw it in the news section of my phone earlier this evening. It would be typical of him to get impatient. 'It seems like a big coincidence,' I say, because it does.

He grunts and shakes his head. 'I don't like the way this whole thing's going.'

Like I care you, you bald fucker.

He fixes me with one of his death stares, and once again I have this terrible feeling that he's somehow reading my mind, which would really not be good. 'So, you're using the Vanishers for this, are you?' he growls.

'I'm using people I know are reliable.'

'That's not what I asked, is it, Fisher? I asked, are you using the Vanishers? Answer yes or no. Which is it?'

I make it my business not to give away any information I don't have to, but when Blisterfield's in this kind of mood, it doesn't pay to hold back. 'Yeah, I'm using the Vanishers.'

'See, that wasn't so hard, was it?' He sits back in his throne-like chair and gives me a leering smile. 'You're a dark horse, ain't you, Fisher? Getting involved with people like that. Got your copper fingers in lots of pies, ain't you? The fucking tales you could tell, eh?'

I try to hold his mocking gaze, but it's never easy having a staring competition with a man who once sucked a rival's eye out.

'I'm reliable,' I say, 'and that's why you use me.'

He just keeps staring at me, allowing the silence to get heavier.

Then he farts. A loud, trumpet-like blast, which he ignores entirely as he picks up his drink – a brandy by the looks of things (he hasn't offered me one) – and takes a satisfied gulp.

Blisterfield is renowned in male underworld circles for practising what has best been described as power farting. This is where the farter shows his general contempt for the fartee by letting rip in his presence without even bothering to acknowledge the fact. Apparently he got it from old-school Libyan dictator Colonel Gaddafi, who was reputed to have unleashed an almost constant barrage of wind when meeting Tony Blair in his Bedouin tent. Blair just sat there and took it meekly, thereby making himself look subservient to the other guy.

At least Gaddafi did it in a big, well-ventilated tent, though, and not in an airless office, and at close quarters. Thankfully, this one of Blisterfield's doesn't smell and, like everyone else, I don't acknowledge it, just sit there and wait for this mentally unhinged lunatic to continue.

He draws out the silence, farts again (a small one this time), then says suddenly: 'What do you want a gun for, Fisher? Planning murder, are ya?'

'Not me, Colin. One of the people I'm using for this job needs to get rid of the other one.'

'Why?'

I knew he'd ask me this, but in my experience it's best to get bad news out of the way at the beginning, while you're still in control of the narrative. 'The one who's got to die has been fingered as a possible suspect to the police. He needs to be got rid of to contain matters.'

'How many are involved in this apart from you?'

'Two,' I lie. If I tell him it's three, he won't like it.

'Best to get rid of both of them. This whole thing's going to blow up when Quinn gets hit. Less people who know about it the better.'

'Even if they're caught, it won't get back to me,' I say hastily. 'There are plenty of layers between us.'

'I hope so, Fisher. I don't like loose ends.' He gives me a look like I might well be one of them. 'I want this job done fast, all right? It's a real pity about Becca. She's an amazing woman, but what's done is done. Hopefully the law will look kindly on her.'

'They'll take into account that she was acting under duress,' I say, thinking that she deserves all she gets for helping keep a man like Blisterfield at liberty.

'They'd better,' he growls. 'How can you punish a mother

like that when she's doing it for her daughter? You're looking after the daughter properly, right?'

'Of course,' I say.

'She'd better not be harmed, Fisher. I never hurt women.'

Which isn't strictly true. He once had a female accountant garrotted when it became clear she knew too much about some of his shadier financial dealings.

'She won't be,' I tell him, although I'm not sure I trust Delvina on that front. I know she has a thing for women, and not an altogether healthy one.

'I've got a gun you can buy from me, Fisher. It'll cost you three grand. I'll take it off the balance of your money. Sounds fair? Course it does. Collect it on the way out and make sure you don't leave your prints all over it.'

'Thank you, Colin,' I say, knowing I've got no choice but to agree. 'I'm sure I'll manage.'

Blisterfield gives me one of his death stares. Sarcasm can mean a couple of broken fingers minimum if he decides it warrants it. This time, thank God, it seems it doesn't.

'You fucking better do, Fisher,' he says coldly, leaving me in no doubt what will happen to me if I don't. 'You fucking better do.'

41

Friday, 9.50 p.m.

'I can't believe I did this,' says Vincent as he and Delvina stare down at Marv's body.

Delvina can't believe it either. She was sure that when it came down to it, he simply didn't have the capacity to commit murder. 'We had to do it,' she says, giving his neck an affectionate squeeze.

Marv sits slumped against the shed door, his head leant forward, one end of a crossbow bolt sticking out of the top of his head, the other jutting out of the underside of his chin where it exited. A second bolt sticks out of his chest. Delvina is impressed with her husband's shooting. There's very little blood, which equates to very little mess in the Chrysler, thank goodness, although she'll still get Vincent to give the interior a good clean tomorrow.

'We won't be able to fit him in the back of the van with that bolt sticking out of his head,' she says. 'And it'll play havoc with the interior.'

'I won't be able to get it out,' says Vincent, the anxiety and guilt obvious in his voice. 'It'll be stuck fast.'

'Then you'll need to take his head off, pet. There's no other way. There's an axe in the shed.'

'Oh Jesus, Goddess, please don't make me do that.'

She strokes his neck, makes soothing sounds. 'This is a time for mental strength, pet. And physical. And I haven't got the physical. That's why you have to do it. I'll take care of him when we're back at the office.'

Vincent takes a deep breath and exhales condensed air. It's cold out here tonight, and deadly silent. 'Okay,' he says at last.

Together they move Marv's body out of the way of the door and onto its side, so that it's resting on the shed's concrete foundations. He's cold now, but not yet as cold as Delvina's usual clients when she takes delivery of them. She waits, drinking in the sight of helpless, dead Marv while Vincent goes into the shed and reappears with a large wood axe.

She steps back and watches as her husband takes another deep breath, lifts the axe high above his head and brings it down on Marv's neck, narrowly missing the end of the crossbow bolt. It's a good, solid blow, but not nearly enough to complete the task, and it takes him another three goes, during which he also chops off the end of the bolt, before the blade finally strikes the concrete and Marv's head rolls off.

Vincent stands there leaning on the axe and panting, deliberately looking away from his work. Delvina can see tears in his eyes, but she's impressed that again he's shown himself capable of ruthlessness.

285

The decapitation has produced very little blood, since it's largely coagulated in the hours since Marv died, and as her husband continues to look away, Delvina leans over and gently picks up the head by the feathered end of the crossbow bolt. She wishes she could take it home and embalm it, humiliating him even in death.

But needs must. Giving the head a last, lustful smile, she carefully places it in the big wicker shoulder bag she often carries with her, and which tonight is empty aside from a few bits and pieces, then turns to Vincent and asks him if he's okay.

He nods, not looking her way.

'I'm sorry it had to come to this,' she says. 'If he hadn't talked, we wouldn't have had to do it.'

'Let's just get on with it,' he says, and together they slowly haul Marv's body round the side of the house and over to the Chrysler, which is backed up in the driveway as far it can go to make the job easier. It's hard work and it exhausts both of them, particularly Delvina, who's never been keen on physical exercise, but finally they get him into the vehicle, along with the head, which almost certainly wouldn't have fitted if it was still attached to the body.

When they're done, she rifles through Marv's pockets and finds his keys. 'We need to get rid of his car,' she says, handing them to Vincent. 'Follow me out of here and we'll dump it somewhere out of the way. But there's something I need to do before we go.'

She grabs the latest copy of the *Evening Standard* from behind the driver's seat and heads into the house.

It's pleasantly warm in there. Marv must have switched the heating on earlier. Delvina considers turning the thermostat down, given how extortionate energy prices are these days, but relents. She doesn't want Elle accidentally freezing to death in the night. She needs to be kept alive, at least for now.

Going up to the bedroom, she takes a leather studded paddle from a drawer in the clothes cupboard where she keeps some of the implements she uses from time to time on her husband, then heads down to the basement.

As she unlocks the door and opens it a crack, she calls out to Elle to put her blindfold on. She waits until the girl calls out that she's ready, then steps inside.

Their prisoner is sitting on the bed, still in her scrubs, the blanket pulled up over her, even though the radiator's on full blast. Delvina takes a few seconds just to stare at this pretty young woman, savouring what she's got in store for her tomorrow when all this is done.

'Is everything okay?' asks Elle nervously.

'Everything's good,' says Delvina, deepening her voice a little so that it's at least partly disguised. 'Would you mind just standing up? I want to take a photo of you holding this evening's newspaper for your mum.'

'Is my mum all right?' Elle asks, getting to her feet.

Delvina steps forward and hands her the paper, positioning it so that the front cover and date are visible for the camera. She notices that Elle smells a bit. 'Your mum's fine,' she says, turning her burner phone to video and pressing record.

She films Elle standing there in silence for several seconds, focusing on the newspaper date and the chains attached to her ankle and wrist. She knows that this video might end up as evidence later, so she's careful only to film the wall behind the girl and nothing else.

Then, without warning, she steps forward and, still filming, strikes Elle hard on the side of the head with the paddle, sending her falling to the floor with an anguished cry.

Delvina lingers on her for a second as she cowers on the ground, then stops the film and puts the paddle down. 'Sorry I had to do that,' she says in a sympathetic voice, helping Elle up and guiding her back to the bed. 'Your mum just needs some encouraging. She's not moving as fast as she needs to.' Elle begins to cry and Delvina gently strokes her hair, imagining the excitement of strangling this vulnerable young woman with her bare hands. 'There, there,' she says. 'It'll be okay. You'll be home soon. I'm going to bring you some warm water and soap so you can wash yourself. Okay?'

'Thank you,' says Elle, calmer now.

It's so easy, Delvina thinks, to manipulate these young women. To terrify them one minute then make them grateful to you the next because you haven't hit them a second time. It strikes her then that when she retires somewhere in eastern Europe, she'd like to abduct a young woman like Elle and hold her prisoner for months, or even years, doing with her anything she wants. Any torture; any torment; any perversion.

The thought gives her a shiver of anticipation as she picks up the paddle and the newspaper and, promising to be back shortly, exits the room.

As the door closes, Elle knows for certain that something is badly wrong. Her face stings from the shock of the blow, but that's the least of her problems. What scares her most is that her captor made very little attempt to disguise her voice, and there was something truly unnerving in it. Lust. The woman – whoever she is – was sexually aroused when she was touching Elle. And that spells danger, because the whole dynamic of this hostage-taking has changed. The man who was looking after her – who she could at least reason with – is gone. And these other two are unpleasant at best. Hitting her like that was sadistic. Elle understands it's to scare her mum, but she knows Mum will already be pulling out all the stops to get them their money, so there was no need.

But amidst the fear, she feels something else. Hope. Because if the woman is aroused around her and attempts some kind of sexual assault, it also offers her an opportunity to escape. It'll require a steel she's never had to show before, but Elle knows that it could well mean the difference between life and death.

42

Friday, 10.10 p.m.

Having finally picked up the supposedly untraceable gun in the underground car park beneath Colin Blisterfield's club, the Crafty Fox, I'm finally on the way to my next meeting.

There's a voicemail from Cotton on my regular phone asking me to call him back, and since it's a good twenty-minute drive to Misty's place, I do.

'Everything all right, Cott?' I ask him, hoping he's long gone from Misty's.

'Where are you?' he asks

I'm suddenly paranoid. 'I'm on the way back from Brighton. I got caught in traffic. Are you still on your date?'

'I had to cut it short. I'm back in the office, and I've been on the phone to the assistant DG. We've identified Elle Barraclough's parents now, and guess what? Her mum's Rebecca Barraclough. The big-shot defence lawyer who got that killer off a few years back, the one who went on to kill again.'

'Fancy that,' I say, resisting the urge to add that she probably deserves it, and hoping that they haven't established a link between Barraclough and Logan Quinn, because that would be a real problem. 'So what's the plan now?'

'The dad's estranged and lives in Australia, so no point talking to him. But the DG wants to monitor developments tonight before we approach Barraclough.'

'What does that even mean? Monitor developments?' I say, playing my part as the man desperate to get this case solved. 'It sounds like the usual bureaucrat-speak to me.'

'It means we keep the phones manned overnight in case we get a call from Barraclough reporting the kidnapping. But right now, without that call, there's no direct evidence that there's been a crime. We've set up surveillance on Cunningham's place and I've got people tracking down possible associates. The DG's still deciding whether it's worth putting surveillance on the mother to check her movements.'

That's something I definitely don't want, because it'll ruin everything. 'Do you need me back in the office now?' I ask him, deliberately yawning.

'No, you've done enough, but I will need you back in first thing. I'll try to sort some overtime for you.'

The amount of money this job's costing me, I might well need it. 'I just want these people caught,' I tell him. 'Keep me posted if there are any developments. I'll leave my phone on.'

'You'll be the first person I'll call,' he says. 'We're going to get these bastards now, Fish. I can feel it.'

And worryingly, this time I know he's right.

*   *   *

Misty's apartment is above a dry-cleaner's in a strip of shops wedged between two big housing estates in a not especially attractive part of Streatham, and twenty minutes later, I'm inside her front door. She's wearing pyjama bottoms and a sweatshirt and is still heavily made-up after her evening with Cotton. Misty's always been an attractive woman, but there's a weariness in her features that I guess comes from being ground down by the vagaries of life. Right now, I know the feeling.

The first thing she asks as we stand in her tiny sitting room is 'Have you got the money?'

'Of course I have,' I tell her, slightly miffed at the quality of her reception. 'I'm a man of my word.' I reach into my jacket pocket and pull out the envelope that I've been carrying round with me all day.

'Why are you wearing gloves?' she asks, and I can see she's nervous.

'It's cold out. And it's also good security not to leave your fingerprints on envelopes containing illicit payments. You don't think I'm going to hurt you, do you?' I add, genuinely surprised.

'I thought I knew you, Fish, but it turns out I really don't.' There's an edge to her voice; it's almost contempt. 'I don't trust you.'

'Well, you'd better count your money then,' I say, more offended than I'm letting on. I've already had one rejection tonight. Before I left Brighton to drive back here, I mentioned in passing for a second time to Elaine about the possibility of a drink one night when all this is over, and she brushed me off, telling me it was best to, in her words, 'keep things official'.

Misty counts the money carefully, keeping one eye on me as if she half expects me to attack her.

'Your turn,' I tell her. 'Where's the drive?'

She reaches into her pyjama pocket and reluctantly hands it over. 'I don't know what you've got planned for Adam, but if it's bad, I'll never forgive you.'

'I just want the opportunity to get my old job back,' I say, 'and this is a little insurance. Nothing more.' I give her a look. 'You definitely recorded tonight's conversation?'

'Just like you requested. We were in bed and I left the room. I didn't hear what was said.'

I'm not sure I trust her either, so I connect my phone to the device using Bluetooth and download the audio onto an app. There's a three-and-a-half-minute recording from tonight, which would be about the length of the conversation I had with Cotton earlier, but just to make certain it's the right one, I take a couple of steps away from Misty and put the phone to my ear. Sure enough, Cotton's dulcet tones are soon ringing out and incriminating him as, at the very least, a serious blabbermouth.

I slip both phone and drive into my pocket. 'Thanks, Misty. Your work here is done.'

'To be honest, I wish I'd never met you,' she says, giving me a look of utter distaste.

I meet her gaze. 'Sadly, it's too late for that now. And by the way, if you say a word about this to anyone, you'll be opening yourself up to a whole host of criminal charges.

Deception for one. Soliciting's another, since you got Cotton interested in you under false pretences. Then there's illegally recording a police officer in the pursuit of his duty, and you can go down for that.' I made that last one up, but Misty looks suitably scared. 'Or you can keep your mouth shut, go find another man and get on with your life. Which would be by far the best move.'

I give her a long stare and she looks away. 'Just get out,' she says with a weary sigh. 'I never want to hear from you again.'

So that's what I do. It's 10.35 and I'm shattered, but I still have one more meeting and I need to hurry.

As always, there's no rest for the wicked.

43

Friday, 10.50 p.m.

Becca's still pacing the floor of her house like some sort of caged animal, eight cigarettes in now, when she gets a text message from an unknown number.

The text contains a video, and the moment she opens it, she gasps out loud. It's Elle, standing against a wall in her nurse's scrubs, a blindfold covering her eyes, chains attached to her wrist and ankle. She looks so young and scared that it makes Becca want to cry. But that would show weakness, and she can't afford that right now. As she watches, the camera focuses in on the copy of the *Evening Standard* Elle is holding, clearly showing that it's today's late edition.

And then, without warning, something black flies through the air and Elle cries out as she's knocked to the floor.

Becca gasps as the camera pans towards Elle. She's conscious but lying there looking terrified.

Then the film ends.

Becca's still in shock at what she's just seen when the phone rings in her hand. It's the same number from which the video was sent, and she answers immediately. 'You hurt my daughter and I will fucking kill you,' she hisses, anger taking over now.

'Calm down,' says the mocking voice. 'Your daughter's fine. That was just a little slap. Nothing compared to what we can do.'

'Why did you do it, you bitch? You didn't need to.'

There's silence on the end of the phone and Becca realises her mistake instantly. She's not meant to know that she's talking to a woman, but the kidnapper's reaction confirms her suspicions.

'You think I'm a woman, do you? And what makes you think that?'

'You're the one from the video footage who drugs the victims in the street. That's my guess.'

'I'd keep the guessing to yourself if I were you. I sent you that video to give you an extra incentive not to talk to the police, and to do what you're told regarding Quinn. I've heard he wants to be moved to a safe house. Is he there yet?'

Becca decides not to lie. 'They're moving him tonight, I believe.'

'So you need to be quick. Are you seeing him tomorrow?'

'I'll try to.'

'Make sure you do. This needs to be done as soon as possible. Then you get your daughter back alive and unharmed.'

'You've already harmed her. Touch one more hair on her head and I'll hunt you down. And I've got influential friends who'll help me.'

'You do your job tomorrow, you'll get her back alive. You don't, you'll never see her again. And don't bother with threats,' the woman adds contemptuously, before ending the call.

Becca can't bring herself to watch the video again, but she knows what she has to do. Bringing up Colin Blisterfield's name on her phone, she texts it through to him with an accompanying message: *THIS IS WHAT THEY'VE JUST DONE TO MY ONLY CHILD. PLEASE HELP.*

He calls her back before she has a chance to call him.

'Christ, that's a fucking liberty doing that to a defenceless woman,' he snarls, 'and a nurse as well. I've got feelers everywhere, babe, and I've put the message out there that if anyone hurts your daughter, they'll be getting a visit from me very, very soon.'

'But you've got nothing yet?'

He sighs. 'Not yet. I told you it would take time. I sent a couple of people to talk to that bloke you mentioned, Jeff whatever his name is . . .'

'Barris.'

'That's him. He's got nothing to do with this.'

'Are you sure?'

'One hundred per cent. My boys aren't the sort of people you lie to.'

Becca takes a deep breath. 'I'm running out of time, Colin. They want me to kill Logan Quinn tomorrow. What am I going to do?' She hates feeling so helpless, but what choice does she have?

'I'll be straight with you, babe. You may have to do him. I can't see any other choice unless I strike lucky tonight and find out who these people are who've got her. But they'll know not to hurt her, because that would mean falling out with me, and that's not a good move for anyone.'

This is not what Becca wants to hear. 'I'm not a killer, Colin.'

'We're all killers, babe. Just that some of us don't know it yet. Listen, if you go through with it, the courts will be lenient, especially after all the mistakes the Old Bill have made with the Vanishers. I'll set you up with lawyers and there'll be no way you'll do any jail time.'

'Please keep trying. I'll be eternally grateful, you know that. I'll do anything to get her back.'

'You'll get her back, I promise.'

'You don't know that, though.'

'I give you my guarantee,' he says with total confidence, and in spite of herself, Becca feels a sense of relief.

'Thank you,' she whispers.

'I'm on this, babe. I won't stop. Day or night. Now go to bed and get some sleep. If I hear anything, I'll call.'

And then he's gone and she's standing alone, knowing that the fate of her whole world lies in the hands of a violent, psychotic gangster.

44

Friday, 11.10 p.m.

The night's turned cold and I'm sitting in my car with the heating blaring out in a secluded corner of a car park facing rugby fields somewhere in Sunbury. We're on the edge of London here, close to green-belt land, a suitably quiet place for an illicit rendezvous, and thankfully there's no one about. Even so, I'm jumpy, and every time I hear a car drive past on the main road, I get a nervous twinge, because as you know, I'm currently in possession of an illegal firearm that I want to be rid of as fast as possible. Once upon a time, when there were actually such things as real-life police patrols, there's no way I'd have considered doing an exchange like this in public, but let's be honest, I've got a hell of a lot more chance of seeing some dogging action, or even a ghost, than I do a couple of inquisitive uniforms, so I try to stay calm and warm while I wait for Delvina, who's already ten minutes late.

I pass the time staring at various crap on my phone and it's another ten minutes before a vehicle finally pulls into the car park, and I put the phone down, instinctively sliding lower in my seat. But then I see that it's Delvina's white Audi convertible, and it's her behind the wheel.

Typical Delvina, she parks a good twenty yards away, and I know that she'll wait for me to come over to her, however long it takes. It's all a power play with her. She has to feel like she's the one in control.

As it happens, I'm keen to get the hell out of here as soon as possible, so I reach down under the seat and grab the brown paper bag containing the gun, putting it in my jacket pocket, then position the mini flash drive containing Cotton's various musings on the Vanishers case so that it's tucked into the edge of my jeans pocket. Then I get out and walk over to the Audi as nonchalantly as possible.

The interior smells of warm, fragrant perfume, and as always, Delvina seems to ooze a thick, dark sexuality that I genuinely have to work hard to resist, even now. She turns to me with a knowing smile and a glint in her eyes that I really don't like.

'Well?' she says. 'Where is it?'

Now, as you can imagine, I don't trust Delvina an inch, and I'm aware that she could be recording this conversation, or even filming it, just in case she has to turn on me later, so I've also brought along a hand-held bug detector that lights up if it comes into close contact with an active listening device or camera, and I run it round the car like a wand.

'What the fuck are you doing?' she demands, looking very put out.

'Being safe and secure,' I say. The bug finder lights up

when it gets near her, but that'll be her phone and I can see that she can't be filming me with that.

'Arsehole,' she sneers as I put it back, then take out the bag containing the gun and hand it to her. It's an old Ruger 9 mm.

She drops her death stare and tears open the bag with all the eagerness of a kid presented with a much-anticipated Christmas present, which is what I've been counting on, because as she removes the pistol, I swiftly take the flash drive condemning Cotton between thumb and forefinger and stuff it into the gap between the two seat cushions, shielding the movement with my body. Delvina doesn't see a thing; she's too busy gawking in awe at the pistol.

The magazine is taped to the side of the gun, and she pulls it free. 'Is there a round in the chamber?'

I shake my head and watch as she points the gun at the floor and racks the slide, just to make sure, then inserts the magazine and racks the slide again so that the gun's ready to fire. There's a gleeful confidence in her movements that demonstrates categorically that she knows exactly what she's doing, just like she boasted yesterday.

I lean over until I'm close to her ear, conscious of her gorgeous scent, and whisper: 'It's a full magazine, more than enough for what you need.' And enough, I also think, if it comes to a stand-off and she attempts a Bonnie-and-Clyde style shoot-out with the cops, which would be a perfect result for me. 'It's also untraceable. Now, if you're happy, I'm off. You'll get the rest of your money as soon as I know the job's done.' I have an urge to kiss her neck – the

301

closeness of her pale, soft skin acting as an unwanted aph-rodisiac – but force myself to pull away.

She notices, though. She always notices. 'You still want me, don't you, baby?' she purrs, turning the now loaded gun so the barrel is pointed vaguely in my direction and giving me a playful smile.

'No,' I say, finding it hard to take my eyes off the weapon. 'I don't. Now, why don't you put that thing away?'

She chuckles. 'Why? Scared I'll use it on you?'

It's this comment that confirms she can't be recording this. It'd be too incriminating. I give her a withering look. 'Even you're not that stupid.' And with that, I climb out of the car, a tiny part of me nervous that she *might* actually be stupid enough to put a bullet in me, and keep on walking without looking back.

One minute later, I'm out of there and driving home, eager to get back to the relative safety of my flat. It's been another long day, with some mistakes on my part (particu-larly that little slip with the Syed kid this morning), but I'm still here and in one piece, and no one's any the wiser about my role in all this. I even get a text from DC Elaine while I'm driving back, asking how we're getting on with the case.

I don't bother answering. I'm still disappointed with her brush-off. I'll text her back in the morning.

It's just turned midnight when I finally get home. My flat's on the first floor of a rambling detached Edwardian house that was once a primary school, which I've rented for the past five years because there's no way on earth I'd be able to afford to buy it. I love the place, though, and I'll miss it when I finally leave.

I park in my designated spot, round the side of the house, then climb out of the car feeling tired and yet pleased with the way things are going.

Which is the exact moment the punch comes, right out of nowhere, sending me slamming into the open door.

45

Friday, 11.40 p.m.

Before I've even got a chance to react, I'm yanked up by the collar so I'm not quite face to face with a man I immediately recognise as Delvina's toerag of a husband, Vinnie, and then hit squarely in the face with two more punches in rapid succession. Vinnie lets go of my collar, and as I drop my keys, he shoves me back into the car. Because I'm still in a state of shock and everything's happening so fast, I make no effort to stop myself, and end up sprawled over the two front seats with the handbrake digging into the small of my back.

Vinnie's straight in after me like some kind of rabid dog, his knee digging into my groin, his face looming in front of mine, and I think he's going to hit me again, but instead he produces a flick knife from underneath his jacket, clicking open the blade, which, though only about four inches long, is more than enough to cause me serious damage, especially with a lunatic like this guy behind it. A second later, the tip of the blade is pressed against my cheek.

Thankfully, he makes no move to stab me, and I stay

stock-still, knowing that fighting really isn't an option right now. If it ever was.

'You're McBride, right?' he hisses, his mouth close enough that I can smell his breath. It's stale, like he hasn't flossed in a while.

'What?' I say. 'Who's McBride?'

He looks momentarily confused, although still angry as well. 'Don't fuck me about. What were you doing just now with my missus? Are you fucking her?'

The bastard obviously followed me here, probably by planting a tracker on my car while I was talking to Delvina. Very sneaky, and something I really wasn't expecting, especially from a lowlife like him.

'Course I'm not fucking her,' I say, careful not to move and get myself jabbed.

'You were kissing her earlier. In the car park.'

'I wasn't,' I tell him indignantly, beginning to get pissed off now that the shock of the attack is wearing off. 'I was whispering something in her ear because I don't trust her not to record what I was saying.'

I can see his anger fading now as he realises he might have made a mistake, so I seize the initiative and keep talking, knowing I'm going to have to come clean. 'I'm the man who supplies her with information for your little sideline, and I was helping her out tonight. So why don't you just take that knife away from my face and we'll forget this ever happened?'

He removes the knife from my cheek but still stays on top of me. 'What's your name?' he demands.

'You don't need to know my name,' I tell him. 'McBride's as good a one as any.'

The knife moves back towards my face and his expression turns cold. 'Tell me your name or I'll cut you. And don't bullshit. Because I can easily check in your wallet.'

This is bad. I really don't want to tell him who I am, for very obvious reasons, but I'm also aware that his old nickname was Slice, on account of the fact that he once sliced open a man's face almost from ear to ear with a Stanley knife, so his threat needs to be taken seriously. I take the least bad option under the circumstances. 'My name's Fisher. Now, if you want to receive the rest of your money for the Barraclough job, you'd better let me go.'

He leans forward, still crushing me. 'You know her mum's the defence lawyer for Colin Blisterfield, don't you?'

'I'm aware of that,' I say carefully, not sure how the hell he knows.

'Well, no one told us. If he ever finds out we were involved, we'll be mincemeat.'

'He won't. Don't worry.'

'That's easy for you to say, Fisher. You're not the one doing the hard work. You just take a nice big cut for doing fuck all. Was it you who told Delvina that the police were on to Marv?'

I notice he uses the past tense here, and I wonder if Cunningham's already dead. In which case, why did Delvina need the gun? 'Yeah,' I say, 'because they are.'

'How did they know about him?'

'He was shooting his mouth off to some mates. A guy

called Leon Dennay gave us his name when we arrested him over something else,' I add, seeing no reason to protect Dennay.

Vinnie shakes his head. 'Fucking idiot. Why did he have to do that? He was on to a nice little earner with us.'

'Yeah, well. He did. And you need to sort that situation. It's either you or him.'

'I've already sorted it.'

'He's dead?'

He nods, his face dropping.

'What happened?'

'It doesn't matter,' he says, glaring at me. 'He's gone. Who are you working for?'

'I work for myself.'

'You know what I mean. You didn't want the girl kidnapped for yourself. Someone else wanted to blackmail her mum and they hired you. So who's that someone else? Because it must be someone with some fucking big balls to risk upsetting Colin "the Voice" Blisterfield.'

I'm surprised he's bright enough to put all this together, and since I'm already in for a penny, I may as well chuck in the whole pound. 'Get off me and I'll tell you. And it *is* someone with some big fucking balls.'

Vinnie hesitates, reluctant to give up his advantage, but then he climbs off me and steps out of the car, keeping the knife down by his side.

My face stings from where I've been punched, and when I wipe it, a smear of blood appears on my hand. My nose is bleeding, but I don't think it's broken, which is something.

307

As I climb out of the car, I can't believe that I've now been assaulted twice in the space of barely twenty-four hours, and this time round I most definitely came off worst.

'Well,' he says as we stand facing each other in the shadows of the trees bordering my block, 'who is it?'

I look around, but we're alone here, with only the sound of the occasional passing car. 'Colin Blisterfield,' I say, 'is the man I'm working for.'

'It can't fucking be. The girl's mum is his lawyer.'

'That's who it is. I'm not bullshitting. But I'd appreciate it if you didn't say anything to Delvina.'

He seems to think about this for a few moments, then takes a step forward so he's right up close, glaring at me, and I involuntarily flinch. 'Then why does the girl – the daughter – have to die?' he hisses. 'Why does Blisterfield want that?'

I step back and frown. This is news to me. 'What are you talking about?'

'Delvina told me that when all this is over, we've got to kill the girl.'

'Well, she's wrong. In fact, Blisterfield stated he wanted her released unharmed as soon as the job's done. And that's what I told your wife. If either of you kill her, we're all in real trouble.'

'Shit,' he says, looking confused. 'Why did she tell me that, then?'

'I don't know, and I need to speak to her right now.'

'Don't,' he says hurriedly. 'She'll know I talked to you.' He looks scared, which would be amusing under different circumstances, but now just annoys me.

'She's got to know not to do anything,' I tell him. 'You leave now, and I'll call her later. That girl can't die, right? You understand that? If she does, we're all dead.'

He nods. 'I know that. I never wanted her to.'

We both stare at each other.

'Sorry about hitting you,' he says.

'There are easier ways of getting the answers you want,' I say with a sigh, thinking that this guy's almost like a child. 'You'd better go.'

'Do you mind if I just get my tracker?' he says sheepishly.

What am I going to say? 'Be my guest.'

He crouches down, and I have to step back as he takes it out from under the rear passenger-side wheel arch, the same place that he planted the one on Elle Barraclough's Mini.

'Cheers,' he says with a nod, as if we've just been shooting the breeze rather than him ambushing and assaulting me, and then he's off out down the driveway and back onto the road. I watch him disappear, standing in the shadows and rubbing my face, wondering why the hell Delvina told him that the girl had to die, and thinking too that by coming here, Vinnie Steele-Perkins has just signed his own death warrant. Because it's far too dangerous to let him live now he knows who I am.

I'm just trying to work out how I can bring this about when my phone starts ringing, and lo and behold, just as I think things can't sink any lower, the snarling T-rex appears on my screen. It's SLAPHEAD WANKER calling.

I almost don't answer it, but if Colin Blisterfield's calling at midnight, it's more than my life's worth to ignore him. 'Is everything okay?' I ask quietly, putting the phone to my ear.

'No it fucking isn't,' snarls Blisterfield. 'I've had Becca on the phone. Apparently your people sent her a nasty video showing her daughter getting smacked about with some kind of fucking bondage toy. She's really upset.'

'I didn't know anything about that, Colin,' I say. 'I can only imagine they were doing it to encourage the mother to deal with Quinn, but there's no call for it.'

'That's right, Fisher. There's no fucking call for it. And if it happens again, I'll be on *you* with a bondage toy. See how you like it.'

'I'll get on to them now,' I say, trying to banish the picture of Blisterfield assaulting me with a bondage toy out of my mind. 'And I'll make sure it doesn't happen again.'

Blisterfield growls, a low, dog-like sound that seems to stretch for a long time.

Then he ends the call, leaving me suddenly feeling very, very tired.

46

Saturday, 12.10 a.m.

When Delvina pulls into the funeral home's car park, she notices that the Chrysler isn't there. She dropped Vincent here in it after they'd dumped Marv's car, and he didn't say anything about going back out. Normally this wouldn't bother her, but with everything that's going on at the moment, especially what happened with Marv, she knows that he's probably feeling under a lot of pressure.

She's about to give him a call when one of her other phones starts ringing. She reaches inside her bag and pulls out the one she uses for her communication with Fisher.

'Yes,' she says, making no effort to hide her impatience.

'The girl's okay, right?'

Delvina frowns, wondering why he's asking this now. 'Of course.'

'Good. Because my employer has specifically said that if her mother does what she's told, she has to be released alive and well.'

'What's suddenly brought this on?' she demands.

'I heard about the video you sent her mother.'

'How?'

'Let's just say my client indirectly knows the mother. And he's called me to reiterate that he wants the daughter unharmed and looked after properly. I'll tell you something else. My client is a very dangerous and vengeful man, so if anything happens to her, he'll come after you.'

Delvina doesn't like the sound of this at all. It's too dangerous to let the girl go. Unlike all the other individuals they've snatched, this one has heard her speak.

So one way or another, she has to die.

'She'll be fine,' she says.

'She'd better be. You're not getting the balance until she's released.'

'That's not what we agreed, Fisher.'

'Suffice to say I don't trust you, Delvina. I know what you're like with young women, remember?'

She knows what he's referring to. A few years back, not long after they'd started the abduction gig, Delvina got a bit too carried away with a young masochistic female sub she'd met online, beating her savagely and finally strangling her unconscious. Afterwards, the sub tried to blackmail her, threatening to report her to the police, and she'd had no choice but to call on Fisher, with his police credentials, to warn her off. Of course the bastard has never let her forget it. 'I told you,' she hisses. 'The girl will be all right.'

'Good. And by the way, is your husband home yet?'

She bristles. 'Why do you ask?'

'Because he paid me a visit tonight. He put a tracker on

312

my car when I was meeting you and ambushed me when I got home. He was asking all sorts of questions.'

Delvina expresses genuine surprise. 'I'll bring him under control,' she tells Fisher. 'He won't say anything.'

'He was also talking about Marv in the past tense. He says the problem's already been fixed. Has it?'

She sees no reason not to tell him, since it was something he requested anyway. 'He's gone, yes.'

'And where's the body?'

'None of your business. But it'll never be found. And we've got rid of his car too, so there's nothing linking him to us.'

Fisher is silent for a couple of seconds, which is unlike him. 'Why do you still need the gun, then?' he asks eventually.

'Because it's useful protection right now,' she says, which is probably as close to the truth as any answer she could give him.

'Well, you might want to think about using it on your husband and making him disappear as well.'

'And how will that look after what happened to my last one? Forget it, Fisher. I'll get him under control and we'll take a nice long holiday after this. And by the way, just in case you were getting any ideas, I've got plenty of evidence that'll bury you, and if anything happens to me, I have ways of making sure it comes out. So it's definitely in your interests to keep me alive and at liberty.'

'Just do your fucking job and stop leaving a mess everywhere,' he says, and ends the call.

Delvina allows herself a smile, pleased that she's riled him, even if what she said wasn't true. The fact is, she's got very little on him. He's too slippery for that. But it's worth sowing the seed of doubt. And at least now she knows where Vincent is. The sly dog. It seems he's got a lot more nous than she gave him credit for. And that could be very dangerous.

47

Saturday, 12.30 a.m.

Do I think Delvina's got evidence implicating me in all this? No, I don't. I'm extremely careful when I speak to her, and when we do talk frankly about our crimes, as we did just then, she incriminates herself just as much as me, and I'm pretty certain she'd be too paranoid to keep any physical evidence of her own confessions.

However, having said that, I'd still vastly prefer both her and her husband dead than alive. Because there's no way they're going to avoid being identified. They've already made some big mistakes, and I'm pretty certain they've made another one tonight by getting rid of Marv's car. As soon as Delvina told me that was what they'd done, I got an instant bad feeling, because unless they dumped it just round the corner from their safe house (and I'm betting there's no way they would have done that, or changed the plates on it), it would have passed through at least one ANPR camera. That ANPR camera would have then sent a message to the national ANPR data centre, known to us as the NADC, flagging up that it was on the move and taking a photo of the driver, who, I'm guessing, wouldn't be Marv. It's another nail in the Vanishers' coffin, and it means that the time Delvina and Vinnie have left could well be measured in hours.

Obviously I've got the recording of Cotton in Delvina's car to fall back on if they're taken alive, painting him as the unwitting inside man, but it's not an entirely foolproof plan and there'll still be a cloud of suspicion hanging over my head if Delvina decides to drop me in it (which I have no doubt she will).

Right now, I'm standing in front of the bathroom mirror, a wet cloth in my hand, assessing the damage that piece of shit Vinnie has done to my face. I'm also trying to work out how to make sure that he and Delvina are killed rather than captured, and timing it so that the Logan Quinn hit still goes ahead.

I go through my options. I could ask Colin Blisterfield if he's got someone who could take them out at short notice. He probably has. He's that kind of man. But he'd need to know where they were in order to get to them quickly, and I've got no way of tracking them . . . Except of course I have. Vinnie used a tracker to get to me. I could just as easily put trackers on his and Delvina's vehicles. I've got several that I bought years ago, and that I've used periodically in the past. In truth, though, it's almost certainly a bad idea to get Blisterfield involved. He could easily conclude that I was a loose end too, and that really wouldn't be good. But tracking Delvina and Vinnie would work. If I know where they are, it gives me far more control over events.

I'm shattered. The last thing I want to do tonight is drive back out and creep round the driveway of a woman who I've just supplied with a fully functioning firearm, but I also know I can't delay things either. It's better to be sneaking round in the dark than in the light of day tomorrow morning, when events might already have moved on.

So, having made the decision, I finish wiping my face, take a last sad look at myself in the mirror and get to work.

48

Saturday, 8.20 a.m.

I won't bore you with the details of how I planted the trackers. It was straightforward, and actually quite exciting climbing over the gates of the funeral home and sneaking round the edge of the driveway out of range of the camera they have above the front door, before doing the honours and getting belated revenge on Vinnie and his witch of a missus. An hour after I'd set out, I was back in bed and, if not calm, at least satisfied that I'd done what I could to protect myself.

But as I walk into the office now, things have already taken a turn for the worse. The place is busy, not only with colleagues from the unit but also plenty of people I don't recognise. Cotton and a few others are gathered round a desktop PC in the centre of the room.

He turns my way and pulls a face. 'Blimey, your bruises are getting worse, Fish. Are you all right?'

It pisses me off that I have to show my face when I look like this. I'm vain at the best of times, and today I look dogshit, although it's more thanks to the cowardly beating I took at the hands of Vinnie than the tussle with Leon

Dennay on Thursday night. I've got the beginnings of a black eye, there's a cut on my left cheek that's swollen and turning a horrible mix of blue and red, and my thick top lip looks like I've had cheap fillers put in. I'm knackered too, having being assailed by several bad dreams, including one where I was being chased by a dildo- and machete-wielding Colin Blisterfield, in what felt like an unwelcome portent of my immediate future.

'That's what the call of duty does to you,' I reply with a rueful smile, nodding in greeting to everyone. 'What's going on?'

'Good news,' says Cotton. 'Marvin Cunningham's car was on the move last night. It pinged two ANPR cameras, and only a few miles from where we found Henry Day's phone in December. Since it hasn't been picked up by any other cameras, we've narrowed down the area where it'll be to about thirteen square miles.'

Exactly as I predicted. I join him at the computer and look down at a map on the screen, covering a section of central Surrey and including all the ANPR cameras in the area, of which there are a lot. Two of them next to each other are flashing red, and I know immediately that this spells the end for Delvina and Vinnie. 'Christ, this is good news,' I say. And in a way it is, because it means we're now approaching the endgame. Whatever happens now, at least it'll be over soon. 'Have we heard from Rebecca Barraclough yet to confirm that her daughter's missing?'

Cotton shakes his head. 'Not yet. But given her relationship with the police, I'm not surprised.'

I'm pleased that so far no one seems to assume that this is any more than a kidnap for ransom and not something to do with her work as a defence lawyer, but that's so often the way with police investigations these days. You're not encouraged to think laterally. It's all about going for the obvious.

'The DG's got a team keeping Ms Barraclough under surveillance,' Cotton tells me, 'in case we need to make a clandestine approach to tell her we know what's happening with her daughter.'

This is less good. If she's under surveillance, it'll be harder for her to kill Logan Quinn.

'By the way, that's not all we've got,' Cotton continues, just to make my day even worse. 'Have a look at this.' As the other people crowded round the desktop drift back to their desks, he punches a couple of keys and a video still of a driver comes up on the screen. Straight away I can see it's Marvin Cunningham. 'This was taken by a camera on the A3 near Wisley on Thursday afternoon,' he says. 'So Cunningham was driving his car then. But now look at this.' He punches a couple more keys, and lo and behold, a second video still of a driver appears. This time Vinnie's not wearing a mask or glasses, although he's still got a cap on. 'This was who was driving Cunningham's Mondeo last night.' Cotton smiles. 'Does he look familiar?'

He certainly does, given that I was on the receiving end of his punches barely an hour after this footage was taken.

Cotton now brings up a video still taken by the camera in Brighton of Vinnie driving the Chrysler on Thursday night and puts it beside the other one.

'It looks like the same guy, doesn't it?' I say, because it quite clearly does.

'Which means we've got to find that car. We're setting up a grid search involving our people and local plain clothes so we don't look too conspicuous. That should get going in the next hour. In the meantime, I've got to run for a meeting with the DG, then I want me and you to head over to Paddington Green. Leon Dennay's still there awaiting court on Monday. I need you to set up a visit with him as soon as possible, so we can show him this photo and see if he recognises the guy.'

Which sounds better to me than traipsing round the back roads of Surrey searching for something I don't want to find, but it also means we're only a few hours away from ID'ing Vinnie and Delvina, who according to my trackers are still at home, where they'll be sitting ducks when we come calling.

49

Saturday, 9.15 a.m.

Becca Barraclough stands at her bedroom window staring out across the street where she's lived for close to fifteen years now, the place where Elle grew up and where she's always felt at home and safe.

But this morning, she feels sick as she looks out. There's a white van she hasn't seen before parked about thirty yards down from her house on the other side of the road. Its rear windows are blacked out and the writing on the side identifies it as belonging to Charlie Drake Decorators. It was there half an hour ago when she went for a run, desperate to ease some of the pressure she's been under, and there was no one inside when she passed. She's been watching it for ten minutes now and no one's come out to it from any of the nearby houses. That doesn't mean anything, of course, but with her senses heightened, and having already been warned that the police know about Elle's abduction, she's getting paranoid.

She googles Charlie Drake Decorators. Nothing comes up. Now she's convinced it's a fake company. Which means that someone's in the back, watching her. It could be the police. It could even be the kidnappers.

The problem is, there's nothing she can do about it either way. She's impotent. Not even Blisterfield seems able to help. She called him earlier for an update, but he didn't answer. All she got was a text message ten minutes later saying that there was no news yet, but that he was, in his words, breaking his back to find Elle, and wouldn't stop until he'd exhausted every line of inquiry. She texted back a thank-you and yet another desperate plea for him to do everything in his power to make sure Elle wasn't harmed.

His reply: *U BET YA.*

It wasn't a response to elicit much confidence, and like it or not, Becca knows she can't rely on him to dig her out of this particular hole. Right now, she's totally alone, the only person who really knows the true torment she's suffering being her daughter, who's trapped and helpless in some unidentified room, being kept prisoner by sadists. The thought makes her want to collapse on the bed and just pray for the world to go away, but there's no time for that now. She has to stay strong. There's no choice.

Becca's phone rings, giving her a start.

It's from a withheld number, and she stares at the screen for several seconds, contemplating whether to answer. If it's the kidnappers again with a video like the one they sent her yesterday, she doesn't think she can face looking at it.

But she can't ignore the call either.

'Hello?'

'Rebecca Barraclough?' It's a man's voice. Not disguised. Deep and confident.

'Yes,' she says. 'That's me.'

'My name's Chris. I'm part of the security detail for your client Logan Quinn. I understand you want to meet him today.'

Becca would rather do anything in the world than meet Quinn. 'That's right,' she says, thinking about Elle and the possibility of her being released if she just does this one thing. 'I do.'

'Are you alone?'

'Yes. I'm at home.'

'Get a pen and paper. I want you to write down the instructions I'm going to give you.'

She sits on her bed, grabs a notebook and pen from her bedside drawer (she uses it sometimes for writing down her dreams when she wakes up in the night) and takes down his instructions.

Twenty minutes later, Becca strides out of her front door and walks down the street to her car. She's wearing a dark trouser suit and carrying the vintage briefcase bag she's used her whole career, containing copies of the contracts her client needs to sign. She looks just like any other businesswoman. No one would guess that she's carrying a vial of cyanide in the breast pocket of her jacket and is on her way to commit murder.

As she pulls away from the kerb, she checks her rear-view mirror. The decorator's van is still there, but Becca knows that if it does contain a police surveillance team, they won't be the ones following her. They'll radio ahead and someone else will pick up her trail.

She comes to the end of the street, waits for a car to pass, then pulls out onto the main road, checking her mirror the whole time, aware that she's being paranoid but knowing too that it's far better to be prepared.

Sure enough, a car pulls out into the road fifty yards behind her. She slows down, takes a right turn into another residential road and sees the car – a black saloon – turn in after her. It's thirty yards back now, and there are two men in the front. They're dressed casually, but something about them doesn't look right.

So when Becca reaches the end of this road, she pulls straight out into traffic, causing cars coming both ways to beep their horns, then accelerates, taking another rapid turn the wrong way down a one-way street, thankful that nothing's coming in the other direction, before taking another right into a large council estate. The thing is, Becca's lived here a long time and she knows these streets well.

Five minutes and a couple more turnings later, she comes out the other end of the estate, and this time she's confident she's lost them. But there's no sigh of relief. Because she knows full well that this could be the beginning of the worst day of her life.

50

Saturday, 10.05 a.m.

Delvina's been working hard all morning in the embalming room cutting up Marv, while his severed head sits on the worktop, eyes open, overseeing proceedings. She takes off his arms and legs, and because he's such a big guy, she chops each limb in half at the joint, then quarters his torso into nicely manageable sections. For this task she uses a set of butcher's knives she bought online and a traditional cross-cut hand saw. It's hard work because of the thickness of Marv's bones, but she finds it intensely pleasurable.

When she's done, she loads the pieces into bin bags, which she tapes shut then stacks in the chest freezer in the corner of the room. The body parts will eventually be distributed among their clients' coffins and cremated, thus disappearing for ever. Marv's a lot bigger than Henry Day, so they'll need at least six funerals to get rid of him, and since they've only got three scheduled for next week and just one the week after, it's going to take a while.

Delvina's tired from all her exertions and decides to clean

up later. She's had a bathroom fitted next door, and that's where she heads now for a long, luxurious shower, before changing into jeans and a shirt and heading back up to the apartment.

Vincent's in the kitchen picking at a greasy fried breakfast and wearing an unpleasant-looking grey tracksuit. Delvina knows he didn't sleep well, because he was tossing and turning half the night and ruining her own sleep. She hasn't confronted him about his visit to Fisher's place, seeing no profit in it at the moment. Right now, he looks tired and sullen and barely looks up when she walks in.

'Are you all right?' she asks him, putting a capsule in the coffee machine and brewing up a double espresso.

'My wife's just been downstairs cutting up my dead cousin, and everything's going to shit. What do you think?'

What Delvina thinks is that when her husband is morose, as he is now, he looks even more rat-like and unpleasant than usual, and right now she just wants rid of the bastard. Permanently.

'I'll tell you what I think. That if Marv had kept his mouth shut instead of shooting it off, he'd still be alive. I'm also thinking that by the end of the day, when Barraclough has done what she's been told to do, we'll be a lot richer. And then we can finish with this life.'

'And what about the daughter?' he says, looking up at her. 'Who's going to have to do the dirty work there? Because I'm not doing it.'

Something significant has shifted in Vincent. He no longer worships Delvina in the same way. It's like a spell has broken. And that suddenly makes him dangerous. She would love to be able to get the gun from her car, stroll back in here, and put a bullet right through the miserable fucker's eye, but that'll just have to wait a while.

'No one's going to be doing the girl,' she says, knowing that Vincent's trying to trick her. 'As long as her mother does what she's told, we'll release her.'

Vincent frowns. 'I thought you said—'

'There's been a change of plan. McBride now says she can be released unharmed.'

She can see that this catches him out. She has no doubt that if she'd persisted with the line that the girl had to die, he would have confronted her about it, given what Fisher obviously told him. Instead he says: 'That's good. I never saw why she had to die.'

'She also needs feeding. Can you go over there and see to her? I have a chiropractor's appointment this morning.'

Vincent looks surprised. 'You're going to the chiropractor with all this going on?'

Delvina shrugs. 'My back's in a lot of pain and there's not much more we can do today anyway. It's as good a time as any.'

'Do you want me to drug her?'

'No. I'll do it when I've got word that Barraclough has done the job.'

Vincent seems to perk up a little. It's like he can see a light at the end of the tunnel. He looks at his watch. 'I'd better get over there soon. I didn't leave her much last night.'

'Good. Do that,' says Delvina, feeling like she's getting a bit more control back.

Fifteen minutes later, she watches from the bedroom window as Vincent drives the Chrysler out of the driveway, thinking that he's soon going to be in for a real shock. Because as far as Delvina's concerned, the girl is going to die. She knows killing her carries some risks – namely upsetting the mysterious Colin Blisterfield (who she strongly suspects will get over it) and, of course, Fisher (which will please her no end, even though it might put their final payment in jeopardy) – but for Delvina, the risk of releasing the girl outweighs them.

But it's more than that. In truth, Delvina wants – no, *needs* – to kill. She hasn't committed murder since she was a thirteen-year-old girl, and that was a killing she was unable to savour. She's been building up to this one. As soon as she found out that the latest victim was female, and that this was probably the last job they would do, she knew it was her opportunity finally to live out her fantasy

And today's the day it's going to happen.

51

Saturday, 10.40 a.m.

'Can you believe they've lost Barraclough?'

It's Cotton speaking. He's just come off the phone to HQ and looks pissed off.

It's good news for me, though, because it means that the Quinn killing will go ahead, and I won't have to pay back Blisterfield any of the money he's given me.

Cotton and I are currently in Paddington Green station, there to see Leon Dennay. He's been charged with conspiracy to kidnap, which means we're not allowed to talk to him about that charge, but because this is a separate matter and he's agreed to speak to us, we can still meet. Usually, setting something like this up would take days rather than less than two hours, but that's the advantage of kidnap cases. Because lives are necessarily in danger, everything speeds up dramatically, and thanks to the high profile of the Vanishers investigation, and the fact that it's something of an ongoing embarrassment, anything related to it goes straight to the front of the queue.

'How the hell did they manage that?' I say.

'Apparently she clocked them straight away and gave them the slip.'

I shake my head. 'That's what happens when you rely on other people.'

Cotton grunts. 'Tell me about it.'

Dennay's already in the interview room when we get there, along with the same bald, miserable lawyer. He gives me a sly grin as Cotton and I take a seat. 'Those bruises don't look good, bro. That can't be me. I hardly touched you.'

The comment stings, just like my face. But I don't want to give him the satisfaction of reacting, so I simply smile back. 'Don't worry, I won't press charges. I've heard that sunshine's really good for bruises, and it's a beautiful sunny day out there today. What's it like in here?'

Dennay's smile disappears. 'What do you want?'

Cotton pulls an A4-sized close-up photo of Vinnie driving Marv's car from an envelope and slides it across the table. 'We'd like to know if you recognise this man.'

'What relevance is this to my client?' asks the lawyer, tetchily.

'We believe this man is an associate of Marvin Cunningham, and potentially one of the Vanishers gang of kidnappers,' says Cotton.

'Will my client's cooperation be noted at his court appearance on Monday if he does recognise this man?'

'And will I get that fifty-grand reward?'

'We can certainly put a good word in at the court appearance, yes,' says Cotton. 'And if this man is one of the Vanishers and he's convicted, then yes, you stand to receive that reward money.'

'I don't know if I want to get bail on Monday,' says Dennay. 'Because how will that make me look in front of my bros?'

Like a snitch, I'm hoping as I sit listening to this back-and-forth.

'Because I'm not a snitch,' he continues. 'The only reason I'm helping you with the Vanishers is because I want the reward.'

'That's very community-spirited of you, Leon,' I say.

'Fuck that,' says Dennay, with an honesty that's rare among criminals. 'I don't care.'

'Do you recognise him or not?' says Cotton impatiently.

Dennay picks up the photo and takes a good look. 'Yeah. I recognise him.'

Cotton: 'So who is he?'

'I want it in writing that I'm getting the fifty grand.'

'Look, we haven't got time for this right now.'

Dennay shrugs. 'Then I ain't going to help.'

'You're going to leave a young woman in serious danger,' says Cotton in what I can only describe as a hopelessly optimistic attempt to get Dennay to show compassion.

'That's not my client's problem,' says the lawyer, also demonstrating how compassionate most defence lawyers really are. 'And you shouldn't try to make it so.'

Cotton gives me a sideways glance. I can see that he's stuck. In truth, to get the reward money authorised in writing will take hours and a lot of phone calls. No one wants to be on the hook for fifty grand.

'Listen, Leon,' I say, deciding to intervene, just because I'm vain enough to know I can get him to cooperate. 'This is a recorded interview. If we've said you're entitled to the reward, which we have, then we can't just back out. If you tell us now, I guarantee you'll get at least a sizeable chunk of that money, probably all of it, if the man you're looking at is convicted of the crime. But that car you see in the picture, we're searching for it now, and we know its approximate location down to a couple of square miles of countryside, so it's only a matter of time, maybe even hours, before we find it. As soon as we do and forensics get involved, we'll have this guy's DNA – and contrary to popular belief, we can get DNA results back very quickly if it's urgent – and then we won't need you, and your possibility of getting bail and that money will disappear. But if that's a risk you're prepared to take, fair enough. Sorry to have wasted your time. I'm sure you've got plenty of other things you could be doing in your cell.' I turn to Cotton, give him a look like maybe we should call it a day, and we both start to get to our feet.

Dennay exchanges glances with his lawyer and I can tell he's going to bite. You might ask – and with good reason – why I've just tried so hard to get him to give up Vinnie's name. It's because it really is only a matter of hours before we get it anyway. And I see no reason in prolonging the inevitable. Plus, the fact that I'm pressing Dennay for it is another reason why no one will suspect me, even if Delvina points them in my direction.

Dennay does indeed bite, greed getting the better of him as it gets the better of so many of us.

'It's Vinnie Steele,' he says. 'He's Marv Cunningham's cousin.'

And bang. That's the final nail in the Vanishers' coffin. If you'll excuse the pun.

52

Saturday, 11.25 a.m.

Becca's in the back of a car, a blindfold over her eyes, off to commit murder.

Everything has been very cloak-and-dagger. When she arrived at the rendezvous she'd been given an hour before, she got another call from the same guy, Chris, telling her to leave her car and keep walking in the direction she'd parked. She must have walked for at least five minutes, crossing a busy junction, before a car containing two men pulled up beside her and the passenger called out her name and told her to get in.

As soon as she was in the back, the car pulled away and the passenger turned round in his seat. He was a good-looking red-haired guy in his thirties, with a full beard, and he gave her a polite smile, told her he was Chris and asked for her mobile phone.

The phone represented Becca's last link with the outside world. If she gave it up now, it meant she had no choice but to carry out the murder of Logan Quinn. That even if Colin Blisterfield located Elle's kidnappers, there'd be nothing she could do about it.

But failure to give it up wouldn't help either. Not any more. So she handed it over without complaint and waited while Chris placed it in a Faraday bag to block the signal, before slipping it into his jacket pocket and running an electronic wand up and down her body to make sure she wasn't carrying any clandestine devices. 'I'm sorry for all the hoops,' he told her, giving her a blindfold to wear, 'but it's essential we keep your client's location an absolute secret.'

She didn't complain – there was no point. Just sat back in the seat, conscious of the vial of poison that she'd pushed into the space on the inside of her cheek shortly before she'd parked earlier, knowing that it could easily break and kill her within minutes. Although, she thought, perhaps right now that would be a blessing.

The journey continued largely in silence. Chris made a couple of half-hearted attempts at conversation, but he quickly sensed that Becca didn't want to talk and soon gave up.

And now finally she's aware of the car turning into a gravel driveway and coming to a halt. She's here. This is it.

'You can remove the blindfold now,' says Chris.

She takes a deep breath and pulls it off, thinking about Elle in that soundproofed room. Knowing that she has to be strong for her.

The safe house where they're holding Logan Quinn is a detached modern house backing onto fields and with no obvious neighbours. It's a bright, sunny day and Becca can hear birds singing. As she gets out of the car, Chris approaches her with a sheepish smile. She can see he's wearing a gun in a shoulder holster beneath his jacket. 'I'm sorry, but I need to frisk you for any hidden weapons,' he says. 'It's procedure. Do you mind? I'm afraid we don't have any female officers in the detail.'

'Do you really have to?' asks Becca, deliberately not looking happy about it. 'It's not like I'm going to kill my own client, is it?'

'You'd be surprised, Ms Barraclough,' he says. 'Stranger things have happened.'

Again it's obvious that he's not about to change his mind, so she calmly raises her arms, praying that he doesn't try putting his fingers in her mouth. If he does, she'll have no choice but to bite him or kick up a fuss.

But his search is cursory, and he quickly finishes and nods to his colleague, who's also armed. The two of them escort Becca inside and through to a spacious kitchen/dining area where a third man – older than the other two, his pistol and shoulder holster on display – sits at the table reading a newspaper. He gives her a nod as she approaches but doesn't bother saying anything. Becca has this effect on police officers. None of them like her.

'This is a secure establishment,' Chris says, stopping next to her. 'Which means that your client's not free to move around.' He motions to a monitor on the wall, which shows a separate living room with a table and chairs, a sofa and a bed at one end. A man she immediately recognises as Logan Quinn reclines on the sofa with his legs crossed and hands behind his head, staring up at the ceiling. He looks irritatingly relaxed, and Becca is immediately filled with a visceral hatred for her client. If it wasn't for him, she wouldn't be in this position, about to commit a crime from which there's no way back. 'I understand you've got some contracts for him to sign,' continues Chris.

Becca nods. 'I do. And I need to discuss a number of matters with him in confidence, so you'll need to turn the camera and any audio off for that.'

'We can turn off the audio, but we can't turn off the camera for security reasons. If he attacks you—'

'He won't attack me. I'm his lawyer.'

'I'm afraid it's more than my job's worth not to keep the camera on,' he says, and there's a firmness in his voice that tells her he's not going to change his mind. 'You can sit with your backs to it if that makes you feel better.'

'Well, I guess that'll have to do, then,' Becca says with a sigh, and immediately feels the vial move in her mouth. As inconspicuously as possible, she pushes it back into place with her tongue. It strikes her now that she's got to think of a way to administer it to Quinn, if indeed she intends to follow through with this crime. And right now, standing here, she's not at all sure that she does. 'Can I have a jug of water and a couple of glasses?'

'He's got glasses and water in there,' says the cop at the table without looking up.

Chris escorts her through a hallway to a door at the end. 'Take this.' He hands her a small key-fob-shaped alarm. 'In case of an emergency.'

338

'I really don't think I'll need it,' she says, but takes it off him. Because in reality, she's definitely going to need to raise the alarm after she's poisoned Quinn. A crime that will be caught on camera for all eternity, however much she tries to hide it. The way the camera's angled downwards to cover the whole room means she won't be able to administer the cyanide surreptitiously.

Chris unlocks both bolts on the door and pushes it open. 'Hope it goes well,' he says and turns away.

'Don't forget to turn off the audio,' she says to his back, then steps inside.

Quinn gets to his feet to greet her, his big boyish smile covering his handsome face. He's dressed casually in a black hoodie, jeans and trainers, looking like he's just about to go for a run, and there's such a vitality about him it's hard to imagine that he could be dead and already going cold within the next few minutes. 'Welcome to my abode,' he says, and for a terrible second, she thinks he's going to try to hug her. But thank God, he doesn't, although she's suddenly very conscious of the vial pressing against her cheek as they shake hands and exchange pleasantries. He looks genuinely pleased to see her, and she has to force a smile in return.

'I've got some contracts I need you to sign before we can go any further,' she tells him. 'They've already been signed by the attorney general, and by countersigning them you agree to give up all the physical and digital evidence you have regarding the murders you've committed.'

He nods, and puts on a serious expression. 'Sure, I

understand. Take a seat.' He motions to the table in the middle of the room, where there are two chairs facing each other.

'Do you mind getting me a glass of water?' Becca says, sitting down and taking the two copies of the contract from her briefcase. She's facing the camera that looks down at her from the ceiling and she wonders whether any of them are watching her on the monitor. She takes a deep breath, tries to stay calm, but her mind is an absolute maelstrom and she can see that her hands are shaking.

Quinn returns with two full glasses of water and sets one down in front of her before taking the seat opposite. 'They look big,' he says, motioning towards the contracts. 'I'm assuming you've read them through.'

I can't do this. Jesus, I can't do this.

'Legal contracts are always big,' she says, trying to concentrate. 'But there's nothing untoward in there.'

'What about the time I'm agreeing to serve. Did you get it to five years?'

She shakes her head. 'They want ten.'

'No way.'

'It's the final offer, Logan,' she says. 'There's no choice.'

Quinn picks up his water. Takes a gulp. Becca pictures Elle standing in chains. The blow knocking her to the floor. Most of all she thinks about how it would break her not to see her daughter again. To have her disappear off the face of the earth like Henry Day did.

'How about seven?'

'I can't ... We can't do seven. That's just ... We just have to compromise.'

How am I going to get the poison in his drink?

He smiles. 'Tell them seven.'

She suddenly has an idea. She can't understand why it never occurred to her before. If she can get hold of all the evidence that Quinn possesses incriminating the people he's been working for, and somehow destroy it, there'll be no need to kill him. Because without evidence, there's no case against any of them.

'Okay,' she says, taking a deep breath. 'I'll go back and see if we can get them to agree to seven. But before I do, I want all the evidence you've got on the individuals who've hired you to commit murder. Both physical and digital. I won't let anyone else see it without your permission. You have my word on that. But I need to know where it all is. Right now. Because it means I've got a much stronger negotiating stance with the CPS, to try to get you down to this seven years you want ...'

She's conscious that she's talking too fast – rambling almost – and there's a desperation in her tone that she seems unable to hide, but now that she's got this idea in her head she has to make it work somehow, because it offers her the slim possibility of a way out.

Quinn just needs to bite.

He smiles at her again. He's looking right into her eyes, and she finds herself struggling to hold his gaze.

'Now, why would I give up everything I've got before the contract's signed? I need it in writing that I'm serving an absolute legal maximum of seven years before I hand over any more evidence.'

341

Becca knows she can't give up. 'Well, if you don't trust me, maybe you should look for another lawyer.'

'Should I trust you?' He's staring at her as he speaks.

She looks straight back, her jaw tightening. 'Yes,' she says emphatically. 'You can trust me completely. I'm your lawyer.'

'Are you okay?' he asks, frowning. 'It's just, you look really jumpy.'

Becca sighs, tries to compose herself. 'It's just stress. I've overworked myself. I think I need a holiday.'

He smiles again. 'Hard work's definitely overrated. Do you know that the biggest regret people on their deathbed have is that they worked too hard? Don't fall into that trap, Becca.'

It feels like he's playing with her, and right now, she can't have that. She needs to get this sorted. And fast. 'Are you going to let me know where the evidence is?'

He sits back in his chair, arms folded. It looks like he's thinking about whether to comply with her request, and she can feel the first stirrings of hope somewhere in her gut.

'Well that's the thing,' he says. 'There isn't any.'

53

Saturday, 11.50 a.m.

Becca stares at Quinn, confused. 'What do you mean? There's no evidence?'

'I mean,' he says, leaning forward, his voice quiet and cold, 'that I brought you here under false pretences. Is there anything you'd like to tell me, Becca? Something you might be trying to hide, for instance. And try not to look too shocked. They might be watching out there.'

'I don't know what you're talking about. I'm not hiding anything.'

'Don't bullshit me. I know what you've smuggled in here with you.'

The shock hits her hard. Somehow the bastard knows about the poison. But how?

And that's when it dawns on her. Logan Quinn set this whole thing up. She stares at him. 'This is all you?'

He nods slowly, still wearing that smile of his. Like a kid with all the cards. 'Don't look scared. Show the camera we're just having a nice, normal conversation.' He leans in closer, his voice low. 'Now, you need to listen to me very carefully if you ever want to see your daughter again, because my colleagues won't hesitate to kill her. You'll be pleased to know that the vial you're carrying in your mouth doesn't contain poison. It contains pure ketamine. Enough to knock out all three of the men out there for several hours. And you're going to administer it to them.'

'How the hell am I meant to do that?' she says, keeping her expression as neutral as possible.

'Once we're finished in here, tell them that you have some new evidence you need to discuss with the CPS urgently. There's a landline phone. Pretend to make the call from that. Then you tell those police officers that someone senior from the CPS will be making arrangements to come here, and that you need to wait until they arrive. Then you sit out there, you make conversation. You ask them if you can make a cup of coffee. You offer them one. Then you put the drug into their cups. It's as simple as that. They won't suspect you. You're a high-flying, high-profile lawyer.'

Becca can't believe what she's hearing. She's not sure whether to feel relieved or not. 'What if they don't want me to make them a drink?'

'They also have water in a water filter. I've seen it when they take me out for exercise. If it works better, slip it in there. But get it into them somehow if you ever want to see your daughter again.'

Now it's Becca's turn to lean forward so their faces are only inches apart. 'Where *is* my daughter?' she hisses.

'I honestly don't know,' says Quinn with a shrug. 'What I do know, however, is that if the people who have her don't hear from me by eight o'clock tonight, she will die. Everything hinges on you getting me out of here. Do that, and she's released. So if you can think of a faster, more effective way than the one I've proposed, feel free to use it. But the clock's ticking.'

'You bastard. If anything happens to Elle, I'll kill you.'

'No, you won't,' says Quinn evenly. 'And if I'm still here tonight, she'll die and there'll be literally nothing that ties me to her murder. I can guarantee you something else as well. No trace of her will ever be found. The people holding her have a foolproof way of disposing of corpses.'

To hear Elle being talked about like this fills Becca with a burning fury. She wants to take Quinn by the throat and throttle her daughter's location out of him. She'd kill him gladly now. Wipe that smirk from his face. Because he doesn't care about Becca. He doesn't care about Elle. He cares about no one. He's a psychopath, pure and simple. Someone who deserves to rot in prison for the rest of his life.

'So,' he says. 'Are you going to help me, and save her?'

What choice does she really have?

'Yes.'

54

Saturday, 12.30 p.m.

You know those times you call the police to report a crime and you get put on hold? Or told that officers will attend when they can, only for no one to show up for hours, days, or even at all. Unless it's an absolute emergency, that's the norm these days. We all know that, especially the police themselves. We don't like it any more than you do, but the way our resources have been pared to the bone means there's nothing we can do about it.

A high-profile kidnap case, however, where the kidnappers have been seen to be outwitting the police for months – now that's different. Because the brass don't like the attention and the bad press, and nor do the politicians. They don't want to give the impression that criminals can act with impunity (even though I can categorically tell you that they do). Now, though, with the Vanishers in the NCA's cross hairs, and the opportunity to rescue a kidnap victim as well, processes that usually take days or weeks suddenly take hours and even minutes.

Which is why, less than two hours after we were given

Vinnie Steele's name by Leon Dennay, Cotton and I are sitting in my car thirty yards down the street from the Travellers Rest Funeral Home, armed with a search warrant for the offices and the apartment above. There are a further two dozen plain-clothes officers dotted round the nearby streets, including specialist firearms teams. The majority of us, including me and Cotton, are armed, the reason being that when we checked Vinnie's record, we discovered that he was charged some years back with possession of a firearm, which was news to me. As it happens, he was acquitted of this offence, but that doesn't matter. He's had a past association with firearms crime and that means we're not taking any chances.

Delvina's been ID'd now too. The NCA analysts back at HQ took a closer look at Vinnie, saw who he was married to, and less than half an hour later, Delvina's photo was in front of Jody Hallam, the woman who'd witnessed Elle Barraclough's abduction.

Neither the Chrysler nor Delvina's Audi are in the driveway of the funeral home, which of course I knew before we got here because the tracking app told me. The last time I checked, they were both somewhere in darkest Surrey, probably at the place where they're keeping Elle. HQ are also trying to track them via their mobile phone signals, but at the moment, the phones registered in their names are switched off, their last locations being, not surprisingly, Surrey.

Although it appears that neither of them are home, as far as the investigating team are concerned, Elle could still be locked inside, so we need to make an entry. We're just waiting for the alarm company to switch off the security system and then we're going in.

Right now, I'm nervous. I know that a search of this place isn't going to elicit anything, because Elle isn't there, but now that we're approaching the endgame, I just want to get things over with. The best thing will be to take Vinnie and Delvina soon, while we're all still armed and pumped up. I know Delvina will have the gun with her. I saw the way she looked at it last night. The power it obviously gave her. She won't be letting it out of her sight for a while yet.

'I don't think Elle's in there,' I tell Cotton. 'The floor plans say there's no basement, and I don't see where else they can keep her without it being a security issue, given that members of the public pass in and out of there. I reckon they've got her somewhere round where we picked up Cunningham's car on the ANPR.'

'Yeah, but there's nothing on the Land Registry saying either of them owns a property in Surrey,' he answers, 'and they won't be renting.'

I shrug. 'They could have bought it through a company. Plenty of people do.'

Cotton looks surprised. That's the thing with the police. Although we're good at looking for evidence of crimes, we don't tend to deal with the financial stuff, so it's easier than you think for us to miss something like this, especially when there's a load of other leads to process.

'Good point,' he says, in the manner of someone who

wouldn't have thought about that in a thousand years. 'I'll get back on to HQ.'

'We can check it ourselves easily enough. We just google Katherine Steele-Perkins, company director.' Which I do as I speak. 'And look, there we go. She's the MD of the Travellers Rest, but also the co-director of DV2 Property Services, along with her husband. So we just need to find out the addresses of any properties that DV2 owns, and then we have potential locations.'

He looks at me. 'Did you just think of that?'

I shrug casually. 'Yeah. I'm not just a pretty face. Do me a favour, though. Let the bosses know that I was a help on this. It's important to me.'

He puts a meaty hand on my shoulder. 'You know I will, Fish. To be honest, we'd have struggled getting to this point without you.'

Which is the grim irony of this whole thing. But I appreciate the sentiment. 'Thanks, Cott. I know I can always rely on you. But listen, if HQ have got someone they're talking to at the Land Registry, get them to call about properties belonging to DV2. It'll probably be quicker than me trawling through the Companies House website.'

Cotton nods and gets back on the phone, while I stare out the window thinking it won't be long before we inevitably discover Elle's location. If possible, I want to be the one who gets to her first and tells her everything's going to be okay. She'll have had a pretty stressful time and it'll be nice to see the relief on her face when the cavalry arrives, with me hopefully at the helm and the bullet-ridden corpses of her captors lying outside.

A few minutes later, Cotton's off the phone, and this time he's grinning. 'You're a genius, Fish. DV2 only owns one property. It's a house in Surrey, just off the A3 near Cobham.' He brings up Google Maps on his phone, types in the postcode, and straight away we can see that it's barely five miles from the first ANPR camera triggered last night by Cunningham's Mondeo, and only a few miles in the other direction from the barn where we found Henry Day's phone. 'That's our place,' he says, barely able to contain his excitement, and no doubt dreaming of glory.

Feeling a sudden burst of nerves, I switch on the engine. I don't even bother waiting for instructions.

'Let's go,' I say, and pull away from the kerb.

55

Saturday, 12.35 p.m.

Delvina is sitting in her Audi, parked on a single-track road in woodland two hundred metres from the cottage. From here she has a view of the main road back to the A3, and she's waiting for Vincent to drive past. He's currently at the cottage feeding their prisoner and checking up on things, and it's taking him a long time. So long in fact that she's beginning to wonder if he somehow drove back a different way, but she knows she's being foolish. There's only one way back. The problem is, Delvina's impatient. She wants to get to work on the girl. The desire's upon her now, and when it's like this, it's almost unstoppable. She's quite literally dressed to kill, in an outfit of black and leather, topped off with stiletto-heeled black ankle boots.

It will be a moment of pure unadulterated power that few people are ever fortunate enough to experience.

But the waiting is driving her mad. What the fuck is Vincent doing? She knows that if she sits here much longer, the doubts will set in. Doubts that she's doing the right thing. And she doesn't want that to happen. This is a mood she doesn't want broken.

She wonders if Quinn's free yet. It was always Delvina's plan to help him escape. The two of them have known each other for a number of years now, ever since she found him online when she wanted her first husband killed. Together they planned Philip's murder, for which Quinn charged a fee of £50,000 plus expenses. His services might have been expensive, but she considered it money well spent, given that he'd done the job exactly as planned and she'd inherited a lot more than fifty grand.

Delvina had been intrigued by the mysterious and deadly Quinn, and they remained in contact online after the killing, finally meeting up in person two years ago, when they embarked on a brief and enjoyable affair. Unfortunately, Quinn was too independent for Delvina, who likes her men to be subservient, but it didn't spoil their relationship, and they continued to stay in touch.

When she heard about his arrest, she knew she had to visit him in prison, if only to make sure he wasn't going to tell the authorities about what he'd done for her all those years ago. Quinn had been pleased to see her, but he was also worried that the police were building a case against him for several murders unrelated to the one he'd been arrested for, and that his life was in danger in prison because he knew too much about certain high-powered individuals he'd killed on behalf of. That was when Delvina came up with the plan to get him out, which they perfected together in subsequent visits, and which used her expertise in kidnapping.

It was only while she was working out the logistics and timing of the Elle Barraclough abduction that Fisher, her long-term contact, approached her offering her and Vincent £450,000 to do what she was planning to do anyway, which was a particularly fortuitous coincidence. The only difference was that Fisher wanted Becca Barraclough to kill Quinn using poison that he was supplying.

Delvina accepted the contract – after all, she wasn't going to turn down that sort of money – even though she had no intention of letting Becca kill Quinn. As soon as he's free and in a safe place, Quinn will call her to let her know his location, as they planned. Her job is then to provide him with the fake passport he stashed before his arrest, as well as several thousand pounds in cash and a ferry ticket to Santander. In return for this, he's paying her two hundred grand and has made a promise to kill both Vincent and Fisher at a time of her choosing. It's not like Delvina to trust anyone – especially a man – but she's known Quinn long enough to be certain that he'll come through on this.

As for double-crossing Fisher, she definitely won't lose any sleep over that, and what's he going to do about it anyway? It's not like he can complain to anyone. It's mildly inconvenient that he's working on behalf of some big-shot gangster who won't be very happy when Quinn disappears into the ether, but in the end that's Fisher's problem rather than hers. As will be the fact that Elle's not going to make it out alive either.

Delvina smiles to herself as she thinks about Elle, a lively, vibrant young woman whose life she's about to snuff out just because she can. It excites her that she's not hamstrung by a false morality. She's an alpha. A warrior. A hunter. Unfettered by the rules of society.

And no one can fucking stop her.

At that moment, she sees the Chrysler through the trees, crossing her vision. She watches as it passes and just makes out Vincent behind the wheel. And then it's gone.

Delvina's smile grows wider as she starts the Audi.

It's time.

56

Saturday, 12.40 p.m.

'I need to make an urgent call to Clyde Faulkner at the CPS,' says Becca to Chris when he lets her out of Quinn's room.

'You can't use your phone here,' he tells her.

'I understand that. Have you got a landline or a satellite phone I can call from?'

'Through here,' he says, leading her along the hallway, where there's a phone on a stand by the coat rack. He doesn't seem remotely suspicious, which Becca supposes is natural. There's no reason to think she's going to do anything untoward. Even so, he waits at the end of the hallway while she pretends to dial Clyde. She then stands there having a make-believe conversation with him in which she says that Quinn wants the amount of time he will serve to be seven years rather than ten. She's sweating as she talks, and she's having to work hard to keep her voice calm and her hands from shaking.

Finally she comes off the phone and turns to Chris. 'I need to stay here and call him back in an hour. Can I wait with you guys?'

He nods, looking like he doesn't care one way or the other. 'Sure.'

They head back to the kitchen, where the other two are sitting at the table. They barely glance her way and don't say anything, which is a reaction she's used to getting from police officers, none of whom have much time for her. Becca leans against the worktop, conscious of the vial in her cheek and trying to work out whether Quinn's lying to her. Is it ketamine? Or is it the cyanide the kidnapper told her it was? Because it's the difference between aiding an offender under duress and triple murder. And the fact that Logan Quinn has admitted to no fewer than twenty-three murders suggests strongly that he wouldn't care a jot about being responsible for the deaths of three more people. But for her own sanity, Becca's got to believe this isn't poison she's planning on administering to these men.

A few feet away from her she sees a used cafetière, with three empty cups next to it. So these guys drink proper coffee. If she's going to add the drug, that's the way to do it. She looks up at the monitor showing Quinn's room and can see him back on the sofa, this time reading a book, as if he hasn't got a care in the world. He's an ice man, she thinks. A complete sociopath. And she wishes she'd never set eyes on him.

'It must have been hard finding someone worse than Oliver Tamzan or Colin Blisterfield to defend,' says the older cop, giving a look of dismissive contempt. 'I'm impressed that you've managed, though.'

'Now, now, Martin,' says Chris. 'We don't need to get personal.'

'It's okay,' says Becca. 'I can understand how you feel. If it's any consolation, I genuinely thought Quinn was innocent when I agreed to defend him.'

'Like Tamzan?' says Martin, raising an eyebrow.

In normal times she would never bother defending herself to a man like this, but these aren't normal times. And she needs to try to get these guys on side. 'Yes,' she says, meeting his gaze. 'I genuinely thought he was innocent too. And I had a lot of sleepless nights after he was convicted of the other attack. I'm not a monster, you know. I'm just trying to do my job. And everyone's entitled to a defence.'

Martin clearly doesn't know what to say to that, so he turns back to his paper.

'It's a fair point,' says Chris, giving her a smile, and she wonders if he's flirting with her.

The third cop, the one who drove her here, asks her if Quinn has really confessed to twenty-two murders.

'I'm not allowed to say officially,' she answers, 'but it's actually twenty-three.'

'Jesus Christ,' he says. 'And he seems like a really nice guy.'

'Well, you know as well as I do that not all criminals look or sound like criminals,' she says.

Becca, Chris and the third cop talk back and forth for another few minutes, and weirdly she finds herself relaxing in their company. In the end, even Martin joins in the conversation. The ice has been broken between them and she knows that it's now or never; there's no point in putting things off any longer. Because the sooner she does it, the sooner she gets Elle back.

Or that's the theory, anyway.

'Do you mind if I make a cup of coffee?' she says.

'Go ahead,' says Chris.

'Anyone else want one while I'm here?'

This, of course, is where it could all go wrong. If no one else wants one, or only one or two do, then she's going to have to think again.

But all three of them say yes. Martin even adds flippantly: 'As long as you don't try to poison us.'

'I think you're probably safe with me,' laughs Becca, putting on the kettle and washing out the cafetière, surprised at how easy this is. As she puts the clean cafetière back on the worktop, her back to the three of them, she casually reaches into her mouth, removes the capsule, clicks off the lid and pours in the contents. She then pretends to yawn as she drops the vial into her jacket pocket.

No one says anything, which means no one saw her, and as the kettle comes close to boiling, she picks it up and pours the water into the cafetière. She knows there might be a camera covering this room too, which would have caught her adding the drugs, but there's nothing she can do about that now. She just has to keep going with the plan and hope for the best.

As the coffee brews, she continues her conversation with the men. She's good at keeping calm under pressure, which is a prerequisite if your job involves standing up in a courtroom and taking on other barristers. They talk about the pros and cons of the taxi-cab rule whereby lawyers are not allowed to refuse to take on clients unless they have a very good reason. Of the three, only Chris knew that rule actually existed, and the other two seem surprised.

'So even if I wanted to turn Quinn down, I couldn't have,' she says, handing each of them their drugged coffee, noticing that her hands have stopped shaking.

The conversation continues. Becca blows on her own coffee and puts it to her lips. It smells just as you'd expect it to smell. As it happens, she could really do with a coffee now, and she actually has to force herself only to pretend to take a sip.

The wait is excruciating. Becca has never been a woman given to self-doubt. Right from childhood, she's been single-minded in her desire to succeed. She came from a good, stable family, had an excellent education, and worked damned hard the whole way through, filled with a burning desire to make the world a better place. When she became pregnant and Elle's father deserted her, she didn't let it bring her down. She kept fighting through, brought her daughter up as a single mother and never deviated from her path to success.

And now she's about to throw it all away in one fell swoop.

When it happens, it happens fast.

Martin's the first to react. All he says is 'What the fuck?' as he tries to get out of his seat and then falls back, unable to. The third guy, the one whose name Becca never got, turns her way, an accusing look on his face, and then his eyes widen, his cheeks puff out and he topples off his chair.

Becca instinctively acts as if she too has been poisoned,

dropping her still full cup of coffee on the table, her head lolling to one side. Out of the corner of her eye she sees Chris jump to his feet, seemingly unaffected. He starts to say something, coming round the table towards her, and then his legs appear to go from under him and he too falls to the floor, making horrible gasping noises.

Becca shuts her eyes, slumping her head forward, and sits like that for a few moments.

Chris's gasps stop and the room falls silent. Becca counts to twenty in her head, then opens her eyes and looks around. None of the three men are moving. It looks like they're unconscious rather than dead, which is at least one good thing, but she's not hanging round to look too closely. Instead she rifles through Chris's jacket, pleased that he still appears to be breathing, until she finds her phone. She takes it out of the Faraday bag and switches it back on. But as she removes the keys from his belt, his eyes jerk open and he grabs her by the wrist.

She cries out and jumps back in shock, dragging him with her. But then his grip slackens and his eyes close again.

Breathing rapidly, she gets to her feet, knowing she's got to move fast now.

Which is the moment she realises that as soon as she unlocks the door and releases Logan Quinn, she's lost all her power. He could grab one of the officers' guns and kill her on the spot. He's ruthless enough. Becca needs to protect herself. She looks down at Chris. His gun is on display in his shoulder holster. She's never used a gun before, only rarely even seen one, and knows how dangerous they can be in the wrong hands. But at least if she's got one, Quinn won't be in control of the situation and she'll have more chance of staying alive.

Becca crouches down beside Chris and very slowly, very gingerly, removes the weapon, making sure to keep her fingers a long way from the trigger. She places it on the table and sees that it's called a Glock 17. She immediately googles *How to fire a Glock 17* and has to stand there watching a demonstration video on her phone, knowing all the time that reinforcements might already be on the way to arrest her.

When she's finished, she can see that the gun is ready to fire, so she picks it up and walks over to the door leading to Quinn's quarters. She remembers the keys Chris used, and she unlocks the door and pushes it open, taking a couple of steps backwards and raising the gun. 'It's me,' she calls. 'You can come out.'

Quinn strides out confidently and Becca continues to retreat, both hands on the gun.

He looks at her, then at the three men on the floor. 'You did well. How long have they been out for?'

'A few minutes.' She stops retreating and points the gun at Quinn's chest with steady hands, exhibiting a confidence she's not feeling. Ten feet separates the two of them. 'I want you to pick up the nearest phone and call the people holding my daughter. Tell them to release her now, along with a phone, and get her to call me. When I hear from her, you can go.'

Quinn smiles. He doesn't seem remotely perturbed by the

gun. 'These men aren't going to be out for very long, and if this room is being monitored remotely, it won't be long before the alarm's raised. I need to be safe before I make the call to the people holding your daughter.'

'No,' says Becca emphatically. 'We're not going anywhere until she's released.'

'If you shoot me, or reinforcements turn up here, you'll never see her again and she'll be dead in . . .' he makes a play of looking at his watch, 'exactly seven hours. Do you want to take that risk?' As he speaks, he walks over to where Martin's lying, passing only feet in front of Becca, leans down and removes the pistol from his shoulder holster. 'Now we've both got one of these things,' he says, pushing it into the waistband of his jeans. 'So are you going to put yours down, or are we just going to waste time?'

Becca stares at him coldly, knowing they can't stand like this for ever, and that if she shoots him, it's over for her. 'Okay. Let's go. You drive, but I'm keeping this.' She points her gun down towards the guy who drove them here. 'He's the one with the car keys.'

'You're a hard bargainer,' says Quinn with a big boyish grin, rifling through the driver's pockets and coming up with the keys. 'And that's why I hired you. But, you see,' he adds, walking up to her, 'so am I.' He points his own gun straight at her head, his eyes suddenly cold. 'Now give me that.'

Becca swallows. Staring down the barrel of a gun is a uniquely terrifying experience, and she can see that the man holding it will not hesitate to kill her. Logan Quinn's ruthlessness is written all over his face, and she really can't compete with that. She hands him the gun and he motions her towards the front door.

And with that, they're out of there.

57

Saturday, 12.55 p.m.

Elle sits on the bed, feeling better – at least physically – than at any time since she first woke up in here, however long ago that was now. The man from yesterday evening came back earlier. He filled her a big bowl of warm soapy water to wash herself with. He also brought her bottled water, a bacon sandwich, a muffin and some bananas. He told her it wouldn't be long before she was released. Either later today or tomorrow. She was worried that the sandwich might be drugged, but her hunger trumped her fear and her vegetarianism, and she ate it in barely a couple of bites. There were three bananas, and she ate two of them, saving one for later, along with the muffin.

She feels awake and alert. But scared too. Mainly that the woman who hit her might come back. There was something deeply malignant about her. Even when she said sorry for striking Elle, her tone didn't reflect her words at all.

The cell door begins to open, making Elle jump. She instinctively turns towards it. All she sees is a gloved female hand on the handle, and then that husky voice again. 'Put your blindfold on, darling. I'm coming in.'

So she *is* back.

Elle tenses and pulls on the blindfold, remaining on the side of the bed.

'Please don't hit me again,' she says, as she hears the woman's soft approach.

'I won't hit you, darling.' The voice is soothing, but once again there's something in it that sets Elle on edge. It sounds like ... excitement. 'You'll be free very soon now.'

The woman's right in front of her now: Elle can sense her presence, smell her perfume. 'I just need you to lie back on the bed for me,' she says gently.

Some deep-seated instinct tells Elle that if she lies back on the bed, then that will be it for her.

The woman's hand is on her shoulder, pushing her firmly backwards. Elle can hear her heightened breathing. Something's wrong. She knows it. The way the woman is touching her, and no longer making any effort to disguise her voice. She's looming over her, and as she does, she grabs Elle's breast and squeezes the nipple painfully.

And that's when something breaks in Elle. She grabs at the woman with both hands, finds the material of a jacket and clutches it tightly, then drives herself upwards with all her strength, using her head as a battering ram that slams into the woman's face.

Her attacker cries out, and knowing that momentum is with her and she can't stop now, Elle uses the woman to pull herself off the bed and immediately headbutts her a second time, then a third, oblivious to any pain as adrenaline surges through her.

The woman grabs Elle's hair and yanks it as she stumbles backwards. Elle butts her again, although this time she only catches the side of her attacker's head. Knowing she needs to see what she's doing, she lets go of the jacket with one hand and yanks down her blindfold, and now she's staring directly into the face of her abductor.

The woman's nose is bloody and her eyes are wild and furious. Before Elle can even think about reacting, the woman drives her own head into Elle's face, sending her crashing to the floor, her shoulder blades striking the side of the bed.

'Fucking bitch!' the woman snarls, and charges towards Elle on spiked heels before launching a kick at her.

But Elle knows she's fighting for her life now, and she's still pumped enough to move fast. She throws up both hands and catches the foot in mid-air, twisting it round and pulling hard, throwing her attacker completely off balance. The woman goes down on her side, although she immediately starts kicking out like a mule, the spiked heel of her free foot catching Elle in the belly and chest.

The outcome of this fight is all about who gets to their feet first, and Elle knows it has to be her. Ignoring the kicks, she scrambles to one side and jumps up so she's out of range.

The woman now turns away slightly, using one hand as support as she tries to push herself up, but Elle's faster. Grabbing the chain that's attached to her wrist, she pulls it tight and jumps on the woman's back, looping it over her head and tightening it round her neck. The woman flails around wildly, trying to scream, but she can only manage a horrible rasping noise as Elle pulls her backwards, using all her strength to hold the garrotte in place. She feels sick doing this to a fellow human being, but knows she has no choice.

The woman's struggles grow weaker, then stop. Elle doesn't know if she's feigning or not, so she counts to five before releasing the chain. The woman falls over on her side. Her breathing is raspy and it's clear she's not conscious.

And now Elle needs to get out of here fast. She rifles through the pockets of the woman's long leather coat, finds a small hunting knife in a sheath, which she takes out and shoves in the pocket of her scrubs, then finally what she's looking for: a bunch of keys. Immediately she starts trying them in the lock on her wrist cuff, finding the right one on the third attempt. She feels a burst of elation as the cuff comes off and her arm's finally free.

But the woman's already stirring, rolling away from Elle and coughing painfully.

Elle tries the same key in the ankle-cuff lock and feels another burst of excitement as the cuff clicks open.

Dropping the keys, she staggers over to the half-open door, her legs stiff from so little recent movement, and starts up the stone steps towards the open hatch at the top.

Behind her, she hears the woman getting to her feet and crying out in a hoarse, rasping voice, and this spurs her on. She clambers through the gap and finds herself on her hands and knees in a comfortable-looking living room. Bright sunlight shines through the window, forcing her to squint for several seconds. But this close to freedom she's just got to keep going, and still half blinded, she gets to her feet and runs into the hallway.

The front door's just ahead of her, and she grabs the handle with shaking hands and pulls.

Except it doesn't open. It's been locked from the inside. Panicking, she tries again, harder this time, causing the door to rattle in its frame. But it's still not opening, and now Elle can hear movement from the living room. The bitch is coming for her.

Turning, she sprints towards the back of the house, searching for another way out. It's not a big place, and she goes through the first door she can find and into a kitchen with a back door into a decent-sized garden.

Taking a look over her shoulder, she sees her abductor in the living room, picking something up from a chair.

That's when Elle sees it's a gun.

She turns and runs for her life, praying that this door isn't locked. But once again she's out of luck, because it is, with no key in sight. There's a window above the sink right next to the door. Panicking, Elle scrambles onto the kitchen worktop, grabs the handle and shoves it open.

'Don't move!' comes the hoarse cry behind her, and Elle can see her abductor's reflection in the glass as she raises the gun.

But there's no going back now. Elle dives through the gap, landing on the patio as a shot rings out and a bullet whistles somewhere overhead. She rolls over, then runs in a low crouch along the side of the house. A high gate separates the back garden from the front, and she's just about to try to climb over it when she realises the woman might come round and cut her off. So instead she sprints to the fence, which backs onto trees, and launches herself at it.

But as she scrambles up, she loses her footing and finds herself stuck with her elbows on the top, trying to drag herself over and realising that she just doesn't seem to have the strength left. That's when a second shot rings out and she feels a burning sensation in her shoulder.

Somehow, ironically, this seems to galvanise some inner strength, and Elle's somehow able to summon the energy to yank herself up and over the fence, falling head-first into the thick tangle of bushes on the other side.

And then, like a frightened rabbit, she's back on her feet and half running, half stumbling into the trees, driven by the fuel of desperation.

58

Saturday, 1.05 p.m.

Vinnie Steele is walking out of the McDonald's at Cobham services, having just enjoyed a Big Mac and fries, when his phone rings. It's Delvina, and he immediately feels a twinge of fear. She hates him eating junk food.

'Hi, Goddess,' he says. 'How was the chiropractor?'

'The bitch has escaped,' says Delvina, sounding like she's got a very sore throat.

'What do you mean? I was there half an hour ago. I fed her and left. She must be there.'

'There's no time to discuss it. You need to get back here right now. How far away are you?'

'Not far. Fifteen minutes.'

'Drive fast. I'll see you in ten.'

Delvina puts the phone back in her pocket, neglecting to switch it off. Right now, she has a much bigger problem.

The woods behind the cottage sit between the single-track road on one side and a field, behind which is a farm and several houses, on the other. She's not sure which way

Elle will go, but either way she's no more than a few minutes from help, which means she needs to be intercepted fast.

Shoving the gun, with its barrel still hot, into her coat pocket, she runs over to the Audi and gets inside, kicking off the spiked heels and putting on a pair of trainers before reversing rapidly out of the drive. She drives slowly along the road, her eyes scanning the treeline for any sign of Elle, but there's nothing. Frustrated, she parks by the side of the road and walks rapidly into the woods. She pulls out the gun, enjoying the weight of it in her hand, knowing that, having been shot, the girl won't get far. When Delvina gets hold of her, she's going to put a bullet in her head, although she'll make her beg for mercy for a few seconds before she dies. It'll be a punishment for trying to throttle her. She curses herself for getting slapdash and letting the little bitch escape. This is Surrey, not the Scottish wilderness, and it's a sunny Saturday. There'll be dog walkers about. You often get them round here. If one of them disturbs things, they'll have to die too. And that's just going to make things complicated.

She heads through the trees in the direction of the field beyond. It doesn't look like Elle's gone that way, because she can't see her anywhere. Which means she's somewhere in this very small area, probably hiding behind a tree or under a bush. But the trees here are well spaced and there aren't that many hiding places.

Delvina slows down, creeping now. Looking and listening. Hunting.

*   *   *

371

Elle lies on her stomach at the foot of a beech tree, partially concealed by brambles. Her shoulder burns from where she's been shot, but, having given it a very brief examination, she can see that the bullet sliced through the flesh at the top of her arm but didn't penetrate properly, so although there's a reasonable amount of blood, the wound isn't serious.

But she can't stay here long. Her bare feet are sore and bleeding from running through the woods, and she's shivering with cold. Worse, she can see her abductor barely twenty yards away, moving slowly across her field of vision, still holding the gun and looking round carefully, no sense of panic about her.

Elle holds her breath, her whole body tense, trying to ward off the terrible exhaustion she's feeling.

The woman disappears from view and a minute passes. Then another. Elle stays absolutely still, trying to control her breathing, telling herself that help won't be far away, that this nightmare is almost over.

More time passes. Two, three, five minutes? It's hard to tell. She almost begins to relax as the risk of discovery slowly fades.

And then she hears it, very close by, coming from behind her. A twig cracking, followed by the rustle of movement. The hairs on the back of her neck stand up.

Suddenly a phone rings, only feet away from her, the loud standard iPhone ringtone that she's heard a thousand times before, and which now causes her whole body to shake because it surely spells discovery and death.

The woman answers. 'Where are you?' she whispers hoarsely into the mouthpiece.

Elle forces herself to look up. Her abductor is right there. Six feet away, phone in one hand, gun in the other.

'Keep going. She's somewhere in the woods,' continues the woman, and Elle knows that any second now she's going to look down and see her. She has to act fast.

Picking up lumps of the moist forest dirt in both hands, she lifts herself into a crouching position. And then, as the woman spots her for the first time, eyes widening in surprise, Elle flings the dirt into her face, the effort making her injured shoulder burn, and immediately dives to one side.

The woman curses hoarsely and the gun immediately goes off with a loud, unmistakable retort, but there's no pain and Elle can tell she hasn't been hit, so she keeps rolling over then leaps to her feet and runs with a speed she's never managed before, trying to keep low, waiting for the next shot.

But the next shot never comes, and now she's out on the road. On the other side is a high, impenetrable hedge running for several hundred metres in both directions, so she takes off in a flailing, exhausted run, her feet banging painfully on the hard tarmac, her shoulder feeling like it's on fire.

There's a car approaching. It looks like one of those seven-seater taxis she and her friends sometimes get after a night out in Brighton. There's a man behind the wheel. He's waving to her. She remembers that the woman has just been talking to her accomplice and she knows this could be him, but she's so exhausted, she's got no choice but to keep going towards him and hope for the best.

The vehicle stops in front of her and the man jumps out. 'Are you all right?' he says, running over. 'Come here.'

That's when she recognises the voice. It's him. The man who brought her the sandwich in the basement this morning. With a desperate scream, she turns round, running back into the woods that she's just come from, but she's not fast enough because he's on her, a hand clasping her mouth firmly shut, and Elle knows that this is it. It's all over.

59

Saturday, 1.15 p.m.

It's all happening now. In the forty-five minutes we've been driving to Delvina and Vinnie's country retreat, Acorn Cottage, they've both turned their phones back on, giving us real-time locations, and now HQ are telling Cotton over the car radio that there have been two separate reports of gunshots coming from the area near the house in the last few minutes.

Up until just over ten minutes ago, Vinnie was in the McDonald's at Cobham services, presumably scoffing his lunch. At that point we were only a few minutes away from him on the A3, but then he received a call from Delvina's phone and since then has been driving back in the direction of Acorn Cottage at high speed, suggesting that something's gone very wrong.

Unfortunately for me and Cotton, given that neither of us would describe ourselves as fighters, we're the nearest car to the scene. Our original plan had been to park close to the cottage, recce the place to see who, if anyone, was in residence, and then set up the operation to storm it, with the specialist armed units going in first. But now that plan's out the window. According to Google Maps, we're only three minutes away from the cottage, with the ARVs still some five minutes behind us, and because we're both armed, that means we're the ones who've got to intervene in what looks like a potentially very dangerous situation.

Even so, I'm pumped up and ready to go. Most police work involves sitting behind a desk, and frankly, up until the last couple of days, the job has bored me senseless for years, so to actually get out and do something exciting, especially when it involves a gun and potentially taking revenge on two people I really hate, is something of a novelty, at least if I don't spend too long thinking about the potential ramifications.

Like getting shot.

'The turning to their place is up here on the left,' shouts Cotton. His face is red and he looks more scared than excited, and who can blame him? I bet he didn't expect to be in this situation when he got out of bed this morning.

'Roger that,' I say, approaching the turning so fast I have to slam on the anchors to make it, which I do in an old-school screech of tyres.

Cotton grabs the seat for support, now looking terrified, and reaches for the gun in his shoulder holster with hands that appear, rather worryingly, to be shaking.

We're on a bumpy single-track road that I can see from the map leads to Acorn Cottage and a few other houses and farms before eventually petering out. We pass a couple of driveways, but there's no one around. Cotton's shouting our current location and status into the radio as I keep driving, my hands surprisingly steady on the wheel, thinking only of dealing with those two arseholes once and for all and getting young Elle Barraclough out in one piece. Play this one right and I'm a hero.

I round a wide bend. And that's when I see Vinnie's Chrysler blocking the road thirty or forty yards ahead, the driver's door open, with him wrestling a young woman I immediately identify as Elle towards the back of the vehicle. I can't see Delvina anywhere, and that's more of a worry, because I know she'll be the one with the gun.

Cotton yells this latest update into the radio as I bring the car to a screeching halt about ten yards away and Vinnie turns to us with a surprised look on his face.

'Can you give us a location on Delvina's phone?' shouts Cotton.

Almost as soon as he says these words, Delvina appears behind Vinnie, using him as a human shield as she steadies herself on his shoulder.

Then, just like that, she opens fire.

I've already released my seat belt, so I'm out of the car in a low crouch, looking round the door with my gun out-stretched just in time to see Elle break free and dive to the ground. I fire back straight away, and even though there are all kinds of strict rules around police shootings, in this sort of situation, where not pulling the trigger may cost you your life, you don't hang about. I get off at least four shots, aiming for both of them, and and it's Vinnie who takes a good couple of hits and goes tumbling backwards.

377

But I don't hit Delvina, who's already running away round the side of the van. There's maybe a split second when I could have shot her in the back, but that would just get me into a lot of trouble, plus I think I'd have missed. I don't want her to get away, though. I take a quick glance at Cotton, which is when I see him still sitting in the passenger seat, his head slumped forward, not moving. The poor sod just wasn't fast enough.

I'm fast, though, and I'm off like a shot after Delvina, yelling at Elle to get behind the Chrysler so she's safe from any gunfire. Over the ringing in my ears I can hear the sound of sirens. Help is only minutes, potentially seconds, away.

Which means I have to act quickly. I jump over Vinnie, pleased to see he's not moving either, and immediately spot Delvina making for her white Audi, which is parked up by the side of the road about thirty yards further on, the gun still in her hand. She's got maybe ten, twelve yards on me, but the thing is, I don't want to catch her up, because there's no way I can afford to take her alive.

I'm holding my gun two-handed out in front of me when I shout: 'I'm catching you, you bitch! You're not getting away.'

She swings round, gun waving, to face me – no more than a few yards ahead – and that's when I pull the trigger, hitting her twice in the upper body.

She goes down fast, dropping the gun, which immediately goes off, stopping me in my tracks as I automatically tense at the prospect that I might be on the wrong end of the bullet.

But thankfully I'm not, and now Delvina's lying on her back on the tarmac, staring up at me, utterly helpless, but alive and conscious.

She opens her mouth, trying to get words out, but those sirens are very close now, so after a quick glance over my shoulder to check the coast's clear and there are no inconvenient witnesses about, I give Delvina a smile and a wink and then, from a distance of about five yards, I take aim through the pistol's sights and, as the bitch's eyes widen as she realises what's coming, I put a bullet straight between them. And this time the lights really do go out.

I take a deep breath. I've never killed someone before and it's a shock to the system. But I'm already planning ahead. Delvina's Audi's a few yards away, and I think of old Cott and the fact that it would be harsh to besmirch his memory, so I jog over to the passenger-side door, hoping it's unlocked (which it is), reach inside and pull out the flash drive I secreted between the seat cushions last night, before lobbing it into the bushes at the side of the road.

See. I'm not all bad.

It's part of the training that every effort should be made to save the life of a suspect who's been shot, so, obviously wanting to appear to play by the rules, I run over to where Delvina's lying on the ground and pretend to give her the kiss of life, knowing full well that, with a goodly part of her brains already sitting on the tarmac behind her head, we're not going to get any dramatic recoveries.

I'm still there, and still pretending, when moments later

379

the cavalry finally arrive and a bunch of other officers, both uniformed and plain clothes, come running over to me.

I get to my feet slowly, my expression one of pained resignation as I shake my head. 'I think she's gone,' I say, stepping away. 'Is Elle okay?'

'She's good,' an armed uniform I don't recognise tells me, then adds: 'You're a hero.'

'I was just doing my job,' I say wearily, but I have to say, I like the praise. Because do you know what? I do feel like a hero.

60

Saturday, 2.05 p.m.

'Look, you're safe now,' says Becca to Logan Quinn. 'Please call the kidnappers and let me speak to my daughter.'

Becca has been driving the car she was taken to the safe house in for close to an hour now, while Quinn sits in the back with the gun drawn, her phone in his hand, giving directions. They're clearly making for a predetermined destination and Quinn's in a hurry, which is no surprise given that this car will almost certainly have a tracker on it, and if the alarm hasn't been raised by now, it soon will be. They've already traversed a section of the M25 and are now somewhere in Berkshire, in a semi-rural area a little south of Windsor.

'We'll call her soon,' he says brusquely. 'Drive for one mile down here and go fast. I'll tell you when to turn right.'

Becca does what she's told, accelerating down the tree-lined avenue of big detached houses. She's glad that the traffic is fairly thin, because on the busier roads Quinn has been ordering her to do some risky manoeuvres, including a lot of overtaking. She's tried to engage him in conversation during the journey, but he's had no interest in talking. The expression on his face is tense. He knows how high the stakes are.

'Take the next right,' he snaps.

She glances in the rear-view mirror. His face is cold, so different from the smiling prisoner she first encountered a few weeks ago who called his arrest a complete misunderstanding. She believed him as well. Bastard.

She makes the turn. The houses give way to pine trees on both sides of the road. About two hundred metres further on, there's a lay-by with several cars parked in it, and Quinn tells her to pull in there.

'Get out and leave the keys in the ignition,' he says.

Becca does what she's told. There are two cars coming the other way. She could run into the road and flag them down, but she knows it's too risky with an armed killer only a few feet behind her.

'This way,' he says, placing a hand on her shoulder and guiding her onto a marked path leading into the woods. In the distance she can hear a couple of dogs barking, but right now there's no one else around.

She glances down and can no longer see the gun, which he appears to have put under his jacket. 'Where are we going?'

'Just keep walking,' he says, holding her close and upping the pace so she's almost running. Then, abruptly, he guides her off the path and through a tight row of pines.

'What's going on? Please let me talk to my daughter.'

He says nothing, just keeps moving her forward, further into the woods. She knows she needs to do something, because this really isn't right, so she makes a decision and suddenly thrusts a hand beneath his jacket, trying to find the gun.

But Quinn is faster. Grabbing her wrist with his free hand, he twists it violently, then kicks her legs out from under her, knocking her to the ground.

When she looks up, the gun is pointing at her head.

'What are you doing, Logan?' she asks uncertainly, slowly getting to her feet.

'You know,' he says, his eyes cold, 'just before I was arrested, I was given another job to do. Unfortunately I wasn't able to complete it. I'll be honest, Becca, I don't like leaving loose ends.' He lifts the gun. 'The target was you.'

'Please don't do this, Logan,' she says, trying hard not to panic. 'If you kill me, there's no going back for you. But if you leave me alive and you're caught, you could still rescind your confession. I'll even represent you.'

'I wouldn't want you to represent me,' says Quinn, making no move to lower the gun. 'As it happens, I think you deserve to die after what you did, defending that murdering bastard Oliver Tamzan.'

So even after all this time, it still comes back to Tamzan. 'I was just trying to do my job.'

'So were the Nazis,' he says, without any hint of irony, and Becca realises then that he's not going to spare her life however much she pleads. Somewhere deep down she feels a grim resignation, but also a mother's instinctive desire to protect her child.

'Even if you kill me, please at least phone the kidnappers

and get them to release my daughter. She's a nurse. She's nothing to do with my job. Allow me to die knowing she's safe. Please.'

Something in his expression softens just a little. He reaches into his pocket and pulls out Becca's phone, and as he does so, it rings. Still holding the gun, he glances down at the screen.

At that moment, a dog bounds up behind him and runs round his feet. And now Becca can see the owners – a middle-aged couple who've appeared on the path, both of them looking towards her.

Quinn moves the gun closer to his body and glances briefly over his shoulder as the man calls the dog.

And that's when Becca spins round and sprints straight into the trees, ignoring the branches that tear into her, keeping low and trying to veer, expecting a bullet any second.

But it doesn't come, and she keeps running until she joins another path and takes a final look back.

Logan Quinn is nowhere to be seen.

61

Saturday, 8.30 p.m.

When a police officer shoots someone, even if it's a lowlife like Delvina or Vinnie, there's a lot of rigmarole afterwards. It's not like Dirty Harry, who bags a few of the bad guys then grabs a quick coffee and goes back out on patrol. You're removed from the scene of the shooting as soon as possible, then taken to a designated suite – in my case it was actually at NCA HQ, where I handed over my gun, was examined by a doctor, and then had to give my account of what happened to a senior officer, before having an initial meeting with a lawyer to discuss the possibility of criminal charges.

Now that that's all over, I'm sitting in the interview suite, alone and nursing a cup of coffee, wondering when they're going to let me go, and how I'm going to get home now that my car's been shot up and taken away as evidence. I haven't even had a proper debriefing. I know that Delvina died at the scene (obviously), and that Vinnie succumbed to his injuries later in hospital. Which serves him right. I know too that poor old Cott died too, hit once in the chest by a lucky bullet that finished him off instantly. Other than that, though, I've heard nothing, and I'm not allowed to talk to colleagues to find out any more.

Right now, I'm something of a pariah through no fault of my own, and will be until the IPCA investigation into the shooting is carried out, which hopefully will be days, but more likely weeks. I'm thinking right now that early retirement is my best option. The lawyer doesn't think there'll be any case to answer, meaning there's nothing really keeping me in the country any longer, so why not? Before this job, my retirement fund made up of ill-gotten gains was worth two and fifty hundred grand (it would have been more but I've spent a fair bit of it over the years). Still, it's no problem because now the job's been done and I avoided having to pay Delvina her last chunk, so I'm three fifty up on the deal, more than doubling the size of the pot. Add to that a reasonably decent police pension, and a life of sunshine, laughter and good food beckons.

My thoughts are interrupted by the arrival of none other than the director general of operations herself, Sheryl Trinder, a short, tough woman with thirty-five years in the force behind her who you definitely don't get on the wrong side of.

But today she's smiling, which is a rarity, at least with me. It was Trinder who gave me my demotion and told me I was in 'the last-chance saloon' after Henry Day.

'Ma'am,' I say, getting up from my seat.

'Sit back down, Fish, you deserve the rest,' she says as we shake hands. She's looking very happy, but then she's going to be the one basking in all the glory, especially now that Cotton's gone.

'I'm so sorry about Adam,' she says.

'He was a good man,' I say. Which is true. He was. And I'll miss him. Although the beaches and sunshine of Thailand will doubtless do a good job of easing the pain.

'But I'm here because of you,' she continues, taking a seat opposite me. 'I want you to know that the whole of the NCA are immensely proud of what you've achieved with this case. I know there was the tragedy with Henry Day, but you've more than made up for that in the last two days, and frankly you were a hero today. And I have absolutely no doubt that you will be exonerated of any wrongdoing in the shooting of those two individuals.'

'Thank you, ma'am,' I say with an earnest smile. 'I really appreciate the sentiment.'

'You can count on the support of all of us here,' she continues, even though that's bullshit. If there's any glitch in the IPCA inquiry, she'll drop me like a stone. Trinder's nothing if not political, which is how you get to the top these days.

'How's Elle Barraclough? Is she unharmed?' I ask her.

'Yes. Apart from a few cuts and bruises, she's fine. And she asked me to thank you for what you did.'

'It's my job. And how about her mother? Have we got hold of her now?' Because that's one thing I really need to know.

Trinder frowns. 'There've been some complications there, I'm afraid. It turns out that Elle Barraclough wasn't kidnapped for ransom like the others, although it was definitely the work of the Vanishers. From what we can gather, it

387

appears her mother was being coerced into helping one of her clients escape police custody. She's being questioned now, but she does at least know that her daughter's safe, and they've spoken to each other by phone.'

'That's good,' I say, distracted by what Trinder's just told me, because that wasn't my understanding of what Becca Barraclough was meant to be doing. She was supposed to be killing Quinn, not helping the bastard. 'Who's the client she was breaking out? And did she succeed?'

'Look, nothing's official yet, so keep it under your hat, but the client is a man called Logan Quinn. He was on remand for murder but was moved to a safe house because he apparently had information about a number of other killings. From what we can gather, Rebecca Barraclough drugged the police guards at the safe house and sprang Quinn. He's now on the run.'

Trindle keeps talking about how Quinn's escape isn't our problem and that it shouldn't detract from the success of the NCA's Anti Kidnap unit, and me in particular, but as you can imagine, I'm no longer listening, because right now I'm trying to work out how the hell this could have happened when it was all so fucking straightforward.

'Anyway,' she concludes, 'I can see you're exhausted, so I want you to take a few days' sick leave and have a good long rest. There's a car waiting outside to take you home.' She gets to her feet and puts out her hand. 'And thank you once again for your help.'

I'm in a daze right now, but I shake Trinder's hand a second time and parrot all the right words of gratitude, then

I'm out the door and heading downstairs, trying to work out my next move. The job I've been paid to arrange hasn't been done. Worse, I've already shelled out three hundred grand of that money to Delvina, and although no one will ever be able to find out that it came from me, I'm not getting it back now. And if you subtract that three hundred grand from the value of my retirement fund, which is what I'm doing in my head over and over again as I race down the stairs, it gives me a balance of minus fifty thousand, a figure that I now owe to probably the UK's least understanding and most psychotic creditor: Colin Blisterfield.

Which leaves me only one course of action. I get the hell out of the country right now, and don't come back for a long, long time. It's hardly practical, given that I'm the subject of an IPCA investigation, but it does mean I'll stay alive a fair bit longer, and in the end, as I'm sure you'll agree, that's the most important thing.

As I formulate the basis of an exit plan in my head, I begin to calm down. I've taken plenty of hits in the past and I've always managed to bounce back from them. And I'll bounce back from this one too, somehow.

In fact, I'm even smiling as I climb into the car waiting for me outside the door, give the driver my address, and settle back in my seat as he pulls away from the kerb.

And that's when I hear it. A loud, rumbling fart from the back seat, followed by a low animal growl I recognise all too well, and then words that literally freeze me in my seat, because I know they mean a world of pain.

'I believe you owe me some fucking money, Fisher.'